P9-CFX-792

What Happened to the Bennetts

What Happened to the Bennetts

Lisa Scottoline

THORNDIKE PRESS
A part of Gale, a Cengage Company

This is a work of fiction. Names, characters, places, and incidents either are the product of the author's imagination or are used fictitiously, and any resemblance to actual persons, living or dead, businesses, companies, events, or locales is entirely coincidental.

Thorndike Press® Large Print Core.
The text of this Large Print edition is unabridged.
Other aspects of the book may vary from the original edition.
Set in 16 pt. Plantin.

**LIBRARY OF CONGRESS CIP DATA ON FILE.
CATALOGUING IN PUBLICATION FOR THIS BOOK
IS AVAILABLE FROM THE LIBRARY OF CONGRESS.**

ISBN-13: 978-1-4328-9475-7 (hardcover alk. paper)

Published in 2022 by arrangement with G.P. Putnam's Sons, an imprint of Penguin Publishing Group, a division of Penguin Random House LLC.

Printed in Mexico
Print Number: 01 Print Year: 2022

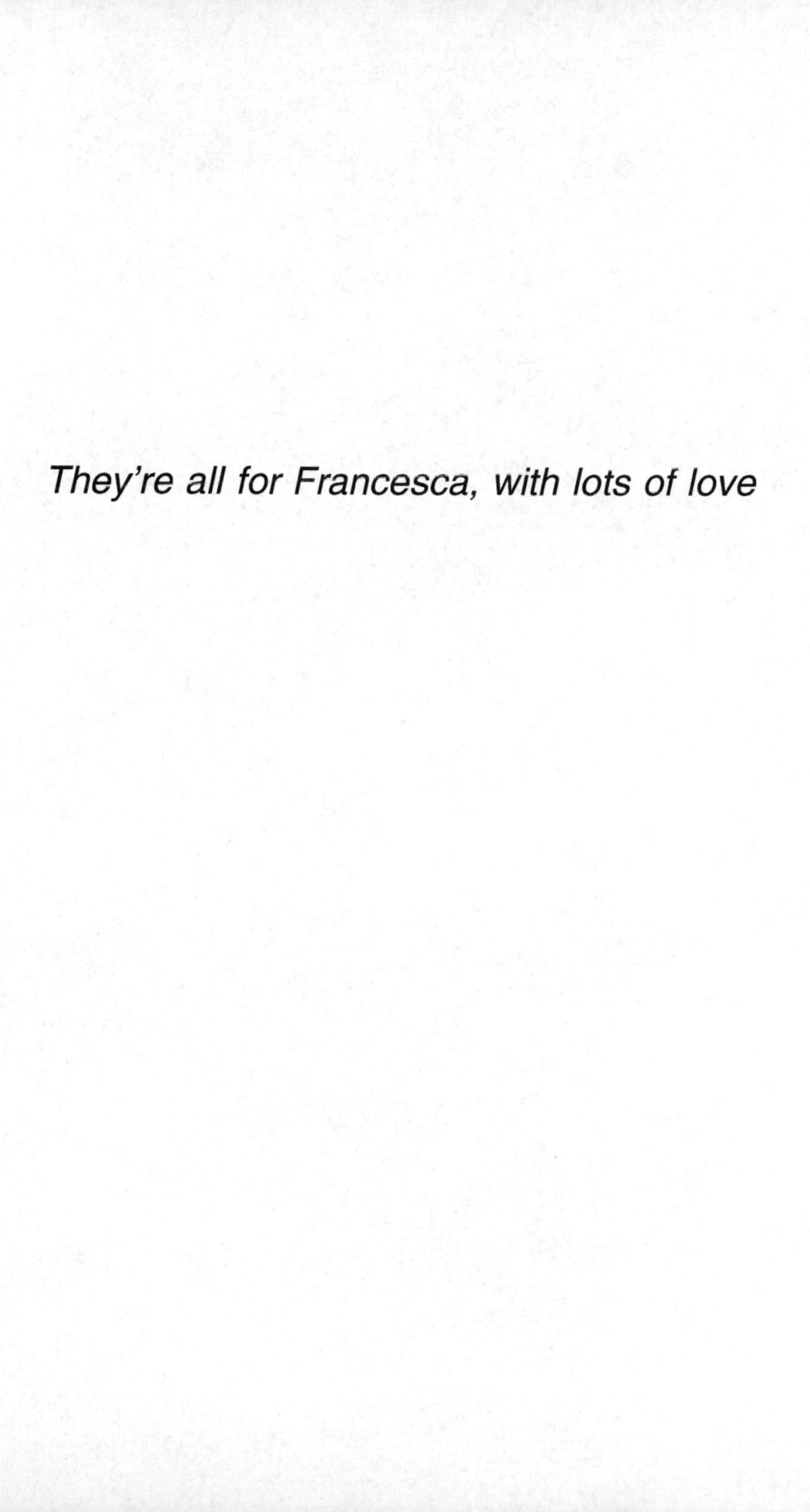

They're all for Francesca, with lots of love

■ ■ ■ ■

Part One

■ ■ ■ ■

Nothing good gets away.

— John Steinbeck's letter
to his son Thom, 1958

Chapter One

I glanced in my rearview mirror at the pickup truck, which was riding my bumper. I hated tailgaters, especially with my family in the car, but nothing could ruin my good mood. My daughter's field hockey team had just beat Radnor, and Allison had scored a goal. She was texting in the back seat, one of a generation that makes better use of opposable thumbs than any prior.

My son Ethan turned around next to her, shielding his eyes against the pickup's headlights. "Dad, what's up with this guy?"

"God knows. Ignore him."

"Why don't you go faster?" Ethan shifted, waking up Moonie, our little white mutt, who started jumping around in the back seat. I love the dog but he has two speeds: Asleep and Annoying.

"Why should I? I'm going the limit."

"But we can *smoke* this guy now."

We had just gotten a new car, a Mercedes

E-Class Sedan in a white enamel that gleamed like dental veneers. Ethan said the E stood for his name, but I said Exorbitant. My wife and kids had lobbied for the car, but I felt like a show-off behind the wheel. I missed my old Explorer, which I didn't need a tie to drive.

"Dad, when I get my license, I'm gonna *burn* guys like him."

I heard this once a week. My son counted the days until his learner's permit, even though he was only thirteen. I said, "No, you're not. You're gonna let him pass."

"Why?"

"We have a right to enjoy the drive."

"But it's boring."

"Not to me. I'm a scenic-route kind of guy." I moved over to let the pickup pass, since Coldstream Road was a single lane winding uphill through the woods. We were entering the Lagersen Tract, the last parcel of woodland preserved by Chester County, where Nature had to be zoned for her own protection.

I lowered the window and breathed in a lungful of fresh, piney air. Thick trees flanked the road, and scrub brush grew over the guardrails. Crickets and tree frogs croaked a chorus from my childhood. I grew up on a dairy farm in Hershey, home of the famous chocolate manufacturer. I loved living in a company town, where the air smelled of sweet cocoa and corporate largesse. Everyone worked toward the same goal, even if it was capitalism.

"He's not passing us," Ethan said, bringing me out of my reverie.

I checked the rearview mirror, squinting against the headlights. Moonie was facing backward, his front paws on the back seat and his ears silhouetted like wispy triangles.

"Come on, Dad. Show 'em who's boss."

"That's well-established," I said. "Mom."

Lucinda was in the passenger seat, the curve of her smile illuminated by the phone screen. She was a natural beauty, with gray-blue eyes, a small nose, and dark blond hair gathered into a loose ponytail at the nape of her neck. She had been on Facebook since we'd left the school, posting game photos and comments. Great save by Arielle!!! Lady Patriots rock!!! Woohoo, Emily is MVP!!! My wife never uses fewer than three exclamation marks on social. If you only get one, you've done something wrong. Or as my father would say, *You're in the doghouse.*

Lucinda looked over. "Jason, speed up, would you?"

"You, too? What's the hurry?"

"They have homework."

"On Friday night? Have you *met* our kids?"

Lucinda smiled, shaking her head. "Whatever, Scenic-Route Kind of Guy."

"Aw, I feel so *seen*."

Lucinda laughed, which made me happy. I love my wife. We met at Bucknell, where she was an art major and I was a workstudy jock slinging mac and cheese in the dining hall, wearing a hairnet, no less. She could've had her pick, but I made her laugh. Also she loves mac and cheese.

"Dad, listen to this." Allison looked up, her thumbs still flying. She could text without looking at the keyboard, which she called her superpower. "My friends just voted you Hottest Dad."

I smiled. "They're absolutely right. There's a reason I was Homecoming King."

"Dude, no. Never say that again." Allison snorted, texting. "We don't even have that anymore."

Lucinda rolled her eyes. "Allison, who came in second?"

I added, "Yeah, what troll came in second?"

Allison kept texting. "Brianna M's dad."

I scoffed. "Ron McKinney? Please, no contest. I got the bubble butt."

Allison smiled. "Stop it!"

"I bet I can twerk, Al. Show you when we get home."

"Nobody twerks anymore." Allison snorted again, texting away. "OMG, they're saying you look like Kyle Chandler."

"Who's that?"

"The dad from *Friday Night Lights.* We watched it together. You remember. Also the dad in *Bloodline.*"

"What's that?"

"A show on Netflix."

"Never saw it."

"Anyway, you look like him, except he's way hotter."

I smiled. "Okay, but can he twerk?"

Allison burst into laughter, and I glanced in the rearview mirror to see her, but the headlights of the pickup truck were too bright. The outline of her head bent over her phone, then I saw the bump of a skinny headband, and the spray of shorter hairs coming from her double ponytail. Those ponytail holders were all over the house, and I fished them from the dog's mouth on a weekly basis.

Ethan kept twisting around. "Dad, if I were driving, I'd speed up."

Allison added, "Seriously."

"Me, too," Lucinda joined in, still on her phone.

"Okay, I'm convinced." I pressed the gas pedal, and the Mercedes responded instantly. We accelerated up the hill, hugging the sharp curve to the left.

Oddly the black pickup truck chose that moment to pass us, a dark and dusty blur roaring by with two men in the cab. It crammed us against the guardrail, and I veered to the right, barely fitting on the street.

Suddenly the pickup pulled in front of us and stopped abruptly, blocking our way.

I slammed on the brakes and we shuddered to a stop, inches from the truck. We lurched forward in our seat belts. Lucinda gasped. Moonie started barking.

"It's okay," I said, instinctively reversing to put distance between us and the truck. I scanned for an escape route, but there wasn't one. I couldn't fit around the truck. I couldn't reverse down the street because of the blind curve.

Two men emerged from the pickup, illuminated by our headlights. The driver was big, with shredded arms covered by tattooed sleeves. His eyes were slits under a prominent forehead and long, dark hair. His passenger wasn't as muscular, but had on a similar dark T-shirt and baggy jeans. The driver said something to him as they approached.

I inhaled to calm myself. If it was road rage, I could defuse the situation. I had a year of law school, so I could bullshit with anybody. Otherwise I was six foot three, played middle linebacker in high school, and stayed in decent shape.

Lucinda groaned. "Should I call 911?"

"Not yet."

"Dad?" Allison sounded nervous.

"What do they want?" Ethan stuck his head between the seats, and Moonie barked, the harsh sound reverberating in the car.

"Don't worry. Lucinda, lock the doors."

"Okay, but be careful."

I climbed out of the car and closed the door behind me, hearing the reassuring *thunk* of the locks engage. The men reached me, and I straightened. "Gentlemen, is there a —"

"We're taking the car." The driver pulled a handgun and aimed it at my face. "Get everybody out."

"Okay, fine. Relax. Don't hurt anybody. This is my family." I turned to the car and spotted Lucinda's phone glowing through the windshield. She must have been calling 911. The carjackers saw her at the same time.

"Drop it!" The passenger pulled a gun and

aimed it at her.

"No, don't shoot!" I moved in the way, raising my arms. "Honey, everybody, out of the car!"

Lucinda lowered the phone, the screen dropping in a blur of light.

Allison emerged from the back seat, her eyes wide. "Dad, they have *guns.*"

"It's okay, honey. Come here." I put a hand on her shoulder and maneuvered her behind me. Lucinda was coming around the back of the car with Ethan, who held a barking Moonie, dragging his leash. They reached me, and I faced the men.

"Okay, take the car," I told them, my chest tight.

"Wait." The passenger eyed Allison, and a leering smile spread across his face. "What's your name, sweetheart?"

No. My mouth went dry. "Take the car and go."

Suddenly Moonie leapt from Ethan's arms and launched himself at the men. They jumped back, off-balance. The driver fired an earsplitting blast, just missing Moonie.

My ears rang. I whirled around.

Allison had been struck. Blood spurted from her neck in a gruesome fan. She was reeling.

No! I rushed to her just as she collapsed

in my arms. I eased her down to the street. Her mouth gaped open. Her throat emitted gulping sounds. Blood poured from her neck. My hand flew there to stop the flow. The blood felt hideously wet and warm.

Allison's lips were moving. She was trying to talk, to breathe.

"Honey, you've been hit," I told her. "Stay calm." I tore off my shirt, breaking the buttons. I bunched it up and pressed it against her neck. I couldn't see the wound. It scared me to death. "Lucinda, call 911."

"My phone's in the car!" Lucinda grabbed Allison's hand, beginning to sob.

Suddenly the gun fired again behind us, another earsplitting blast.

We crouched in terror. Lucinda screamed. I didn't know who had been shot. I looked around wildly, shocked to find that one carjacker had shot the other. The driver stood over the passenger, who lay motionless on the street, blood pooling under his head. The driver dropped the gun and ran to the pickup. I spotted his license plate before he sped off. A sudden brightness told me another car was coming up Coldstream.

"Dad, here's Allison's phone!" Ethan thrust it at me. My bloody fingers smeared the screen, which came to life with a photo of Moonie in sunglasses.

I thumbed to the phone function and pressed 911. The call connected. I held the phone to my ear to hear over the dog's barking.

The 911 dispatcher asked, "What is your emergency?"

"My daughter's been shot in the neck. Two men tried to carjack us on Coldstream Road near the turnpike overpass." I struggled to think through my fear. Allison was making gulping sounds. She was losing blood fast, drenching my shirt. My hands were slick with my daughter's lifeblood, slipping warm through my fingers.

"Sir, is she awake and responsive?"

"Yes, send an ambulance! Hurry!"

"Apply direct pressure to the wound. Use a compress —"

"I am, please send —"

"An ambulance is on the way."

"Please! *Hurry!*"

Allison's eyelids fluttered. She coughed. Pinkish bubbles frothed at the corners of her mouth. "Daddy?"

My heart lurched. She hadn't called me that since she was little.

I told her what I wanted to believe: "You're going to be okay."

Chapter Two

The waiting room of the emergency department was harshly bright, and the mint-green walls were lined with idealized landscapes of foxhunts. Green-padded chairs had been arranged in two rectangles, forming rooms without walls. The front section held a handful of people, but we had the back to ourselves. Wrinkled magazines lay on end tables, ignored in favor of phones. There was a kids' playroom behind a plexiglass wall next to vending machines.

I had been in this waiting room so many times over the years, for so many reasons. Allison's broken arm. Ethan's random falls. Once, a moth flew into Lucinda's ear. Every parent knows the local emergency room, but not like this. Never before had I seen anyone look like us, right now.

The three of us huddled together, shocked and stricken. Allison had been taken to surgery. My undershirt was stiffening with drying blood, and Lucinda had spatters on her Lady Patriots sweatshirt and bloody patches on her jeans. She had stopped crying and rested her head on my right shoulder. Ethan's T-shirt was flecked with blood, though the fabric was black and it didn't show except for the white *N* in Nike. He slumped on my left, and I had an arm around each of them.

"She'll be okay, right?" Lucinda asked, hushed.

"Yes," I answered, but I was scared out of my mind. "How was she in the ambulance?"

"Okay. She didn't panic. You know her."

"Yes." I nodded. Allison had a high pain threshold. At lacrosse camp, she broke her arm in the morning and didn't tell her coach until lunch.

"The EMT was in the back, I had to sit in the front. He was nice. He talked to her. He called in her vital signs."

"How were they?"

"Her blood pressure was low." Lucinda started wringing her hands. I remembered her doing that when her sister Caitlin was dying of breast cancer, five years ago. I hugged her closer.

An older couple shuffled in together and took a seat in our section, glancing around. The husband had a walker with new tennis balls on the bottom, and he walked ahead with concentration. His wife noticed us, then plastered her gaze to the TV, showing the news on closed-captioning.

Lucinda wiped her nose with a balled-up Kleenex. "Jason, do you know what she said to me in the ambulance? She told me not to worry."

Tears stung my eyes. "What a kid."

"I know." Lucinda sniffled. "I wonder how long the surgery will be."

"They have to repair the vein. I think it was a vein, not an artery."

"How do you know?"

"If it were an artery, like the carotid, the blood would have pulsed out." I hoped I was right. Any medical information I had was from malpractice depositions, of which I'd done hundreds. I was a court reporter, which made me a font of information about completely random subjects. It wasn't always a good thing.

"We were supposed to look for a homecoming dress tomorrow. She found one she liked at the mall. She saw it with Courtney."

I remembered. Allison had shown me a picture on her phone. The dress was nice, white with skinny straps. She would have looked great in it. She had the wiry, lean build of an athlete. She worried it would make her butt look flat.

Allison, your butt isn't flat.

Dad, you don't know. You just love me.

I had so many nicknames for her. Al, Alsford, The Duchess of Alfordshire, and The Alimentary Canal because she ate like a horse. She called me Dad or Dude. I was an *involved* father, according to my wife. I was *present in my children's lives.* I sold raffle tickets and bought gigantic candy bars that I gave out at work. I taught both kids to pitch and saw that Allison was the better athlete.

Lucinda sniffled again. "I assume they'll keep her a few days, don't you?"

"Yes."

"I suppose I could pick it up for her."

"Pick what up?"

Ethan looked over, his eyes glistening. "The dress, Dad."

"Right." I was too upset to think, it just didn't show. I couldn't follow the conversation. My wife talked more when she was upset, but I talked less. I was lost in my own thoughts. I was *lost.*

Lucinda wiped her nose. "I hope she can still go to homecoming. She's so excited. I think she really likes Troy."

"I know." Troy was Allison's boyfriend of

two months, already lasting longer than her last boyfriend. I liked Troy because he was as smart as she was, a true scholar athlete. He was on the quiet side, but I learned from having Ethan that there's more to introverts than meets the eye. My son had a circle of friends, but needed time to himself.

"I got her a hair appointment the same day as the dance. They all want to get in the morning of, but they don't want to miss the game. It was impossible, but I got her in." Lucinda's voice carried an unmistakable note of mom pride.

"Way to go."

"She wants beachy waves."

Beachy waves. I'd been hearing that a lot. I knew it was a thing. Allison had beautiful hair, but she thought it didn't have enough volume.

Dad, I hate my hair, it's so flat.

Like your butt?

Lucinda was saying, "Do you think they'll tell us something soon?"

"Yes, as soon as they can. They know what they're doing."

"Right, they do. It's a good hospital."

"It is." I squeezed her hand. We had often discussed the relative merits of Paoli Hospital, routinely rated among the top in the Philadelphia area. Lucinda had researched the hospitals before we moved here, and she became an expert on them and schools, comparing what the districts spent on instructional costs versus the state and national medians. My wife did the homework; we had that in common. Her mother had been the same way and her father had been a CEO of PennValue, a big insurance brokerage in Allentown. My father used to say she *came from money,* as if it were an actual place. Moneytown.

"Dad, do you think Moonie's okay?" Ethan looked over, his eyes pained. They were blue, a shade lighter than Allison's. I was the only brown-eyed one in the family. Well, me and Moonie.

"Yes," I told him. We had left the dog in the police cruiser, since the Mercedes was being impounded by the police.

"Don't be mad at him." Ethan hung his head, showing a gelled whorl of light brown hair, combed from a low side part. I supposed the style started with Justin Bieber, but Lucinda and I both hoped it would end soon.

"I'm not. Why would I be?"

"I thought you would say it was his fault, but it wasn't."

"No, it wasn't." I managed a smile to reassure him, but Ethan didn't smile back.

His face was rounder than Allison's, his eyes were narrower set and his build skinnier. I tended to define him in relationship to his sister, which I knew wasn't a good thing, but as an only child, I found their differences fascinating. His skin tone was lighter, too. He had a sprinkling of small freckles on his upturned nose, since he got my thin Irish skin.

Ethan's face fell. "It was my fault."

Lucinda reached for his hand. "Ethan, no, it wasn't. Why would you say such a thing?"

"I should've held him tighter. If I had, Allison would be fine. I shouldn't have let him jump out."

Lucinda's gaze met mine, her expression agonized. We both knew our son could not bear this burden. He was the more sensitive of the two, carrying his hurts around like a backpack. Meanwhile he began looking down at his hands, where blood had dried within the lines in his palm.

"Ethan, listen." I squeezed his shoulder. "It's not your fault."

"Why not?" Ethan's troubled gaze lifted to me, and his lip caught on his braces, like it did when his mouth went dry. I knew he wanted an answer, since he was the kind of kid who needed to be reasoned with, not just told.

Because I said so, my father would have said, but that didn't work with my son.

"Ethan, you're saying Allison would be fine, but for your letting go of Moonie, right? But that's bad reasoning. Your letting go of Moonie is just the but-for cause." I was dredging up first-year torts class, from before I dropped out. "There's a bunch of other but-fors, and none of them is the real cause."

"What do you mean?"

"Well, think about it. How about, 'Allison would be fine, *but for* the fact that we won the game'? Or 'Allison would be fine, *but for* the fact we stayed late to celebrate'? Or 'Allison would be fine, *but for* the fact we have a new Mercedes'?" I spotted Lucinda wince, so I moved on. "But-for is the same trap as what-if. You drive yourself crazy with possibilities. There's only one cause, and it's the carjackers. *They* did it. It's *their* fault."

"But Moonie —"

"Not Moonie, not you. *Them.*" My face went hot. I suddenly felt like I was raging inside, my emotions all over the lot. "The two of them, they're scum. Violent, stupid, evil men. They aren't worth one hair on your sister's head. They're the ones at fault, and I want them to *rot* in jail. I want them to suffer every damn day of their miserable lives and —"

"The one's already dead, Dad."

Lucinda's eyes flared. "Honey, we were talking about Ethan."

"I *am* talking about Ethan. I don't want Ethan to blame himself for what that *scum* did to Allison."

Ethan looked down. "I get it, Dad."

Lucinda looked shaky. "Your dad's just upset, is all."

I turned away, trying to calm down. I wished I knew how Allison was doing in surgery. I loved that child to the marrow. She was everything I could've asked for in a daughter. Strong, smart, funny, bold. More blunt than tactful. More sensitive than she looked. My father always said she was like a draft horse, that way. Big and strong, but not always rough and tumble. Growing up, we had a great brown draft, named Chocolate Soldier.

He's a gentle giant, that one. Don't use the shank on him.

Allison worried more than she should have, about everything. Hair, body, GPA, extracurriculars, PSAT practice courses, and blackheads *in the T-zone,* whatever that was. She looked like Lucinda, but her blue eyes were narrower, and she had a long, straight nose and a big smile, now that her braces were off. She had brown hair that she wanted to highlight *and* lowlight. To her, nothing was as good as it should have been. I never understood. I wouldn't have changed a thing about her. *Good enough for government work,* my father said all the time.

I shifted in the chair. My mouth had gone dry. It was impossible that Allison was lying on an operating table, down the hall behind double doors. Every instinct told me to be at her side. Then I remembered I had been at her side on Coldstream Road. She had bled in the street with me right there.

The thought made me furious, and inside I boiled over with rage at the carjackers, at the world, and most of all, at myself.

Daddy?

I spotted two men in suits entering the waiting room, looking around in an official way. They had to be the county detectives, who were supposed to meet us here.

I jumped to my feet.

CHAPTER THREE

The detectives headed in our direction. The older one looked to be in his late fifties with a thick bristle of gray hair, hooded brown eyes, and a sunglasses-tan. His sunburnt cheeks were jowly, and his lips a somber line. He was tallish and lean, holding a folder with a gold emblem on its brown plastic cover. The other man was younger, and his dark sport coat looked boxy on his frame. His hair was slicked back and his nose had a pronounced bump.

I extended a hand to the older one. "I'm Jason Bennett, I assume you're the detectives."

"Yes. Bill Willoughby, Sergeant Detective of the Chester County District Attorney's Office. This is my partner, Jim —"

"Did you get him?" I interrupted, unable to hold back.

"No, not yet. My partner is Jim Balleu. We're sorry about your daughter. We know this is a difficult —"

"I gave the cops descriptions of the driver, the pickup, the license plate, everything. I don't know if they told you —"

"Yes, they did. Now, if we could speak with you."

"Sure, of course. Please." I gestured to the chairs, then realized I hadn't introduced Lucinda and Ethan, so I did.

Detective Willoughby sat down. "Mrs. Bennett, we're sorry to disturb you now."

"I understand." Lucinda nodded.

"We won't keep you long." Detective Willoughby opened his folder, which held a fresh legal pad and a silver Cross pen. Detective Balleu sat down next to him and tugged a reporter's notebook from his jacket pocket while I started talking.

"You shouldn't have a problem catching the guy. He drove a black pickup, a Chevy. Maybe five or six years old."

"We got that message." Detective Willoughby made a note in his pad.

"Plus you have the other guy, dead at the scene. You must be able to find out who he is. His wallet or phone are probably on him. His fingerprints must be on the gun."

"We will, rest assured —"

"I mean, you have to find the driver. He's the guy who shot my daughter. He *shot my daughter.*" I spat out the words. I couldn't help it. All that rage exiting my body, blowing through the doors. "I want you to catch him and prosecute him to the fullest extent. I want him in jail for the rest of his life."

Lucinda dabbed her eyes. Ethan slumped, his hands in his lap.

"Okay." Detective Willoughby nodded. "Now, if you could tell us what happened."

"Like I told the cops, they pulled in front of us, then said they were going to take the car."

"And you resisted?"

"No. Why would I? I care about my family, not a car."

Detective Willoughby furrowed his short brow. "But one of the perpetrators was killed —"

"*I* didn't kill him, I didn't kill anybody." I realized they thought I had done it. I wished I had. I should have. "The other carjacker killed him. Didn't the cops tell you? I told them."

Lucinda recoiled. "My *husband* didn't kill anybody. He would never."

Detective Willoughby looked from Lucinda to me. "So you're telling me perpetrator one killed perpetrator two?"

"Yes." It bothered me the cops at the scene hadn't told them. I wondered what else the cops hadn't said. I needed to have faith in these guys.

Lucinda cleared her throat. "We were trying to help our daughter. We were bent over her, and Jason was trying to stop her bleeding. I heard another shot, and then, um, well —"

"I'll tell it," I interrupted, to save her from having to continue. "We heard the shot, turned around, and saw that the driver had shot the passenger."

Detective Willoughby glanced skeptically at the other detective, which made me mad.

"Don't tell me you don't believe me."

"We didn't say —"

"You didn't have to. Don't start with me, not tonight. My daughter's in there fighting for her life."

Lucinda grimaced, her eyes flying open, and I realized I had said the wrong thing. We hadn't acknowledged that Allison was *fighting for her life.* I hadn't even known I thought it until it came out of my mouth.

"Mr. Bennett, you can understand, it's unusual for one perpetrator to —"

"It's what happened." I raised my voice, unable to control my tone. It wasn't like me, but I didn't care. "I'm telling you the truth."

Lucinda took my arm. "Honey, calm

down. Really."

Detective Willoughby pursed his lips. "Sorry, we got off on the wrong foot."

"Accusations will do that," I shot back. I couldn't apologize. Not tonight.

"So let's begin at the beginning. What happened?"

"They pulled in front of us and blocked the road. Then they got out of the truck and walked toward us."

"Were their weapons drawn?"

"No, not at first. They were talking." I remembered something I hadn't before. "The driver said to the passenger, 'You go left, Junior.' "

Lucinda looked over.

Ethan blinked.

I added, "Good, so you know his name, or his nickname, if you didn't find out from his wallet."

Detective Willoughby wrote in his pad. His Cross pen gleamed in the overhead lights. "You heard him?"

"No. I was still inside the car."

"Then how do you know what he said?"

"I read his lips. I could see his face in the headlights."

Detective Willoughby blinked. "So you don't know what he said for a *fact.*"

"Yes, I do. I read lips."

Ethan perked up. "He really does. My sister says it's his superpower."

I forced a smile for Ethan, then faced Detective Willoughby. "I lip-read, as a registered merit reporter."

"Is that like a court reporter?"

"Yes, but licensed in specialized areas."

"What does that have to do with reading lips?"

"My job is about accuracy. Lip-reading increases my accuracy."

"You work in court?"

"No, we're private. Court reporters in court are state or municipal employees." I wanted to talk about my daughter, not my job, but Detective Willoughby was taking notes.

"Your business is located where?"

"West Chester. Can we get back to what happened?"

"Okay, please resume."

I went on to explain, telling every detail as best as I could, remaining in emotional control by defaulting to work mode, as if the question-and-answer were a transcript. I visualized my sentences the way I would write them, in the old-school Courier font we still use, so heavy on the page that it was embossed. The testimony would form an official record, considered the truth in any court of law, and on the final page of the original, I would sign under my oath, warranting that the words were true and correct.

Just then an older doctor in a white coat appeared at the entrance to the waiting room. He had short gray hair and thick wire-rimmed glasses, and his gaze swept the room.

Lucinda straightened. "Is that her doctor? Does he want us?"

I stood up, but the doctor crossed to the older couple, shook their hands, and they rose as a group and left.

Lucinda sighed, anxious. "They came in after us, didn't they?"

I sat down. "I don't remember."

Ethan interjected, "It's not like Cheesecake Factory, Mom."

Detective Willoughby closed his folder, slipping his Cross pen inside. "Okay, I think that will do for tonight. We'll follow up in the days to come."

Detective Balleu flipped his pad closed. "Yes, thank you."

"So can we talk later?" I rose, shaking their hands.

"Of course." Detective Willoughby nodded. "We'll keep you apprised of any developments as they occur. We'll do our best to bring this man to justice. By the way, we ask you not to talk to any reporters. Or post about this on social media."

"We weren't planning to."

Lucinda added, "Of course not."

They both bade us a quick goodbye, and left.

In the next moment, the gray-haired doctor reappeared in the threshold of the waiting room, catching my eye behind his glasses. His somber gaze communicated something man-to-man, something primal. I didn't know if I was imagining it. It couldn't be. Suddenly I wondered if he'd moved the older couple to give us privacy.

No, no, no. I found myself shaking my head.

The doctor walked toward us, his lined face falling into grave folds. "Mr. and Mrs. Bennett? I'm Mark Chen, head of emergency surgery."

Lucinda jumped up. "How is she?"

"Please have a seat." Dr. Chen gestured to the chair, then sat down opposite us, and we both sank into the chairs.

No, I thought. *No, this cannot be. No, I do not want to hear this.*

Dr. Chen took Lucinda's hands. "I'm sorry, Mrs. Bennett, Mr. Bennett. Your daughter passed away. We tried everything.

There was nothing we could do."

No, you cannot say that, no, no, no, and no.

My heart wrenched so deeply that I lost my breath. It felt like a shock wave blasting me in the chest. The world blurred, fuzzy and far away. The doctor, the waiting room, the TV.

"No!" Lucinda wailed, which brought me to my senses. I reacted reflexively, pulling her closer, trying to steady her. Ethan burst into tears, so I gathered him under my other arm, holding on to both of them.

I wanted to cry, I wanted to scream, I wanted to wail and howl in disbelief and fury. Lucinda sobbed, tears pouring from her eyes. Ethan cried like a little boy, a sound I didn't know I remembered until now.

I knew we could not all fall to pieces at the same time. I was Daddy. I was the center, and the center had to hold. I tried to make sense of it. My voice came out choked. "What . . . happened?"

"The gunshot severed her jugular veins and tore other vessels and muscle. She sustained significant blood loss." Dr. Chen's eyebrows sloped like a roof sagging under snowfall. "I'm so sorry. We tried everything."

"Explain it to me, please." I needed to understand. I was trying to comprehend something incomprehensible.

"The external jugular vein is large and on top of the muscle that enables you to turn your head. It was severed by the bullet, which went through the front of her neck on the left and exited out the back, causing her to lose a massive amount of blood."

My gaze fell to the doctor's hands. I realized they were the last to touch my daughter alive.

"A young person has roughly ten pints of blood. At a fifth of blood loss, a body goes into shock. Your daughter lost almost half."

I flashed on the horrific memory. I couldn't speak. I could barely hear him.

"We transfused her, but she had a cardiac arrest."

I shook my head. "Her . . . heart? Her heart is . . . perfect, it's strong. She's an athlete, a superb athlete."

"Yes, but with significant blood loss —"

"I tried to stop it with my shirt."

"That was the proper protocol. You did everything right. You did everything you could have."

I knew why the doctor was saying that. I could see it in his knowing eyes and hear it in his gentle tone. He didn't want me to blame myself. But I hadn't asked because I wanted absolution.

I would never absolve myself.
Ever.

CHAPTER FOUR

The next hours at the hospital were a blur, and I traveled through them numbly. Dr. Chen told us they had to perform an autopsy on Allison, which made Lucinda cry harder — *they can't do this to her, we can't let them* — the prospect eviscerating her as if she were the one being emptied of her organs, reduced to a hollowed-out shell of a mother.

I held her close. She wanted to see Allison's body, and they showed us to an operating room. We left Ethan in an anteroom with a nurse, guessing that it would have been too much for him, and we turned out to be right. The OR was empty, chilly, and immaculate, filled with gleaming equipment and lined with cabinets. The overhead fixture was shaped like a saucer, and only a few lights had been turned on, illuminating a gurney of molded plastic, which held a body covered by a white paper sheet. There was a large bump at the head and little bumps at the feet.

Lucinda burst into new tears, and I managed not to fall to pieces when I walked her to the gurney and moved the paper aside, just enough to see the beautiful face of my daughter. It wasn't possible I was seeing her this way, now. It couldn't be happening.

Her eyes were closed. Her skin was pale. Her hair was darker at the hairline, dried sweat from the game. Her headband was gone. A faint reddish line from an oxygen mask encircled her mouth, where only hours before had been a blue mouth guard. She still wore a retainer at night.

I didn't dare lower the paper sheet another inch. I knew we couldn't handle seeing the wound on Allison's neck. I covered her face again, and Lucinda collapsed, sobbing against our daughter's chest.

I rubbed Lucinda's back, but didn't succumb to emotion. I couldn't. Lucinda bent over to hug Allison, crying so hard I worried she would never stop. In time, a nurse came to the window and caught my eye, and I sensed they needed the room.

I signaled to her for a few more minutes, stalling, not wanting to leave my daughter here, behind, for good, forever. I found myself reaching under the sheet to touch

Allison's cheek one last time. It was cool but soft in the way of young people, full of promise. I felt my heart break. Tears blurred my eyes. My daughter could've done anything, she could've been anyone. I wanted her to be whatever she wanted to be. I wanted her to be *alive.* I had taken *alive* for granted.

Anguish tore me up, and I understood why mourners shredded their clothes. I found myself saying *I am so sorry I am so sorry,* then I realized I was entering dangerous emotional territory, my rage resurfacing. I clenched my teeth so hard I couldn't say another word.

Lucinda mopped her eyes before we collected Ethan, and she sagged as we were led to the police cruiser, where Moonie barked with happiness, oblivious. Ethan scooped the dog up, buried his face in his coarse coat, and hugged him in the back seat, crying all the way home.

Somehow we got upstairs, and Lucinda and I brought Ethan into our bedroom, cuddling with him. The bedroom was dark except for ambient light from the window that faced the street. The curtains were open, and I could see the cedar shakes of the Brophys' roof and the zigzag tree line of the Whitmans' windscreen across the street.

The blue Nittany Lions flag in front of the Corbuzes', next door. All the markers of my life, still in place. Except everything had changed.

Lucinda's tears subsided, her sobs finally ceasing. Ethan fell asleep in time. I closed my eyes to the rhythm of his respiration, one breath after the other, in and out of his lungs. I didn't know what to do or what to think. I didn't understand. It had all happened so fast. It was as if she slipped through my fingers. My hands were still sticky with her blood, dry now, flaking off. It itched. It seared.

I needed to reconfigure who I was. I was still her father, but she was gone. I had only one living child now, just a boy, my son.

I would always be Allison's father, even without Allison. Lucinda whispered, "You awake?"

"Yes."

"I don't know . . . our baby girl."

I hugged her tighter, in the darkness.

"It's . . . this is . . . unreal."

"I feel the same way."

"We're here . . . without . . . her. She's too . . . young . . . she has everything . . . her whole . . . *life.*" Lucinda began to cry again. "Why . . . why her . . . why? She was so . . . great . . . she was just a *great kid* . . .

and now, now, that's *it*? That's her . . . life? Her whole . . . entire *life*?"

I closed my eyes.

"She wasn't even sixteen . . . we were just talking about . . . what kind of . . . party . . ."

I swallowed hard. Allison's birthday was January 18. It would have been her sweet sixteen. Most of her friends were already sixteen. She hated that. She was competitive.

"She doesn't . . . get to graduate? Go to . . . college? Get married?"

I couldn't even get that far.

"This happened . . . to her? This is what happens?"

I felt the same, that this was unfathomable.

"What will . . . we do? What? How?" Lucinda fell silent a moment, then whispered, "Do you know what's . . . the worst?"

"Everything," I whispered back, without thinking.

"Yes," Lucinda said, after a minute. "She was . . . my best friend."

"I'm so sorry, honey," I said. It was true. Lucinda and Allison were best friends. Lucinda had other girlfriends, like Melissa. They were field hockey and lacrosse moms, walking buddies, yoga on Mondays and

Thursdays. But none was as close as Allison.

"We were . . . two peas . . ."

She didn't have to finish the sentence. I said it all the time. Mother and daughter were so much alike they were almost the same person. They looked alike, they even had the same walk, slightly duck-toed. They both talked too fast. They were both all over everything. Intense, strong.

"I loved her . . . I love her so . . . much . . . Ethan loved her . . . we loved her . . ."

"We always will."

Lucinda cried harder. Tears filled my eyes, but I held them back. I was already feeling the weight of the awful tasks ahead. I would have to call the funeral home in the morning. Make an appointment to choose a casket. We would tell Allison's friends, our friends. Troy, the new boyfriend. The coaches, the school. Lucinda would cancel the coveted day-of appointment for beachy waves. She would have to pick out Allison's dress.

Not for homecoming.

Forever and ever.

I awoke to Moonie's barking downstairs, then the doorbell ringing. I reached for my phone to check the time. Three-fifteen a.m.

I had no idea who would be here at this hour, then realized it could be the detectives. Maybe they had caught the guy.

I jumped out of bed and flew from the room, still in my bloody undershirt. I hurried downstairs to find Moonie barking and jumping around the entrance hall, his nails clicking on the hardwood.

I looked through the window in the front door and saw two men in suits. The one in front was a trim, fit African-American about my age. He spotted me, then held up a bifold wallet that read FBI under a golden badge. Behind him stood a younger White man with short brown hair, wire-rimmed glasses, and a blocky build, holding up his own FBI bifold ID.

I didn't know what the FBI wanted, but I opened the door. "Hello —"

"Mr. Bennett, I'm Special Agent Dom Kingston of the FBI, out of Philly. This is my partner, Special Agent Michael Hallman. Our condolences on the loss of your daughter. I'm sorry to disturb you at this hour. May we come in?"

"Okay." I stepped aside, and they entered to Moonie sniffing their shoes. "What's the FBI's involvement? I thought Chester County was handling this."

"Not anymore." Special Agent Kingston

looked grave.

"Did you catch the guy?"

"No, not yet. May we speak with you and your wife?"

"It's the middle of the night, and she finally got to sleep."

"It's important. Can you wake her?"

"Now?"

"Time is of the essence."

Chapter Five

I was on the couch between my wife and son, and we sat opposite Special Agents Kingston and Hallman. Puffy-eyed and exhausted, Lucinda had changed into a chambray shirt and jeans before coming downstairs, taking off her blood-spattered clothes. Ethan still had on his Nike shirt and jeans. I would have let him sleep, but Moonie's barking woke him.

We had exchanged introductions in the family room, where Special Agent Kingston seemed to take command merely by his presence, which was quietly authoritative. His face was a long rectangle, with a strong jawline and a small mouth. His hair was cut short, with a hairline beginning to recede. He was about my height, too, and muscular in a dark, well-cut suit. Special Agent Hallman ceded him the floor, with an impassive expression on his round face. Dimpled cheeks emphasized his youth.

Special Agent Kingston cleared his throat. "Mr. and Mrs. Bennett, and Ethan, let me begin by saying we're very sorry about your loss."

"Thank you," I said for us all. Ethan glued his gaze to the FBI agents, and I realized he had never seen a real one before, though I had, back when I took a job for the government, working on depositions at Guantánamo Bay. All of the federal agents I met were just like these two, steady and professional in demeanor.

"As I said, we're sorry to disturb, but time is of the essence. We have been in contact with the Chester County detectives and the officers at the scene."

"Okay," I said, not sure where he was going. "So why is the FBI involved?"

"I'll come back to that in a moment. First, we have identified your daughter's murderer as one John Milo."

My jaw clenched. Now I knew the name of the man who had ended my daughter's life. It felt surreal, hearing it in a family room filled with Allison. Her most recent school photo dominated the mantel; we had sprung for the eight-by-ten. The coffee table was cluttered with bottles of Holo Taco nail polish, tubes of watermelon ChapStick, a black ponytail elastic, and a tub of peppermint Mentos gum, which she loved so much we called her *gum pig.* Her Adidas slides and a pair of worn red Toms were piled by the entertainment center. My daughter surrounded us, but was absent. It was a family room without the family.

"We have also identified his accomplice, the man killed at the scene. His name is George Veria, Jr. He goes by Junior."

Ethan looked over. "Dad, you were right. Remember, you read his lips? You said his name was Junior."

I had forgotten, my alleged superpower. I nodded at Ethan, but my thoughts flashed back to Coldstream Road. It struck me that Allison's backpack, purse, and hockey stick were still in the car. Overnight, my daughter's belongings had become her personal effects.

"Jason, we understand that Junior Veria was shot by John Milo, not by you."

Even if I remained angry that anyone had questioned this, I was relieved to hear that the suspicion had ended. "Good."

"Both men were members of the George Veria Organization, or GVO, a dangerous criminal network that distributes and sells OxyContin, fentanyl, and other opiates in central and southeastern Pennsylvania."

"Oh no," I said, aghast. Lucinda reached

for my hand. Ethan hugged Moonie, a speck of dried blood on the dog's front paw.

"First, let me give you some background. A carjacking usually occurs for one of three reasons. Number one, the car is stolen to flee the scene of a crime. Number two, the car is stolen because it's a specific make, as part of an auto theft ring." Special Agent Kingston counted off on slim, nimble fingers. "Number three, the victim is in the wrong place at the wrong time."

Lucinda interjected, "Was it because they wanted a Mercedes?"

"No. We have reason to believe that they needed your car to flee another crime. There was a double homicide last night, about an hour before your daughter's. We believe it was committed by Milo and Junior. They needed to ditch their pickup, so they took your car."

I tried to process the information. It was hard to think about what had happened before Allison was killed.

Dad, they have guns.

I asked, "Why take a car with a family in it? Isn't that risky?"

"They had no choice. They take what comes."

"Where was the double homicide? Who was killed?"

Special Agent Kingston paused. "Milo and Junior killed two men in Jennersville. Their names were Walter Jersey and Gary Reid. They were retail-level drug dealers in the same organization."

"So they killed their own men? Why?" I flashed on Milo shooting Junior. "What is it with these guys? They turn on their own?"

"Infighting is not uncommon in a criminal organization. They jockey for power."

"But why kill lower-level men? How does that help them move up?"

"We don't know. There are a few likely scenarios."

"Like what?"

Special Agent Kingston pursed his lips. "It's possible that Milo falsely accuses the other two of skimming, then kills them to curry favor with the boss. The kingpin of the organization is Junior's father, George Veria, Sr. They call him Big George. There's nepotism even in crime families. Junior was being groomed for the top spot. So if Milo wanted the top spot, he'd have to kill Junior."

It made a horrific sort of sense. "Do you think Milo *planned* to kill Junior at our carjacking?"

"No. We believe he exploited the opportunity presented by the dog attack."

Ethan looked down at Moonie. I hugged my son closer.

"That brings me to why we're here." Special Agent Kingston leaned forward intently, his dark-eyed gaze bracketed by crow's feet that looked earned. "Obviously, Milo can't tell Big George that he himself killed Junior. We believe Milo will say you put up a fight, disarmed Junior, and shot him. In effect, Milo will frame you for Junior's murder."

Lucinda gasped. Ethan looked over. I felt my chest tighten. I hadn't seen this coming, but it was a logical assumption. It was what the Chester County detectives had believed, too.

Special Agent Kingston frowned. "Big George was very close to his son. We believe the organization will target you and your family in retaliation. We believe you're in danger, right now."

"Oh no!" Lucinda recoiled, her lips parting.

I struggled to process the information. "But won't they find out from the news that Milo killed Junior?"

"No. We won't release that information."

"Why not? It's the truth and it would prevent me from being framed."

"If we reveal that Milo killed Junior, he'll

flee. It will hurt our chances of apprehending him."

"But if you're right, then why didn't Milo kill me last night? Or kill all of us? He could still have lied to Big George."

"Excellent question." Special Agent Kingston smiled with grim approval. "We recovered only one weapon at the scene, a .45 caliber revolver. The bullet recovered from Junior's body was a .45 caliber. We don't have a complete ballistics report yet, but we believe it's from Junior's weapon. In other words, Milo shot Junior with his own gun."

"How do you know it wasn't from Milo's, if you don't have his gun?"

Special Agent Kingston hesitated. "The round recovered from your daughter was a .22 caliber. We know it came from Milo's gun, so Milo was carrying a .22 caliber weapon."

It was hard to hear. I willed myself to stay in control. I couldn't imagine the horrific insult of the bullet, tearing my daughter's neck apart.

"A logical question would be, why did Milo switch guns to kill Junior? We believe it was an abundance of caution, in case word of the ballistics leaked. Big George would never have believed you could disarm

Milo, Jason. He's big, you saw. He started with the organization as muscle and worked his way up."

My mind reeled. "But my fingerprints aren't on the gun."

"Milo couldn't do anything about that. He had to take a chance. He couldn't go back without his own gun. He couldn't explain that to Big George."

"But how did Milo get Junior's gun? We were right there."

"We had the same question." Special Agent Kingston's eyes narrowed. "So let me ask you, did you see Milo shoot Junior?"

I remembered, with a sickening sensation. "No, we were with Allison. Our backs were turned to them."

"That's what we thought." Special Agent Kingston glanced at Special Agent Hallman. "While you were with your daughter, Milo must have taken the gun from Junior and shot him. Later, did you notice if Milo was holding a gun in each hand?"

I thought back. "No, I saw him drop a gun. I guess I assumed there was nothing in his other hand."

Lucinda shook her head, stricken. "I don't remember."

Special Agent Kingston paused. "You asked me why Milo didn't kill you all. The reason is simple. He ran out of bullets. Junior's gun had only one round left. He would have finished the job with his own gun but for the car coming on the scene."

The words landed an impact of their own. My mind reeled. All of us, dead. Lucinda. Ethan. I tried to process what he was telling me. "Why would Junior carry a partially loaded weapon?"

"We believe he committed the homicides in Jennersville, using his gun." Special Agent Kingston frowned with concern. "Bottom line, your family is in danger. You're eyewitnesses to the murder of your daughter. You need to enter the witness protection program."

"What?" I asked, shocked.

Lucinda's hand flew to her mouth.

Special Agent Kingston pursed his lips. "We're here to take you to a safe, temporary location, right away."

"Tonight?"

"Yes. Now."

Lucinda gasped. Ethan's eyes filmed.

I shook my head, reflexively resisting. "Go, now? Leave? We live here."

Lucinda recoiled, aghast. "I mean, our daughter was just . . ." she said, hushed. "We have to hold her funeral, and Ethan has his friends, his school —"

"I don't want to go," Ethan interrupted, anxious. "I don't want to go where I don't know anybody else."

Special Agent Kingston nodded grimly. "I know this is a lot, after such a tragedy. But your lives are in jeopardy."

I couldn't process it that fast. "But I own a business. So does my wife. We're self-employed. We work. Our businesses are here."

Lucinda shook her head. "And I can't leave my mother. She's in assisted living. She has no family but us."

Special Agent Kingston leaned forward, urgent. "We can guarantee your safety if you enter the program. You'll be relocated to a comparable neighborhood. You can have a new life and start over."

I felt my world turning upside down. I didn't want a new life. I wanted my old life back. I wanted my daughter back. Instead I said, "How will I support us? What will I do for a living?"

"The government will sell the business and help you establish yourself in another profession." Special Agent Kingston checked his watch. "There'll be time to discuss it later. We need to go now. They could be on their way."

"How would they find us?" I couldn't

wrap my mind around it. "The police haven't even released Allison's name."

"Word gets out. Information leaks. They have your plate number. They could have a scanner."

Lucinda kept shaking her head. "What about my mother? Our friends? What do we tell them? We just *vanish*?"

"There can be no further communication —"

"No! Are you serious?"

"I'm sorry, but —"

"We don't *have* to go, do we? You can't make us, can you?"

Special Agent Kingston pursed his lips. "No. It's your choice. You can choose to stay, but we strongly advise against doing so."

"Then we're not going," Lucinda shot back.

"We're totally not," Ethan added, teary. "This is where we live."

I rose. "Gentlemen, we need to talk this over."

"As I said, time is of the —"

"We're going to talk this over." I held out a hand to Lucinda. "Honey?"

Chapter Six

I took my seat at the head of the kitchen table, and Lucinda and Ethan sat down in their chairs. The lamp glowed softly overhead, and the air still smelled of the garlic bread we had with a spaghetti dinner, another lifetime ago. Allison's chair was empty, as it would be forever.

"Jason, do you believe this? It's too much." Lucinda shook her head, her face ashen. Her eyes were bloodshot and puffy. Her fine nose was red at the tip, and her nostrils swollen. Her face was heart-shaped, curving to a pointed chin, but she worried about the wrinkles in her forehead. I had never noticed them before tonight.

"No. It's unreal, I know." I took her hand across the table. "But I think we should go."

"You do?" Lucinda's eyes widened. "Really?"

"No!" Ethan cried out, teary. "Dad, please, no. Can't we please stay? We can be careful. We'll watch out. We can do it."

My heart ached for him. "I know this isn't what you want, or what we want. But it's not safe to stay."

"It is if we're careful! It's called 'situational awareness,' we learned about it in assembly!"

"It's not that easy, Ethan."

"But we have a burglar alarm. We never use it. We could start using it!"

"It's not good enough. We didn't get sensors on the windows, only the doors." I had cheaped out, not that it mattered now.

"So we'll get the sensors on the windows or whatever!"

"It's not enough, buddy."

"It is, we'll be fine. I don't want to go. It's not fair!"

"I know it's not." I turned to Lucinda, who was trying not to cry, her lower lip trembling. "What do you say, honey?"

"I don't know. I can't decide, I can't." Lucinda wiped her eyes, biting her lip. I had never seen her so distraught, even after her sister Caitlin died. She looked worse than heartbroken. She looked broken.

"Let's talk it out." I squeezed her hand.

"I can't decide so fast. They're waiting."

"It's okay. Tell me what you're thinking."

Ethan touched her arm, anxious. "Mom,

can't we stay? Please? We *live* here!"

"I don't know, honey," Lucinda answered, then turned to me. "What about Mom? She has no one. I don't want to leave her, but I don't want us in danger."

"I know." I loved my mother-in-law, who suffered from Alzheimer's and lived at Bay Horse, an assisted-living facility nearby.

Ethan interjected, "Mom, we'll be okay if we just use the burglar alarm!"

"Buddy," I said gently. "Let your mom and me talk. We know what you think and we know why."

Ethan sniffled, wiping his eyes. "Okay, but it's really not fair."

Lucinda let go of my hand and placed her palms on the table. "I can't leave my mother, just like that. I have to make sure they take good care of her. You know, you have to be there, on the scene."

I knew what she meant. Lucinda was hands-on, a great daughter and mother. She visited her Mom twice a week, and when the kids were in elementary school, she was class mom and chaperoned on every field trip. She was the one who brought the orange slices and snacks after the games. She collected for the coach's gifts, which somehow ended up costing me extra money.

"Her main nurse, Susan, is usually on top

of things, but Marjorie, who comes on Monday and Wednesday, never gets it. If she doesn't understand my mother, she pretends she doesn't hear it."

I knew my wife was right about that, too. Bay Horse was a great facility, but it wasn't perfect. My mother-in-law's care was paid for by her inheritance from my late father-in-law, though I had been truly staggered by the cost of assisted living in the Memory Care wing.

"Sometimes I think they're mean to her just because she has money. They think her life was easy, but it wasn't. It never has been. She always worked in my father's office, she just didn't get paid." Lucinda's face fell. "She would do anything for me and Caitlin. Remember how good she was when Caitlin got sick? She dropped everything."

"Yes. So did you." Both my mother-in-law and Lucinda had rallied to take care of Caitlin through her cancer treatments. "Well, family is always different."

"That's why I want to be there."

I didn't know what to say, having inadvertently proven her point.

"We shouldn't stay, but . . . it's so much to give up. Ethan's school, his friends, everything he does." Lucinda looked over at him. "I know this is terrible for you, to go. I know that, honey. Your father does, too."

Ethan sniffled. "Then can't we stay?"

"I'm trying to figure it out with your dad." Lucinda turned to me, stricken. "And I hate to leave our friends, Melissa and all of them, everyone. The house. This house. Our *home.*" She started shaking her head, exhaling slowly. "I remember the day we brought her home from the hospital, don't you?"

"Sure." I knew she meant Allison.

"She was so little, in that car seat. We had to put it on the floor, right here. We didn't even have a table. The furniture was backordered. We had nothing, remember?"

I did. A big, empty house. A small baby girl. We were in heaven.

"Even the color of the kitchen, she and I picked it out together."

I remembered. One weekend, mother and daughter had watched an HGTV marathon, then gone to the paint store. They had chosen Tuscan Gold, which Allison had loved.

It reminds me of the sun in Rome.

Al, you've never been to Rome.

I can imagine it.

You can imagine Rome?

Can't you, Dad?

I couldn't think about that now. Allison would never get to Rome. We had never traveled out of the country. I hadn't been able to take that much time off. I felt a wave of regret, of things not done, milestones not achieved, my daughter's very life ended, my wife and I surviving her, the one thing every parent dreads.

"What about her trees?" Lucinda gestured out the window, to the backyard.

I looked outside, where it was still dark. I could barely see the outline of the two evergreens that Allison used as goalposts. She had named them Scylla and Charybdis, since she had been studying Greek mythology at the time. She had showed me Edith Hamilton's book.

Dad, how the hell do you pronounce Charybdis?

Don't say "hell."

But that I can pronounce.

"And what about this?" Lucinda rose and crossed to the threshold of the kitchen, then ran a finger down the white molding. We tracked the kids' growth on it over the years, the names and dates wiggly in the paint, with lines written in pencil, crayon, pen, and Sharpie. My anguished gaze stopped where Allison had crayoned in big letters, *IM SOOOOOOOO BIG!!!!!!!*

Lucinda shook her head. "I don't know what to do."

I did. "We can't look over our shoulder for the rest of our lives. We can't, honey. It's not safe to stay."

Lucinda's gaze shifted to Ethan, and her lovely face fell into lines of deep sorrow. She didn't say anything, but I knew what she was thinking:

We lost our daughter. We cannot lose our son.

"I would never forgive myself," Lucinda said quietly.

"Neither would I," I told her.

I knew it was true.

I was already not forgiving myself.

Chapter Seven

We left our lives in silence. I sat in the back seat of the nondescript white van, with Lucinda asleep on one shoulder and Ethan on the other. Special Agent Kingston did the driving with Special Agent Hallman in the passenger seat. Moonie was in the back in his crate, asleep. We'd had fifteen minutes to pack, and I'd grabbed clothes and cash from the safe. Lucinda took her best jewelry and some clothes, then hurried to Allison's bedroom. I found her there in tears, stuffing mementos into Allison's quilted bag, a birthday gift from one Vera Bradley freak to another.

Mom, this is the new pattern! I love it!

Deep inside me was the most profound sorrow I had ever known, one that had unpacked, settled in, and taken up residence. I felt the mute agony of loss, my heart so heavy it weighed on my lungs, making it hard to breathe. I didn't feel entitled to, when Allison could not.

Special Agent Kingston glanced at me in his rearview mirror, so I turned away, to the window. The morning sun climbed the sky, trying vainly to brighten the interior of the van through its smoked glass. I watched traffic zoom past, eyeing the uniformed drivers delivering paper goods, a florist singing along to music, a white van with a red cross on the door and a windshield placard that read BLOOD DELIVERY.

I looked away. I didn't want to think about trying to stop Allison's blood, trying to keep it inside her with my palm, absorb it with my shirt, do anything to conserve it, my daughter's very life-blood. I wanted to cry, but I was the center, still holding.

We passed a big green sign for the Port of Wilmington, heading south on I-95. I hadn't traveled this way often. We had gone to Baltimore a few times to take the kids to the National Aquarium. I remembered Allison loved the puffins, pressing her tiny hand on the glass, and when her fingers had bowed backward at the knuckle, I realized she was double-jointed. It would become her claim to familial fame, and she could twist her elbow around or put her entire fist in her mouth.

Al, you're a freak of nature.

Jealous much?

The sun came up, and we left I-95 and switched to Route 1 continuing south. Traffic congested through Smyrna, and as we passed Dover Air Force Base, military planes flew overhead like gray shadows behind the cloudy haze. There were fewer trucks as we headed toward the coastline, then fewer cars. The FBI agents didn't exchange a single word. They knew where we were going, without conversation or GPS.

We passed an Arby's, a Chick-fil-A, a McDonald's, and a Dunkin' Donuts, then got off Route 1. We drove through a series of beach communities, their quiet streets lined with houses, many of which were built up on stilts. Each one was different from the next; modern glass affairs, old weathered clapboard with screened-in porches, new multi-story homes with siding in colorful aluminum, flying novelty flags with lobsters and cartoon fish.

Seagulls scored the sky, and in time the houses grew fewer and farther apart. The landscape changed dramatically, and I shifted upward to take it in, trying to get my bearings. There were wooded patches here and there, but in time there were almost no trees, nor even land.

We drove through vast stretches of marsh, populated with tall green and brown reeds and a variety of water plants I couldn't identify. A myriad of canals and creeks with brown, murky water snaked through the foliage. Random ponds appeared around every corner, their surfaces covered with moss and algae.

I felt an increasing sense of dislocation. I was a suburban dad, a farm boy at heart. It disoriented me to see the vanishing of terra firma, as if the land beneath my very feet were disappearing. Or maybe it was simply my mood, because I knew nothing would ever be familiar again.

I heard myself say, "I didn't realize there was so much swamp down here."

Special Agent Hallman turned to me. "We're driving on the border of a nature preserve."

"Oh."

"But the fact is, about ninety percent of Delaware is wetlands. By the way, it's not a swamp, it's a marsh."

"Good to know. I didn't realize there was a difference."

"There is. A swamp is generally standing water. What you're seeing is saltwater tidal marsh. It flows into the Delaware Bay."

"Sounds like you have the facts."

"I'm local. I grew up in Lewes."

Special Agent Kingston smiled. "Now you know why we call him Wiki. He's Wikipedia Brown."

Special Agent Hallman chuckled, and the van began to slow. Brownish sand drifted onto the asphalt, gritty under our tires, and we turned onto a street that had just a few houses. They were set back from the road, blocked from view by thick scrub pines and arborvitae.

I glimpsed shingled façades, generous porches, and second-story decks to take advantage of the view over the marsh. We passed a small, decrepit house with rusting junk in its front yard, an eyesore among an enclave of nicer homes. There were no cars parked on the street or in the driveways, and I gathered they were vacation homes for the well-heeled, unoccupied this time of year.

I cleared my throat. "What's the name of this town?"

"Reeford," Special Agent Kingston answered, looking in the rearview mirror. "Your house is at the end of the street, a dead end. Three bedrooms, two and a half baths. You have the marsh out back and the beach out front, on the bay."

I could tell he was trying to cheer me up,

which I appreciated. "Sounds nice."

"We'll be in the au-pair suite, which is detached. It gives your family privacy. Fenced-in backyard for the dog, too."

"Thanks." I tried to wrap my mind around it. I hadn't even noticed the street name. "How long do we stay here?"

"Six months through the application process. Then you make a permanent move. We'll be there in a few minutes. You might want to wake up your wife and son."

I didn't reply. I didn't want to wake them. I wanted Lucinda to stay in whatever dreamworld she was in, because it had to be better than this one, in which her beloved daughter, her best friend, no longer lived. Ethan, too. He adored his sister, and I didn't know if he was strong enough to live a life in which he had seen her shot to death, feeling like it was his fault. I didn't know if we could get him professional help in the witness protection program. I didn't know anything about the program except what I had seen in the movies. It was the one thing I had never had a deposition about.

We reached the end of the street, then turned onto a large square of driveway. It was of crushed seashells lined with thick railroad ties, holding back brush and trees.

Shards popped under our tires as we slowed to a stop, and Special Agent Kingston shut the ignition.

The sudden silence brought up the sounds of Ethan's snoring, still congested. Lucinda didn't wake up, but stirred, lifting her head from me and shifting sleepily to the window.

"Jason, you wanna wake up —"

"Hold on." I got up, eased around Ethan, and left the van, orienting myself. "Mind if I look around a sec?"

"Take your time." Special Agent Kingston reached for his phone.

I took in the house, elevated on stilts, which was large and traditional in style, with a brown clapboard façade weathering tastefully. A wooden staircase led to a front porch with two rocking chairs and a front door of forest green. There were plenty of windows, their frames a faded white, on both floors. Underneath were outdoor shower stalls next to air-conditioning units and propane tanks on elevated platforms. Next to the house stood a smaller version without the porch, presumably for the FBI agents.

I could see the fenced backyard on the right, and on the left a trail to the marsh, with its tall reeds, brownish creek, and vast expanse of cloudy sky. The air was heavy and smelled briny and organic, like decomposing matter. I turned away and was about to go back to the car when on the other side, I spotted a path to the beach.

On impulse, I went that way. The sand was a coarse light brown, mounded with brackish seaweed and hollow dried reeds that snapped when I stepped on them. The path led over a small dune dotted with grass and cactus, lined with a wooden fence. I kept going to the long stretch of beach, which was completely empty.

The bay's shoreline was an endless slow curve. The water was gray-blue, lapping against the beach, and the waves rippled in striations of dark blue and black. The breeze smelled fresh and salty, and the sun emerged from a screen of cirrus clouds, glittering briefly on the water.

The sight sent me back in time, and I found myself remembering when I had taught Allison to float on the bay side of Long Beach Island. I remembered putting my hands under her wiry little body as she lay on her back, her skinny arms out, palms up. She was only three, but fearless.

Let go, Daddy! Let me go! I can do it myself!

Keep your head back. Stay straight.

Let me go!

So I did, and Allison had floated, squeezing her eyes shut as water sluiced into her ears.

It had been so hard to let her go, then.

It was impossible now.

I heard my throat catch, emitting a sound I never had before. I couldn't believe my daughter was gone. I was alone, on the edge between land and sea, earth and heaven, life and death.

Suddenly a magnificent blue heron flew overhead, flapping its angular wings, leading with its long neck, graceful and strong, the hue of heaven itself.

Tears came to my eyes. I took the heron as a sign. It resonated within me. It felt like Allison's soul, beautiful, strong, and proud, set free, taking flight.

I love you, Al.

I missed her so much. I loved her even more. But I had failed her, as a father.

My daughter believed I had superpowers, but I didn't. I'd thought I was a good dad, but I wasn't. I hadn't saved her life. I had let her down. It broke me in pieces, wiped me out, annihilated me. I couldn't be the center anymore. I couldn't hold another second.

I fell to my knees in the coarse sand.

And I cried and cried, for my beloved baby girl.

Chapter Eight

I woke up Monday morning after a restless night, and my first thought was for Allison. I closed my eyes again, hoping it wasn't true. Hoping it hadn't happened. I knew it had.

I lay on my back, tried to think of what we did yesterday, but it was a lost day. Lucinda and Ethan had taken to bed, alternately crying and napping, and I had showered, checked on them, and unpacked our few belongings. Somehow we had gotten through the day and the night.

I made myself open my eyes. It was the beginning of the rest of my life, like the posters used to say. They meant everything can change for the better. They never say it can change for the worse.

I missed my daughter with every cell in my body. I knew I would think of her every morning. It had been like that after my father passed. I would think, *Maybe I dreamed it.*

My heart actually ached, which I hadn't known was physically possible. I had lost my mother, my father, and Caitlin, but I had never felt like this. Paralyzed, in pain, stuck between mute disbelief and abject despair. Lucinda slept next to me, her back turned. Thank God she had finally gotten some rest. She had been crying most of the night.

I looked around the bedroom for a minute, orienting myself. The walls were painted white, and the room was sunny, with a panel of windows on each side. The right side overlooked the driveway, and the left, the marsh out back.

A cool, briny breeze and the call of seagulls wafted through the screens, billowing curtains in a blue seashell pattern. Beachy watercolors hung on the walls, and we had a blue bedspread patterned with fish. Two white dressers sat opposite the bed, also white, matching the night tables. The only incongruous note was a first-rate alarm system. It worked like ours at home, but had sensors on the windows and motion detectors.

I got out of bed, slipped into a T-shirt and gym shorts, remembering to disable the alarm. I left the bedroom, and on the other side of a center hall were two more bedrooms, one large and one small. The little one was less desirable, but Ethan had taken it, perhaps by habit. If Allison had been here, she would have bounded into the bigger room and staked her claim with a huge grin.

I peeked into Ethan's room to find him asleep in his clothes, cuddled with Moonie. He looked lost in the queen-size bed, which had a pine headboard. Otherwise the room held a pine dresser and a desk-and-chair combination. I remembered we had bought a desk for Allison, the mistake of rookie parents.

Dad, please take this stupid desk out of my room.

You're supposed to do your homework there. Develop good study habits.

Okay, boomer.

I closed the door and padded downstairs to the living room, which was furnished with a beige couch and matching chairs around a white coffee table. Against the wall was a white entertainment center with a flat-screen TV. I tried to imagine us living here. A nice house, but not ours. A house holding its breath for a household. I didn't know if we could make it one without Allison. I didn't know if I wanted to try.

I crossed the room, unlocked the dead bolt on the front door, and opened it wide, breathing in the marshy air. Out front was the driveway, and trees and brush hid the house from the street. The FBI van was parked with its back to the house. It had a Delaware plate, not a government one.

I went to the kitchen in the back, which was a long rectangle edged with builders-grade appliances and oak cabinets, white Corian countertops, and a double sink. Beyond was the laundry room, powder room, and a back door, which I opened.

I stepped outside onto a small deck, complete with blue canvas director's chairs around a teak table and a Weber propane grill. Ducks sailed silently past, and I thought I saw a loon but I wasn't sure.

I went back inside to the kitchen and opened the refrigerator to find milk and half-and-half, a six-pack of Diet Coke, and apples and oranges in plastic bags. We had barely eaten yesterday, picking on grapes and apples. The freezer held cans of orange juice concentrate and a plastic bag of Dunkin' Donuts ground coffee.

"Bingo." I found the new Mr. Coffee and brewed a pot. I was always the first one up, since morning chores were in my DNA. On a normal Saturday at home, Allison would be upstairs listening to Lady Gaga over the costly whine of the Dyson blow-dryer we'd gotten her for Christmas.

Dad, Mom, this is sick!

It better be, I had said. I cringed inwardly at the memory. Looking back, I hated that I had said that. I was frugal, like my father. We had to be, on a farm, but it had stuck with me. Now I would buy her a million Dysons. I would pay anything.

I found a mug that read NANTICOKE WILDLIFE AREA, poured a black coffee, and went back into the living room, where I sat down on the stiff couch, found the remote, and turned on the TV to see if the news was reporting anything about what happened.

I sipped coffee, switching around to find some news. My heart started to pound. I didn't know if I could watch an account of Allison's murder, but I had to know. I waited through a traffic report, a weather forecast, and a feature about a baby panda, as well as a report of a trash fire, of a tractor-trailer overturned, of stock prices, of gas prices. Nothing about Allison's murder or the double homicide.

I heard footsteps on the porch and startled.

We can guarantee your safety if you enter

the program.

"Hello?" I rose, nervous.

"Jason, it's Dom. You up?"

Special Agent Kingston. I remembered we were on a first-name basis.

"Sure," I called back. I crossed to the door and opened it to find Dom standing there. He had on a white polo shirt and khaki pants, and a shave so fresh there was cream in his ear. He held a bag of groceries, and on his broad shoulder hung a black messenger bag.

"Good morning." Dom smiled, his teeth nice and even. "I got fresh eggs and produce. I knew I could improve on the oranges."

"Thanks." I accepted the bag from him, surprised by his thoughtfulness. "Anything new about Milo? Did you find him?"

"No, I'll let you know."

"Do they have any leads? I mean, on top of what I gave them?"

"Not yet." Dom lingered on the step. "Mind if I come in?"

"Oh, right. No, of course not." I felt vaguely awkward, I didn't know how to act. I wondered if he'd check in on us every morning or if we were supposed to become friends. I held open the door. "Come on."

Dom stepped inside, looking around. "You

like the place?"

"Yes, thanks." I headed for the kitchen, and he fell in stride on the way.

"We tried to take into account that you're a family. Normally it's a crappy motel off 95."

"Thanks." I set the groceries on the counter. "I guess we're not the usual . . . whatever you call us."

"Applicants." Dom put his messenger bag on a kitchen chair. "Anyway, the investigation into your daughter's murder is in full swing."

"How, if you're here?" I unpacked eggs, big oranges, and romaine lettuce and put them in the fridge.

"Wiki and I aren't on the investigation team."

"What team are you on?" I put a block of Cabot cheese and a pack of sliced turkey into the fridge.

"They call us The Babysitters Club."

"Funny." I smiled.

"It gets old." Dom chuckled. "My team gets you through the application process, then hands you off to the U.S. Marshals. They run WITSEC."

"So who runs the investigation?" I put away apples and grapes, and packets of vanilla Yoplait.

"Agents on the investigative team."

"I meant their names."

"Joe Watanabe is the case agent and Matt Reilly is the laboring oar. Reilly briefs me, and I keep you in the loop." Dom leaned against the counter.

"Can I talk to them directly if I want to?" I put away two-percent milk and a tub of Turkey Hill vanilla.

"Yes. They'll be talking to you soon, to get any information you may have."

"But nothing new on Milo?" I pulled out a green pack of cookies and folded the empty grocery bag. "They have so much to go on."

"This is too soon."

Maybe he was right but I had barely slept, replaying what had happened. I still couldn't get Allison's blood from under my fingernails. I didn't know if I wanted to. I was half-in and half-out of my own life. My new life. Our new life.

"From now on, if you make a list, I can get whatever you need. Food, supplies, whatever."

"So we don't do the shopping?"

"No. Don't worry, I get Tate's. Best chocolate chips ever." Dom smiled slyly, gesturing at the cookies. "They're good for breakfast, too."

"Is that a hint?" I opened the bag, releasing a sugary smell. "Want one?"

"No, I want two."

Dom accepted the cookies eagerly, reminding me of Allison.

She'll eat you out of house and home, my father used to say.

I took a bite of the cookie, which tasted buttery and delicious. "Wow."

"Right?" Dom grinned, chewing.

"My daughter loved chocolate chips," I heard myself say.

Dom's smile faded, his sympathy plain. "I'm sorry, really. I have two girls, sixteen and twelve. I can't imagine what you and your wife are going through."

"Thanks." My throat went thick. I had to change the subject. "Coffee?"

"No thanks, already had a cup. Then I run."

"I run, too." I finished the cookie.

"I'll run with you."

I used to run with Allison, I almost said. It was our thing. "You don't have to."

"Yes, I do. It's my job."

"Like a bodyguard?"

"Exactly."

It was strange, thinking I needed one. "Does the FBI know that I run? Is that why they picked you to be our . . ."

"Case agent?" Dom supplied. "No. We all run, except Wiki. He sits."

I smiled.

"What if I want to go to the hardware store or something?"

"We go for you. We can get you a couple of bikes, for exercise. We go with you if you ride."

"How about the dog? Do we walk him?"

"No, let him out in the backyard." Dom chewed his second cookie. "How's your wife?"

"Not great," I said, without elaborating. I didn't feel comfortable talking about Lucinda with him. "What about Ethan and school?"

"He's in eighth grade, right?"

It was strange how much Dom knew about us. "Yes, it's his last year of middle school."

"We get him a tutor or you homeschool."

My heart ached for my son. All of his friends would be moving on to high school without him. The same with Allison. She would never graduate, never even be a junior. She would be fifteen forever, but I couldn't go there.

"By the way, I have goodies." Dom brushed off his fingers, dug into the messenger bag, and slid out three Apple laptops and old-school flip phones. They landed on the kitchen table with a clatter and a sealed white envelope. "This is for you guys."

"Thanks. Who pays for this?"

"Taxpayers. Our budget is good, but we're careful." Dom winked. "The Tate's were my treat."

"Thanks," I said, liking him. I was scrupulous with business deductions, too. Then I realized that didn't matter now.

"The laptops are cleared with secured Wi-Fi. But there's no email account. Please don't start any new ones. You can't communicate with anybody, whether by email, text, or phone. Agreed?"

"Agreed."

"The phones are basic but they'll do. I loaded our numbers so you can reach us anytime. Call us for any reason, day or night. We're here for you. One of us will be in the apartment at all times."

"Thank you." I examined the flip phone, missing my iPhone loaded with contacts, email, and documents on Dropbox. Then I realized they didn't matter anymore, either. I wondered about my pictures of Allison. "All of my photos are in my cloud. Do we still have access to that? My wife uses the cloud for her photos, too. You know, she has a photography business."

"No, not yet." Dom's tone turned official. "Don't access your cloud under your name, until we clear that."

"Okay." I understood we were living under FBI rules now.

"By the way, there are security cameras around the property. Obviously, for your safety."

"Where?" I asked, surprised, then realized I shouldn't have been. "Not in the house, right?"

"Correct. Outside. Back door, front door, and in the trees."

"In the trees, really?"

"Yes. We monitor them in our apartment." Dom slid me a laptop, opened it up, and hit the power button. The screen came to life with the unfocused background of Apple's Catalina. "Wiki set these up. They're good to go. Feel free to go online — except, as I said, don't communicate with anyone."

"What's the password?"

"Hold on." Dom leaned over the laptop and hit a few buttons, and the browser came into focus. "There's a document with the passwords in the envelope. Feel free to reset them. It's your computer, not ours. In other words, it has no spyware, in case you were wondering."

I hadn't been. I was still processing the

security cameras in the trees.

"As far as social media goes, you can't go on Facebook, Instagram, or any platform that shows you as a live user. You can't open any new accounts under pseudonyms. Obviously, you can't buy anything. You can't use any credit cards. You can't do anything more active than looking. Understood?"

I nodded.

"When you get a chance, we need your passwords for your current social media accounts, so we can monitor them."

"Okay." I caught sight of the TV playing in the background. "You know, I didn't see anything on the news about my daughter or the double homicide."

"There won't be, as I said."

"It's hard to believe. Can I check online?" I heard myself, asking permission like Ethan. I logged on to Google and searched my name and *carjacking,* which was a disturbing sensation. I got no results. "Nothing."

"Correct."

"Let's try Allison Bennett and —" I hesitated, not wanting to say *murder.* I typed it in anyway, and there were more than a few entries, which horrified me. I skimmed them, realizing that each one represented a grieving family, the ripple effects of violence.

But none of the entries was Allison. "So there's *no* mention? It never happened officially?"

"Correct," Dom repeated.

I didn't know whether to be happy or heartbroken. I rested my hand on the laptop, its metallic surface smooth under my fingertips. "Okay. Thanks."

"You're welcome." Dom smiled. "I'll get going. Call me if you need anything, or come up anytime and knock. Anything you need, just say so."

"I will, thanks," I said, preoccupied. I was itching to go online and learn everything I could about John Milo, Junior Veria, Big George Veria, and the double homicide in Jennersville.

"I'll see myself out. Catch you later." Dom headed for the front door and left, and I sat down. A moment later, I realized I had forgotten to ask him the most important thing.

I hustled after him.

Chapter Nine

"Dom?" I caught him when he was at the bottom of the stairs, and he looked up, then I remembered the cameras in the trees. I descended the stairs, scanning the branches, but didn't see anything. The morning was sunny and clear, and a cool breeze blew off the bay. Seagulls called overhead, a constant backdrop I would have loved on vacation, but not now.

When I reached the driveway, I asked, "How many trees have cameras?"

"Four, in front of the house."

I blinked. "That many?"

"Yes. They're cheaper than personnel. Safer. It's our go-to."

"I don't see them."

"Good." Dom smiled.

"Where's the camera on the porch? You said there was one at the front door."

"In the ceiling fixture."

I looked up at the fixture, wrought iron

with yellow glass, like an old-time lantern. "Is there one on the back door, too?"

"Yes, and several out back."

"Can they hear us, too?"

"No. No audio."

"The house isn't bugged, is it?"

"No," Dom answered, his tone official again. "The intent is to protect you, not spy on you. Now, was there something you needed?"

"I wanted to ask you about arrangements for my daughter's . . . funeral." I still couldn't believe I was saying the words. "Do you know when her body will be, uh, available?"

"It will be released in about seven days. It takes longer when there's an autopsy."

I winced inwardly, but stayed on track. "Uh, Lucinda and I were talking last night. How do we make arrangements for the funeral? And where do we have it? Do we pick out a casket down here, or what?"

"You can choose online or I can get you some brochures." Dom hesitated. "But Jason, you can't go to the funeral. For security reasons."

"What?" I didn't understand. "I'm talking about Allison's funeral."

"I know, I'm sorry. You can't go."

My mouth dropped open. "But it's my

daughter, our daughter. Of course we go to the funeral. We're *holding* the funeral."

"No, it's not procedure."

"Look, I get that we don't invite her friends or our friends. But we go. *We* go. We're her family."

"You have to follow procedure —"

"And not go to my own daughter's funeral?" Suddenly I wasn't sure Dom and I were going to be pals. Our Tate's moment was gone. "You can't tell me there's a procedure for my daughter's funeral."

"There is, and if you think about it, you'll realize why." Dom pursed his lips. "The only link Milo and Big George have to you is your daughter. So let's say they put out feelers. They start calling area funeral homes." Dom paused, his eyes flinty in the dappled sunshine. "They know you'll want to go."

"What if their feelers don't go this far?"

"Delaware's not that far."

"So why didn't we go farther? Delaware was your choice, not ours. I'd fly anywhere to bury my daughter. I'd do anything, go anywhere, to lay her to rest as a family . . . with . . . love." My voice broke so I stopped talking.

"How would you fly? Under what name? We haven't begun to clear your new identity." Dom's gaze softened, and I could see he felt for me, so I couldn't even be mad at him.

"Can't you make a temporary one?"

"No."

"Why not? Teenagers can get a fake driver's license. Why can't the FBI?"

"That's not procedure."

"Then fly us on military transport. When I went to Gitmo, we flew military transport."

"We don't have military transport at our disposal. We're not the military."

"Then get a private plane. You can't tell me you don't have that. What does the FBI Director fly? Commercial?"

"It's not like the movies." Dom frowned, pained. "We have budgets."

"I'll pay for it." I couldn't accept it, not for Allison. "She has to have a funeral."

"Oh, don't get me wrong, she'll have a funeral. We'll clear a funeral home and we'll bury her properly. My fellow agents will attend —"

"What?" I recoiled. "The *FBI* will bury my daughter? Who goes? What agents?"

"The Babysitters Club goes. We have female agents, too. We pose as couples, as families."

"Really? Why? If you use a secured funeral home, why go through this charade?"

"We backstop ourselves."

I tried to think. "Wait, I have an idea. If there's going to be female agents dressed as fake moms, why can't Lucinda go as one?"

Dom shook his head. "Milo saw your wife. He knows what she looks like."

"What if it's not Milo who's watching?"

"They have her picture. She takes selfies with the moms on the team and her friends. They're all over her Facebook page. I knew what she looked like before we met. Make no mistake, they'll kill her."

"What if one of *your* daughters was shot to death?" I knew it was cruel, but let him feel what I felt. "Could you even *keep* your wife away?"

"If my family were in the danger yours is, I wouldn't allow them to go. Jason, I know this is hard. You can all watch the ceremony on closed-circuit TV."

"On TV? *On TV?*" I looked down, hands on hips, fighting for emotional control. I wondered if the cameras in the trees were recording us. Or if Special Agent Hallman was watching on his laptop.

"Look, our goal is to keep you safe. This is the first test. Unfortunately, it's the hardest. If you want, I can explain this to Lucinda."

"Oh no you can't," I told him, looking him in the eye.

I went back inside the house, crossed to the kitchen, and poured myself a glass of water, my mind reeling. It seemed impossible that we wouldn't be going to Allison's funeral. My daughter, buried without me. I didn't even get to see her one last time to say goodbye. I had assumed there would be a viewing, private, just us. I wanted to give her a note, a wish I hadn't acknowledged until this very moment.

I sipped the water, trying to recover. At my father's viewing, I had slipped a note under his hand, which held a rosary of chalky blue plastic. I had touched his skin, and makeup came off on my finger pads. I remember him feeling cool, hard, and oddly tacky. I didn't want to think about what my note to him had said.

I hope I am as wonderful a father as you. Love you, Dad.

I set the glass in the sink, trying to shoo the thoughts from my mind. The house was still quiet, and my gaze fell on the open laptop. I went over, logged on to Google, and searched for images of John Milo. The screen showed a line of John Milos from all over the country. I added *Philadelphia* to the search, and one face jumped instantly off the screen.

Him. I reacted viscerally, as if my body remembered Milo. His eyes glittered darkly. His cheekbones were set high, and he had marble slabs where cheeks should have been, ending in a broad jawline. I shuddered, then moved the mouse to his image, clicked, and saved it to the desktop in a folder. I didn't know what to label the folder. I didn't label it.

Next I searched under *George Veria, Jr.*, and after some doing, found a photo of Junior. The image was grainy and pixelated, taken from a newspaper a few years ago. His eyes were round and brown, his nose thick, and his cheeks puffy. I flashed on his disgusting leer at Allison. Nevertheless, I saved the image to the desktop folder.

My next search was for Big George Veria, Sr., and I identified him because his son looked so much like him, the origin of his son's wide nose and fleshy lips. Big George's eyes were smaller than Junior's. He was graying, and there was a V-shaped ridge in his short forehead. He'd been photographed at the federal courthouse on Market Street, a grim expression on his face and his tie flying as he hustled along. Junior hurried at his side, grinning in a badly fitting suit, and on his right was Milo in long hair and a black leather jacket.

I saved the picture, started the search of articles about Milo, and one of the most recent entries was from *The Philadelphia Inquirer:*

ARREST IN HOMICIDE OF AREA MAN

A suspect has been arrested in connection with the June 10 shooting death of Daniel Mozer, 27, of Avondale, Pennsylvania. John Milo, 32, of Kennett Square, Pennsylvania, was apprehended when he attempted to flee the victim's residence but was attacked by the victim's pit bull. Authorities believe that the murder was committed in connection with the enforcement of a drug debt. District Attorney Jay Gold praised the performance of the Criminal Investigation Unit (CIU) of PSP Avondale, saying, "Troop J of the PSP continues to excel in keeping the community safe."

Milo was taken into custody and charged with homicide, robbery, assault with a deadly weapon, and weapons offenses. Counsel for Milo issued a statement on behalf of his client, denying culpability. No further details have been released.

I felt my heart begin to pound. It had to be the same John Milo. Avondale was in southern Chester County, about an hour from our house. But something didn't make sense. If Milo had been arrested for murder last year, why was he on the street? If he had been caught fleeing the scene, they had him dead to rights. He should have been convicted.

I skimmed the other articles, but there was no mention of his trial or sentence.

I paused a minute. Not every murder trial made the news, though I would have thought this one would have. Another possibility was a plea deal, but even that would've made the news at sentencing.

I checked the article for the name of the defense counsel, but it wasn't specified. That didn't make sense, either. Most criminal defense counsel were shameless self-promoters, crowbarring their name into the news. They should be touting the representation of Milo.

I logged on to the database of the Courts of Common Pleas, using my office manager's access code. That didn't break any FBI rules, and I wasn't asking anyway. The database contained orders of all of the judges, whether published or not. If Milo's case had gone to trial, it would be here.

I plugged his name into the search function, and an unpublished opinion popped onto the screen under the caption *Commonwealth of Pennsylvania v. Milo:*

> For all of the foregoing, the case is hereby dismissed with prejudice. It is SO ORDERED.

I blinked. Milo had gotten off scot-free. I clicked and scanned the court opinion. The defense lawyer had gotten the case thrown out before it went to the jury, suppressing evidence on procedural grounds. It was skillful lawyering, so it didn't make sense that defense counsel wasn't taking credit.

I navigated back to the docket, a list of pleadings filed in the case. I clicked on the Entry of Appearance, the first filing by any defense counsel. Appearing for the defendant was Paul Hart of Lattimore & Finch.

After I had searched under Milo's name, I looked under Junior's and his father's. They had been arrested many times but had beaten every rap on procedural grounds: improper search, wrongly included testimony, wrongly excluded testimony, and for darker reasons, witnesses who recanted — or in one grim case, had simply vanished. It gave me the chills. And every victory was won by Paul Hart of Lattimore & Finch.

I mulled it over. Lattimore & Finch was one of the most prestigious firms in Philadelphia, comprised of Ivy League graduates and Supreme Court clerks. I'd met plenty of them, and they represented Fortune 500 companies, banks, and insurance companies. Since when did they represent a thug like Milo?

I scrolled to the Lattimore & Finch website and searched under *Paul Hart.* A thumbnail of a blond preppy popped onto the screen, with horn-rimmed glasses and a bow tie. I couldn't believe people still looked like him, but the Main Line was full of the whale-belt and seersucker shorts crowd. Hart's face was lean, and he had a longish nose and a smile that was client-ready, with veneers that were the rich-guy flex.

I skimmed the bio. Hart was a year older than I was; Princeton grad, Harvard Law, Law Review Comment Editor, Assistant U.S. Attorney for the Eastern District of Pennsylvania, Chairman of the White-Collar Criminal Group at Lattimore & Finch. No wonder Hart hadn't wanted his name in the paper. Lattimore & Finch did not want to be publicly associated with John Milo.

I stared at Hart's photo. Once I had

admired lawyers so much that I had wanted to become one, but that was before I knew better. I was raised to believe that law led to justice, but I grew up to learn that law could perpetrate injustice, like letting killers go free on technicalities. I valued procedural safeguards, but form was too often elevated over substance.

Now I was living that reality. Milo was on the street to kill my daughter because of lawyers like Hart. I wondered if he knew what he had wrought. I would never understand lawyers who weaponized the law against justice.

And now I knew the cost.

Allison.

Chapter Ten

I climbed the stairs, my head buzzing with what I'd learned online. I didn't know if I would tell Lucinda yet, because I still had to tell her about Allison's funeral, which would devastate her. She and Ethan hadn't come down to breakfast yet, and I wanted to check on them.

I reached the landing and heard them talking in his bedroom, so I opened the door. They were sitting against the headrest and looking at one of our old photo albums. I recognized its maroon cover instantly, though I hadn't known Lucinda had taken it from the house. I couldn't imagine looking at it. I knew I couldn't.

"Hey guys." I masked my emotion, crossed to the bed, and kissed Lucinda on the cheek. "How are you?"

"We're hanging in," Lucinda answered, looking up with a wan smile. Her eyes were puffy, and her reading glasses were on top of her head.

"Hi, Dad." Ethan smiled, though his eyes were glistening. I didn't know what had made Lucinda show him the album, but if she had been hoping to make him feel better, it looked like it was working.

"What're you doing, looking at pictures? Aren't you guys hungry?" I sat down on the edge of the bed, glancing at the photo album. It was open to a picture of Allison holding baby Ethan in the hospital, on the very day she'd first met him, a look of goofy puzzlement on her face. With effort, I put on a smile, like I'd put on a tie for work.

"Look at her little face." Lucinda tapped the photo with her fingernail, and it made a sound. "She looks confused, doesn't she?"

Ethan nodded. "She looks pissed."

They both chuckled, but I swallowed hard. I knew that everyone grieved differently, but somehow I hadn't expected to grieve so differently from them. "Guess what, we have new laptops and phones."

"Really?" Ethan shifted upward, instantly distracted.

"There are rules, though, and you can't communicate with anyone. No texting, no WhatsApp, no Snapchat, no social media, no nothing."

"What about video games?"

"No online ones, otherwise fine. I'll play with you."

"No Facebook?" Lucinda interjected, and her resigned expression told me she knew the answer.

"No, nothing where people can see you're online."

"I wonder what people are saying about us. They must be starting to talk." Her troubled gaze strayed back to the photo, and so did Ethan's, then I gave in.

"Where did you get the album?"

"From her room. It was on the bed, I remembered she'd asked me for it. She was taking pictures of some of the older photos. She wanted to post them on Insta."

I remembered when Lucinda had told her we used to send prints to be developed.

Mom, did you have a horse and buggy, too?

"Dad, you should see this other picture. It's funny."

"Oh?" I braced myself. "Show me."

"Let's see." Lucinda started paging back through the photographs, passing Allison at three years old, laughing as she held our gray tabby cat Max in one of Ethan's baby blankets. Her eyes sparkled, her grin spread ear-to-ear, and I could almost hear her giggle.

My heart ached as Lucinda turned the

pages. It was too soon for me to do this. I struggled to even accept that Allison was gone. That Milo murdered her. That lawyers like Hart had enabled him. She should be alive, flesh and blood, not encased in a photo album, flattened behind plastic.

"This is the one we like the best, so far," Lucinda said softly. Her fingers grazed Allison's face in the photo, which she had taken. "It was Easter, remember? She was trying to find the eggs."

Ethan nodded. "Those plastic ones. You guys would put, like, a jelly bean inside, or a dollar."

"Yes," I said, suppressing my sorrow. The photo was of Allison at maybe six years old, racing across our backyard, her hair blowing behind her. She had on a yellow dress and shiny black shoes, like a baby chick at speed.

Ethan pointed. "I like this picture the best. She looks like herself in it. She's always mad when I find more eggs than her."

"I know." I forced a smile. My daughter was born wanting to win, and as she grew into a teenager, I used to tease her about it, especially where Ethan was concerned.

Al, why do you have to be so competitive? Let him win for once.

Hell to the no.

Lucinda sniffled. "This picture makes the cut."

I looked over. "What do you mean?"

"I'm making a video for the funeral."

My heart wrenched. I dreaded telling her we weren't going to the funeral, but I wanted to wait until we were alone. Or maybe I wanted to stall.

Ethan pointed at another photo. "Dad, what do you think of this one?"

I looked over to see Allison at about ten, licking rainbow sprinkles off a vanilla ice cream cone. Nobody loved ice cream more than my daughter. Her favorites were vanilla, butterscotch, and mint chocolate chip, but not the green color, nothing artificial. I never minded going to Wawa to pick up a pint of Häagen-Dazs while she studied for finals.

Ice cream has superpowers, Dad.

Her words echoed, but I was doubting the very concept of superpowers. Maybe there was no such thing. Unless you were a lawyer named Paul Hart.

I wondered how he would tell his wife she couldn't go to the funeral of her own daughter.

I told Lucinda in the living room, while Ethan was upstairs getting dressed.

"What?" Her eyes filled with outraged tears. "We can't go? The FBI *pretends* to be mourners? They fake-cry while we watch on *TV*? You have to be kidding me! Did you say we don't accept it?"

"Yes, absolutely, I pushed back —"

"Did you?" Lucinda shot me a resentful look. "Or did you go along to get along? You should have raised holy hell."

I didn't reply, I let her vent. We'd had this argument before. She claimed I was *conflict-avoidant,* though I considered myself easy-going, like my father. Plus in my profession, I watched lawyers fight all day, arguing for the sake of arguing. What I knew from being a court reporter was that court wasn't the answer.

"Why didn't they tell us that before we came here, huh?" Lucinda's eyes narrowed, her anger curdling to suspicion. "They wanted us to take the deal, that's why. They knew we wouldn't if we weren't able to go to the funeral. It's bait-and-switch!"

"I don't think they intentionally deceived us." I thought of Dom. "I trust him."

"Why?"

"I think he cares about us —"

"Jason, really?" Lucinda scoffed. "They only care about us because we're witnesses. It's called the *witness* protection program, not the *victim* protection program."

"Whatever the reason, they're trying to protect us."

"We'll see about that." Lucinda called upstairs, "Ethan, Dad and I are going next door!"

CHAPTER ELEVEN

"Dom, got a minute?" I called through the screen, standing next to a simmering Lucinda.

"Be right there," Dom called back, then opened the door. "Hello, Jason, Lucinda."

"Hi," Lucinda answered, clipped, and we entered their apartment, which we hadn't seen. The window overlooked the driveway, and the small living room had a blue couch, matching plaid chairs, and an entertainment center with a small TV and a video game console. The tiny kitchen had an oak-veneer table covered with several laptops, empty mugs, and a sports section. I assumed Wiki was in the shower since I could hear it running.

Dom smiled politely. "How are you, Lucinda?"

"How do you think?" Lucinda folded her arms and planted her feet. "You told my husband we can't go to our daughter's funeral. You kept this from us intentionally. You knew we would never come here if we knew."

Dom blinked, his smile fading. "We didn't keep it from you —"

"Why didn't you tell us?"

"All right, I should have. I'm sorry. The issue wasn't top of my mind that night. The moment was exigent. We were concerned about your safety. That's our priority."

"Whatever, I'm telling you now, you are *not* keeping me from my daughter's funeral. If you try, I'll contact the hospital myself, get my daughter's body, and arrange for her burial."

Dom frowned. "Please don't. The Verias can guess which hospital your daughter was brought to. We've already sealed her medical records. Hospital employees have been instructed to direct inquiries to a number we monitor."

"Hospitals follow the HIPAA laws. They don't give out personal or medical information."

"Generally, that's true. But don't you think somebody would leak information for five grand? How about ten? It only takes one employee to tell them you called. They'll find out where you are."

Lucinda shook her head. "But this is our

daughter. I'm willing to take a risk to bury her."

"Risking your life? Ethan's?"

"You're exaggerating," Lucinda shot back.

"Why would I?"

"To get us to do what you want."

I cringed inwardly. My wife was nothing if not direct. I wondered if she was right. Maybe I *compartmentalized,* like she said.

Dom pursed his lips. "I can prove the danger, if I have to."

"Then do."

"This way." Dom crossed to the kitchen table, hit a few keys on the laptop, then angled its screen to face us. We walked over together and looked at a color video showing our house, the Corbuzes' next door with their blue Nittany Lions flag, and most of our street. The scene was sunny and still, and according to a clock at the bottom with the time and date, in real time. "So you see, we have a team monitoring cameras on your house. This feed is raw investigative material. It's against procedure to show it to you, but you need to understand why we cannot let you go."

Lucinda fell abruptly silent.

I couldn't ignore the pang I felt at seeing our street. The front yard. The lawn and beds, with my fresh mulching. Our *home.*

Without us. Without Allison. "So this video is from the investigation team? Watanabe and Reilly?"

"Yes."

Lucinda lifted an eyebrow at the unfamiliar names, and I made a mental note to explain later.

"Now, I'll rewind." Dom rewound the video, and time ran backward onscreen, our street going from sunshine to darkness and back again at top speed. The Patels walked their rescue greyhounds up and back. The Slater-Dobbs rolled recycling bins back and forth. Everyone drove in and out of driveways, opening and closing SUV hatchbacks and trunks.

Dom slowed the video, saying, "Now, watch. This is what happened eight minutes after you left the house, that first night."

I watched the dark screen of our street at night, holding my breath. Suddenly a sedan cruised slowly past our house, silent as a shadow. I didn't recognize the car, which went down our street and vanished around the corner.

My heart started to pound. "Is that them? Veria and company?"

"Yes," Dom answered.

Lucinda gasped. "You mean, we got out just in time."

"Correct." Dom eyed the laptop screen.

"My God." Lucinda's hand flew to her mouth, and I felt the gravity of the threat in a way I hadn't before.

"Dom, who was driving? Was it Milo?"

"No. We believe it's someone else. Lower-level."

"Who?" I was already thinking of researching the name.

"I'm not going to divulge that."

I tried a different tack. "Is lower-level lower than retail-level?"

"It's the same."

"How do you know who it was?"

"The license plate."

I squinted at the video. I could barely see the outline of the car in the darkness, much less read the plate. "How can you tell, in the dark?"

"Our lab did."

"Aren't you going to arrest him?" I asked, but I knew the answer from my one year of law school.

"Not enough evidence —"

"Can't you pick him up anyway? Ask him where Milo is?"

"— and again, we don't want to tip them off."

My thoughts raced. "Let me ask you something else. Milo and this organization have been arrested plenty of times, but they always get off. Is that right?"

"Yes."

Lucinda looked over. "How do you know this, Jason?"

"I researched it online."

"Hold on." Dom pressed a key, and the video rewound further. He stopped at another view of the same car, then pointed to the bottom of the screen. "This is him, ten minutes later, circling the block. He did that until midday. We believe they were trying to determine if you were coming back. By now, they'll have concluded you've entered the program. That's why it's against procedure for you to go to Allison's funeral, as hard as that is to deal with." Dom closed out the video as he spoke.

On impulse, I slid my flip phone from my pocket and took a photo of the screen. Dom turned around at the click. "Jason, did you just take a picture?"

"Yes."

"Please delete it. I wasn't supposed to show you that."

"I won't tell." I slipped the phone into my pocket.

Dom looked pained, like I had broken faith with him, but Lucinda glanced over with approval.

So I had chosen the right side. We were united, husband and wife, allowed this tiny act of defiance in return for not burying our murdered daughter.

I wanted to know who that driver was.

Chapter Twelve

I toweled off in the bathroom, reviewing the long, crummy day. Something told me every day from here on out would fit that description. Showering before bedtime used to relax me, but my old routines weren't working. I had felt uneasy since I had seen Dom's video of the car cruising our street, but hadn't had the chance to study my photo or fill Lucinda in on anything, since Ethan was around. I made much of the phones and laptops to distract him, but it only went so far.

I slipped back into my shorts and entered the bedroom, where Lucinda sat cross-legged in bed, her laptop open. She was in a T-shirt, her hair up in a loose ponytail, but she was upset. Her cheery red reading glasses incongruous.

I crossed to her and sat down. "Honey?"

"Everyone's worried about us."

"You're not on Facebook, are you?"

"No, Next Door, the neighborhood Patch. It doesn't show when you're online."

"Oh, right." I knew the platform, with postings about local contractors, lost dogs, and spotted lantern flies.

"Allison's friends have been texting her and she's not replying, so they tell their mom, who tells another mom, who tells another, who calls the Corbuzes or one of the other neighbors, and asks if they've seen us, and they haven't." Lucinda scanned the screen, miserably. "It's terrible to put people who love us through this. I feel so guilty. We have to let them worry? Let them wonder?"

"It can't be helped. You saw the video."

"I know, but can you imagine how Melissa is feeling? We always walk on Saturday morning. She's probably texting me and calling."

I had no reply. Melissa was my wife's best friend after Allison.

"I just wish we could let her know."

"That would defeat the purpose."

"Would it? She wouldn't tell anybody. And what about the other moms? We were planning for the semifinals, who brings what, all that. They'll be calling, too."

"We don't have any choice." I sat down, glancing at the TV. A commercial was ending, and the eleven o'clock news came on, with the lead story. The screen showed a burning storefront that I recognized instantly.

"That's my *office*!" I jumped to my feet, horrified. Flames raged from the front window of my office and the Chinese restaurant next door. I couldn't believe what I was seeing.

"No!" Lucinda tore off her reading glasses. "Oh my God!"

The voice-over said, *"We're live in a strip mall in Newtown Square, where fire destroyed several businesses, including a restaurant, a court-reporting business, a nail salon, and a dry cleaner. . . ."*

Lucinda rose, stricken. We watched together, stunned.

"Authorities believe the blaze started after hours in the nail salon. No injuries were reported. Fire companies from neighboring Montgomery County were called to the scene. . . ."

"He said 'after hours,' right?" I asked, panicky. "So no one was there, right? No injuries?"

"Right, he said that."

"Man, oh man." I raked a hand through my wet hair, reeling. The TV screen changed to gray smoke billowing from the restaurant, then the report ended with a photo of an overturned tractor-trailer.

Lucinda touched my shoulder. "Honey, I'm so sorry."

"What does this even mean? Marie must be so upset." Marie was my office manager, a first-rate court reporter and single mom.

Lucinda shook her head. "They're probably trying to call you."

"Totally. What's she going to do now? What are any of them going to do? This is awful. My company, *gone*? How does the government sell it now?"

Lucinda hugged me, and I clung to her for a moment. I loved my employees, and so did she. We threw our holiday party every year at the house. I hosted Happy Hours on Fridays at Baxter's. Our softball T-shirts read, our word is law. The six of us had worked together for years, and we knew each other's kids, attended birthdays and graduations. They would have been devasted to hear about Allison. Now, this.

"I'm insured, but when does that settlement come through? How do we keep anybody employed now? Can they even get severance pay?"

"Jesus." Lucinda sank onto the bed, and I sat next to her. It had taken my whole life to build that business, and I owed so much to my employees. I made sure they got bonuses, and I made a standard thirty percent commission on their deps. My net annual income had grown to $420,000, a sum I never would have dreamed of. My father worked around the clock and never cleared a hundred grand.

It's only money, he said all the time.

Oddly, I thought of my conference room, newly renovated for out-of-town counsel or solo practitioners. Mechanized pull-down screens. Quality grease boards. State-of-the-art audio and projection equipment. I even sprang for the oak credenza, not veneer. I said I wanted to be buried in it, so we called it the Jason Bennett Memorial Conference Room. "My conference room."

Lucinda shook her head. "All that work."

"Yours, too." My wife had picked out the carpet, a navy blue pattern, all wool. The ergonomic chairs, Herman Miller with lumbar support, not the knockoffs. Glass, not plastic, mats under the desk chairs.

"What about the steno machines?"

"They're insured, but jeez, that's forty grand."

"All your plans."

"They were gone already." I had wanted to open an office in Philly in two to three years, then maybe franchise in the mid-Atlantic.

"We should call Dom."

"I wonder if he knows already."

Suddenly my cell phone rang, and I got up and went to the night table. I flipped the phone open, and it was him. "Dom, are you seeing this? My office is on fire."

"Your *office, too*?"

Horrified, we watched the video on Dom's laptop. A raging conflagration engulfed our home, turning it into an orange fireball. Flames streaked from the windows, upper and lower. Black smoke billowed from the roof. Firefighters swarmed the front lawn, their silhouettes hazy against the fire, aiming hoses at the blaze. Fire trucks lined up along the curb, boxy shapes amid the smoke.

My house. Our *home*. I *loved our house*. I knew every imperfect inch. I had patched its drywall and painted its baseboards. I had fixed the hose on the back of the washing machine. My proudest moment was locating the leak in the wall of the family room. A patch of the stone façade had needed re-pointing.

"Oh my God," was all I could say.

Lucinda shook her head. "They did this, didn't they? They burned our house down."

"And my office," I added, as if nobody

had figured that out yet. "Did you not know about that, Dom?"

"The team probably knew but they didn't get a chance to tell me yet. We're spread thin tonight." Dom looked from me to Lucinda. The FBI agents were dressed like us, in T-shirts and gym shorts. Wiki stood behind Dom, letting him take the lead. "I have more bad news. Your studio was vandalized."

Lucinda moaned, stricken. "Are you sure? How do you know?"

"We got a report from the locals. It happened in the early evening, we think. I was about to call you when we heard about the house."

"Did they take anything?"

"We're not sure yet. What did you have there of value?"

"My camera's a Nikon D6, only a year old. The backup camera's not worth as much, but it's still valuable, and the lenses cost a fortune. The 105 mm 1.4, I use it all the time, is a two-thousand-dollar lens." She shook her head. "I keep them in a closet. I never even got a safe. I've been there for six years and never had a problem."

"I'm sorry, honey." I put my hand on her shoulder.

Dom nodded. "Anything else of value, Lucinda?"

"The backdrops, I rent them both. They're Oliphants, the best. I had a projector and screen, for showing clients the photos."

"What about the photos? They're backed up, right?"

"Yes, but does it matter? What the hell is going on, anyway?" Lucinda sank into the kitchen chair. She rubbed her face, leaving pinkish streaks. "My studio, his office, our *house.* All my photos of the kids. Allison's *room,* all her things."

"I know, honey." I sat down and put an arm around her, eyeing Dom. "So obviously, this is a coordinated attack. They're trying to scare us."

"Yes, it's witness intimidation. Milo must have convinced Big George that you killed Junior. They're both after you, but for different reasons. Big George wants revenge. Milo doesn't want you to testify."

"I have a question," Lucinda interjected. "You have the house burning on video, so you had to know it was happening. Why didn't you stop them? Did you let them burn it down?"

I blinked, confused. "Dom, you'd stop them, right? Even if it means showing your hand?"

Dom recoiled. "Of course we would."

Wiki spoke up. "Just so you know, we're the ones who called it in. We cooperate with the locals. No one will know how the fire was discovered."

I didn't understand. "But how did they set the fire, if you were watching? You have a team on the cameras, don't you? How did this happen?"

"We don't know. To be clear, this isn't our jurisdiction. The investigative team has someone on the cameras, not us. They're investigating, as we speak."

"The investigative team is investigating itself? Great. When did the fire start? How did it go up so fast?"

"We assume they used an accelerant." Dom paused, chastened. "We will sort this out financially. I will do my best to make sure you get a fair settlement."

"What about the businesses? Everything we owned is gone."

"Jason, Lucinda, there's something you need to understand. Our job is to protect you and your family. Your property isn't our charge —"

"Something else we weren't told," Lucinda interrupted. "But what about my mother? What if they do something to her? She's a person, not property. Will you protect her?"

Dom hesitated. "No, I'm sorry, truly, but extended family is not in the budget. We don't have the manpower —"

"Are you serious?" Lucinda raised her voice. "You protect my mother or I won't testify to a single thing!"

I understood her anger. "Dom, my mother-in-law is family. Move her here, then you don't need extra manpower."

"We can't do that in her condition."

"I'll take care of her," Lucinda shot back, agitated. "I did it before, I can do it again. And what if they figure out who my friends are? All they have to do is look on my Facebook page. Are they going to go after them, too?"

Dom put up his hands. "Okay, I hear you. I'll share your concerns with my boss. We did not anticipate they would go this far."

"You should have," Lucinda snapped.

I didn't pile on. I could tell from Dom's expression he felt bad enough.

"Listen, I promise you." Dom raised a finger. "I will defend your lives and Ethan's with my own. You have my word."

Wiki nodded, his young face solemn. "Mine, too."

Lucinda fell silent, and so did I. They had just made a vow to take a bullet for us, and

I gave their words the weight they deserved. My wife and son were all I had left, all that mattered now. Losing everything clarified my priorities on the spot. If the FBI could keep my family safe, that was all I really needed. My anger ebbed away.

I thanked them both.

Lucinda said nothing, folding her arms.

Chapter Thirteen

I tried to sleep but couldn't, thinking about the house, the office, Lucinda's studio. I didn't know how the government would value my business or hers, but it paled in comparison to one thing.

Allison.

I opened my eyes and checked the clock. Its glowing digits read four-fifteen a.m. The bedroom seemed oddly bright, and I realized the glow was coming from Lucinda's side. I turned over to see the covers over her head and light coming from underneath, like a girl reading with a flashlight.

"Honey?" I lifted the covers, dismayed to find her on the laptop.

"I didn't want to wake you." Lucinda closed the laptop, but not before I glimpsed the screen, groaning.

"Facebook?"

"Don't worry, I'm on my summer intern's account. Remember her, Rebecca Robertson? I made her an account so she could contact my clients. I never bothered to close it."

"What if Rebecca realizes you're using her account?"

"She forgot about it, I'm sure. She hasn't posted since July." Lucinda's expression darkened. "I checked Melissa's page, and it's awful. She knows about the house fire, and the fire trucks are still there. Our street is cordoned off. They saw on the news that your office burned, too."

"Oh no."

"So she drove over to my studio, and cops told her that it was vandalized. You should see what she posted." Lucinda reopened the laptop, pressed a key, and the screen woke up Melissa's Facebook page. The header showed her and her husband, Seamus, with their daughter, Courtney, in Avalon.

I shifted up on my elbows and read the glowing screen.

I'm sending all the love in the world to my dearest friend Lucinda and to Jason, Allison, and Ethan.

It jarred me to see Allison's name, and I had to remind myself that Melissa didn't know. I read on.

I don't know where you guys are or what happened and I am worried sick. I know you will see this and I am begging you, please please call me, Lucinda. Any time of day or night, I just need to hear your voice and know that you're OK. I know that you are a wonderful loving family and these rumors cannot be true.

I blinked. "What rumors?"

"I don't know." Lucinda moaned. "I wish we could tell them we're in witness protection."

"No. We can't. Don't."

"What if something happens to them because of us? They should be warned, they could be in danger."

"We'll talk to Dom in the morning."

"Look." Lucinda started scrolling through the comments, already 175 of them. "Everyone's worried. Look at these comments."

I scanned them, and they were mostly parents of Allison's and Ethan's friends:

Judy Wright-Cobb We love you Lucinda and the Bennetts! We hope you are okay and we are praying for you! Please be safe! XOXO

Sally Liatsis What is going on? This is so

crazy! I just saw them at the game! What happened? They could have been kidnapped! I'm so worried about Lucinda! She is the best!

Deb Gallagher What if they died in the fire? Did anybody think of that? What if they were asleep when it broke out? They could all be dead!! Why haven't the police announced anything? #Fishy

April DelVecchio Did you see her studio was trashed, too? She took pics of us two years ago and it's still my header. This is like a mystery in our own backyard! Connect the dots to foul play! Lucinda, I love you and I'm worried about you!

Ali Choudhoury I've been texting and calling Lucinda and she's not responding. My son Jake knows Ethan and he isn't, either! I hate to be alarmist, but something must really be wrong. This is not like them. Not at all!

I got the gist. I put an arm around Lucinda, and her laptop slid to the side. "Honey, it's better not to go on Facebook."

"It helps me. It's our life."

Not anymore, I thought but didn't say.

"I hate that they're upset and there's nothing we can do. It's a terrible way to treat people. They love us." Lucinda met my eye, exasperated. "They're not going to *forget* about us."

"They have to."

"But what will happen? What will they do?" Lucinda shook her head. "The FBI isn't doing its job. How good can they be if they let the house burn? Your office? My studio? Why didn't they anticipate that? It's like they didn't think it through."

"You heard him. Their focus is on us, not property."

"I hope to God we made the right decision, coming here." Lucinda looked away, and I touched her arm.

"Of course we did. You saw, we got out just in time. They'd kill us, honey. They wouldn't think twice. You get that, right?"

"Yes," Lucinda answered, her voice hushed. She slid off her reading glasses, her eyes glistening.

"Ethan will take his cue from us. He didn't want to get out of bed. He didn't want to go downstairs. He wasn't even excited about the laptop."

"He needs time."

"We have to make sure he doesn't contact

anybody. If you figured out a way, he might, too."

"This is just so terrible. . . ." Lucinda heaved a sob, out of nowhere. "I'm trying, I'm really trying . . . but she's all I think about. . . ."

My heart wrenched. I reached for my wife, hugging her close while she began to cry.

"And . . . she's so young, just a kid . . . it's so *wrong,* that she . . . isn't with us . . . she's in some morgue, all alone . . . and now we won't even be at her funeral . . . I just want to . . . I wish we could change it all . . . go back . . ."

"I know, I know," I repeated, having nothing else to say.

The only way out of this hell was through, and all I could do was wrap my arms around her and hold her until she finally fell asleep at dawn.

Chapter Fourteen

I woke up, put on the same T-shirt and gym shorts, and disabled the burglar alarm, leaving Lucinda asleep. I peeked in on Ethan, who snored cuddling Moonie, so I went downstairs. I opened the front door onto a sunny morning, then went to the laptop in the kitchen without making coffee. I wanted to see if there was any report of our house fire.

I sat at the table and searched online, but didn't find any. I searched for the fire in the strip mall, but there was no new reporting of that, either. I searched for news about Lucinda's studio, but it was likewise absent. If the FBI had shut the media down, I wasn't sure of the point. Our neighbors had seen the fire, and they would wonder why there was no mention.

I thought of my employees, with no word from me. They had to be putting things together. I made a mental note to talk to

Dom about getting them severance. I thought of the physical damage to the office fixtures, then realized I hadn't checked my cloud, which held my office files in Dropbox.

I logged on and onto the screen popped the case files that automatically backed up. The first one, *Clennic v. Exxon,* was a big antitrust case in which I'd had a deposition on Friday afternoon. Before the weekend, a lifetime ago. Back then, I had been looking forward to the weekend, starting with Allison's game.

Dad, do we have a chance against Radnor?

Absolutely. You can beat them.

You should get an Academy Award. Best Dad.

I wiped my eyes, feeling raw and empty. My mouth tasted bitter. I knew my life would forever be divided into Before and After. I didn't know how other fathers survived their own children. I wished I could talk to one, just one. I wished someone would tell me. It wasn't possible, yet people did it every day. I just didn't know how.

I stared at the laptop. It was Monday morning, and I didn't have to leave for the office or a job. I had nothing to do. I had always worked: on the farm after school, work-study during college, construction in the summers, and legal research at a law firm while I was in law school. My first dollar bill was hanging in the office that had just burned to the ground.

I remembered something. I picked up my phone, opened it, and scrolled to the photo of the car driving past my house, which I had taken from Dom's laptop. I couldn't enlarge it on the phone, and it was too small to be able to tell the make or model.

I held the photo up to the laptop and used the Photo Booth app to take its picture, then saved it to the desktop. It gave me a larger view of the car, and I made it even larger. I wished I had Adobe Photoshop, but I couldn't order anything online. I made the photo one click bigger and tried to discern the make of the car. The outline looked like a BMW.

I scrolled to the BMW site and scanned through the lower-end models, a remarkably similar silhouette. Then I noticed something on the photo. There was a shadow on the right side of the car's bumper. It could be a flaw in the enlargement. Or it could be a dent, but an oddly vertical one, as if the driver had backed into a pole.

Who's the driver?

I went back online and searched through

the court index, then called up the most recent cases with George Veria, Jr., or Milo as defendants. I clicked the first one and skipped ahead to the Facts section, where the facts to support the charge were explained in detail. Most people didn't realize that a vast amount of information was available to the public in legal papers, especially in a criminal case.

The Facts section described how Milo had attempted to sell cocaine, and the transaction had been observed by police and caused his arrest on the spot. I kept reading, and paragraphs set forth the locations at which the other codefendants had been caught selling drugs, specifying what they had attempted to sell.

I skimmed the pleadings, getting an idea of where GVO was doing business — on street corners they actually called "stores." GVO operated all over Chester County, in Downingtown, Thorndale, Coatesville, Parkesburg, and most recently New Cumberton, as well as the towns around Kennett Square like Toughkenamon, Avondale, West Grove, even as far west as Paradise in Amish country. Some towns were more rural than others, and they represented an array of ethnicities and economic levels, evidence that opiates had spread everywhere.

"Jason, you up?" Dom called through the screen door.

"Yes." I closed the laptop, pocketed the phone, and went to the door to find him in running clothes, carrying a brown bag. "Good morning. Come on in." I let Dom in, and he handed me the brown bag.

"Purina kibble. How are you?" Dom smiled, uncertainly, as if unsure of our new footing after last night.

"Okay, thanks. How did you know I was up?"

"You open the door at the same time, every day. People are creatures of habit. It's my job to notice yours. You'll see what I mean when we get to work, in about two weeks. I'm trying to give you and Lucinda some time."

I sensed he was trying to clear Allison's TV funeral, which I appreciated. "Anything new on Milo's whereabouts?"

"No, not yet. We're on it."

"What about the fires?"

"On that, too."

"I looked online, and there's nothing more in the news about them."

"There won't be. Again, I'm sorry." Dom winced, and I felt a flicker of our former connection.

"Don't beat yourself up. Look, after last night, I'm grateful we're safe."

The crease in Dom's forehead relaxed. "How's Lucinda?"

"She barely slept."

"We have a doctor who can get her Ambien or something."

"She'll never do that, she's too organic. We're worried about Ethan, too."

"If he needs to see somebody, we can do that."

I had wondered about that. "You can get him a therapist in witness protection?"

"Yes." Dom met my eye, earnestly. "This goes without saying, but I care about your family, not only because you're witnesses."

"Thanks," I said, glad to be reassured. In my experience, things that go without saying sometimes need to be said.

"Hey, you wanna go for a run? I waited."

"No," I answered reflexively. The last time I had run was with Allison.

"Don't worry. You're safe." Dom pointed at a fold in his maroon polo shirt. "Waist holster. That's why the dark shirt."

"Are you a good shot?"

"The best."

I didn't think he was kidding. His manner was steady and calm. He exuded reliability.

"Anyway, *I'm* safer with you than alone." Dom grinned crookedly. "Not a lot of brothers in the neighborhood."

I laughed, uncomfortably. "So why did you choose it?"

"It's deserted this time of year." Dom started for the door. "Come on, let's go. Lucinda and Ethan will be fine. Wiki will keep an eye on them. You can't help them if you don't stay strong."

"Okay," I agreed reluctantly.

"Good. I'll tell him." Dom texted, and I slipped into my socks and sneakers, which I had left on the living room floor. Dom set the burglar alarm, produced the key from a pocket in his running shorts, and locked the door. We went down the porch stairs.

I inhaled deeply, realizing I hadn't been outside in some time. The air felt cool and fresh, but I didn't feel entitled to it. The sky was a sheer blue, and the sun rose behind a mound of white clouds, backlighting them. It hurt my eyes, as if it were too pretty to see. Maybe it was too soon to go running without Allison.

"Dom —" I started to say.

"Warm up." Dom stretched at the bottom of the stairs, one leg, then the other, methodically.

"Usually, I don't."

"You should."

"I know, I'm old. Forty-seven." I realized he knew already. "Listen, I don't think I can —"

"Let's go." Dom took off, and I hesitated, then went after him, running across the driveway. We turned left at the street, going away from the bay beach. Coarse brown sand drifted across the asphalt, gritty under my sneakers. Dense scrub pines and oaks lined the street, and there were no other houses in sight. Seagulls squawked, and a silvery plane glinted overhead.

We ran without talking, and I tried to match Dom's stride, which was longer than Allison's. It felt so strange to run with him. He was all business, facing front and pumping his corded arms. Allison and I didn't take running so seriously. She used to shove me, and I'd tickle her.

Dad, cut it out!

Ha! You can dish it but you can't take it!

Dom glanced over as he ran. "There's a three-mile or a six-mile loop around the marsh. Which one you want?"

"Three." I didn't know if I could make it even that far. My legs felt already like lead. My arms ached. My wind was lousy.

"You okay? I can slow it down."

"No, it's okay." I couldn't stop the memories of Allison. She always chewed gum while she ran, yakking away. She would give me an earful about Troy and his nosy mother. Or her new French teacher, who overshared. Or her beloved field hockey coach.

"When was the last time you ran?"

"With my daughter," was all I could answer. I knew he meant when, but I didn't remember when. Anything that happened before Coldstream Road was gone. "Usually, we run three times a week, or four, but I'm already tired."

Dom fell silent a moment. "That's grief, man. It gets in you. Your body carries it. It's *embedded.*"

"You think?"

"I *know.*"

I didn't know whether to ask or if it was prying. We hadn't talked, except about cookies. I still didn't know if we were supposed to be friends. I hadn't had a close friend since my father. Lucinda was my best friend.

Dom cleared his throat, his arms pumping. "I lost my partner. I wasn't always in The Babysitters Club."

"Oh?" I sensed it rattled him, still. Beads of sweat popped onto his smooth, high forehead.

"I used to work undercover, until a buy-bust went south." Dom's tone softened. "It messed me up."

"How long ago?"

"Three years, this winter. I kept going after, I thought I was fine. I wasn't. My body knew. I slowed down. I was tired all the time. A beat behind, mentally." Dom shrugged. "Finally I did the counseling thing. Not ashamed of it. Now it's a different life. Denise likes it better. Undercover's dangerous."

"I bet." I noted his wife's name.

"And I like this gig. Wiki's a good guy."

"He seems like it."

"Let him talk to your son. He'll take him out on the marsh, tell him all about it. He knows about the birds, the grasses, the muskrats." Dom chuckled. "He's like a light switch. You throw it, and he talks."

"Good to know."

"Meantime, keep a routine. Run. Stay strong. You gotta get them through this. You gotta get Lucinda through this."

"Right," I said, because it struck a chord. It sounded like something my father would say. The center *did* have to hold. I wasn't crazy.

"It's a lot, plus the house burning down."

"I didn't see any mention of it online."

Dom nodded, wiping his brow.

"Why? I mean, the neighbors know it happened."

"Damage control."

"But our friends aren't stupid. They're putting it together. They're connecting the house fire to the office fire."

"How do you know?"

Shit. I'd let my guard down. I didn't know whether I should tell him about Lucinda going on Facebook. She wasn't doing anything wrong, so I did.

"She's lurking under an intern's name?" Dom pursed his lips.

"She followed the rules."

"She'll be tempted to post."

"No, she won't," I said defensively. "Let's deal with what she knows, rather than how she knows it. Facebook changes the ball game. All her friends are online. They know about the house, her studio, my business."

Dom picked up the pace, but didn't reply.

"Were you able to talk to your boss about my mother-in-law?"

"I emailed last night. He said he'd get back to me."

My side stitch was killing me. "What about Melissa, Lucinda's best friend? We think you should get a message to her, saying we're in the program. She's posting about a search party. If you don't get ahead of this, she's going to raise a posse."

Dom smiled slyly. "Torches and pitchforks?"

"Yes." I chuckled. "So what do you think?"

"About a message to them? We never have."

"Did you ever have to? Have you ever had a family as applicants?"

"No."

"So, we come with connections. Friends, school, employees, *people.* Normal families are connected, and we're a normal family. You have to bend the rules."

"No, we don't." Dom shook his head. "We're not negotiating. That wasn't the deal. The deal was that you follow the rules."

"You just said you never had a family before. There's new rules when you have a family. You guys *have* to compromise. I am, I'm not going to my daughter's funeral."

We ran in stride, breathing hard. I prayed the stitch would go away. Ahead was a line of mailboxes painted with fish, seashells, and crabs. Some had family names. Lovell, Sinclair, Tyson. The houses were obscured by the woods. There were no signs of occupants, like recycling bins or delivered newspapers.

"Dom, listen, who's the usual applicant?

Gang members? Murderers? Drug dealers? Have you ever even had an applicant with no criminal record?"

"What's your point?"

"So usually, you're putting up a witness that's a criminal himself. Somebody who's flipping, right?"

Dom looked over, flinty-eyed.

"I know the lingo. I'm a badass court reporter."

Dom burst into laughter. "Okay, yes, a snitch."

"Okay, and their credibility is terrible. I bet the defense always makes the same argument. 'Were you lying then or are you lying now?' "

We passed a row of crudely hand-painted signs — FREE FIREWOOD, TORO MOWER FOR SALE, FOR SALE CAR RUNS GOOD — clustered in front of one house with a front yard full of washing machines, a refrigerator with the door off, a few battered cars, a truck rusting on cinder blocks, and other junk. The mailbox read THATCHER, and an old man smoking a cigar in a BarcaLounger watched us run past.

"There's one in every neighborhood." Dom rolled his eyes. "I got a guy like that on my street. Drives me nuts."

I wanted to stay on point. "Anyway, we're

good witnesses, law-abiding citizens. Not even a speeding ticket. We'll put Milo away forever."

Dom smiled. "Now you're talking."

"We're great witnesses because we're a normal family, and on the other hand, because we're a normal family, we have family and friends. You can't have it both ways." My side stitch began to subside. "You can't get the value of a normal family but not accommodate us. That's the argument you have to make to your boss."

"And what do you want?"

"Protect my mother-in-law and Melissa. Get somebody on their street or some cameras, do whatever you do. And tell Melissa we're in WITSEC."

Dom fell silent. "It's up to my boss."

"What will he say?"

"I don't know."

"Come on, you know."

Dom pumped his arms. "I think we can swing surveillance of your mother-in-law. Maybe the friend. Melissa."

Thank God. "That would be great."

"But no message to her."

"Why not?"

"What if she tells her friends?"

I had made the same argument to Lucinda. "She won't if you warn her our lives are at stake."

"Where does this end? How many friends do you want us to notify?"

I could deal with a slippery-slope argument. "She's the only one. You need to get ahead of this. I know this woman, and she's connected to the field hockey moms, the lacrosse moms, the choir moms, the drama moms. She's —"

"The kingpin?" Dom supplied.

I laughed. "Bingo. These are suburban moms. The Vera Bradley Organization."

Dom burst into laughter. "Tell me about it. My wife's one."

"So then you know, and please get it done. It would really help Lucinda. This is killing her."

Dom wiped his brow again. "I'll talk to Gremmie."

"Your boss?"

"Yes, Richard Volkov. We call him Gremmie. The Gremlin from the Kremlin."

I smiled. "He's from Russia?"

"No, Cleveland."

My mood lifted. "One more thing. My employees. I want to pay them severance. I have money in the corporate account. It has to happen this week. I don't care how."

"I'll talk to Gremmie."

"Thanks." I hated to have to ask for

everything. My father taught me to be self-reliant, and I was. Until now.

"So, Jason, where you from, originally?"

I started to answer, then stopped. "You know the answer already. Why don't *you* tell *me*?"

Dom snorted. "Okay. You grew up on a twenty-one-acre farm in Hershey. Your father, William, was a second-generation farmer —"

"A *dairyman,* not a farmer."

"I stand corrected. Your mother died of a heart attack. You were only nine. That must have been tough."

"It was." I loved my mother, but didn't remember much about her. A round face framed with red curls and a sweet smile. A faint warm feeling of soft arms, kisses, kind words, rosewater, and More 100s.

"What was Hershey like?"

"Heaven. I felt like I went to school in a candy store."

"I bet. I'm a chocoholic."

"Me, too."

"You don't get sick of it?" Dom looked over, surprised.

"Never."

"I worked in a McDonald's and never want to eat it again."

"Chocolate's different."

"Agree. Should be a controlled substance."

I smiled. "Nowadays Hershey has the Medical Center and all, the place is booming. Back then, it was about the company. Every T-shirt I had was an irregular from the company store. We had dish towels covered with Hershey bars. Salt-and-pepper shakers shaped like Kisses." I thought back, surprised the memories came so easily. I felt my throat catch, for some reason. "My father *idolized* Milton Hershey. Milton *S.* Hershey. We all called him MS. To be a dairyman for him was a badge of honor. We had a tiny farm, like only fifty head, but he kept us going. We had a picture of him on our mantelpiece." I heard myself yammering, my emotions all over the lot. "So tell me, *then* what did I do?"

"Star linebacker in high school. Majored in political science at Bucknell. Graduated magna. One year at Dickinson Law School, dropped out."

I hated the word *dropout,* even if I was. "I couldn't afford it."

"Hey, no judgment." Dom shrugged. "Your father died when your kids were little. You sold the farm."

"We had debt. I had student loans to pay."

"Grew your court-reporting business, got

licensed as a merit reporter. One of only thirteen in the country chosen to go to Guantánamo Bay. The youngest, too. You got clearance."

"I did, Top Secret." I couldn't help but smile. "No civilian was ever prouder of clearance. You would have thought I was a four-star."

Dom laughed.

"How about you? I don't have a file on you."

"I grew up in West Philly."

" 'West Philly born and raised'?"

Dom smiled. "Everybody says that. I never know whether to thank Will Smith or hit him."

"I like Will Smith."

"All White people do."

I sensed I'd stuck my foot in my mouth. I felt momentarily like I didn't know what to say, or how to act. I didn't have any close friends who were Black, and only one of my employees was Black.

Dom added, "Relax, I like Will Smith, too."

I laughed. "So then what about you?"

"University City High, Temple Criminal Justice Program, Quantico. Then, like I say, worked undercover for twelve years. Now, The Babysitters Club."

"Where do you live?"

"Villanova. I was raised by my grandmother and my Uncle Tig. He had a check-cashing agency at Gibbons and Masterman. I was there every day, working after school. My grandmother hated it. Said it wasn't safe. She was right. He got held up four times. Never got hurt, luckily. That's why I went into law enforcement. I saw what he went through."

"I get that."

"Still, I loved that job. I felt useful."

"I felt the same way. It's a different world in a family business." I added, "Your own world."

"You work for *yourself.*"

"Exactly."

Dom fell silent a moment. "I don't know what made me think of that job. I haven't seen my uncle in too long."

"It must be hard, away from home for months with us . . . applicants."

"It's the job."

"What do your neighbors think you do? Do you say you're in WITSEC?"

"No, I say I travel a lot, work in procurement. Nobody knows what that is, and it sounds too boring to ask about."

I smiled. "Do you like it? WITSEC?"

"In this case, absolutely." Dom brightened. "Your family's nice, and you can't beat the location. Normally I'm in a crappy motel with a sociopath."

I burst into laughter.

"Only one problem."

"What?"

"Can we pick up the pace, gramps?"

Chapter Fifteen

After the run, I climbed the stairs, excited to tell Lucinda I'd made progress getting protection for Mom and Melissa. I reached the second floor and checked on Ethan, not surprised to find Lucinda dozing with him. Moonie was curled at the foot of the bed. Lucinda opened her eyes and motioned me over.

I went to the bed and kissed her. "Want coffee?"

"No." Lucinda brushed a strand of hair from her face. Moonie raised his head from his paws.

"How about breakfast? I'll make eggs."

"No, thanks. Where were you, so sweaty?"

"I went for a run with Dom."

Lucinda lifted an eyebrow, and I translated disapproval, since my wife's eyebrows contain our marital vocabulary.

"He asked." I looked at Ethan, asleep in the Call of Duty T-shirt Allison had given him. "How's he?"

"Okay."

I started to sit down, but Moonie growled at me, which was strange. "Moonie, no."

Lucinda shifted upward. "Moonie?"

The movement woke Ethan, blinking. "What's going on?"

Moonie growled louder, baring his teeth. His round brown eyes bulged as they fixed on me.

"Moonie, no." I straightened, and Moonie jumped up, still growling.

Lucinda recoiled, surprised. "Be careful. I think he wants to bite you."

Ethan reached for the dog, who allowed himself to be taken. "He thinks you're mad at him."

"Why?"

"You know, for what happened."

Lucinda and I exchanged looks. I sensed we weren't talking about the dog. "Well, I love him and I'm not mad at him."

"Good." Ethan flopped back down with the dog, who snuggled against him, eyeing me.

I sat down and patted Ethan's foot. "Buddy, how you doing?"

"Okay."

"How about pancakes?"

"Nah."

"*Banana* pancakes?"

"No, thanks." Ethan leaned back, closing his eyes.

"Why don't you get up?" I wanted to keep him on a normal schedule. "It's a nice day. Let's go take a beach walk. Maybe we'll see a heron."

"A what?"

"It's a bird. They're huge, and blue. They're amazing. Dom says the other agent knows all about them. He knows about the marsh, too. Maybe we can take him along."

"No, that's okay. I'm tired."

Lucinda shook her head, warning me off.

"Okay, maybe another time. Guess what, I have good news. Dom's going to get protection for Mom and Melissa."

"That's great." Lucinda smiled.

"Plus, I asked him to send her a message, saying not to worry about us."

"Will he do it?"

"He said it wasn't likely, but I pressed him. I told him they should get word to Melissa or she'll raise a Facebook posse."

"Wait," Lucinda said. "You didn't tell him I went on Facebook, did you?"

"Yes, but you weren't doing anything wrong."

"Still, you told him?" Lucinda's eyes flared, which meant more disapproval.

"I had to tell him how I knew."

"That was between us. You should have discussed it with me."

Ethan perked up. "Mom, you went on Facebook?"

Lucinda turned to Ethan. "Not on my own account. I went on under my intern's."

Ethan shifted up in bed. "Can I go on Insta?"

"No," I answered, because Lucinda was giving me a see-what-you-started look. "Dom doesn't want us to —"

"Jason," Lucinda interrupted. "Is Dom pissed at me now?"

"No, it's not a big deal."

"It's not a big deal to *bust* me? To the *FBI*?"

Ethan looked from his mother to me and back again, and I realized the conversation was taking a wrong turn.

"Honey, it's okay, really. He's going to talk to his boss and —"

"Oh, great." Lucinda rolled her eyes. "What did he say, exactly? Tell me."

"I thought you wanted me to get protection after the fire —"

"What fire?" Ethan interrupted, and we both looked over, remembering at the same moment that we hadn't told him yet.

Lucinda touched his arm. "Ethan, something happened last night while you were asleep. These criminals, the men who, you know . . . they set fire to the house."

Ethan recoiled, his lips parting. "They burned our *house*? Did they burn our stuff? Inside?"

Lucinda's eyes began to glisten, so I answered for her. "Yes, I'm afraid so."

"*All* our stuff?" Ethan looked stricken, his eyebrows sloping down. "I had ashes in my room. Wendy's and Max's. Their ashes. That's like their *graves.*"

He meant our old dog and cat. He hadn't talked about those pets for years.

Our vet had given us the cremains in small cedar boxes, and Ethan put them in his bedroom, which Allison had teased him about.

Bro, you're the crypt keeper.

"Remember, Dad? Do you know if they burned up?"

"I think they did, I'm sorry," I answered gently.

"But you can't burn ashes." Ethan ran a dry tongue over his braces. "Dad, can we go check? People go back to their houses for stuff that didn't get burned up. I see that on the news."

"We can't do that now."

"Why not? Or maybe the FBI guy can do

it? Dom, your friend?"

Lucinda caught my eye at *your friend.*

"Ethan, I'll talk to him. We have a right to ask."

"You and your rights," Lucinda said, edgy.

"What's that mean?" My heart knew what she meant before my brain did. I flashed on the night Allison was murdered, when Milo started tailgating and I didn't want to speed up.

We have a right to enjoy the drive.

I knew that was what she meant, but it felt unsayable. Marriage was reading each other's minds, but knowing what had to remain unsaid. It killed me to think she blamed me for Allison, even though I was already blaming myself, a fact I had managed to suppress until now.

Lucinda hugged Ethan. "Let's go back to sleep, honey."

Ethan snuggled against her, with Moonie. "I'm tired."

"I'll go eat," I said, my throat suddenly thick.

Shaken, I turned away.

Chapter Sixteen

I went downstairs, trying to sort my thoughts. I never felt right when Lucinda and I were at odds. Our marriage was solid ground, the terra firma of my life, but this was disturbances-in-the-field time. If Lucinda really blamed me for Allison's murder, I had no idea what to do.

I walked to the front door, driven to get some air. I hadn't been to the marsh yet and it was closer than the beach. I left the house, went down the stairs, and crossed under the stilts holding up the house. Out back was a path through underbrush, and I made my way through the scrub pines, needles scratching my forearms.

My shirt clung to me, and humidity weighed the air. I reached the clearing and took in the view of the water. Sun shimmered on the surface, making shifting shadows of darkness and light. Ducks flapped their wings as they landed. The mosquitoes and horseflies buzzed. I inhaled, but it smelled like decomposing things.

"Jason?" Dom called behind me.

"Oh, hi," I said, startled, then remembered about the cameras.

"I spoke with my boss, and it's confirmed. They're putting a surveillance team on your mother-in-law's nursing home and Melissa's street, for the foreseeable future."

I forced a smile. "That's great, thank you."

"And we're arranging a way to pay severance to your employees. We'll have to work out the details."

I forced another smile. "Thank you again."

Dom cocked his head. "What's the matter? I thought you'd be happy."

"Lucinda's pissed I told you she was on Facebook. You didn't tell your boss, did you?"

"Yes, and he says no-go on the message to Melissa."

"That's a bad call. Did you tell him she's not going to quit?"

"Yes, I tried. In fact, he told me she reported your family as missing to the locals."

"Oh no." My chest went tight. "Now what happens? What do the police do?"

"Nothing."

"Do they know we're with you?"

"Yes, but only at the highest level."

"Did you make my argument?"

"Yes, that's why I got protection."

"Can I talk to him?" I asked, on impulse. "You just talked to him, right? Let's call him now. What did you say his name was? Gremmie?"

"No, he doesn't know we call him Gremmie. Richard Volkov." Dom slid his phone from his pocket, pressed speed dial, and said into it, "Hey, I'm here with Jason Bennett. You got a sec to talk to him? Thanks. I'll put you on speaker." Dom pressed the speaker button. "Richard, I have Jason Bennett."

I didn't hesitate. "So you're Dom's boss?"

"Yes." Special Agent Volkov cleared his throat. "Please accept my condolences. We know this is a difficult time for you and your wife. We appreciate your cooperation and —"

"Thank you, but why is it so hard to find Milo?"

"The investigative team is working around the clock on —"

"Then I want to talk directly to them."

"Mr. Bennett, first let me say we've had a major development in your case. We learned that Milo has fled the country. We believe he's in Mexico."

"Wait, what?" I couldn't process it fast enough. "He got away?"

"No, we don't look at it that way. We will apprehend him there and bring him to justice. We have extradition with Mexico."

"That's still *away.* He *got away.*" I fought for emotional control. "How did he get to Mexico? How did that happen?"

"We're as disappointed as you, but —"

"*Disappointed?* Is *that* what you think I am?" Try furious! I felt my jaw clench. "He *cannot* get away with killing my daughter."

"He won't. We're liaising with DEA, DHS, and the Mexican authorities. This case is our top priority."

"How do you know he's in Mexico?"

"I can't divulge that."

"Where in Mexico?"

"I can't divulge that, either."

"Is he connected with drugs there, like a cartel?" I couldn't believe I was saying the words. I didn't know anything about drug cartels. It was like a TV show.

"We can't divulge that information, either."

"He's not Mexican, is he?"

"No."

"How did he get there? Did he fly?"

"We don't believe so."

"When did this happen?" I looked at

Dom, who hadn't said a word about this on our run. "Why am I just hearing this now?"

"We were just informed. I just told Dom."

Dom nodded, sympathetic. "I was about to tell you."

At least Dom hadn't kept it from me. "I want you to keep me posted, both of you. I want to know everything as soon as you know it. Getting blindsided makes it worse."

Special Agent Volkov said, "Dom will keep you apprised."

"Good, and I really think you should get a message to my wife's best friend Melissa. You have to give her an explanation."

"It's not procedure."

"You're making a mistake. Like I told Dom, we're a family, we have friends, and you have to deal with that."

"I'll take it under advisement."

I tried to collect my thoughts. "Do you think Milo's leaving has to do with our house fire and my office?"

"We don't believe he set either fire, if that's what you're asking. You have my apologies. We did not anticipate they would do that."

You should have, I thought but didn't say, like Lucinda would have. "Do you know who set the fire?"

"Not at this juncture."

"It has to be someone who works with Milo and Big George, right?"

"We have reason to believe it's someone within GVO."

"Who? What are their names?"

"I can't divulge that."

I wanted to ask him if it was the BMW driver, but I didn't want to get Dom in trouble, since he had shown us the video he wasn't supposed to. I knew that Special Agent Volkov wouldn't have confirmed or denied anything anyway. "How's our house, have you seen it?"

"Not personally."

"I assume the fire is out?"

"I understand it is, as of early this morning."

"How much damage was done?"

"I'm told it will have to be torn down."

I felt a deep pang. "Do you have agents there now?"

"Yes. We're salvaging the contents."

"Then I have a request, from my son. There were some things in his room, small cedar boxes with the cremains of pets. Obviously it's not about the pets."

"Dom mentioned your son's issues to me."

I glanced at Dom. My son's *issues* were now known to the FBI. Suddenly I understood what had bothered Lucinda. "If you have an agent on the scene, can I speak with him?"

"Yes. I'll tell him who to call."

It turned out that one Special Agent Devi Gupta was at the house, and she FaceTimed me on Dom's phone so I could see for myself. The sight broke my heart, and my only consolation was that Lucinda was spared. Anything she could imagine wasn't as bad as it was. Seeing it made it real, and reality was awful.

Our house was charred and smoldering. The support beams were still standing, but the living room and family room were mostly gone. I could see clear to the fireplace in the family room, its bricks blackened. The blaze had ravaged the façade on the second floor, marring its white clapboard with smudges that streaked upward from the windows. The roof was open in ragged patches. Grayish smoke drifted upward, hazing the sky.

Firefighters were dragging hoses back to trucks, and workmen in boots were raking debris and carrying Hefty bags to a blue Dumpster in the driveway. Shingles and burned wood lay strewn all over the lawn, deeply rutted and churned up with footprints, full of standing water. Lucinda's rosebushes were smashed and broken. I had mulched the beds after she put in some bulbs a week ago, staining my hands brown.

I cleared my throat. "How bad does it look inside?"

"I don't know," Special Agent Gupta answered, her tone sympathetic. "Only firefighters are permitted in, given the structural damage."

"Can you look for the contents of a room on the second floor, the bedroom on the end of the hall? That's my son's. I'm looking for some little cedar boxes."

"Hold on, let me see."

Special Agent Gupta crossed the ruined lawn toward a pile of debris, as the phone screen jolted along. She passed a drenched pile of my old law hornbooks; Torts and Contracts, the green covers now black. Then our family-room television, charred, found randomly among drinking glasses. A stack of dishes, a pile of Lucinda's handbags. The detritus of our family.

Special Agent Gupta muted the call, and I waited. After a few minutes, she came back on, then we jolted along again. "Sir, items from your son's room are in a row ahead. We'll give a look and see if the boxes are here, okay?"

"Thank you," I said, and onto the phone screen came Ethan's Rubik's Cube collection, their unnaturally bright colors standing out on the muddy lawn. Then there was a pile of sneakers and clothes.

Special Agent Gupta kept scanning the row, and among a slew of old video games I spotted the two cedar boxes.

"Those!" My heart lifted. "That's them."

"Great." Special Agent Gupta picked up the two cedar boxes, showing them to the camera.

"I really appreciate that. That's very kind of you." My throat caught, my emotions raw. I felt like a wreck, like I was the burned-out house, a shell without structure, unable to bear weight.

"So, mission accomplished?"

"Yes, and if you see any of our family photographs, that would make my wife so happy. She's a photographer."

"I did see some."

"If you could box them with the cedar chests, could you send them here?"

"Sure, I'd be happy to."

"Thank you."

"Anything else?"

I thought of something else. "Yes, one last thing."

■ ■ ■ ■

Dom pocketed the phone. "I'm glad you got the cedar boxes."

My chest was still tight. "But what does it mean that Milo's in Mexico?"

"It means we go after him there."

"It's not that easy, I know that." I couldn't help but despair. "He killed Allison and now he's out of the country."

"It's not easy, but it's doable. DEA knows the players as well as we do. Better."

"Dom, tell me the truth. Don't bullshit me."

"I'm not bullshitting you. I never will." Dom's expression was sympathetic, which softened me.

"Are you telling me that the DEA knows of Milo, Junior, and the organization? Small-time drug dealers in the Philadelphia suburbs?"

"Yes. GVO is not small-time."

I wanted to believe him, so badly. "You can't pretend this is good news."

"I'm not trying to. But it's not a disaster, either."

"To me, it is. Our chances of getting him are worse than before."

"It's a setback, at most."

"What is this, semantics?" I threw my hands in the air. "He got out when you guys were looking for him!"

Dom winced, and I could see I had landed a blow, which conflicted me. The man had vowed to take a bullet for us.

"Dom, I don't mean you, *per se,* and I didn't tell your boss you showed us the video."

"I noticed." Dom met my eye. "Thank you."

"I think it was a BMW. Was it? Was he the guy who burned down my house and office?"

"I don't know either of those answers. Honestly, they don't tell me. It's strictly need-to-know, and The Babysitters Club does not need to know." Dom shook his head. "My job is keeping you and your family alive, and if possible, happy. That will be harder if we don't trust each other. You have to trust *me.*"

"Can I?"

"Yes." Dom cocked his head. "But can I trust *you*?"

"Of course." I felt taken aback. "Why wouldn't you?"

"When I showed you the video, you took that picture of it. Now you're trying to identify the car and who was driving. It's exactly what I wanted to avoid."

I realized he was right. "Fair enough."

Dom extended a hand, with a smile. "Let's start over."

I shook his hand, smiling back. "Okay."

"We'll get this guy, Jason."

"I believe you," I told him, trying.

Chapter Seventeen

I went back inside the house, got online, and searched *Mexican cartels,* wanting to learn all I could. I clicked and clicked, reading one grim article after another, passing one hour after the next, going down a gruesome wormhole of Sinaloa, Jalisco, and Pablo Escobar, the truly horrifying numbers of murders, beheadings, and other carnage.

I made a pot of coffee and a cheese sandwich as the afternoon wore on, and Lucinda and Ethan didn't come downstairs. I stayed online and plugged in *Mexican cartel* and *Avondale, John Milo, George Veria, Big George,* and *George Veria, Jr.* to see if there were any reported connections. I knew it was probably futile, but it was all I had to go on. There were no articles.

On impulse, I plugged in our last name to see if there was any new mention of us. The first entry caught me off guard, and the link read WHAT HAPPENED TO THE BENNETTS? Astonished, I clicked and was taken to the website of one Bryan Krieger, who called himself America's premier citizen detective, above a photo of a middle-aged man in wire-rimmed aviators, with salt-and-pepper hair and a darker beard. Above him was a heading, CASES, and the first one was THE BENNETT FAMILY.

Aghast, I clicked and read:

Folks, it looks like a bona fide mystery in the Philly suburbs, where an entire family disappeared in one night — Jason Bennett, wife Lucinda, daughter Allison, and son Ethan. Not only that, their house burned down, his court-reporting business burned down, and the mom's photography studio was trashed, all in one night. And the family vanished into thin air.

My ears pricked up when I heard about it from my cousin. Your favorite citizen detective (me!) is leaving NYC now to investigate. Legacy media is missing the story, but we sure won't. Looks like Jason runs a successful business, but who knows? His website lists lots of clients, but again, really? The site shows pictures of the office staff, and there's a sweet young thing. Is that what's going on here? Did

Jason have an affair, then kill his family and run off?

I recoiled. I hadn't known there was such a thing as citizen detectives, much less that they were speculating about me and my family. The "sweet young thing" could only be my employee Justine Vanderlost, who happened to be gay.

Folks, you know what I always say, look to the nearest and dearest! We'll never know what goes on behind closed doors, and I'm working on a theory of family murder. Familicide happens. John List comes immediately to mind, right? But where are the bodies? When will they turn up? Let's crowd-source this case!

I shook my head in disbelief. I scanned the comments from the online community:

JellyBelly Rick, I get why he would burn down the house, since it could be the crime scene, but why his office? And why burglarize the wife's studio? Do you think that was for the insurance money? And how could he collect, if he's a fugitive? And most of all, WHERE ARE THE BODIES?

Dark Horse I was thinking the same thing, Jellybelly, but he could have done it to make it look like someone else! We have to dig deeper. I'm going to investigate, too, and I'll keep you all posted here. I don't live that far away, I'm at the Jersey shore.

Slim Jim I know you ladies think you're experts, but you assumed right away that the father killed his family. What if it was the mother? What if she pulled a Susan Smith and drove her family into the river?

Professor Outlaw Slim Jim, you need to educate yourself. Familicide, or the murder of an entire family, is more commonly committed by men than women. A study published in the Howard Journal of Criminal Justice reports that in 71 cases of familicide, 59 of the perpetrators were male. The "family annihilator" is usually a middle-aged man, a good provider who "appears to neighbors to be a dedicated husband and devoted father." I'm paraphrasing Prof. Jack Levin, Professor of Sociology and Criminology Emeritus at Northeastern University in Boston. Bottom line, do the reading. The odds are, it's Daddy, not Mommy.

Suddenly I heard Lucinda and Ethan coming downstairs and closed the laptop. It was almost five o'clock, and they had been in Ethan's bedroom the whole day. I hadn't seen Lucinda since our fight this morning. I didn't know what to expect from her.

I rose as they trundled into the kitchen, downcast. "Hey, how are you guys?"

"Okay." Ethan plunked down at the table, resting his face on his hand, and I ruffled up his brown hair, soft under my palm.

"Hey, buddy. You must be starved." I tried to catch Lucinda's eye, but she was looking around the kitchen.

"Jason, how old's that coffee?"

"Too old, but come here." I took her arm and drew her close to me, kissing her on the forehead. "I love you."

"Love you, too." Lucinda leaned into me and linked her arms around my waist. "Sorry if I was cranky before."

"No worries. Food's on the way. I ordered us something special. It's being delivered any minute." I let Lucinda go, and she went to the coffeemaker, so I turned to Ethan. "Buddy, how you feeling?"

"Okay."

"I got your favorite thing for dinner."

"Cool."

I noted he didn't ask what I meant. His

blue eyes looked washed out, and his skin was pale, which happened when he was sick. "You getting a cold or anything?"

"No, just tired." Ethan looked over as Moonie trotted in. "He pooped in my room."

"That's weird. Moonie, come." I motioned to the dog, who followed me to the back door, and I watched him go down the steps, then left him. I came back into the kitchen, dismayed to see Lucinda on my laptop, looking at the citizen detective website.

"Jason, what's this?" Lucinda unhooked her reading glasses from her collar and slipped them on, as she read the website. "This is about *us*?"

"Don't let it bother you."

"They're saying you killed us. You *murdered* us."

Ethan scooted over, leaning on his forearms. "What? Dad killed us?"

Lucinda recoiled. "Jason, they can't say this about you. It will ruin your reputation."

I waved her off. "Honey, we're getting different names. My reputation no longer matters."

"But this is outrageous." Lucinda read the screen, eyes flaring behind her readers, which magnified them. "They're calling you a *family annihilator.*"

I held her shoulder. "It's nothing."

Ethan looked upset. "Dad, who are they? How can they investigate us?"

"They're not going to. They're people who follow true-crime cases, that's all. It's their hobby."

"Like *Dateline*? Like *48 Hours*?"

"Right," I answered, and Moonie started barking at the back door. I ignored him because Lucinda was typing, her jaw set with determination. "Honey, what are you doing?"

"Checking my page."

Moonie kept barking, so I let him in. He trotted to his food and water, sniffing the unfamiliar kibble.

"Oh no." Lucinda frowned at the laptop. "Jason, some of our friends think you murdered us, too. This is crazy!"

Ethan leaned over. "It's not my friends, is it? What are they saying?"

I went over and read posts from the other parents, whom I knew from school or the games:

Julie Carruthers Jason always seemed like a nice guy, but the quiet ones are trouble.

Melody Frank-Yoli Agree! Still waters run deep!

Susanna Burlemann Don't talk trash about the Bennetts. What kind of friends are you?

Ethan's eyes rounded. "Mrs. Carruthers is Jared C's mom. What does that mean, 'Still waters run deep'?"

"It means quiet people hold things in."

"I don't do that, and I'm a quiet person."

"Right, it's just an expression. Don't pay it any attention."

Lucinda sighed. "Oh no. Melissa reported us missing."

"I know." I had a lot to tell her, but I looked over at Ethan. "And in the good news category, the FBI got the boxes of ashes from the house."

"Cool," Ethan said idly, distracted by Facebook. "Mrs. D, Kyle's mom from soccer, she thinks you killed us, too, Dad. That means Kyle thinks it and all the guys are gonna start thinking it."

"We can't control what people think or say, so we can't let that bother us." I patted Lucinda's shoulder. "Honey, there's something I have to tell you."

"What?" Lucinda asked, looking up. Her

skin was fair and when she was upset, like now, her face and neck mottled slightly.

"I talked to Dom and his boss. I have bad news, a setback. The FBI says Milo is in Mexico, but don't give up hope." I wanted to play it down in front of Ethan. "They work with the Mexican authorities and other federal agencies. They feel confident they're going to get him."

Lucinda's eyes flared. "They're not going to let him get away, are they? He's not going to get away with it, is he?"

"No, no, honey." I squeezed her shoulder. "They're all over it, I talked to Dom's boss. They'll get him down there."

Ethan looked taken aback. "Like on *Pablo Escobar*?"

Lucinda started shaking her head. "How could they let that happen? They're looking for Milo, and he gets out of the country. They have cameras on our house, and it burns down. Can't they do anything right?"

I heard a knock at the door, which had to be Dom. "Coming!"

Dom called through the screen, "Okay!"

Lucinda shot me a look. "What does he want?"

"He's bringing dinner." I kept my voice low so Dom couldn't hear. "And don't blame him for Milo. It's not his fault. He's not on that team."

Lucinda's eyes flashed. "Whose team are *you* on?"

I let it go, left the kitchen, and went to the door. "Hey, Dom."

"Hey." Dom handed me the pizza box hastily, and I knew he'd heard the exchange.

"Thanks." I let the door close and went to the kitchen, setting the pizza box on the table. "Surprise!"

"How nice! Ethan, look, pizza." Lucinda forced a smile, trying to rally.

I opened the box, revealing a glistening pizza topped with mushroom slices.

"Wow, smells great!"

Ethan looked at the pizza, stricken, which I didn't understand.

"What's the matter, buddy? Mushroom's your favorite, isn't it?"

"It's not my turn, it's Allison's. She gets peppers."

Lucinda jumped up. "Moonie, no!"

I turned around to find the dog pooping on the floor.

CHAPTER EIGHTEEN

It was growing dark by the time we finished dinner, and I stood in the backyard, waiting for Moonie to go to the bathroom. Truth to tell, I needed some air. My pizza surprise had been a flop, and Ethan had eaten in teary silence. Even now, I could hear him in the kitchen with Lucinda, answering her only in monosyllables.

I inhaled heavy, brackish air off the marsh, which I was getting used to. The odor that had smelled moldy now seemed organic, and all around me stretched patches of water, cordgrass, and tall reeds. The sun dipped low in the sky, its waning rays bronzing the water. Jagged treetops pierced a sky washed with purple and pink streaks. Sounds filled the air, seagulls and owls, crickets and tree frogs, and random squawks I couldn't identify. I had never been among so much water, and now it surrounded me. I felt oddly like an island, unto myself.

I startled at a sudden motion in the trees, and a shadowy silhouette emerged from the woods beyond our fence. Moonie ran barking to the back of the yard.

"Who's there?" I froze, alarmed until I recognized the figure as Special Agent Hallman.

"Sorry, my bad!" Wiki called back. "I didn't mean to scare you. Okay if I come in?"

"Sure." I went to meet him, and Wiki entered the backyard. He finger-combed hair from a damp forehead and smoothed down his blue polo shirt, which clung to his bulky frame. His khaki pants were wet to the shins and his sneakers soaked. Moonie sniffed them, then took off.

"What were you doing back there?" I asked, then realized he was probably keeping us safe. "Do you patrol?"

"We don't call it that, but yes."

"Thank you." It made me feel good, and bad. "How often do you do it?"

"A few times a night."

"When, so I'll know when to expect you?"

"We change it up, per procedure."

"Oh, I see." It made sense. "Thanks for doing that."

"It's our job, but I like it. It clears my head. I get sick of answering email."

"I hear that," I said, since I used to have the same complaint. I could imagine my inbox right now. All the lawyers wanting answers, all the depositions that had to be scheduled or postponed. I wasn't sure if I missed it or I didn't.

"How're you doing?" Wiki pushed up his glasses.

"We're hanging in."

"How's your boy?"

"Okay." I realized yet another person knew about Ethan's issues.

"I hear he likes video games. If he ever wants to play, I'll play with him."

"Thanks, Wiki," I said, touched.

"Which games does he play? I play Apex, Minecraft, Star Wars Battlefront, Call of Duty—"

"He likes Call of Duty."

"Good. Tell him, anytime. We want this to be as easy as possible on your family. That's why we picked this location. It's mostly salt marsh, but there's mud flats and wildlife. Here, you have everything. Plant life, the birds, geology. I think I told you I grew up in Lewes. I live in Dover. Went to U of D."

"That must be difficult. So near but yet so far, all that."

"Nah. It suits me. I'm divorced, no kids. I'm a loner, not like Dom. Everybody loves

Dom. He can deal with anybody. He was even best man at the wedding of one of our applicants." Wiki chuckled. "Your family is in great hands."

"Thanks."

"You should take your boy to the ghost forest. He would love it. Text me if you go, I'll keep an eye on you. The tide will be in, but the walk is easy. On a full moon like tonight, it'll be amazing."

"What's a ghost forest?"

"This way," I said, taking Ethan's hand, and I led him into the woods. Moonlight filtered through the trees, lighting a skinny trail that Wiki had described. My flashlight shone a jittery cone of light on the tree trunks and underbrush. Moonie tugged at the end of his leash, but Ethan began to lag.

"I don't care about a ghost forest."

"Wiki said it was cool."

"I don't want to go. Let's go back."

"It won't take long. He's keeping an eye on us. Don't be afraid."

"I'm not. I think it's dumb."

"Give it a chance." Moonie sniffed a bush, then urinated, which was a victory. I was hoping the dog would poop outside for a change.

"Ugh, my feet are wet. It's a swamp."

"It's not a swamp, it's a marsh. Do you want to know the difference?"

"No."

I let it go. We tramped through the woods, following the flashlight. "Wiki says ghost forests are springing up all over the mid-Atlantic, and Delaware has quite a few. Unfortunately, it's the result of climate change. The glaciers are melting, so the sea level rises and salt water flows into a forest and kills the trees."

"Fascinating."

I let that go, too. "Anyway, the salt water kills the trees but doesn't knock them over, so what's left is called a ghost forest."

"Let's go back."

"No, keep going. I want to see it. We're almost there." I noticed the trees beginning to show less leaf and the foliage growing wetter. The footing, also, got wetter. "Wiki was telling me there's all kinds of native plants like spartina, or cordgrass, and the birding is supposed to be incredible this time of year."

"Birding?" Ethan snorted, which I ignored. My son was an indoor cat. Allison had been the one who'd lived outside, 24/7. She'd go running even when I wouldn't.

Al, it's raining.

Your hair gonna frizz, dude?

I shooed the memory away. I had to stop comparing Ethan to his sister.

"Ethan, you know, birding is a big deal here. There are Snowy Egrets and Clapper Rails. Also Great Blue Herons and not-so-great Blue Herons."

"That's dumb, Dad."

I was trying to make him laugh. "Lots of birds migrate through here in October. There are bird sanctuaries, but we have our own private view."

"Wiki told you this?"

"Yes."

Ethan snorted again. Moonie panted, trying to strangle himself on the leash. We splashed along.

"He said he'd play Call of Duty with you. He's a gamer."

"Is he supposed to be my new friend, like Dom is yours?"

I sighed inwardly. "I don't know what to tell you, Ethan. I like the guy. I like them both. They're trying to help us."

"Well, I don't need their help and I already have friends. Zach, Christopher, and Scott and the other guys. I don't need an old-guy FBI friend."

"He's thirty-five."

"That's old."

"We're getting closer." I noticed the surroundings grew brighter as the tree branches grew bare, and we came to a clearing. We could hear the flapping of wings and more calls and squawks, the chirping of crickets and other insects. The moon was as round as a bullet hole.

"This must be it," I said, turning off the flashlight. I waited while my eyes adjusted, and Ethan let out a whistle.

Everywhere around us were dead trees, their bleached trunks white as skeletons, their branches denuded of life, reaching jagged in all directions, glowing like a field of lightning strikes against the black sky. They rose from a blanket of dark cordgrass rippling in the breeze, undulating as if alive. Snaking everywhere was tidewater, obeying the pull of the moon.

The place struck me as a convergence of life I couldn't see and death that was staring me in the face. Tears came to my eyes, and grief ambushed me, as if it had been lying in wait, all along. Maybe it wasn't a good idea to go to a ghost forest so soon.

But Ethan gasped in delight. "Dad, this is so cool!"

It is? I cleared my throat. "Yes, it sure is."

"How did it get like this, again?"

"The salt water kills the trees," I managed to say, my throat thick.

Ethan touched my arm, looking up.

"Are you okay?"

"I'm fine," I said, clearing my throat again.

"Dad, you're not."

I felt exposed, despite the darkness. "You're right. I'm sad about Allison."

"But you don't cry like Mom. She cries all the time. Me, too. You don't."

"I do when I'm alone."

"Why? You cried when Aunt Caitlin died."

"I don't know." I held back tears.

"Mom said you told her you're not crying because if you start, you're afraid you won't stop."

It caught me up short. I forgot when I had said that, but it was how I felt. I looked down at Ethan in the moonlight. "I love you, buddy. You know that, don't you?"

"I love you, too, Dad."

I put my arm around his shoulders, pulling him close. "We have each other. We're going to be okay."

"Mom's upset we can't go to the funeral."

"Me, too. How about you?"

Ethan hesitated. "Is it okay if I'm not? I don't want to watch it on TV, either."

"Yes, of course, that's okay." I gave him a squeeze. "We know you love Allison and you miss her."

Ethan fell silent. "She woulda thought this

was cool. I wish she was here."

"Me, too."

"Like, I can't believe she's not . . . alive. I keep forgetting."

"I know. It's horrible."

"I wake up and remember." Ethan looked up at me, and I could see his stricken grimace, the moonlight glinting on his braces.

"I do, too," I said, hugging him against my side.

"Do you think she's a ghost? I mean, really? Do you think she's in heaven, or do you think she goes flying around?"

I wasn't ready for this conversation. "Well, I believe she's always with us. Her soul is with us."

"I believe that, too. I talk to her, Dad. Is that weird?"

"No, not at all. I talk to her, too, and I hear her voice. I think of conversations we had."

"So do I. It comes into my head. That happened with Pop, too. I remember things he said. Like he always said, 'Cheese and crackers' and 'Hot damn!' "

I smiled, surprised. "You remember that? You were so young then."

Ethan nodded. "There's times when you say something he woulda said, or you do something he did. Like you suck your teeth."

"Oh no." I smiled.

"I miss Pop."

"I do, too. They say time heals all wounds. I think it's true with Pop. I think of him a lot, but I don't always feel sad."

"That will never happen with Allison. I'll always be sad about her."

My heart hurt for him. It was too much to deal with at his age. Not only the loss, but the horror. "You don't know that yet, honey. Now is really, really hard, and I have to hope this is the hardest it will ever be."

"No, Dad. It will always be hard."

"Not forever, honey."

"Forever."

I feared he was right, but it wasn't what I should say. I looked into his face, placing a hand on his shoulder. "Buddy, listen. This is a hard thing, very hard. We can get a counselor, if you want to talk to somebody about it."

"I know, Mom already told me. She calls it a shrink. She said she went to a shrink after Aunt Caitlin died."

I was glad that Lucinda had told him. It should come from her, since I had given away enough of her secrets. "She did go, and it helped her. I saw it help her."

"Have you ever been to a shrink?"

"No, but I might go now."

"Zach P goes every Thursday after school. Miles saw the number in his phone and started making fun of him, then everybody started calling him crazy."

"That's wrong. It's wrong to call somebody crazy, and it's good to talk to a therapist. We could go as a family."

"But we're not a family anymore."

"What do you mean?" I remembered I had thought that in our family room, that first night. "We're still a family, Ethan."

"Not without Allison, it's not the same. Nothing is the same."

"It's not the same, but we're still a family." I tried to figure it out, because Ethan needed to be reasoned with. "Think of it like this. We're still a family, and Allison is still in our family, even though she's not here, physically. She'll always be in our family." I thought it over. "The people you love, like Pop and Allison, even the pets you love, like Max and Wendy, they never leave you, not as long as you love them. You'll always have them as long as you love them. And you'll love them forever. That's what lasts forever. The love."

We both fell silent, listening to the sounds of the things we couldn't see. The water flowed inexorably to the bay, a hushed rushing.

"Dad, I feel her here. Do you?"

"Yes," I answered, then my cell phone pinged with a text alert. I slid it from my pocket and checked the screen. It was from Lucinda.

Come back ASAP. I'm at Dom's. We have a problem.

Chapter Nineteen

We found Lucinda, Dom, and Wiki in the apartment, gathered around Lucinda's laptop. She was upset, her skin mottled and her neck blotchy. Dom and Wiki looked grim, their hands on their hips. The tension in the room was palpable the moment I entered, breathless.

"What's the matter, honey?" I went to her side.

"Mom, you okay?" Ethan dropped Moonie's leash, and the dog trotted off, sniffing.

"I'm fine." Lucinda forced a smile, then looked at me. "Melissa went to see Mom at Bay Horse."

"Why?" I asked, surprised.

"She went looking for me. She knows I go Monday nights."

"Oh no." I had forgotten, with so much going on. Lucinda visited her mother every Monday night, and I usually stayed home with the kids. We used to go with her, but my mother-in-law no longer recognized anyone but my wife and sometimes Allison.

"Look." Lucinda gestured at the laptop, and the screen showed a Facebook post by Melissa.

> Lucinda, I'm with your mother. You didn't show up or call. Something must be keeping you away or you would be here. What's going on? Please let me know you're okay!

My heart sank. Under the post was a photo of Melissa, a freckled-faced redhead with rimless glasses, uncharacteristically somber. She sat next to my mother-in-law, Claire Romarin, whom I loved like my own mother. Claire had been a beautiful woman in her day, the origin of my wife's wide-set eyes, straight nose, and pretty mouth, but my mother-in-law was frowning in the photo, distraught.

Lucinda glared at Dom. "My mother's confused. She doesn't know what's going on. She doesn't remember Melissa and she doesn't know where I am. All this could have been prevented. All you had to do was tell Melissa we're in the program. She wouldn't have told anyone and she wouldn't have gone to Bay Horse."

"I'll talk to my boss —" Dom started to say.

"A little late, don't you think?"

"We have procedures."

"And look where they got us! It's bad enough I'm abandoning my mother, now she's worried sick about me!"

Dom's expression was grave, and I knew he felt terrible, which frustrated me more.

"Okay," I said to Lucinda, "here's what I think, honey. We can't look back."

"Why not?" Lucinda looked over, shedding my arm.

"Because it's not about blame. It's about what we do next."

"Don't take their side, Jason!"

"I'm not." I was aware of Ethan looking from Lucinda to me. "We're missing the big picture, playing the blame game." I turned to Dom. "This post reveals where my mother-in-law lives. I think that puts her in danger. Did you get surveillance on her yet?"

"Unsure. I made the request this morning. Normally it takes a day or two." Dom gestured to Wiki, who slid out his phone and started texting. "We'll check."

Lucinda's hand flew to her mouth. "I didn't even think of that! They could go there and kill her, for God's sake!"

"Honey, we will deal with this. We can deal with it."

"How? My mother's in danger!" Lucinda turned to Dom, angry tears in her eyes. "You let Milo get away. You let our house burn down. Now my mother has a target on her back because you wouldn't tell Melissa we're okay!"

Dom pursed his lips. "Lucinda, we will —"

"You can't let anything happen to my mother! She's a wonderful person, *wonderful*! She's been through hell! She lost my sister, she's losing *herself.* She never did anything wrong to anybody, not once!"

"Honey, it's going to be okay." I put an arm around Lucinda again, but she looked alarmed, beginning to breathe oddly, her chest heaving.

"Jason . . . my heart's pounding, so hard . . ."

"Okay, here, sit down." I eased her into a chair, and Lucinda's eyes rounded with fear.

"Jason . . . I think I'm having a heart attack. . . ."

"Mom!" Ethan rushed to her side, and Dom knelt in front of her.

"Lucinda, do you feel pain in your left arm?"

"I don't know . . . my heart's beating

so . . . fast."

I told Dom, "She has a heart murmur."

Ethan hugged her, stricken. "Mom, what's wrong?"

"I'll be . . . fine." Lucinda patted him with a trembling hand. Her frightened gaze met mine.

"Honey, we need to get you to the hospital. Dom, should we call 911 or is it quicker to take her?"

"Let's take her."

"I got her." I lifted Lucinda up and carried her to the door, while Dom hurried ahead and flung it open. Wiki took Ethan, and we all hustled down the stairs followed by Moonie.

Dom ran ahead to the white van, opening the passenger door. "Jason, put her in. I'll drive."

"Stay calm, honey." I eased Lucinda into the seat, and she breathed with effort, her mouth slightly open.

"I'm scared," she whispered, which wasn't like her.

"It's okay," I told her, but I would never discount the worst-case scenario again. I was living the worst-case scenario.

"Mom!" Ethan wedged his way to her, starting to cry. "Be okay!"

"I'll be fine." Lucinda forced a smile, jittery.

I put my hand on Ethan's shoulder. "Ethan, stay here with Wiki."

"Jason, no, you can't go!" Dom hustled to the driver's side.

"Yes, I am!" I reached for the back door, but Wiki restrained me with a surprisingly strong grip.

"Jason, stay." Wiki met my gaze with new authority. "You'll jeopardize her safety. Dom's got this."

"Dom?" I called to him, and he met my eye with a nod, giving me the answer I needed.

Lucinda looked over, agonized. "Love you," she mouthed through the window.

I didn't have to read her lips.

Meanwhile Dom had started the engine and was already taking off. Shards from the driveway flew as the van zoomed into the street. Ethan wrapped his arms around my waist, and we watched the van disappear into the darkness, its red taillights swallowed up by the night.

I stood behind the screen of the front door, looking out. The driveway was dark, still, and quiet except for the natural sounds. There was nothing to see, but I was too nervous to sit down. I assumed Dom and Lucinda were at the hospital and I was on tenterhooks.

Ethan curled up on the couch with Moonie, teary and exhausted. The TV was on, but we weren't watching. I tried to shake off the frustration building up inside. I hated staying behind while my wife was being taken to the hospital by an FBI agent. It should have been me. What if there was a decision to make? I had to be there. She would have been there for me, no question.

Ethan emitted a sigh, and I crossed to the couch and sat down next to him. Moonie whipped his fuzzy head around, growling.

"No," I snapped. "Ethan, what's the matter with Moonster?"

"He hates it here."

"I get it." I put an arm around Ethan, and Moonie resettled on my son's far side.

"Dad, will she be okay? You said she has a heart murmur." Ethan pulled his knees up to his chest, wrapping his arms around them. "What's that?"

"It's common."

"Why didn't you guys tell me?"

"It didn't matter enough."

"I'm worried about Muggy, too." Ethan called my mother-in-law Muggy, since he hadn't been able to say *grandma* when he was little. “I don’t want the bad guys to get her.”

“They won’t. The FBI’s going to protect her. Wiki said so.”

Suddenly my cell phone rang on the end table, and I dove for it, checking the screen. “It’s Dom,” I told Ethan.

“Dom, how is she?”

“She’s fine. It’s a panic attack.”

Thank God. I repeated for Ethan’s benefit, “So it’s not a heart attack, it’s a panic attack?”

“Yes. They’re going to give her something to calm her. We’ll be back tonight.”

“Thank you.” I exhaled with relief. “Can you put her on?”

“No, she’s with the doctor. I stepped outside to make the call.”

“Can I call her? She usually has her phone —”

“No. It’s too risky if you’re overheard.”

“Okay. Tell her I love her.” I felt resigned. An FBI agent was telling my wife I loved her. We ended the call, and I set down the phone.

Ethan frowned. “What’s a panic attack?”

“It means Mom’s upset about Muggy. It got to her. All at once.”

“She’s not gonna die?”

“No, not at all. She’s not even sick. We

don't have to worry, and she'll be home soon." I gave him a hug, masking my concern. Lucinda had never had a panic attack in her life. I felt like we were beginning to fall apart at the seams.

Moonie started growling.

And though I had sympathy for everyone in the family, I was running out of patience with Moonie. "Hush," I told him.

Chapter Twenty

Lucinda rested her head on my chest, with one leg over me in the darkness of the bedroom. She called it her "husband cocoon," I assume because she thought I kept her safe. Now we both knew that was sheer fantasy.

"I'm so stupid," Lucinda said softly. "I mean, it *felt* like a heart attack."

"No, don't say that. That's how they feel." I had read about panic attacks online, getting up to speed.

"I feel like a drama queen."

"No, you're not," I said, meaning it. My wife never complained. She got things done, no matter what.

"I never thought I was the kind of person to have a panic attack."

"It's human, and you're a human being. Everybody has a breaking point."

Lucinda fell quiet. The chirping of crickets wafted through the open window, carried on the cool, loamy air. I sensed I had said the wrong thing, so it was time to change the subject.

"At the hospital, how did it work? Were you able to tell the doctor about Allison?"

"Yes, Dom cleared it. *Cleared.* Now I speak FBI." Lucinda chuckled, without mirth. "He stayed with me, though. I made him hold my hand."

"Good." I smiled.

"I felt silly."

"Nah. You like your hand held. Everybody does." I reached for her hand and gave it a squeeze. "See? The circuit is complete."

" 'We fit.' Remember, we used to say that?"

"Of course." I felt a glimmer of happiness, like a splinter of light in the dark, a door cracking to a room that used to be mine, in a house where I no longer lived.

"Dom waited outside when I talked to the shrink."

"How did that go?"

"Well. Mostly I cried."

"Aw, honey." I held her closer, feeling terrible for her.

"He gave me Ativan, but it makes me groggy. I don't think I need it, really."

"Take it, at least until the funeral."

Lucinda sniffled. "I'm sorry I freaked

Ethan out."

"He'll be fine," I told her, though I wasn't sure.

"It was just seeing Mom. We're abandoning her."

"We don't have any choice," I told her, knowing I was repeating myself.

"She doesn't know that." Lucinda shifted position. "The shrink said we have 'acute grief and . . . PTSD.' He said we should all go to counseling, not just Ethan. Would you?"

"Sure," I answered. I hadn't thought about PTSD. It made it so real.

"I keep remembering that when it happened, you were handling it. Like you just *handled* it. You took your shirt off. You knew what to do."

"I don't feel like I handled it," I said, surprised. I felt exactly the opposite. I felt ashamed.

"But you did, you really did. You did more than I did, I didn't do *anything.* I just held her, freaking out. I didn't do anything to help her, I mean I didn't try to stop the blood, I didn't get the phone, and I messed up when I tried to call from the car."

"You tried, don't blame yourself." I realized that as guilty as I felt, Lucinda felt worse.

"But I do, I always thought I was good in an emergency."

"You are. Remember when she got hit with a ball? On her forehead? You went into action."

"Then, I knew, but this . . . this was too much. I couldn't even believe it was really happening, and the blood was so warm, it just was *so warm.*" Lucinda sniffled, beginning to cry. "I told the shrink . . . I think about her all the time, but . . . when they started putting those EKG monitors on me . . . I said, 'Please don't let me die' . . . and I feel guilty . . . I wanted to . . . live."

"Oh, honey, that's okay." I felt the words like a weight on my chest.

"And I do, I don't want to . . . go under but I feel like I am . . . but I have Ethan, and I have you, and we have to . . . I just feel wrong . . . like we're a train leaving the station . . . leaving Allison . . . our baby girl . . . and my mom, we just *leave* them . . ."

"No, we don't, we won't, honey." I didn't know how to console her because I felt the same way. It was important to go on, but impossible to go on. And in the end, that was what I told her.

But by then, she was crying too hard to listen.

Chapter Twenty-One

The week leading up to the funeral started off badly. The FBI had no news on Milo's whereabouts. They were liaising with another federal agency, OCDETF, the Organized Crime Drug Enforcement Task Force, which went after the major drug traffickers. Dom said it would add *jet fuel* to their manhunt. I put on a brave face for Lucinda, but despaired we had lost Milo.

I continued running with Dom, picking his brain about the case, but learned nothing new. He commiserated, but kept telling me to keep the faith. I sensed Lucinda's panic attack had been a turning point for him, and he sympathized with our position more than before. Dom's boss was still refusing to get a message to Melissa, despite the fact that she and our other friends had searched the Lagersen Tract after a neighbor posted that Coldstream had been closed off by police action. The community was speculating, the consensus being that I had murdered my family. Marie and Justine from my office were asked to comment, but didn't. God only knew what they were thinking.

Lucinda worried about her mother, and I worried about her and Ethan. All he wanted to do was stay in his room with Moonie, sleeping off and on. On Thursday, he didn't wake up until mid-afternoon, and I got him downstairs while Lucinda took a shower. He wanted banana pancakes, even though it was almost dinnertime, but I made them anyway, then sat with him. His hair was messy, his head in his hand, his face downcast. He barely ate, pushing a square of pancake around in the syrup, holding his fork loosely. Moonie sat on the floor next to him, his round brown eyes on him, hoping for a scrap.

"Buddy, you don't like the pancakes?"

"I'm not that hungry."

"The first one sucked, then I got my groove, right?"

"They're fine."

"How you feeling?"

"I'm okay. I'm just tired."

I felt pained for him. "No, you're sad, and I know that. I'm sad, too. This is a hard time. It's okay to be sad, like we said."

"I'm not sad, I'm tired."

I eyed him, suddenly not knowing how to talk to him, draw him out, or even wake him up. Every instinct told me to get him outside. It was in my DNA.

There's nothing fresh air can't cure, my father used to say.

I knew it wasn't that easy, but my deepest fear was that Ethan would spiral down, become depressed, even think of suicide. I read those headlines, and so did Lucinda.

"Ethan, how about we go for a walk? You haven't seen the beach yet. We can walk on the beach. Have it all to ourselves."

"Maybe another time."

"Remember our hikes, in Sedona? They were great."

"Yeah."

I remembered our last family vacation, three years ago. The dry, hard flatness of Arizona felt completely different than Pennsylvania, but I took to the desert right away. I loved the dark orange of the craggy rocks, striated with veins of gold, amber, and the richest red. Green underbrush sprouted from crevices, with prickly pear cactus and vegetation I had never seen. One morning, Ethan and I followed a trail until it wound uphill, but he had stopped, worried.

Dad, we should turn around. It's too high.

We can do it.

Ethan hesitated. *You go first.*

No, you go first, and I'll back you up.

I'm not Allison, Dad.

You can do it. You're stronger than you think. Go on.

Ethan turned away, heading up the rock. I watched him climb, and when he reached the top, he threw his hands in the air and hooted with joy. I'd been so proud of him, and he'd been proud of himself. He was the kind of kid who needed a push to fly.

I got up, went over, and touched his shoulder, knobby under my palm. "Ethan, let's go out. If not for a walk, then in the backyard."

"No, I said I'm tired."

"Do it for me. We have to make sure Moonie goes to the bathroom. The dog poops inside because we're not out enough."

"That's not why."

"Humor me." I lifted him out of the chair, which he allowed, pressing the chair away noisily. "Come on."

Ethan moaned, and I steered him to the back, with Moonie trotting behind. I opened the screen door and we went out together onto the deck. The sun had dipped behind the trees, making fiery crowns of their jagged peaks. The air had its characteristic organic smell, and seagulls called overhead. I scanned the sky for a heron or something interesting to point out to Ethan, but didn't see one.

"Dad, it's too hot for a walk."

"It's not that hot," I said, though it was humid.

"I'm barefoot."

"Where are your sneakers?"

"I think upstairs."

I hid my dismay, and Ethan pointed to Moonie, who was running toward the fence, barking. "Dad, is that the FBI guy?"

I looked over to see Wiki approaching the fence. He waved to us, and I waved back. "Yes."

"What's he doing there?"

"Keeping an eye out."

"For us?"

"Yes. He's a nice guy. Let's say hi." I had been trying to put Ethan and Wiki together all week. I started Ethan down the stairs. "He's the one that wants to play video-games with you."

Ethan rolled his eyes.

"Buddy, these men are keeping us safe. You can say thank you." I shot him a look as we reached the ground. Wiki was already coming through the gate, his glasses slipping down his nose and sandy brown hair damp. He lumbered toward us in a navy blue polo shirt and khakis, tugging his shirt away from his trunk. It struck me that he was hiding the outline of his gun.

"Hey, guys." Wiki grinned in his easy way, gesturing at Ethan's Call of Duty T-shirt. "Cool shirt. I have the same one. I've been hoping to run into you guys. I have something to show Ethan."

"Terrific." I smiled. "Thanks for keeping us safe."

"Yes, thanks," Ethan said after a moment.

"Not a problem. Wanna see something cool?" Wiki dug into his pocket and pulled out a small white object shaped like a thick tooth, vaguely whitish and chalky. "It's belemnite, a fossil. It's a cephalopod, related to the squid."

Ethan looked, but didn't reply.

"Wow," I said, though I forgot what a cephalopod was. "Did you find it around here?"

"No, but it's native. I brought it from home to show Ethan. I knew I'd run into him sooner or later." Wiki turned to him. "I told your father, I grew up here. In school we used to go to the Mount Laurel Formation along the canal. We would find plenty of them."

I glanced at Ethan for a reaction, but he was looking at Moonie, digging in the far corner of the yard. I asked Wiki, "How old is it?"

"It's from the Triassic."

I nudged Ethan. "Hear that? It's like Triassic Park."

"Dad, it's *Jurassic* Park."

"I know, I was joking."

"It's even older than that," Wiki continued, his tone vaguely professorial. "The Triassic is before the Jurassic, about two hundred and fifty million years ago. All the landmasses were joined together. It was called Pangea. Did you ever hear of that?"

"Remind us," I answered for us both.

Ethan was still watching Moonie.

"During the Triassic, there was a mass extinction of marine and land species, and when life returned, it was all about the land animals. Dinosaurs were beginning to evolve." Wiki pointed to the fossil. "Ethan, where do you think its mouth is? Take a guess."

Ethan shrugged.

"Here, at the front, where it's wide. It had eyes and ten arms with suckers."

"Moonie's chewing something." Ethan ran off abruptly. "Moonie, no!"

I sighed inwardly. "Sorry. He's not himself."

"Not a problem."

I watched Ethan pet the dog, surprised that his arm was so thin, popping out of his T-shirt like a matchstick.

"So how are you doing, Jason?"

"Okay," I answered, but I found myself scanning my son. His knees seemed more prominent than usual, and his scapula stuck out. He always had a wiry build, but he'd never been skinny.

"Thanks for running with Dom. He's so fast, I can't keep up."

"Neither can I." I managed a smile, preoccupied. Ethan had lost weight, a lot, and we hadn't even been here a week.

"He's hyperactive. He's gotta run to burn it off."

"Right." I knew Wiki was trying to make conversation, but I was thinking about Ethan. He was missing meals, since our mealtimes were all over the lot.

"He said you grew up in Hershey. We used to go there on field trips, too. It's pretty there."

"Yes." I was trying to remember what I'd seen Ethan eat in the past few days. Sometimes he ate with Lucinda, and there was snacking. The breakdown in our routine made it hard to tell.

"I loved that ride through the factory, even though it was fake. The smell was great. The gift shop was the big thing. I ate so many Reese's Pieces I threw up on the bus home."

"Yikes." I only half-listened.

"He told me you were at Gitmo, too. That must've been cool. Dom said you had to be the 'best of the best' to be chosen. What did you do there? Were you in court?"

"The 806 hearings? No." I watched Ethan, wondering if Lucinda had noticed how thin he had gotten.

"What's that mean, 806?"

"It's what they called the detainee hearings. The court reporters weren't in the proceedings." I flashed on the hearings, which were about alleged abuses that took place during detainee interrogations, in the wake of 9/11. The litigation took so long, most of the pretrial proceedings were ongoing, even today.

"Where did you work, if you weren't in the courtroom?"

"We had our own housing unit. They gave us the audio recordings, and we made a same-day transcript."

"You know what I don't get? Why do they need a court stenographer, if they have audiotape? Like, can't they use dictation software?"

I got this question so often I could answer on autopilot. "Audio can't distinguish when different speakers interrupt each other or cross talk, and at Gitmo, there were accents to deal with."

"The beaches must've been nice."

"We didn't get much R & R, but Glass Beach was." I noticed Ethan running across the lawn, and his legs looked positively spindly. "I didn't swim. They got brown sharks."

Wiki snorted. "How about boating? My dad has a boat we take down the Chesapeake."

"Only once. We cruised the river until we got to the sign that says if you go farther, they shoot you."

Wiki laughed, and I seized the moment to go.

"You know, I should get Ethan inside."

"Right." Wiki held out the fossil. "He can have this."

"Thanks." I smiled, touched. Wiki didn't have Dom's ease with people, but I liked him, too. "It's nice of you to give it up."

"Not a problem. I still have my collection from fifth grade."

I laughed, but I wasn't sure he was kidding.

Chapter Twenty-Two

I set the fossil on the table just as Lucinda came into the kitchen in a white T-shirt and shorts, her hair wrapped in a towel. Her eyes looked puffy, so I knew she had been crying in the shower. I stepped toward her and kissed her on the cheek. "Hey, babe."

"Hi." Lucinda met my eye in a tacit thank-you, then sat down. "What's that, a shell?"

"No, a fossil Wiki found."

"He gave it to me." Ethan picked it up, examining it.

"Nice, right?" I ruffled the top of his head. "Buddy, why don't you go take a shower, too?"

"Okay." Ethan left the room with Moonie trotting after him, and I sat down across from Lucinda, patting her hand across the table.

"Want coffee or anything?"

"No, thanks."

"Are you hungry?"

"Not really."

"You haven't eaten since morning, right?"

"Guess not." Lucinda shrugged.

"What about Ethan? Did he have breakfast with you?"

"No, he was in his room."

"I made him pancakes and he barely ate." I had just cleared the dirty plate. "I don't know if he ate the whole day. Do you?"

Lucinda blinked. "If he's hungry, he'll eat."

"Look, I think we're losing structure. So from now on, after my run, I'll wake you guys up and you come downstairs. I'll make breakfast for everybody." I squeezed her hand. "Then maybe at twelve-thirty or so, I'll make lunch. We can make dinner together at six, or I'll do it, I don't mind."

"Okay, but why?" Lucinda took the towel off her head and finger-combed her damp curls.

"I want us to eat together. Get Ethan back to a routine. At home, we ate together when we could."

Lucinda eyed me, pained. "Can't we take it easy on him? Does he have to do chores?"

I remembered Allison used to tease me about that, too.

Dad, let me sleep in. There's nothing to milk here.

"It's not that, honey. He's spending all day in his room, it's not healthy. He looks pale. He doesn't go out. We live across from a beach, and he hasn't even seen it." I caught myself when Lucinda cringed, realizing she hadn't, either. "As a pattern, I don't think it's good, and he looks thin to me."

Lucinda frowned in thought. "You know, now that you mention it, I touched his back this morning and it felt spiny."

"Right. We have to get a scale."

"There's one in the bathroom. I lost three pounds. My shorts fit great." Lucinda half-smiled, but it faded. "Jason, what? You're worried about his weight, for real?"

"I'm worried about our structure. I know how to fix it. I need you to work with me."

Lucinda's eyes flared with alarm. "I remember he didn't eat the pizza. I thought it was because it was Allison's turn."

I could see her mind racing. "Don't worry —"

"Oh no, I think you're right!" Lucinda straightened in the chair. "Boys can get eating disorders, too. These are *just* the conditions that can cause it. I mean, look at what he's gone through, he'll want to exert control in some way. It's about control, not food. We have to get on top of this."

I was beginning to regret bringing it up. "Okay, but —"

"He told me he still feels like it's his fault because he let Moonie go." Lucinda's forehead knit. "We need to get him into therapy."

"We will, and in the meantime, we'll make sure he eats. We can get him on a scale —"

"No. That makes it a thing. You're not supposed to make weight a *thing.*" Lucinda rubbed her face. "I've been enabling this, I think. We hang in his room and talk about Allison. I thought if he got his feelings out and rested, he'd feel better."

"He would, and you didn't cause this."

"But I'm enabling it. I *am* enabling it. It's just that it's hard."

"I know, honey, I really do." I watched her face fall, then went and put my arm around her. Her wet hair felt cool. "Don't worry, we're going to get through this."

"How?" Lucinda shot back.

Chapter Twenty-Three

Lucinda rallied to make fish tacos for dinner, Ethan's second favorite meal. Taco shells were lined up in a white serving platter, waiting to be filled. She slid a Pyrex dish with three pieces of fresh flounder under the broiler, drizzled with olive oil, lemon juice, and cracked pepper. Chopped parsley sat in a fresh green pyramid on the cutting board, next to diced avocado and raw purple onion.

I had already set the table, so I was off duty, leaning against the counter, having a bottle of Stella Artois. It was cold on my tongue, and I felt my spirits lift. I loved hanging with her in the kitchen, and it did my heart good to see her rise to the occasion. Ethan's weight loss was a wake-up call for both of us.

"This is going to be a great meal," I said, patting her on the back.

"I think so, too." Lucinda cracked the

oven door, then straightened up, brushing a strand of hair from her face. She looked flushed and pretty, a glimmer of her old self. "The fish was so fresh. Wiki got it at a fish market. You should see the menu. They have fresh scallops, sea and bay."

"I always forget which is which."

"The sea scallops are the big ones. Just remember that the sea is bigger than the bay." Lucinda smiled. "I like Wiki. He got all the right things and he was back in no time."

"I like him, too." I took a swig of Stella, then passed her the bottle and she took a sip.

"He reminds me of a big, goofy kid. It's funny, for an FBI agent."

"Like a puppy with a waist holster."

Lucinda laughed, a sound that warmed me.

"Honey, Dom's a good guy, too. You should give him a chance."

"I know he is. He was great at the hospital, and I think he really does care. I've been hard on him, and he's just the messenger. I'll make it up to him." Lucinda checked the wall clock. "Dinner should be ready in five minutes."

"Should I wake Ethan?" I had gone upstairs about an hour ago, dismayed to find him asleep with Moonie.

"In a minute or two. Smell that fish?"

"Yes." I found myself salivating. "I'm hungry."

"Me too." Lucinda cocked her head, her hair flowing to her shoulders. "The smell always reminds me of Rubette's."

"That clam place your parents loved?"

"Right, in Barnstable."

"Remember when I met them, for the first time?" I smiled, flashing on that night. I dressed up in a suit and tie, eager to impress Kevin and Claire Romarin, who arrived in shorts and T-shirts. That was when I learned rich people never overdress. Only poor people do, when they want to look rich.

Lucinda smiled. "You ate two baskets of Ipswich clams."

"Your parents caught us making out, by the pay phone."

"They loved you from the start. Like me." Lucinda gave me a look that still made my heart stop.

"I love you."

"I love you, too."

We both turned at the sound of Ethan coming downstairs with Moonie, the dog's nails clicking on the hardwood. Lucinda and I exchanged glances as he entered the kitchen, rubbing his eyes.

"Hey buddy." I went over, ruffled up his hair, and kissed the top of his head.

"Hi," Ethan said sleepily. His gaze found the parsley, avocados, and onion, and a smile spread across his face. "Fish tacos?"

"Yes," Lucinda and I answered, in eager unison. She shot me a look, *Don't make it a thing.*

"Yay, I'm starved!" Ethan practically cheered.

"So am I." I breathed an inward sigh of relief.

"Perfect timing." Lucinda grabbed red oven mitts made to look like lobster claws, which we'd found in a kitchen drawer. "I think we're good to go."

"Fish tacos in three . . . two . . . one . . ." Ethan began to count down, and Lucinda slid out the Pyrex dish, containing three beautiful flounder fillets sizzling in olive oil.

"This fish looks amazing." I set down the beer.

"Thanks." Lucinda started to bring the Pyrex to the counter, but she stumbled over Moonie, bobbling the dish. The flounder fillets slid onto the floor, breaking into pieces, and in the next moment, Moonie started gobbling them up.

"Oh!" Lucinda gasped, holding the empty dish.

"Moonie, no!" Ethan rushed to the dog, trying to pull him back, but the fish was all over the floor anyway.

Lucinda looked up, and I met her eye, and for some reason, she started to laugh. I started laughing too, because it was so silly, our secret plan foiled.

Ethan looked over, then burst into laughter, too. "Mom, you really messed up! Pop would say, 'You screwed the pooch!' "

Suddenly there was a knock at the door, and I heard Dom calling through the screen, "Jason?"

"Come on in!" I called back, and Dom let himself in, carrying a big blue IKEA bag, eyeing us with a grin.

"What's so funny?"

"I dropped an awesome dinner, that's what." Lucinda grabbed a roll of paper towels, tore one off, and wiped her eyes.

Ethan giggled. "Moonie had fish tacos."

Dom smiled. "You want me to go for Chinese or something?"

"No, thanks." Lucinda started cleaning up the fish. "We'll have eggs."

"Need help, babe?" I asked, but she waved me off. I looked over at Dom. "What's in the bag?"

"The stuff you wanted from the house. Devi dropped it off."

"You mean Max and Wendy?" Ethan asked, his face falling.

"Yes." Dom took the cedar boxes out of the bag and handed them to Ethan, who cradled them against his chest.

"Thank you."

"You're welcome." Dom looked over, meeting my eye. "And that other thing you wanted? They were able to salvage it."

"I don't remember," I said, watching Ethan. He was trying not to cry. I could smell the smoke clinging to the boxes.

"This?" Dom started pulling something out of the bag. "From the kitchen?"

The sight hit me like a punch in the chest. It was the kitchen molding with the measurements of the kids, growing up. I had forgotten that I had asked for it, but the timing couldn't have been worse. The molding showed the various hash marks in crayon, pen, and Sharpie, with the dates wiggly in the painted surface. The splintered edge of the wood had been blackened.

I could feel the mood in the room change. I felt ashamed that we had been laughing. Allison had been murdered not that long ago. We were already having fun, without her.

"Thanks, Dom." I took the molding from him as if it were a foreign object, something from another world, which it was. Our old world crashing our new one.

"That's from our —" Lucinda started to say, stunned, but didn't finish. She wiped her hands on a fresh paper towel.

I forced a smile. "I thought we might want to save it."

"How did they get it?" Lucinda advanced uncertainly, her heartbroken gaze on the molding.

"I told them if it wasn't damaged, they should salvage it." I held out the molding, and Lucinda took it from me, scanning the measurements, with Allison's *IM SOOOOOOOO BIG!!!!!!!* staring her in the face.

"I should've told you."

"No, it's okay." Lucinda bit her lip, her gaze still on the measurements. "I want it. We should keep it safe."

Ethan looked from her to me. "I'm going upstairs," he said, turning away.

CHAPTER TWENTY-FOUR

The next morning, Dom and I ran together under a cloudy gray sky. I was breathing hard even though we had just left. We usually ran in silence in the beginning, which gave me time to warm up. The street was deserted, as usual. There was no breeze, and the air hung heavy. We ran past the trees, our footfalls scruffy in the gritty sand. The seagulls squawked above, flying in and out of clouds.

My side stitch started in. "This is rugged," I heard myself say.

"I can slow down."

"Good, I have no pride."

Dom slowed the pace. "What you lack is swag."

"I never had swag. I had a hairnet."

"Whatever that means."

"You don't wanna know, and I can't talk with a side stitch."

Dom smiled. "You had swag in your

Gitmo days, Mr. Top Secret."

"That's *Colonel* Top Secret to you, sir."

Dom chuckled. "Hey, sorry about last night. Seemed like I came in at the wrong time."

"I wanted to surprise her. Unfortunately, I did."

"Was she upset?"

"Yes." Lucinda had cried most of the night, though she wanted the molding. We talked about how we both felt guilty for having fun. "I think we're going to be sad for a long time. We *should* be. That made it worse, you know. We were having a good time."

"I know what you mean, but life has to go on."

"Not just yet," I shot back.

Dom fell silent for a few strides. "I didn't mean to be flip. You know that's normal, the ups and downs. All that is normal. It's part of grief."

"I know."

"You do know. You lost your dad."

"Yes." I had thought of that, but it never helped. "This is different. Maybe all deaths are different, but my father, I expected. I had time to prepare. We knew, he knew." I thought back. "I held his hand in hospice. I helped him change. I swabbed his mouth.

He was at peace. He passed away. I never knew the term could be apt, but it truly applied to him. He passed."

"You were blessed."

"But this is different." My chest felt tight. "You're not supposed to bury your child."

"I know." Dom's voice softened. "How's Ethan?"

"Not good. It's time to set up therapy for us, as a family."

"That's a good idea."

I flashed on that night, on Coldstream. The gunshot, the blood. "How do you deal with violence, in your job? I mean, when you were undercover."

"I'm trained for it. You're not, and neither is your family."

"You don't get PTSD?"

"No, just nightmares." Dom smiled wryly.

"On another topic, about my mother-in-law. Is there any way we can let Lucinda visit her? Just once, so they can lay eyes on each other? My wife is worried about her."

"Why? She's in Bay Horse. That place is nice."

"Yes, but Lucinda still worries, and I get that." My side stitch began to ebb away. We ran past the house with the junk in the front yard. "We got the funeral coming up. I just need one thing good to happen for her, just one."

"Why not a phone call? I bet I can get you a phone call."

"No, my mother-in-law won't know what's going on. I'd settle for a Zoom. We could say that we couldn't make the visit, so we're doing it on the computer."

"What about the staff?"

"Call the CEO. He'll keep it confidential. You're the FBI, for God's sake."

"The problem is the staff, the other patients, the visitors. If the community knows you're missing, the staff has to know, too." A sweat broke on Dom's forehead. "Your wife can't suddenly have a Zoom call with your mother without raising suspicion. Why is she doing that? Where is she? Why didn't you call in? It's a can of worms."

"We have to figure out another way. Put me on the phone with Gremmie. If I have to beg him, I will."

"You won't have to beg Gremmie, I'll beg Gremmie."

"Dom, let me mention something else. Did you ever go online and see these citizen detectives, they call themselves?"

"Yes, what a pain in the ass."

"Well, there's a lot of them, and one in particular, Bryan Krieger. He's writing that

I killed my family and I'm on the run."

"I saw that."

"So you knew?" I asked, surprised.

"It's my job to know. I'm all about the Bennetts."

"Why didn't you tell me?"

"Because it's bullshit and you shouldn't bother with it."

"You say that, but Lucinda saw it online. Ethan, too. The thing that worries me is that they're not gonna stop, either. The one citizen detective, Bryan, he's going to investigate." I had gone online last night and checked the website. "He drove by our house and took pictures of it burned to the ground. He did the same thing with my office and Lucinda's studio."

"I saw. You can't pay any attention to that."

"How do you guys deal with this? You must have experience."

"Uh, no." Dom snorted. "Not a lot of citizens trying to find out what our usual applicant is up to. Anyway, I'll talk to Gremmie."

I felt ragged, running slow. "Any progress on Milo?"

"No, sorry."

"I'm worried we lost him, Dom. I'm worried we'll never get him. That he'll never go to trial. That he'll never pay for what he did to Allison."

"Trust me. We're all over it. I'll keep you posted." Dom glanced over, pained. "You getting any sleep? You don't look it."

"I'm fine," I said, but I wasn't. I'd spent most of last night researching Mexican cartels, as if you could learn anything about Mexican cartels from Google. "I want to talk to Gremmie myself, okay? About Milo and Bryan Krieger?"

"Okay. Just don't call him Gremmie."

"I won't if you get me that Zoom call."

Dom laughed. "Maybe you *do* have swag," he said, then took off.

Chapter Twenty-Five

I sat at the kitchen table while Lucinda held the phone, waiting for a cue from Dom. He had set up a FaceTime call with my mother-in-law on a secured iPhone. I was grateful, and Lucinda was over the moon. The CEO of Bay Horse had agreed to keep the call confidential, and none of the staff in Memory Care knew that the young female lawyer visiting my mother-in-law was really an FBI agent.

Ethan hung out with Dom in the living room, waiting for the call to start. I was happily surprised he'd wanted to take part.

Lucinda looked over, her eyes animated with anticipation. "I'll talk to her first, then bring in you and Ethan."

"Fine." I leaned out of view, to avoid confusion. My mother-in-law's Alzheimer's was in Stage IV, moderately severe. Every illness was awful, but Alzheimer's had a unique sort of staged cruelty. Lucinda felt as if she were losing her mother bit by bit, like a death in life, a purgatory no different from hell. Stage V was the final stage of the illness, but the neurologist had no idea when she would enter that stage.

Dom motioned to us, holding another phone to his ear. "Okay, they're ready. Call, and Special Agent Lingermann will answer."

"Thank you." Lucinda pressed the button, and the phone rang once, then connected.

"Hello, Mrs. Bennett," answered Special Agent Lingermann, and I leaned over to see what she looked like. Tall and youngish, with an angular face, horn-rimmed glasses, and a professional smile. She was wearing a stiff white shirt and a dressy suit that female lawyers hadn't worn for a while, but it was a good effort.

"Yes, hi, is she there?"

"Yes, and she's sitting at the desk. I explained to her that you're going to be on FaceTime, but I'm not sure she gets the concept."

"We'll figure it out."

"Okay, here we go."

I moved away as my mother-in-law popped onto the phone screen, still lovely despite her advancing illness. She kept her feathered haircut coiffed by weekly visits to

Bay Horse's beauty salon and maintained its dark blond color, so there was practically no gray. She had on a navy blue cardigan with a gold necklace, and the only jarring note was the plastic doll she cradled, as if it were a real infant. The doll's head was of grimy plastic, with blue eyes and painted-on blond curls, and its trunk was made of flesh-colored fabric.

My heart lurched when I remembered where the doll had come from. Allison always had a special relationship with her grandmother, so good we called her The Muggy Whisperer. It had been Allison's idea to give Muggy her old Bitty Baby, since we had seen that other patients in the wings had stuffed animals.

"Mom, hi, it's your daughter Lucinda!" Lucinda was saying, and I returned to the present. I wondered if memories were good things, if they came embedded in grief, and Lucinda had more than her share. My father-in-law had fallen ill with leukemia right after he retired, and the disease had taken him a year later. Then Caitlin had come down with breast cancer, enduring chemo, radiation, and surgery that Lucinda had seen her through until her death. Then after Caitlin's passing, my mother-in-law began to show signs of forgetfulness, in a cascade of calamity that would've been hard to believe if I hadn't lived it. Lucinda handled it all, though I knew it had taken a toll.

"Cindy, I don't see you." My mother-in-law was looking around the room, her cloudy gaze jittery. Deep folds creased her forehead and bracketed her mouth.

"Look at the screen, Mom. See me now?" Lucinda waved, smiling. "I'm on the screen. I can't come in person, but we can visit this way."

"I don't understand," my mother-in-law said, frowning. The doll slipped, throttled under her forearm. "I don't understand."

"I'm on the phone. I know it's confusing."

Lucinda was *mirroring the patient's feelings,* one of the guidelines her doctor had given us.

"I don't know what we're doing." My mother-in-law tugged a strand of her hair on the side, a gesture when she became agitated.

Lucida shot me a worried glance. My mother-in-law's anxiety had worsened lately, so the doctors had tweaked her dosages. Her mood had returned to her typical temperament, cheerful and agreeable but off, somehow. She laughed easily but at nothing, emitting an odd chuckle. Still it was easier than the anger I had seen in other patients.

Special Agent Lingermann reappeared behind my mother-in-law, pointing at the phone screen. "Mrs. Romarin, here's your daughter, right here. That's her, right now."

"Don't be silly!" My mother-in-law chuckled. "Oho! That's just a picture!"

"No, it looks like a picture but it's not." Special Agent Lingermann pointed again. "Your daughter is on the phone right now. You can talk to her."

"Stop! I think you're being silly. Oho!"

"Mrs. Romarin, all you have to do is talk. She'll talk to you. You'll see. Just talk."

Suddenly my mother-in-law refocused on the phone, bursting into a smile, a brief flash of her old self. "Cindy!"

"Yes, it's me, I'm here!" Lucinda's face lit up, and I felt a surge of happiness for them both. The bond between mother and daughter was palpable, and my mother-in-law was still the only person who called my wife Cindy.

"Mom, I'm here. It's so good to see you. I miss you, Mom!"

"I miss you, too, dear! Oho, how funny to see you! How funny!"

"I want to hear how you're doing. How

are you doing?"

"I'm fine, dear!"

"Are you having a nice day?"

"Yes! Very nice! Everyone is very nice here! Oho! Oho!"

"I'm good, and everybody here is good, too." Lucinda smiled, and my throat caught, watching her. I had no idea where my wife found the strength to pretend Allison was alive.

"That's good! It's good to be with you, dear!"

"The sweater looks so nice on you, Mom. Navy blue is *your* color."

"Thank you!" My mother-in-law beamed, smoothing her sweater. The doll slipped down farther, its blue plastic eyes fixed on us. "I think it's very smart, myself. Navy blue is a *very* smart color."

"Yes, you look very pretty today."

"Oho! Thank you! You're very nice! You're very nice!"

"So are you. You taught me to be very nice. I'm your daughter. You're my mother."

"Yes!" My mother-in-law burst into laughter, as if Lucinda had said something hysterically funny. Lucinda smiled anyway, her eyes shining with love and pain. She told me once that she was grieving her mother while her mother was still alive, then we found out it was called *pre-grief.*

"Mom, do you have your book? Your special book?"

My mother-in-law blinked. "No."

"It should be there on the desk. Do you see it? You know, your special book?"

"I don't see it. It's not here. It's gone."

Lucinda pursed her lips. The special book was a construction paper booklet that had photos of us, with captions explaining who we are. The kids had made it when my mother-in-law first moved into Memory Care, and the special book was the way of introducing Ethan and me into the visit, suggested by her doctors.

Lucinda motioned to me. "Mom, I'm here with my husband Jason. Would you like to say hello to Jason? He'd love to say hello to you."

"Oho! Oho! Yes, yes, I'd love to say hello."

I leaned in, waving. "Claire, how are you, you gorgeous lady?"

"Oho! Oh my, you're silly, you're so silly!" My mother-in-law giggled, which gave me a bittersweet kick. My father had adored her, saying she had class, and they'd share a cigarette like two naughty kids. It was the only time I saw her smoke, since my starchy father-in-law disapproved.

I waved again. "It's so nice to see you, Claire."

"Well, it's nice to see such a handsome young man!"

Lucinda laughed. "He's not *that* young."

I interjected, "But I am *that* handsome."

"He's *so* handsome! My, my! Oho! Oho!"

I laughed, my spirits lifting. I tried not to think about the future or the way her illness would end. I tried not to think about the past because there was Allison. Death was everywhere, in the present, in the past, in the future. I wondered why we bothered with time at all.

Lucinda motioned to Ethan. "Mom, your grandson Ethan is here. He would like to say hello to you, too."

Ethan hurried over, grinning and turning his head sideways, being goofy. "Hey Muggy, it's Ethan! Your grandson —" he started to say, but grimaced. "Why does she have Allison's doll?"

I touched his arm. "Ignore it," I whispered, realizing he didn't know about the doll.

My mother-in-law blinked, frowning. "My Jo is gone. I don't see my Jo."

Ethan managed a smile. "No, I'm Ethan, your grandson Ethan. My name is Ethan."

Lucinda touched his hand. "Ethan, Jo is

what she calls her hand lotion. She calls it Jo."

"What? Why does she call it a name?"

"It's by Jo Malone."

Ethan's face fell, and I took his hand. He didn't know about the lotion, either. The doctors had told us that we should *provide sensory experiences* for my mother-in-law, so Lucinda bought lavender hand cream, since my mother-in-law used to grow lavender at the Cape. It had been a big hit, so Lucinda had bought lavender body lotion, a pillow, a candle, and sachets, which I hadn't even known existed. My wife didn't believe less was more.

Lucinda was saying, "Mom, your Jo is usually on your bureau in the front."

Ethan tried to smile. "I'm Ethan," he said, but my mother-in-law wasn't looking, turning to the left.

"I don't see it. I don't know where it is. I don't see my Jo."

"Muggy?" Ethan said, his voice wavering, and I put my arms around him, trying to sit him down on my lap, but he resisted, stiffening. "Muggy, it's me!"

Lucinda was saying, "Mom, look under the lamp on the bureau."

"I don't see it. I don't know where it is." My mother-in-law was tugging her hair again. The doll dropped, but she didn't notice.

"Muggy, it's Ethan your grandson!" Ethan tried again, but when my mother-in-law didn't react, he turned away. "I don't want to do this anymore."

My mother-in-law was tugging her hair, her forehead buckling. "I think that girl took my Jo. She takes things! She takes everything!"

"What girl do you mean?" Lucinda kept her smile on, for show. We knew other patients in Memory Care had delusions the staff was stealing.

"She took my Jo!"

"Special Agent Lingermann?" Lucinda asked, raising her voice. "Do you see a bottle of Jo Malone anywhere? It should be on the bureau in the front."

"No," Special Agent Lingermann answered, offscreen.

"She took my Jo! She took everything!"

"Special Agent Lingermann, how about the night table?"

"There's nothing like that on the night table, the desk, or the bureau."

Lucinda nodded. "Mom, is Susan there today?"

"Susan? I don't know her."

Lucinda frowned with concern, and I read

her mind. Susan was my mother-in-law's favorite nurse. We didn't know if my mother-in-law had forgotten her or if she was just too agitated right now. We both looked for details that could signal deterioration.

Lucinda said, "Mom, you love Susan. She has short hair. She's usually there today."

"I don't know."

I understood my mother-in-law's confusion. The nurses' schedule was so chopped up and hard to keep straight. Susan came on Tuesdays, Thursdays, and Saturdays, Linda came on Wednesdays and Fridays, and there was a roving nurse on Mondays and Sundays, whose name even I forgot, not to mention night nurses. Bay Horse tried to keep the staff regular in Memory Care, but they could only do so much.

"Special Agent Lingermann, can you find out what's going on? Go ask someone, where's her lotion and special book?"

"Mrs. Bennett, I don't know if I should do that."

"Dom?" I looked over at Dom, who nodded. "Dom says it's okay."

"Okay, be right back." Special Agent Lingermann nodded, then left.

"I don't like this," my mother-in-law said, frowning.

"I'm sorry, Mom." Lucinda smiled, with effort. "I'm very happy to see you. You look very pretty."

"She took my Jo!" My mother-in-law began to rock, holding her arms like she was still holding the doll. Her expression slackened, as if her lovely features slid off her face. The dulling of her affect happened when she was disengaging from stressful situations, pulling the mental plug on her surroundings.

"Mom? Mom, it's your daughter Lucinda."

My mother-in-law didn't look up, rocking the imaginary baby.

"Look at the phone, Mom. Tell me about your baby."

My mother-in-law didn't look up, rocking.

Special Agent Lingermann reappeared. "Mrs. Bennett, your mother was right. There's a new nurse on the wing, and she took away the hand lotion."

"Why?" Lucinda looked angry, but I felt relieved it wasn't a delusion.

"The new nurse is allergic to the fragrance in creams and lotions. She gets hives. She took away anything with any scent. They're in a box in the main office."

"She went in my mother's underwear

drawer? She took her sachets? They barely smell anymore." Lucinda frowned. "What about the special book? That's not scented."

"I'm sorry, I forgot to ask about the book."

"Special Agent Lingermann, can I talk to the supervisor? Her name is Joyce."

"No, we can't do that. I didn't ask about Joyce."

I checked, but Dom shook his head no.

Lucinda pursed her lips. "What's this new nurse's name?"

"Gabrielle Hook."

Suddenly my mother-in-law rose and walked offscreen.

"Mom? Mom?" Lucinda called, raising her voice. "Where are you going?"

Special Agent Lingermann answered, "I think she's upset. She went to the bathroom. She closed the door."

"Can you check on her?"

"I think we should end the call. The nurse told me we should wrap it up. She said it's almost dinnertime."

"But she doesn't just get up and go. Mom? Mom!"

I patted Lucinda's arm. "Honey, maybe she's tired. It's so new, with the phone."

"Oh no." Special Agent Lingermann cringed. "I think she's crying."

Lucinda grimaced. "Can you please go

see her? Tell her I want to talk to her?"

"I'll get the nurse. We should end the call."

"Mom?" Lucinda said as the screen went dark.

Chapter Twenty-Six

I entered the bedroom, which was dark except for the moonlight glowing through the curtains. Lucinda was under the covers, her back turned away. An empty glass and a bottle of wine sat on the night table. She had gone upstairs after the call with her mother, and I'd gotten Ethan to bed, then come to check on her.

"How you doing?" I sat down on the bed, putting a hand on her arm. I couldn't see her features in the darkness, just her outline.

"I'm wallowing. I'm having myself a good wallow."

"You're entitled."

"I drank three glasses of wine."

"Good girl." I patted her arm. Usually my wife was a lightweight. She didn't drink because it disrupted her sleep. "Want more? You're allowed."

"God, no. I wish we hadn't called Mom. It just upset her."

"No, it didn't," I rushed to say. "She was happy to see you. She was really happy."

"She's not happy, ever. I just didn't realize it before. She's miserable all the time."

"No, she's not."

"She's not even *there.* And now, neither am I."

"Yes, she is." I'd never heard Lucinda talk like this. "She smiles, she laughs."

"She makes sounds and noises. It's not really a laugh."

"It's a laugh," I said, but in truth, I wasn't sure what it was.

Lucinda fell silent, and I knew it was killing her to leave her mother. I remembered a time, not long after Caitlin had passed, when Lucinda, Ethan, and I had been leaving the house to go to Allison's lacrosse final, but Bay Horse had called, saying Mom was agitated and Lucinda should come right away. Lucinda had wanted to go to the game, and Allison was already there, waiting for us. The finals had been a big deal, against Central Bucks West, and even Ethan had been psyched.

Lucinda's face had fallen. *I should go see Mom.*

You sure? It had been her decision to make, but I'd felt for her. *Why not go after the game?*

That'll be too late. Lucinda had buckled her lip. *You go, Monaco.*

Monaco was our code for when one of us was going in our representative capacity, as if we were ambassadors of a small country, the country of us, trying to be in two places at once, tag-teaming our children's soccer semifinals, select choir recitals, and *Annie Get Your Gun.* I put the memory out of my mind, as Lucinda shifted on the bed.

"Jason, you know what I realized, talking to Mom?"

"What, honey?"

"That we both lost a child, her and me."

"Right." I cringed. I hadn't thought of it, either.

"I saw her go through it, after Caitlin died. She spent, like, a month in bed. We went through it, all of us. We cried together, like normal people. Allison was at Caitlin's funeral, remember? She was only eleven."

I thought back. It had been Allison's second funeral. Her third would be her own.

"I can't help but compare, you know? Allison was so much younger than Caitlin when she died. Is it harder for us, or easier?"

I had no answer. It hurt to think about. "You can't compare."

"Right, you can't, and at the end it's the same. You don't want to outlive your child, no matter how old your child is. It's because you can't handle it."

"I'm sorry, honey."

"I can't handle losing Allison, I really can't. I don't want to get out of bed, ever. Ever, ever. I use Ethan as an excuse. I want to lay around all day. I give up, I do."

I felt alarmed. I rubbed her back. I knew the only thing that could bring her out of it. "You have to think about Ethan."

Lucinda didn't say anything, but I knew she was listening. Ethan was my best argument. She would never let him down. We both knew she loved the kids more than me. And I loved her more than the kids. I didn't know if that made me a good husband or a bad father. Or both.

"Lucinda, your mother lost Caitlin, but she was still there for you. She was always there for you, and you'll be there for him. You're not going to fall apart because of him."

"Maybe you're right."

"I know I am." I needed her to believe it.

"You know, I never really noticed it before, she was holding the doll and I really started to think about that doll, and I think she got upset because she dropped it."

"I thought she was upset because of the hand lotion."

"No, she was upset because she *dropped* the doll. I know her. She never missed a stitch, her whole life. She did petit point. She's a perfectionist." Lucinda sniffled. "I know how she feels, because Allison's gone and Ethan's not eating, and it's a disaster. A *disaster.*"

I fell silent. She was right.

"Jason, remember in college, that photography class I took?"

I didn't follow the conversational turn. "Sure."

"I loved that class, and the teacher, she said something really great once. She said, 'Whenever you're taking a portrait of someone, you and your subject are in the present, but if you're any good, you can see their past, and even their future.' "

"You think that's true?"

"I don't know. I try, in family portraits, but I know they're not really *art,* with everyone worried about their hair or their neck or whatever, just trying to look better, or thinner, or younger."

I wasn't sure how this applied, but I didn't interrupt.

"All we have are memories, and right now I have memories of her and I have memories of Allison, and they're with me all the time, and my mother doesn't even have that."

"True, but she has the present."

"But she doesn't have me. I can't check on her in the bathroom, or hug her, or touch her, and she needs help, like with her eyebrow pencil or plucking her chin hairs."

I hadn't known my wife did those things for her mother.

"Let's be real with each other. I was saying I wanted to call for her sake, but really, I wanted it for me. I miss her. Is it okay to miss your mommy, at my age?"

"Of course it is."

"I keep thinking of that story you told us about some farmer who got his arm caught in a hay baler. 'Traumatic amputation,' you called it, right?"

"Yes." I had told that story at the dinner table, and that was when I learned farm life shocked suburbanites.

"So that's how I feel, like when Allison died, somebody pulled off my arm. Just *yanked* it off. Now she's gone, and today, somebody pulled off my other arm, because I can't have my mother anymore, and it's not about her, or Allison, it's about me." Lucinda shifted in bed. "I'm spraying blood all over the place."

"I'm so sorry, honey." I patted her back, but it was as if she couldn't feel my touch, or even hear me.

"Jason, it's too much, what we've lost. Allison, our lives, the house, the business, my cameras, my lenses, my jewelry, all of it is gone, gone, gone, and at some point, it's just too big to overcome, you can't overcome it. It's not possible to lose *everything* and still go on. I'm telling you I'm spent, I'm done —"

"You just feel that way now," I interrupted. I couldn't let her say those things, or think them, even if they were true.

"— and if I'm being real with you, and I'm *trying* to be real with you, I don't think I can be here. I can't do this."

"I'm here, honey, I'll do it." I squeezed her shoulder.

"You can't, Jason, you can't do it *for us,* it's not like Monaco, you can't go it alone. Nobody can. You can't give me our family back, you can't give me our past back, and I don't know what to do because I can't live in the present and I sure as hell can't deal with the future. Neither can Ethan. We're falling through the cracks, like Mom, we're falling."

"I won't let that happen," I said, stricken.

"What can you do about it?" Lucinda asked, beginning to cry.

Chapter Twenty-Seven

The weekend was miserable, with Lucinda nursing a hangover and finishing the video for Allison's funeral. I dreaded its coming, mentally counting down the days, and gloom settled around the house like a fog on the marsh. Ethan retreated to his bedroom with a grumpy Moonie, though I made sure he got some food and fresh air. By Sunday night, I let him stay in his room.

I sat at the laptop in the kitchen, on autopilot. I checked the wall clock, and it was midnight. I had been online for hours, scrolling mindlessly. The house was quiet. I felt raw, exhausted, and broken, alone with my thoughts.

What can you do about it?

I was failing Lucinda and Ethan. I had to pray we could start a new life, but I was having my doubts. A program designed for criminal defendants wasn't tenable for us. Maybe after Milo was caught, we could walk away, although God knew when that would happen.

I scrolled online for news of Milo, but there wasn't any, then I found myself checking the website of the citizen detective Bryan Krieger. The first page had photos of our burned-out house, office, and Lucinda's studio, and a new headline turned my stomach.

BIG INTERVIEW WITH MELISSA DELUCA, LUCINDA BENNETT'S BEST FRIEND!

I recoiled, dismayed. The audio file of the interview had been posted an hour ago. I put on a pair of wireless earphones, clicked the link, and listened to the intro, which began with suspenseful music. Bryan Krieger introduced himself, sounding younger than I'd expected, and Melissa thanked him. I startled to hear her voice, familiar yet from another world, one in which I used to live.

I listened, visualizing the interview as if it were one of my transcripts:

Bryan: You're Lucinda Bennett's best friend, right?
Melissa: Yes, and let me say, I would

never discuss Lucinda's business with a total stranger. I'm doing this only because I'm trying to find her. I contacted you because I want to get the word out that they're missing and put pressure on the police.

Bryan: We should explain how you found me.

Melissa: Some friends saw your website and mentioned it to me, so I emailed you. I feel like the police are not being responsive to me or the community, which I don't understand. I'm a taxpayer. They owe us accountability but they don't even call me back —

Bryan: That's infuriating.

Melissa: I agree. And believe me, I know that I'm not in law enforcement, but I have common sense and I care about Lucinda and her family.

Bryan: I feel the same way, though I don't know the Bennetts. I feel as if I do from your posts and photos.

Melissa: I appreciate that and I know you're not a professional, either, but both of us are trying to solve this disappearance. I'm desperate to get the word out about Lucinda. We need to find her, Jason, and the kids. You have no idea what a wonderful family the Bennetts are.

Bryan: I'm sure, this is so upsetting.

Melissa: Right? Can you imagine? Your best friend and her family vanish off the face of the earth? As soon as she didn't go to her mom's, I knew there was real trouble. Something is really wrong. The police say I'm jumping to conclusions, but I'm telling you it's true. I know when I'm being condescended to.

Bryan: Melissa, obviously, you know Lucinda better than anyone. My wife has a best friend, too, and her best friend would do anything for her.

Melissa: That's how I feel. It's girlfriends that get us through everything. Lucinda was — I mean is — a great friend.

Bryan: I know that you don't suspect Jason, but let's discuss him. You have to understand, the husband is the first person we look to in cases like this. Anyone who watches Lifetime TV knows that, right?

Melissa: Jason should not be a suspect. I don't suspect him at all.

I smiled, appreciating the vote of confidence. I always liked Melissa, and it felt good to hear her defend me, conviction resonating in her voice.

Bryan: You strike me as an educated and sophisticated woman, so you know domestic abusers don't appear to be so on the outside.

Melissa: I do know that.

Bryan: So you can't always tell by appearances.

Melissa: Yes, that's true.

Bryan: No marriage is perfect. Mine certainly isn't. Is yours?

Melissa: No, and I'm not here to say Lucinda's marriage was perfect. It definitely wasn't.

I blinked, surprised. I didn't think my marriage was perfect, but it was pretty good. I would've thought Lucinda would say the same thing.

Bryan: What is it that makes you say that their marriage was *definitely* not perfect?

Melissa: Well, there was a rough patch.

Bryan: When? I'm curious if it was close in time to their disappearance.

Melissa: Well, uh, in truth, it was. It was over the summer. She felt like Jason was spending too much time at work.

I remembered. I had been working all the time last summer, and Lucinda had been unhappy. We had fought about it once or twice, but I hadn't thought it was a rough patch.

Bryan: So Jason was working late at the office?
Melissa: No. When you're a court reporter, you're not working at your own office. Jason would be in someone else's office, but he worked nights.
Bryan: So he could have been anywhere.
Melissa: That wasn't my point.
Bryan: Did Lucinda know where he was on those nights?
Melissa: Yes.
Bryan: But she had to rely on him telling her where he was. He could have been anywhere.
Melissa: I think he was where he said he was —
Bryan: Now during this time period he was working late, did you or Lucinda think he could be having an affair?
Melissa: No, he's not like that. He's a great guy.
Bryan: I did see pictures on his website of an employee named Justine. She's very attractive. Do you know who I mean?
Melissa: Trust me, he wasn't having an affair with Justine and I'm not going to talk about her personal life. Lucinda trusted

Jason and I do, too.

Bryan: Then why do you say the marriage wasn't perfect? What was the rough patch over the summer about, if he wasn't having an affair? I suspect he was, and I don't know why you're lying for him.

Melissa: What? I'm not.

Bryan: Were *you* having an affair with him? Is that why you're so involved in this? You're acting like you're worried about her, but really that's to deflect suspicion —

Melissa: No, no, that's not true! I would never, he would never, we weren't having an affair! *She* was!

I wasn't sure I heard correctly. Melissa sounded so upset, I must have been mistaken. I clicked stop, pressed rewind, then play and listened again.

Melissa: No, no, that's not true! I would never, he would never, we weren't having an affair! *She* was!

I was stunned, in disbelief. It shocked me to my foundations. It couldn't be right. I clicked PLAY to see if she took it back or corrected herself.

Bryan: Are you saying that Lucinda had an affair over the summer?

Melissa: I didn't mean to, it's only because your accusation was so ridiculous and —

Bryan: Who was she having an affair with?

Melissa: I'm sorry I said anything, I'm not going to tell you. I told the police his name and I need pressure on them to look into all possible leads, and he's one. He might know something, or where she was last, or help the police in some way. He's one of her clients and well connected, and you can never tell where these things lead to —

I listened, horrified. My head was spinning. I couldn't process it fast enough. Lucinda had an affair? She had cheated on me, last summer? With a client?

Bryan: If Lucinda was having an affair, that's all the more reason that Jason would kill her, isn't it?

Melissa: No, that's not what happened —

Bryan: You just supplied the perfect motive! He killed her in revenge and took the kids. Or he killed the whole family.

Melissa: No, no. Jason would never —

Bryan: What if he found out about her infidelity and killed her? Isn't that much more likely? It happens every day! Why are you trying to protect Jason?

Melissa: No, you've got this all wrong, we should stop this interview —

Bryan: No, please —

There was a click on the audio, and it ended in silence.

I was reeling. It wasn't possible. I found myself rising, wanting to go ask Lucinda if it was true, to confront her, but the strangest thing happened. My body went numb all over, as if my muscles were frozen. I didn't know if I could take a step. It was as if my body were absorbing the shock, *embodying* the shock.

I stood there, trying to make sense of what I had just learned, letting my body metabolize the revelation.

It took me a few minutes, and when I did, I went straight upstairs.

CHAPTER TWENTY-EIGHT

I entered our bedroom to find Lucinda sitting on the bed, her laptop in front of her. I closed the door behind me, since Ethan was asleep down the hall. I didn't say anything, I couldn't say anything, not yet. I didn't know how to begin the conversation. I knew I was angry, but I didn't *feel* angry. I felt shock.

Lucinda slid off her reading glasses, lines creasing her forehead. "I can't believe how long this took me. Maybe I'm more of a perfectionist than I thought. Take a look."

I walked to the bed, on autopilot.

Lucinda gestured at the laptop. "I picked the song, that was the hardest part. I went with Sarah McLachlan. I know everybody uses it, but I love it when she says, 'weep not for the memories.' "

My gaze fell to the freeze-frame of the video, which was of Allison as a toddler, climbing out of her crib. My throat thickened, but Lucinda didn't notice, focused on the video.

"Here, listen." She clicked PLAY, and the first few notes of a guitar grabbed me by the heart. I struggled to stay in emotional control, and the music played behind another photo of Allison, one I had taken. She was raising her lacrosse stick in the air after a goal, and I shared that moment with her through the lens, as if we were still connected through space and time. I couldn't take my eyes from the photo.

"Please turn it off," I heard myself say.

"Sorry, I know." Lucinda pressed stop, and the video froze, blurring my daughter's pretty face. The music ended abruptly, and the bedroom fell completely silent.

"You had an affair," I said calmly. A statement of fact, not an accusation, not really. My voice sounded so soft, it was almost a whisper. I never was a yeller. Neither was my father.

"What?" Lucinda looked up, blinking.

"You heard me." Another statement of fact. It wasn't an accusation when it was true. The truth had a ring, and I could hear it, leaving my own lips.

"I didn't —" Lucinda started to say, but her gaze met mine, and I saw agony behind her eyes.

"Tell me the truth."

Lucinda's hand went to her mouth, her eyes glistening, and her features seemed to collapse, her eyebrows sloping down, her mouth drooping. "I'm so sorry. I didn't mean for it to happen."

So it was true. And her confirmation made it worse.

"Jason, I'm sorry, so sorry, I love you, I swear. It was a mistake, a horrible mistake, it's over now —"

"I'm surprised, so *surprised.*"

"I'm so sorry, I'm so sorry." Lucinda's eyes brimmed with tears. "It just happened, I met him doing corporate portraits, last summer —"

"You slept with a corporate portrait? You hate that work, you hate those accounts."

"I made a mistake, a terrible mistake —"

"Don't tell me, let me guess. Doctor? Lawyer? Indian chief?" I realized I was finding my voice, and it was sarcastic. Maybe humor would cushion the blow, it always had. "Did he do the folded-arms? Wear a stethoscope? I always think that's a bit much, don't you? Like, we get it, you're a doctor."

"It didn't last long, I broke it off, and it didn't matter, *he* didn't matter."

"That makes it worse. I can't believe you

would cheat on me with somebody who didn't matter." I couldn't imagine who she had been with. "So who was he? Who was it that it *just happened* with?"

"You don't know him. A lawyer in Philly."

"Who? I can't wait to look him up."

"Paul Hart."

I gasped. I recognized the name instantly. "Not the Paul Hart who represents Milo?"

Lucinda frowned, taken aback. "No, of course not. He's a partner at Lattimore. They don't represent people like Milo."

"Yes, they do. A lawyer at Lattimore named Paul Hart represents Milo. He represents Big George, Junior, and GVO." I met her eye, each of us absolutely aghast.

"That can't be!"

"I read the pleadings. He's represented GVO for years." I felt sick to my stomach. She had slept with the man responsible for Milo being free to kill our daughter.

"No, that can't be true!"

I couldn't say another word. I couldn't stay in the room with her.

"Jason, wait." Lucinda rose and came after me. "It can't be the same one!"

"Leave me alone." I hurried from the room, hustled downstairs, and crossed to the screen door, but I stopped on the threshold. If I went out, Dom or Wiki could see me on the security cameras or on patrol. I didn't want to answer questions about what was going on.

I rested my hand on the doorknob, steadying myself. I felt shocked, blown out of my shoes, like a percussive wave following a blast.

I inhaled again and again. The driveway was still and silent. Night cloaked the marsh. The lights burned through a sheer mist. It had been raining, and the air off the marsh smelled more ripe than usual. I couldn't see a single star in the sky, only a cloud cover, impenetrably black.

Tears stung my eyes. I felt a betrayal that went deep, cutting profoundly to the core.

I feel betrayed, I heard a voice say out of nowhere, and I realized it was a memory surfacing. It was Lucinda, and we were in our apartment in Carlisle. I had just finished my first year at Dickinson Law. I had been in the Law Review office all day, checking cites and doing legal scutwork. I had come home and told her I was dropping out.

Why do you feel betrayed? I asked her. I'd expected she would be unhappy, but not like this.

You can't drop out. You're doing great. You just made Law Review.

I can't afford to stay. It's no way to start a

life, a hundred thousand dollars more in debt.

The big firms will recruit you. You'll make it back in no time.

I won't be able to pay off the loans for ages. It keeps me up every night. I hate debt.

You sound like your father.

That's not why, I shot back, but she was right. They were my father's words coming out of my own mouth. He hated debt. He didn't trust banks. He knew dairymen who had been foreclosed on. He squirreled away cash in the house.

Let me ask my father, Jason. He'd be happy to help.

I can support my own family.

If you could, you wouldn't drop out.

I blinked, pained. *This isn't who you wanted me to be, is it? You wanted me to be a lawyer, and you'd be the wife of a lawyer.*

Lucinda wiped a tear away. *That was our plan.*

Plans change, honey.

Not this one. Not without a fight.

I'm still me. I promise you, I'll take care of you. I took her in my arms, but Lucinda didn't lean against me the way she always did.

I could almost feel her now, even as I stood at the door, looking out into the darkness. It struck me that I hadn't asked her why she'd had an affair, maybe because I knew, at some level. It all went back to that stifling afternoon, to an apartment in Carlisle.

That's the way marriage was, I realized in that moment. There was a thing you always worried about, barely a crack, running down the middle between the two of you, and you hope it will go away, but it can widen like a tectonic plate, break open beneath your feet, and swallow you whole.

Suddenly headlights appeared in the driveway, and a black Tahoe pulled in and parked beside the van. It must be the replacement agent that Dom had told me about, since he, Wiki, and the rest of The Babysitters Club were going to Allison's funeral tomorrow. The agent's name was Matt Reilly, and he was from the investigative team. I was going to pick his brain tomorrow, but I was in no mood tonight.

I stepped out of view. Luckily, the downstairs lights were off.

Special Agent Reilly emerged from the driver's seat, talking on the phone. He looked about my age and dressed FBI-casual, in a white polo and khaki pants. He fetched a duffel from the Tahoe while he kept talking.

I was too far away to hear what he was saying.

But when he walked past our front door, I read his lips.

CHAPTER TWENTY-NINE

I stood stunned, replaying what Special Agent Reilly had said:

Milo is a psycho. You couldn't pay me enough to run him, but if he delivers Big George, he's worth it.

It was beyond belief.

I watched as Special Agent Reilly crossed the driveway and walked to the agents' apartment. I waited for the sound of his footsteps on the stairway, a muted thumping that disappeared after a moment. The night returned to its heavy silence, the air weighed with humidity.

I exhaled. I hadn't realized I had been holding my breath. I went over the words again, visualizing his lips moving. I was sure I read them correctly. The driveway was well-lit.

Milo is a psycho. You couldn't pay me enough to run him, but if he delivers Big George, he's worth it.

My mind reeled. It could only mean Milo was working with the FBI. They must have made a deal with him, using him to get evidence to convict Big George. Milo had flipped and become their informant.

The revelation took my breath away. The FBI had been lying when they said they were looking for Milo. They knew exactly where he was. He wasn't in Mexico at all. They probably had surveillance on him. He could be wearing a wire. The government wasn't protecting us, they were protecting *him.*

Allison's killer.

I wondered if Dom knew. I trusted him, but I couldn't be sure. Maybe I had just been reaching for a friend. Maybe he set me up so I wouldn't suspect anything. He was a lot like me, a family man, a fellow runner, about my age. Maybe our friendship was as phony as my marriage.

The worst thing was if Milo was cooperating with the FBI, he would never be punished for killing Allison. God knew if he would get any time in jail. They couldn't let him walk, could they? They couldn't without asking us, could they? What about Allison? What about justice?

My thoughts raced. I didn't know the law. The law was with the government. It was me against them, with their power and might, their treachery and corruption.

I was sick of feeling helpless.

I had to do something.

Chapter Thirty

I stood behind the couch across from the TV, waiting for Allison's funeral to begin. I couldn't bring myself to sit on the couch with Lucinda, and she sat next to Ethan, who had decided to watch. I hadn't said a word to Lucinda this morning, and we had avoided each other while we showered and changed. Of course I hadn't told her the FBI lied to us about Milo. This wasn't the time, and I had to think.

The TV flickered on, and the funeral started. The screen showed strangers in suits gathered around a glistening walnut casket, which rested on a bier of white roses. The camera must have been mounted in a tree, since the angle was high and the view distant.

Lucinda sniffled, and Ethan emitted a moan. I swallowed hard, but the remoteness of the scene muted its impact. I would have cried my eyes out at my daughter's funeral, but I wouldn't at this TV production.

I eyed the FBI agents pretending to mourn my daughter, wondering if any of them knew Milo was their informant. They had no business being at Allison's funeral. They were protecting the scum who killed her.

At the head of the fake mourners stood a priest I didn't know. He began to pray, but I could barely listen to a word. Lucinda started to cry and Ethan, too. The FBI agents bowed their heads, and my gaze found Dom and Wiki. They were to the right of the priest, where I should have been. Again I wondered how much they knew.

The service ended, and Dom stepped to a table that held a vase of white roses and an open laptop. He pressed a key, and Lucinda's memorial video began to play. The notes of the Sarah McLachlan song sounded tinny through the microphone. The photos of Allison were too far away to see.

The music wafted over me, and I felt oddly remote. This was the day Lucinda and I buried our daughter, our firstborn child, and it should have been a burden we bore together. But no longer. She and Ethan cried, and I put my hand on Ethan's shoulder.

I returned my attention to Allison's casket and made a vow to get her justice.

I was her father.
I would be, as long as I lived.
And even after.

CHAPTER THIRTY-ONE

After the funeral, I stayed downstairs, sipping a glass of water and looking out the kitchen window. I found myself scanning the trees for cameras, then I glanced around the kitchen, newly distrustful. I wondered if the FBI had bugged the house or loaded spyware. I eyeballed the ceiling fixture, then my laptop.

I heard Lucinda coming down the stairs, and she entered the kitchen, her eyes teary and bloodshot, her dress wrinkled. I set down the glass and started to leave, but she stopped me, taking my arm.

"Jason, we have to talk."

"No we don't —" I began, then stopped myself, in case the kitchen was bugged. I raised a hand, and Lucinda fell silent. I motioned to the front door. "I need some air, don't you? I'll show you the marsh. I have a spot there."

"Okay," Lucinda answered, puzzled. She

followed me to the door, and we stepped outside. If Special Agent Reilly was monitoring the cameras, he would see we weren't doing anything out of the ordinary. We had just buried our daughter, and it would make sense that we would want time alone. I led the way down the steps and to the path that led through the scrub to the marsh, and finally to the water's edge.

Lucinda looked around, puzzled. "What are we doing out here? What's going on?"

"I needed air." I stepped away, not wanting to stand close to her. "What is it you want?"

"Why are you acting so —"

"What do you want?"

"I know you're hurt, and I'm so sorry, I was going to tell you about Paul."

My gut twisted. "I was better off not knowing about Paul. But now that I do, I don't know how to stay with you. I don't see how we go forward."

"But we have to." Lucinda's blue eyes pleaded with me. "We love each other, and we're in the program —"

"That's not a reason. I have a decision to make." I didn't see how we went forward, but I didn't see how we *didn't* go forward, either. All I could think of was the day I told her I was dropping out of law school.

"You think Paul Hart's better than I am, because he's a lawyer? You're wrong. You have it upside down."

Lucinda got flustered. "I don't think that —"

"Yes you do, and I thought better of you, but I was wrong. You know, honey, this is a strange world we live in, and everybody lies." I found myself spilling my guts. "The lawyers lie, the cops lie, FBI lies, the government lies. Not me. I didn't, I don't. I may not be a lawyer, but I took an oath, as a court reporter. My oath is that everything I write down is accurate, which is another word for *truth.* The transcript, the exhibits, everything — when I sign my name to it, it's true. I watch lawyers every day, and I sit in the same room and hear them lie. I know they're lying, they know they're lying. I write down their lies. I record their lies in a true and correct copy. And you know what? I'm the *only* one who keeps my oath. That's me." I had never thought about it before this very minute. "I made an oath, and I kept it. I made a vow to you, and I kept it."

"I'm sorry —"

"That's who I am, but you threw me away in favor of a *liar.*" I felt tears, but I blinked them away. "And I get it if you felt that way when I dropped out, but *all* our time together didn't teach you anything different? All we went through together, even before Allison? Your sister, your mom, your dad? I was there for you, and it didn't make one damn bit of difference? You know what your biggest crime is, honey? *You haven't been paying attention.*"

Lucinda's eyes flared with pain, and I knew I had hit home.

"Anyway, this isn't the time. What do you want?"

Lucinda wiped a tear away. "I swear," she said, her tone hushed, "I know it never should've happened, but I love you —"

I didn't want to hear that. "What do you want?"

"I don't know where to start."

"What do you have to say?"

Lucinda heaved a sigh. "It turned out Paul was very controlling, very demanding."

"Aw, your fling wasn't fun? My heart goes out."

"No, it's not that." Lucinda pushed a strand of hair from her face. "He wanted me to leave you, and he was going to leave his wife. He wanted us to get married."

"Why are you telling me this?" I shot back, angry. "I don't need to hear this."

"I'm getting to it. Please." Lucinda flushed, upset. "The relationship turned bad pretty quickly, he was pushing me. He got angry about it, really angry. He's used to getting what he wants."

"Just spit it out."

Lucinda inhaled, straightening. "At the end, he made a threat."

My jaw clenched reflexively. "He threatened you?"

"No, he threatened *you.*"

I blinked.

Lucinda pursed her lips. "One time we were having this fight about him wanting me to leave you. He said, 'I could have Jason killed. I know people.' I didn't think anything of it, but I didn't know he represented people like Milo." Her blue eyes sharpened. "What if Paul sent Milo to kill you? What if our carjacking wasn't random?"

I felt taken aback. "But it was. We know why they carjacked us. They needed a car after the double homicide."

"Isn't it too coincidental? What if Milo targeted us to kill you? Let's say he stops us in order to kill you, for Paul, but he changes his plans on the fly. He decides to kill Junior for his own reasons. Junior's gun has only one bullet left, and like Dom said, he couldn't finish the job because a car was coming. In other words, Milo *double-crosses* Paul."

I followed her reasoning, but I didn't see it. "It's possible, I suppose —"

"Milo would tell Hart the same story that he tells Big George. That you put up a fight, the gun went off, and it killed Junior."

"What about the double homicide?"

"You have to change the way you're thinking about the night." Lucinda bore down, the lines in her forehead deepening. "Dom told us the FBI has categories of when cars get carjacked. The most common reason is someone needing a getaway car. So if Milo wants to kill you, he has to stage a crime first, to avoid suspicion that you're the real target. So he kills two people the police won't worry about, like lower-level drug dealers."

"He killed two people to avoid suspicion for killing a third? It's crazy."

"No, it's counterintuitive, and that's why it worked. The FBI assumed the double homicide was the primary crime and the carjacking was the getaway. They never suspected our carjacking was anything but random *because* of the double homicide. But I think it's the other way around. *We* were the primary crime, and the double homicide was to make us look random."

"I didn't think of that," I said, wondering aloud.

"You couldn't have. You didn't know I had an affair, and I didn't know Paul represented Milo. If we hadn't gotten into WITSEC, Milo would've killed you. It would've worked, if we hadn't left."

As horrible as it was, I sensed she was right.

"Jason, how did you know that Paul represented Milo? I couldn't confirm that."

"I used Marie's login to get into the court system. Hart's name is on the pleadings."

"So we both had pieces of the puzzle, and they fit."

I thought of the thing we always used to say, *we fit.*

Lucinda rubbed her face, leaving pinkish streaks. "I feel so terrible. Allison's death is because of me. I brought Milo into our life."

"Don't say that," I told her, meaning it. I wanted to reach for her, but didn't. "Milo was the one with the gun. You're not responsible for Allison's death, any more than Ethan is."

Lucinda looked at me, teary and vulnerable. "But I feel so guilty."

"Good. Feel guilty for cheating on the best husband ever."

Lucinda managed a shaky smile. "I don't deserve you."

"Agree." I wasn't kidding. "We done here?"

"We have to tell Dom and Wiki, when they get back." Lucinda wiped her eyes. "The FBI should talk to Paul. He could know where Milo is."

"We can't do that." I had yet to tell Lucinda that the FBI had been lying to us. I had been up all night doing research and formulating a plan.

"Why not?"

I met her eye. I'd tell her most of my plan, but not all.

I didn't trust her anymore, either.

CHAPTER THIRTY-TWO

The rest of the day, I avoided Lucinda, staying downstairs on the laptop while she stayed in our bedroom. Each of us nursed our grief, and our wounds. My feelings for her tore me up inside, love bollixed up with betrayal. We traded off on Ethan, spending time alone with him. At dinner, we faked it for his benefit. I wondered if there was a married couple who hadn't.

Online I checked in on citizen detective Bryan Krieger, and he had put up a new podcast, which took me aback:

> Folks, if you listened to my last podcast, you know I revealed a bombshell! Lucinda was having an affair with one of her clients, according to her best friend Melissa. That only adds fuel to my theory that Jason killed her after he found out about the affair, and either he took the kids or killed them too. But Melissa refused to tell me

who Lucinda's lover was, so I got busy. And guess what I found out?

I continued reading, with a bad feeling:

I began at the beginning, with Lucinda's website. She took engagement pictures and family portraits. I ran down every lead I could, calling a bunch of middle-management bros and lacrosse dads, and got no suspects. Then I went through the corporate portraits, and I could just smell that I was in the right place. Melissa said Lucinda's lover was well-connected, and I got the impression he was prominent.

A feeling of dread came over me, and I read on.

I noted she photographed three executives, over the summer. I called the first one, a CEO, but he's super old. I reached the widow of the second one, a retired CFO, who died two months ago. I called the third one, named Paul Hart, a partner in the white-shoe law firm of Lattimore & Finch. Hart wouldn't return my calls to his office, but I found his home number and called him there. After I tried many times, his wife Pam answered. PAY DIRT! I reached her after she had definitely had a few drinks. Listen to what she told me:

I recoiled, dismayed.
I put on my earphones and clicked PLAY:

Bryan: Hello, my name is Bryan Krieger. Is this Pam Hart?
Pam: Yes, the one and only.
Bryan: I was wondering if I could talk with you about the Bennett family —
Pam: I don't know them, but what the hell, I have nothing better to do. I've seen every show on Netflix. Ha!
Bryan: First, may I ask, is your husband Paul home?
Pam: You don't know him very well, do you?
Bryan: I don't know him at all.
Pam: Neither do I, and I'm married to the guy twenty-six years! Ha!
Bryan: I can see you're brutally honest —
Pam: That I am! I got honesty *and* brutality! Ha!
Bryan: I'm investigating whether your husband was having an affair with a woman named Lucinda Bennett. She's a photographer who took his photo last summer.
Pam: I don't know anybody named Lucinda, but if she had a pulse, I'm not

surprised Paul's screwing her. She wasn't the first and she won't be the last! Ha! Ha! Are you trying to shock me?

Hart's wife laughed, and the audio ended.

I sighed inwardly. Now the gossip about Lucinda would begin. Her secret was out. I knew she would try to keep it from Ethan.

My heart hurt for her, knowing what she would be going through, yet I couldn't justify my sympathy for her. I didn't know how it would end for us.

I set that aside for now.

Tomorrow, everything changed.

■ ■ ■ ■

Part Two

■ ■ ■ ■

"The fight don't stop until the casket drop."
— Kaboni Savage,
quoted in *U.S. v. Savage,*
970 F.3d 217, 291 (3d. Cir. 2020)

Chapter Thirty-Three

"Don't worry, buddy." I smiled at Ethan, putting a hand on his shoulder. We all stood in the driveway, since it was Tuesday morning and he was leaving for his first therapy appointment. Lucinda was going with him, only one parent permitted per FBI procedure, which worked for my plan.

"I don't want to go, Dad." Ethan looked up, his worried eyes communicating what we couldn't say in front of Dom, waiting by the Tahoe.

"Everything's going to be okay." I gave him a hug, then walked him to the Tahoe and opened the door. "Love you."

"Love you, too. See you later."

"Yep." I forced a smile, not knowing when I would see him again. Ethan reached for another hug, and I squeezed him quickly, not to arouse suspicion.

Lucinda smiled convincingly. "Later, honey. Love you."

My throat caught. She wasn't supposed to say that. It wasn't in the script. "Love you, too," I said lightly, as she got inside the Tahoe.

"See you, Jason." Dom opened the driver's side door.

I waved goodbye, and Dom got into the Tahoe, started the ignition, and drove off, but I didn't have time to watch them go. I was on the clock.

I hurried upstairs to the agents' apartment and knocked on the door. "Wiki?"

Wiki came to the door with a smile. "Good morning."

"Good morning." I smiled back, trying not to think about whether he knew Milo was an FBI informant.

"Sorry to bother you, but something's wrong with the outdoor shower." I faked a frown. "Maybe you can give me a hand with it."

"Not a problem, I can give it a shot." Wiki opened the screen door to go. "There's a toolbox in your laundry room."

"I found it and I put it in the shower." I went down the stairs and led Wiki to the outdoor shower, which I opened. I let him go ahead of me, closed the door partway, then stopped. "Hold on, I have to hit the head. Be right back."

"Okay."

I padlocked the shower door quietly, then took off running. I turned right out the driveway, running as fast as I could down the street, feeling light and fast. There wasn't a moment to lose. The shower door was thick wood, but I didn't know how long it would hold.

I reached the house with the junk in the front yard, and old man Thatcher sat in his BarcaLounger next to a refrigerator, reading the newspaper with his cigar plugged wetly into his mouth. Thatcher looked up, his hooded eyes flinty, when I ran up to him, but I didn't have time for small talk.

"Mr. Thatcher? I have cash and I want that white Civic." I had noticed the car on my last run, with the handwritten sign in the windshield that read $1200. I pulled out my wallet, which held $3000 from the safe at home.

"Okay." Thatcher brightened, standing. "Don't you wanna take it for a spin?"

"No. I need a plate, too. Fast." I thrust the money at him, and Thatcher took the stack, counting it while he spoke.

"There's one on it. What'd you say your name was?"

"I didn't."

"I seen you, runnin' with that other fella."

"I'd appreciate you keeping this to yourself."

Thatcher lifted an unruly eyebrow. "It'll cost you."

Minutes later, I was racing down the street in the Civic. I pulled into a beachy gas station and pumped some gas, paying in cash. I broke my phone and tossed it in the trash. My mind raced. Wiki would be out of the shower by now. He would call Dom. Dom would tell Lucinda, who would give him our cover story, that we had a big fight and I took off for a few days alone, a habit of mine. I hoped it would give me a head start.

Five minutes later, I was back in the Civic, hitting the gas. If I hurried, I would make it in time.

I glanced at the trees as I whizzed past, wondering about cameras. Traffic and red-light cameras on the main road. Security cameras on the shops. The FBI would collect the surveillance tape.

But I would be gone.

I had failed my daughter, but I would not fail my family.

They could not survive in the program, so I had to eliminate the threat against them.

I had a plan I prayed would work.

If it didn't, there was Plan B.

B was for bait.

Chapter Thirty-Four

Straddling the Delaware state line, the Brandywine Valley was home to sunny pastures, colonial-era houses, and watercolor landscapes painted by favorite son Andrew Wyeth. I raced past the entrance to Longwood Gardens and its historic cemetery, but I was heading for a different cemetery. I was going to Junior's burial. I had found the obit online.

I took a left, then a right, passing quaint fieldstone homes and McMansions set back from the winding roads. Horses grazed in dappled sunlight under trees aflame with fall foliage. The air smelled fresh and earthy in a familiar way, unlike the marshy humidity of our house. I regained my emotional footing, despite where I was heading. In time the road narrowed to one lane, and I passed clapboard Cape Cods and ranch homes crowbarred onto land that used to be farms.

I spied a sign ahead, HARTWOOD CEMETERY & MEMORIAL GARDENS, and scanned the area for the FBI or local police. The houses were split-levels with driveways, and only one or two cars were parked on the street. If the FBI were surveilling the funeral, an agent sitting in a parked car would have been obvious. I didn't see any. The street was quiet and still, and the only person out was a ponytailed woman running with a German shepherd. I looked around for unmarked vans, but there weren't any of those, either.

Pillars of tan fieldstone marked the cemetery entrance, and I entered and turned left onto an internal road. The cemetery was parklike, with old oaks interspersed between rows of gray tombstones and only a few scattered mourners. Junior's service was at the top of the hill, a large group of mourners under a blue tent. Long black limos and a line of cars with neon-flagged windshields were parked near them.

I headed that way, my gaze straying to the trees for cameras. I didn't see any, but assumed they were there, now that I knew standard operating procedure. I was hoping the FBI wouldn't recognize me in a cap and sunglasses, even if they were already onto me. No one at Junior's funeral would know me, since I was betting Milo wouldn't be there. He would have to stay away because he was pretending to be a fugitive, and Big George would buy it, unaware that Milo was working for the FBI.

I cruised uphill, feeling a tingle of fear. I would expect most if not all of GVO to attend the funeral, since it was the boss's son who had died. I would keep my distance, but there was no turning back. I approached the line of flagged cars at the curb, scanning them for the dark BMW that had been sent to kill me and my family. Dom had said its driver was a lower-level member of GVO, so he should be here.

I kept going, my face forward and my expression impassive. Two uniformed limo drivers stood together, smoking by the cars. A placard in the window read COLON FUNERAL HOME, KENNETT SQUARE, PENNSYLVANIA. There were a few black SUVs, a red Miata, and a BMW two-door in a dark blue color.

I had to know if it was the same BMW. I cruised forward and passed the BMW, and I didn't know if the plate matched. But then I noticed something on the passenger side of the bumper; a shadow-like vertical dent, like from backing into a stanchion. I remembered seeing that on the photo I had taken of Dom's laptop screen. It *was* the same BMW.

My mouth went dry but I kept going, aware that limo drivers were looking over. I reached the head of the line, forcing a pat smile for the drivers, then drove forward as if I were visiting a different grave. I parked behind an old white Kia with a faded VFW Post 5467 decal, grabbed my drugstore bouquet, and got out of the car.

I made my way down the grassy aisle between the mounded graves, keeping Junior's funeral in my peripheral vision. The seated mourners under the tent were facing me, and beefy types in suits stood apart from them, positioned at the perimeter like bodyguards.

I passed gravestones shaped like an angel and a Celtic crucifix, then a row of granite tombstones with textured tops. I found myself wondering what type of tombstone we would get Allison. I couldn't begin to guess what kind she would've wanted. She was too young to have thought about it. She was too young to die.

I shooed the thought away. I couldn't afford to be emotional now. I read the names etched into the smooth granite: Gavin, Forster, DiJulio, Rodriguez, and Sanchez. Ahead an elderly man leaned on a cane at the foot of one of the graves, whose headstone read HELEN WESTERLY, BELOVED WIFE AND MOTHER. He had to be in his late seventies, stooped in a loose tan sweater and baggy jeans, his head bent in an old VFW cap. I noticed that his wife had died two years ago.

We fit.

I suppressed the thought, focusing instead on the opportunity presented by the mourner. If I picked a grave near him, the FBI or the bodyguards at Junior's funeral would assume we were together. I approached, and the old man looked over.

"Hello," he said, smiling with yellowing teeth.

"Hi," I said briefly, but his hooded eyes lit up behind his bifocals.

"Nice to see a new face. I've never seen you here before."

Uh-oh. "Right, I don't live here anymore. I came to visit my dad." I scanned the names on the tombstones: Harvey Villard, James Hernandez, Arthur E. Nielsen. I set the bouquet down on the Villard grave.

"Where do you live?"

"California," I answered, since it was far away. Oddly, I found myself not wanting the old man to think I was a bad son. My father always said I was a good son. He deserved a good son.

"I was there once. Coronado."

"Right." I had never been.

"I'm here for my wife Helen." The old man returned his attention to the tombstone, pushing up his bifocals. "I visit every day. I miss her every day. People say time helps, but it doesn't." He looked over, his cloudy eyes searching my face. "Does it help you?"

"Honestly, no," I told him. I missed my dad every day. Now Allison, all the time. I was in pain, standing there. I just couldn't let myself feel it.

"Sorry to disturb you. My wife always said I'm too friendly. She said I could chat up a parking meter. I'll leave you to it." The old man looked down. "You won't mind if I talk to Helen."

"Not at all." I regained focus, eyeing Junior's funeral. I found Big George sitting in the front row of the mourners, broad and squat in a dark suit. He had lost weight since the photos I'd seen online, and his hair had gone grayish-white at the temples. He wiped his eyes with a handkerchief, his head tilted down. He had lost a son, I had lost a daughter. No one expected to bury his child, even if the child had been a thug.

I scanned the mourners, men, women,

and kids of all ages, even toddlers and babies. Worlds separated us, but they came together at the death of one of their own, heartbroken, devastated, and reeling. I tried not to project a kinship where there wasn't one. They were the criminal organization responsible for Allison's murder.

The priest stood at the head of the casket between large flower arrangements. An oversize photo of Junior rested on an easel, and I shuddered at his baby-faced menace. The photo brought back his glittering leer at Allison, the earsplitting gunshot, my daughter's eyes, terrified.

I put the thought from my mind. Milo wasn't there, I had been right. There were about fifty adult mourners, mostly rough-looking men in ill-fitting suits and a handful of young women in tight dresses. A short, shapely woman with long curls was crying more than the others, and I wondered if she was Junior's girlfriend or wife.

I glimpsed someone else I recognized in the back row. Paul Hart. I felt my jaw clench, surprised he was here, publicly associating himself with Big George and GVO. Hart's blond hair and horn-rimmed glasses stood out in the crowd, so did his well-tailored suit. He sat next to an attractive redhead in a chic black dress, too young to be his wife Pam.

The priest closed his missal, and the funeral was coming to an end. I found my eyes glued to Hart as the mourners rose. A bolt of anger shot through me. The man wasn't even faithful to Lucinda. He didn't deserve her for a minute. It killed me that I could never give her what she wanted, even if it was the wrong thing to want.

"I miss her cooking," the old man said out of nowhere.

I nodded, distracted. Funeral directors were distributing red roses, and mourners began putting them on Junior's casket.

"She made noodle and tuna casserole every Sunday. Matter of fact, I still got one in the freezer. Got the date on it and all. I won't eat it. Can't bring myself to."

"I couldn't either," I said idly. The mourners were getting in line to pay their respects to Big George, shaking his hand and speaking with him. I tried to read their lips, but I could only catch words here and there, nothing of import.

"She used the wide noodles, not the skinny. Egg noodles. I know that doesn't sound fancy, but it hit the spot. It was hearty."

My attention shifted to the line of cars behind the limos. I was waiting for the mourners to disperse. I wanted to see who went to the dark blue BMW.

"Now, this might sound strange, but I don't ever want to taste that noodle casserole, ever again. As much as I loved it, I don't wanna taste it, *ever*."

"I get that." I kept my eyes on the funeral. Big George headed off first, climbing into the first limo with two beefy men. Other men got into the second and third limos.

"Say, would you like a hankie? You gotta let your feelings out. It's not like it used to be. Everybody cries nowadays."

"No, thank you." I watched the departing mourners. One of the women tottered in high heels to the red Miata, and two of them went to the black Yukon, including the shapely one. A group of men went to one of the Escalades, and Hart and his girlfriend got into a charcoal Mercedes, 500 class. No wonder Lucinda had wanted a Mercedes. She wanted me to be Paul Hart.

"I wasn't gonna offer you *my* hankie. I got better manners than that. You didn't think I was gonna do that, did you?"

"No." My eyes found three men talking near the dark blue BMW and a maroon Lexus. The limos idled at the curb. I waited to see which man would go to the BMW. My hunch was the one standing closest to the car. His face was turned away, so I couldn't get a look at him. He had longish dark hair and was of average height, with skinny shoulders in a dark suit.

"Helen was Pennsylvania Dutch. She could even speak it. Not many people can. The Amish maybe, but not English, that's what they call us."

The man closest to the BMW turned, and I caught a glimpse of his face. He looked about thirty or so, with eyes set close together and a black goatee. He waved to the others and walked to the BMW, keys in hand. I felt my heart begin to pound. He was what a killer looked like, a normal person. I wondered if he had burned down my house.

"Lotta people don't know Pennsylvania Dutch is really German, not Dutch. You know that?"

"Yes, well, it was good talking with you —"

"Don't do it."

"Pardon me?" I looked over, but the old man's gaze bored into me.

"You're in over your head, Bennett."

I recoiled, shocked.

"Don't do it. You don't know what you're getting into."

I edged away, off-balance. He wasn't a real

widower. He must have been with the FBI, here for Junior's funeral.

"You're gonna get yourself killed."

I turned on my heel and walked quickly toward the car. I didn't run because I couldn't arouse suspicion.

The first limo was pulling away from the curb, followed by the second, the third, and the flagged cars. The BMW was taking off.

I jumped in my car and joined the back of the line.

Chapter Thirty-Five

I felt stunned by the old man, blindsided. I followed the line of funeral cars at a safe distance, trying to recover my composure.

You're gonna get yourself killed.

I never would've guessed he was an FBI agent. His age and folksy manner had thrown me off. I could have sworn I heard authentic grief in his voice. Maybe I was the one grieving, my emotions bollixed up.

Maybe the old man had been pulled out of retirement for the ruse. His appearance wouldn't have aroused suspicion from anyone at Junior's funeral. They would have dismissed him, as I had. It made me wonder if the other scattered mourners were real or undercover FBI.

I cruised forward, traveling behind the line of cars as they wound their way past clapboard houses. The road was two lanes, and there was almost no traffic. The maroon Lexus was in front of me, and the dark blue

BMW was three cars up. Hart's big Mercedes was a few cars ahead of the BMW. I had to assume that the funeral procession was going to the same place. In any event, it wasn't suspicious that I was following them. Nobody passed a funeral.

I returned to my thoughts, trying to process what had just happened. The appearance of the old man could mean I didn't have the head start I hoped for. The FBI had been there for its own purposes, but now they'd be onto me.

I stayed behind the line of funeral cars, and we snaked along the winding road. I knew it led to Kennett Square, a town I knew reasonably well. I didn't know where they were going, maybe to a restaurant or back to the house. I was hoping to see where Big George lived, since I hadn't been able to find his address online.

Suddenly I noticed a black SUV in my rearview mirror, following close on my bumper. There was the silhouette of a man behind the wheel, but I couldn't make out his face.

I traveled behind the Lexus, keeping an eye on the BMW ahead and the SUV behind. The SUV accelerated, coming closer.

It made me edgy. Was he FBI? Did he work for GVO? Or was he just an impatient local driver? He couldn't pass me because the road was winding. He wouldn't be able to see the orange neon placards, so he might not know it was a funeral.

I told myself to stay the course. The SUV began to tailgate me, only a foot from my bumper. Was he following me, the funeral cars, or the road to Kennett?

Alarmed, I fed the car some gas. The SUV sped up.

When I slowed, the SUV slowed.

My thoughts raced. If the driver was FBI, he could be trying to talk to me, to get me back into WITSEC. They couldn't arrest me, I hadn't done anything wrong.

I checked the BMW ahead. It was still in line. So was the Mercedes. The chrome grille of the SUV filled my rearview mirror. I still couldn't see the driver's face, the sun glaring on his windshield.

The road wound its way through horse pastures, then a field of cows. I was feeling more and more unnerved. My hands gripped the wheel. I flashed on being tailgated that night on Coldstream Road.

I blinked my eyes clear. I felt my teeth grinding. My heartbeat accelerated. We came to a fork in the road. I didn't want to leave the line of funeral cars. I had to see where the BMW was going or where Big

George lived. I continued forward.

The SUV honked, loud. I jumped. Either the SUV driver was an FBI agent, trying to get my attention. Or a GVO guy, who knew I didn't belong. Or a civilian losing his temper.

In the next moment, the SUV drove up and tapped my bumper.

"No!" I gripped the wheel. The driver of the Lexus looked back, his head wheeling around.

I couldn't afford to draw attention. Ahead on the right was a road. I wanted to follow the BMW, but I didn't know if I could. The Lexus slowed down, the driver twisting in the seat. I could see he was on the phone, his head down and to the right.

I was in trouble. The road to the right was getting closer. I couldn't keep following the funeral. It was too dangerous.

I turned right, watching the BMW drive away.

I glanced in the rearview mirror and froze. The SUV was still behind me, accelerating. He had to be following me.

My mouth went dry. I hit the gas and the SUV did the same. The road plunged into a tall cornfield. I accelerated, the SUV on my tail. Birds flapped squawking from corn rows.

The SUV driver leaned on the horn, harder.

A bolt of terror electrified me. Whoever was driving the black SUV wasn't FBI. Running civilians off the road wasn't procedure in any book. The SUV had to be GVO.

I floored the gas pedal. My car struggled to accelerate to seventy-five miles an hour, then eighty-five. I clenched the wheel, straight through the cornfield. Bugs hit my windshield. My tires rumbled on the dirt road. Stones pinged the car.

My heart hammered. The cornfield went on and on. I didn't know if we were going toward town or away.

Boom! The SUV slammed into my fender, harder than before.

My neck jolted. My teeth clenched. I slammed the pedal to the floor. The engine whined in protest. It couldn't go any faster.

The cornfield ended ahead. I raced toward a fork at the finish. The curve to the right was gentle. To the left was sharper, more dangerous at speed.

I had a choice. I throttled the wheel. The car rattled. The tires bobbled. Sunlight spilled in the clearing. The open road zoomed toward me.

At the last minute, I cranked the wheel to the left, braking just enough not to crash. I took the dangerous way, hoping it was less predictable. I skidded, fishtailing. I struggled to control the car. I narrowly avoided hitting a pasture fence across the street.

I checked the rearview. The SUV wasn't behind me anymore. He'd bet I'd go right.

I raced away, orienting myself. I was heading toward Kennett Square. I would be in civilization soon.

I glanced in the rearview. The SUV was stopped on the road, his taillights red. He must have been trying to decide whether to come after me.

I flew ahead, keeping one eye on the rearview. The SUV didn't follow.

I left him behind. My heart pounded all the way into town.

I tried to puzzle it out, my mouth bone dry. The SUV had to be with GVO, a bodyguard keeping a lookout for the FBI or maybe even a rival.

You're in over your head, Bennett.

Why did the old man say that? Had he been trying to warn me? Had he spotted the SUV driver? Did he know the SUV driver would chase me? Or was the old man connected with whoever drove the SUV?

I didn't have answers.

But I was already getting another idea.

Chapter Thirty-Six

My heartbeat returned to normal. The SUV wasn't following me anymore.

I drove through Kennett Square, looking for the limos or funeral cars. The town was a few charming blocks of artsy boutiques, organic restaurants, and quaint brick row-houses, their windows thick with muntins and authentically bubbled glass. There was a small business district, where brightly colored banners hung from gas-lit lamps and tall oak trees shed dappled sunlight on sidewalk cafés.

I had been here plenty of times. When the kids were little, I had taken them for the annual Mushroom Festival; the surrounding farms produced over half the mushrooms sold in the country. The town's demographics were an uneasy mix of undocumented workers who worked on mushroom farms, and the well-heeled horsey set that rode with Cheshire Hunt and owned horse farms where Olympic riders trained.

I drove through the center of town. People went to and from the bank, lawyers' offices, and a drugstore. There was no traffic except for a fleet of empty school buses rattling uphill toward the high school. I kept my eyes peeled for the GVO funeral cars.

The ice cream store on the corner had a line of customers on this balmy day. Allison loved the place, and Lucinda would take her after away games at Kennett or Unionville. I put them both from my mind, on a mission.

I drove past the brick clock tower, then spied the sign that read COLON FUNERAL HOME, in front of a beautifully maintained colonial house with a wraparound porch. It had been the funeral home the Verias used for Junior. On the side of the building was a parking lot, and three limos lined up in front of a few regular cars.

On impulse, I pulled in to the parking lot. I adjusted my sunglasses, left the car, and hustled toward the front door, which was propped open. I went inside, and there was no one around. Immediately to my left was an open doorway through which I heard the noise of a vacuum cleaner. The cloying fragrance of refrigerated flowers wafted from the room, and I guessed it was where

Junior's wake had been held. Outside the room was a lectern with a white guestbook, closed.

I opened the guestbook and wasn't surprised to find the pages blank. The members of a criminal organization weren't supplying their names and addresses. I ducked inside the room.

The room was a long, carpeted rectangle, empty except for a man in a blue jumpsuit pushing a vacuum that was so loud he didn't hear me enter. White folding chairs had been lined up against the wall between ornate floor lamps, and at the front of the room was a display of flower arrangements on wrought-iron shelves.

The man looked up, shutting off the vacuum cleaner. "Can I help you?"

I thought fast. "Yes, about the Veria funeral. I'm with the courier service. I think they're at the luncheon — I forget where it is, do you know?"

"They went back to the house."

Duly noted. "Right. I'm supposed to get the cards from the flowers."

The workman frowned. "Bill usually does that."

"The Verias sent me. I do what I'm told."

"Okay. You can take that, too." The man pointed to a small box near the baseboard.

"Extra Mass cards and stuff."

"Great, thanks." I hustled to pick up the box, and the man switched the vacuum cleaner back on.

I went to the front of the room, and each flower arrangement had a white card in a plastic holder, displayed to show the sender. They were of varied shapes and sizes, from massive sprays of calla lilies and gladiola to smaller ones of daisies. Some had themes; a green-sprayed carnation bouquet within a little Philadelphia Eagles helmet and a spray of red miniature roses in a ceramic baseball for the Phillies.

I took the cards and put them in the box, moving quickly. I waved to the man on the way out, and he nodded. I hurried from the room, out the entrance, and to the car, then climbed inside and left the parking lot.

I drove a few blocks away, and when the neighborhood turned residential, I pulled over under a tree and tugged the box onto my lap. Inside were the white cards from the flower arrangements, but I moved them aside in favor of a thick black folder embossed with the name of the funeral home.

I opened the folder.

It contained an invoice for George Veria.

With a home address.

■ ■ ■ ■

Big George Veria's house was a massive McMansion with a fieldstone façade on the north and south wings, forming a U-shape around a circular driveway that held a catering truck and parked cars. The front lawn was manicured, with surprisingly tasteful plantings in a parcel of about twenty acres. A tall fence of black wrought iron ran along the front of the property, protected by a gate with ornate scrollwork. Beside it was a call box with a visible security camera, plus white cameras mounted in the trees.

I parked on the opposite side of the street, a distance from the house, eyeing the magnificent place. Whoever said crime didn't pay didn't know what they were talking about. My thoughts turned to Milo, and I knew he would be inside. He wouldn't have risked showing his face in public, but he was safe among Big George's crime family.

I scanned the cars parked out front, wondering which was his. I couldn't remember exactly which cars had been at the funeral, so I couldn't spot any new ones. None of them had their neon placards in the windshield. My gaze found the charcoal

Mercedes that belonged to Paul Hart. He and his girlfriend were inside, too.

I straightened in the driver's seat, having gotten the lay of the land. I twisted on the ignition. My plan was to get to Big George and bust Milo, but I had always known I couldn't do it this way.

I had to start on more familiar terrain.

Chapter Thirty-Seven

I sat in my car, edgy and waiting. Night had fallen, and drizzle dotted my windshield, but I didn't turn on the wipers. I didn't want to be seen by security cameras.

I was parked between two commercial Dumpsters on Buckingham Street, a narrow backstreet in Center City, Philly's business district. Buckingham afforded me a clear view of Colonial Towers East, a monolithic office building across from me on Eighteenth. On my left was Colonial Towers West, and on my right the service entrances to the stores and restaurants around the block, closed now.

You didn't know I had an affair.

I suppressed the thought. Paul Hart was inside Colonial Towers East, and I was here for a reason. Milo was a confidential informant, so he had to have entered into a cooperation agreement. Those agreements were in contract form, drafted by the government and negotiated by defense lawyers. Since Hart was Milo's lawyer, that meant Hart had negotiated the agreement.

I connected the dots that had taken me here. Hart knew Milo was a confidential informant, but Big George didn't. So sooner or later, Hart would have to meet with Milo without Big George's knowledge. I assumed they would meet in some out-of-the-way location, alone and probably at night. They couldn't risk meeting in the open and they couldn't talk on the phone, since they would assume the FBI was listening in. My plan was to follow Hart until he met with Milo, then take proof of that secret meeting to Big George.

I waited, and my dashboard clock ticked to eight forty-five p.m. I knew Hart was inside since I'd looked up his website, on a Tracfone with Wi-Fi I'd bought today. According to his schedule, tonight Hart was at a fundraiser for U.S. Senator Mike Ricks, who was rumored to be considering a presidential run. Tomorrow night, Hart would be at a fundraiser for U.S. Representative Barbara Caldwell, rumored to be vying for Ricks's seat. The lawyer must have been hedging his bipartisan bets, having no interests except self-promotion.

Nine fifteen p.m.

I straightened in the driver's seat, eyeing Colonial Towers East. Its sleek modern lobby was a bright layer of floor-to-ceiling glass under the rest of the darkened building, its mirrored façade vanishing into a black, foggy sky. I turned my attention to the entrance-and-exit of its underground garage. I assumed Hart would be among the last to leave the event, sprinkling his business cards like corporate confetti.

Nine-thirty.

Cars began leaving the parking garage, turning right onto Eighteenth. I got a decent look at the drivers' faces in the streetlight. They were well-dressed men and women, on phones or smoking. No Paul Hart in his charcoal Mercedes.

I watched and waited, checking each driver. A line of big black Escalades left the garage, one of which held Senator Ricks himself. I caught sight of Senator Ricks in the back seat, a tall, gray-haired politician with the requisite toothy smile. But still, no Paul Hart. The caravan diminished to only a few cars, and I worried I had missed Hart. Maybe he had been a passenger in someone else's car or was still inside.

Nine forty-five.

Suddenly I spotted Hart walking inside the lobby of Colonial Towers East, which had a glass façade. He nodded at the security guards at the front desk as he passed them.

My heart began to pound. I started my engine as Hart exited the building, briefcase in hand. He reached the sidewalk and stopped before he crossed the street, waiting for traffic. His head was turned to the right, and I followed his line of sight to a black hired car parked in front of Colonial Towers West. So he hadn't driven himself.

I left my parking space and cruised slowly up Buckingham. Two men under umbrellas met Hart on the sidewalk and they started talking, so I braked a short distance from the top of the street, waiting for them to finish. I couldn't read their lips with an obscured view.

Hart waved goodbye, stepped off the curb, and started to cross Eighteenth. Suddenly, out of nowhere, a dark sedan sped down the street and struck him, head-on.

I gasped, shocked. I couldn't believe what I was seeing. It took everything in me not to shout.

Hart screamed. The impact of the sedan catapulted him into the air, propelling him down the street. The sedan didn't stop.

My heart thundered. It was an intentional hit-and-run. I didn't see what kind of car it was, I had been watching Hart.

Instinctively I accelerated and turned onto Eighteenth Street. People were running down the sidewalk toward the scene. Hart lay motionless in front of the entrance to Colonial Towers West.

I glanced over, horrified, as I drove by. Security guards raced to him from the building. A crowd was beginning to gather.

"Jason?" I thought I heard someone say, as I sped off.

Chapter Thirty-Eight

I raced down Eighteenth Street. The sedan was two blocks ahead of me. In the dark, I couldn't see its make or model. There was no traffic between us.

We flew toward Market Street, one after the other. I swerved to avoid an SUV, the sedan swerved to avoid a cab. People pointed from the sidewalk.

The traffic light turned red but the sedan didn't stop. Pedestrians jumped out of the way. Cars on Market Street screeched to a halt, honking.

I kept going, too. I chased the sedan to the next block, veering around a boxy white SEPTA bus.

The sedan steered left onto the Benjamin Franklin Parkway, the main artery out of the city, lined with streetlights and oversize banners. A Honda tried to pass in front of the sedan, forcing it to slow down.

I slammed the pedal to the floor, getting

close enough to identify the sedan. It was the dark blue BMW from Junior's funeral. It had the dent on its fender.

Questions flew through my brain. Why would GVO kill Hart? And why now? Did Milo know? Was Milo driving the BMW?

I began to lose ground, my Civic no match for the BMW. The BMW took off, tearing around Eakins Oval in front of the Art Museum and heading for the expressway.

Traffic stopped at a red light on the parkway. I tried to collect my thoughts but they raced everywhere. I couldn't shake the horrific image of Hart being struck by the BMW. I took no pleasure in seeing his grisly death. I wondered what Lucinda would say. Whether she would mourn him.

My chest tightened. I realized I hadn't asked her if she loved him. Maybe I didn't want to know the answer.

A car honked behind me, and I looked up at the stoplight, which had turned green. I pressed the gas and went forward, without knowing exactly where.

Then I remembered something.

Jason?

I gritted my teeth. Someone had recognized me at the scene. A lot of lawyers in the city knew me. It could have been anyone.

Plus the BMW driver would remember the Civic. And security cameras must have picked up the BMW and the Civic, giving chase. The Philadelphia police would want to know who was driving the Civic.

So would the FBI.

It was time to change things up.

Chapter Thirty-Nine

The convenience store was cramped and dusty, an old indie off the expressway. It was next to a body shop, closed at this hour, but the reason I'd come. The entire store was one long skinny rectangle, and fluorescent lighting flickered overhead, affixed to a sagging drop ceiling. There was no one else in the store and no cashier in sight. An old TV played behind the counter, showing a commercial.

I went through shelves stuffed with sleeves of Slim Jims, shiny turquoise bags of Herr's chips, and dusty boxes of Pepto-Bismol. The air smelled like cigarette smoke, which never happened anymore in public. The odor took me back in time, since my father used to smoke.

I found what I needed and went to the counter, and an older man appeared from the back, taking a final drag. He caught my eye behind glasses that slipped down a nose with broken capillaries. His gray hair was greasy, and he needed a shave, but the flesh of his cheeks draped a polite smile.

"Can I help you?" He stubbed out his cigarette in a crowded ashtray with a plaid beanbag base.

"Yes, thanks." I set the stuff on the counter and pulled a twenty from my wallet. "Also, do you know who runs the body shop next door? I need my car repainted and I don't want to go to some expensive chain." Of course that wasn't the real reason. The real reason was that chains kept records.

"Sure. The owner, Ed." The man opened the cash register and made change. "He's out for two weeks, gettin' over an operation."

I masked my dismay. "I need it sooner."

"Ed's cousin has a shop."

"Can you call him?"

"Sure."

"Tonight?"

The man didn't ask why, and I saw myself in his eyes. I was a man who needed a car painted fast, for reasons nobody wanted to know. I sensed I was leaving my old legal world behind and entering one where lawyers conspired with criminals and ended up dead anyway.

The man slid my change and bag across

the counter. "I'll call him."

"Thanks." I added, "Got a bathroom?"

In the bathroom, I shaved one strip of my hair, then the next. I had cut it down first with a scissors, then shaved my way through a few razors. Clumps of cut hair and globs of shaving cream filled the small, filthy wastebasket next to the sink. The job was messier and took longer than I expected, but it was working. I was getting balder by the minute. I couldn't risk being recognized again.

I met my own gaze in the mirror, realizing how much I looked like my father, now that my hair was gone. I had his warm brown eyes, wide-set, and his straight nose and small mouth, bracketed by his laugh lines. The thought gave me comfort, and I found myself smiling. My father had been my best friend, and it had been just him and me for almost as long as I could remember. I had been devastated when he died, and I lived by his advice.

Better safe than sorry.

I watched my smile fade. I couldn't deny the facts, literally staring me in the face. I had made safe choices, one after the other, on the belief they would protect me and my family. Yet here I was, with my family in pieces and Allison gone. Playing it safe hadn't kept them safe.

I remembered way back when, I used to wonder why my father idolized Milton Hershey, but never aspired to *be* him. I sensed he didn't know if he was capable of it, or simply didn't want to try. He never tried to swing for the fences, but he could have. He had stayed in his comfort zone, and so had I. I didn't know if we were afraid of failing, or of succeeding.

I knocked the shavings into the trash, then rinsed off the razor and resumed shaving, my thoughts running free. I had to change my appearance, but I sensed something different was happening, something more. I was stripping down to something essential, revealing my rawest self. I was shedding whatever I used to be.

I was becoming someone else. Maybe who I should have been, all along.

Not my father.

Myself.

I looked at my reflection with new eyes.

No more playing it safe.

Chapter Forty

Remy Whitman Towing & Auto Body was a rectangle of white painted cinder block, grimy with age. The lights were dim, owing to fluorescent lighting that had blown out in sections. The concrete floor was stained and hadn't been swept in ages. Overflowing Rubbermaid trash cans, red plastic five-gallon canisters, and half-empty jugs of antifreeze lined both walls. Signs on the cinder-block wall read WE WORK WITH ALL INSURANCE COMPANIES and 100% COLOR MATCH GUARANTEE. Battered gray cabinets with faded decals were in one corner, and a freshly painted car door hung on a metal rack.

Remy turned out to be a tall, skinny hipster with a neck tattoo of Felix the Cat. He had on a Carhartt knit cap, brown flannel shirt, wide-leg jeans, and work boots. "So what color you want?" he asked me, eyeing the Civic.

"Anything dark." I needed it to be markedly different.

"I got black."

"Perfect."

"Done. Two coats takes two days."

"I need it tomorrow morning, so one coat."

Remy nodded. "It's gonna cost you four hundred bucks and it's gonna take all night. Okay?"

"Okay."

"You can wait in my office." Remy gestured at a dirty blue door on the side wall. "There's a coffeemaker and a bathroom. Feel free."

"Thanks."

"You need a new plate?"

"Yes, thanks."

"Anything else?"

I didn't hesitate. "How about a gun?"

"I can't do that."

"You know anybody who can?"

"I might," Remy answered, in a way that told me he did.

Remy's office was barely big enough for a desk, a file cabinet, and an old wooden table that held a microwave, a coffeemaker, and a small TV playing on low volume. The desk was basic metal, its surface cluttered with invoices, parts catalogs, an old sports section, and menus from vegan restaurants. There was a no-frills bathroom at the far end, and the walls were covered with old calendars, a Van Halen poster, and a Felix the Cat clock, its plastic tail still.

I started brewing a pot of coffee, glancing at the TV screen. It was eleven o'clock, and the news was coming on. A red Breaking News banner popped onto the screen, with the chyron LAWYER DEAD IN HIT-AND-RUN. I found the TV remote and turned up the volume.

The anchorwoman was saying: "Attorney Paul Hart was killed tonight by a hit-and-run driver on Eighteenth Street, at around nine forty-five this evening. Hart was fifty-one years old, a nationally known lawyer at the Center City law firm of Lattimore & Finch. The driver was reportedly in a late-model BMW, dark blue in color. Authorities have no suspects at the present time. We will keep you posted on any developments as they occur."

The video showed uniformed Philly cops talking with crime techs, while cruisers idled next to a black Medical Examiner's van and a boxy white Mobile Crime Unit. Yellow crime-scene tape cordoned off the street, and a blue tent had been erected on the sidewalk in front of Colonial Towers East. Presumably Hart's body was still there. The anchorwoman moved on to the next story, a fire at a warehouse.

Hart's murder shook me up. I didn't know what was going on. Hart was Milo's and Big George's lawyer, but he had just been killed by their organization. I was in over my head, but I wasn't about to turn back now.

My Tracfone pinged with notifications, since I had set alerts for any related news. I slid the phone from my pocket and checked the screen. The first few were news outlets, but the last one was from Bryan Krieger's citizen detective podcast. I clicked, and the banner blindsided me:

I SAW JASON BENNETT TONIGHT! Click here for the bombshell development!

I read on, horrified.

HUGE NEWS! The Bennett case just exploded! Lucinda Bennett's boyfriend Paul Hart was killed by a hit-and-run driver tonight! I was THERE and so was JASON BENNETT! I saw him with my own eyes! I'm cracking this case wide open!

My mouth went dry. I hadn't seen Krieger,

but I hadn't been looking at the crowd. I didn't know if I would have recognized him from the website anyway. I kept reading.

> I went to a political fundraiser because I wanted to ask Hart about Lucinda Bennett, after my interview with his wife Pam. I couldn't get to him at the fundraiser for all the muckety-mucks, so I tried after, outside the building. I was walking down the street when I saw a car run him over, killing him! And guess who was driving right behind — Jason Bennett! Click below for my blockbuster interview with a bystander!

Krieger had been following Hart, and neither of us knew about the other. I clicked to listen to the podcast:

> Bryan: I'm Bryan Krieger on the scene of the hit-and-run of lawyer Paul Hart, and I found an eyewitness. What is your name, sir?
>
> David: David Fishman. My God, that was terrible! Are you a reporter?

My gut clenched. I knew David Fishman. He was a partner at Shafritz Ferguson, a law firm that used me from time to time.

> Bryan: Yes, I won't keep you, I need to get

the facts.

David: I still feel so shocked!

Bryan: The man who was struck by the car was Paul Hart, a lawyer. Do you know him?

David: No, but I know of him. I'm a lawyer, too.

Bryan: Were you at the fundraiser tonight?

David: No, I was working late. My office is in the West Tower, and I was leaving the building. I came right after he had been hit. I saw him on the sidewalk and I tried to help. Oh my God, this is upsetting, I've never seen injuries like that!

Bryan: I heard you say, "Jason?" Why did you say that?

David: I looked over and I saw a car going past and I recognized the driver.

Bryan: And who was he?

David: Jason Bennett. I saw his face clearly in the light from the building. It's weird because I don't think he drives a Honda, but I got a good look at him. He was facing me as he went by.

Bryan: How do you know Jason Bennett? Have you used his services as a court reporter?

David: Yes, and I know him from Bar Association conferences and things like that. Last month, we had a fairly long conversation. I was thinking about using him for an upcoming matter.

I remembered the talk. I had chatted him up, trying to get more business.

Bryan: Have you heard that the Bennett family has disappeared?
David: Yes, that's why I was surprised to see him.
Bryan: Have you told the police what you saw?
David: Yes. They want me to go down to the Roundhouse and make a statement.

I groaned. So he had told the Philly police he had seen me.

Bryan: You said a Honda. Can you confirm that Bennett was driving a white Honda Civic?
David: Yes.
Bryan: Did you get the plate?
David: No, I should go —
Bryan: The Civic was following the other car at a high rate of speed, wasn't it?
David: Yes.
Bryan: Weren't they fleeing together, like they were in cahoots?
David: Uh, I don't know, I don't really want to get involved. Did you say you were —

Bryan: Isn't it possible they were in it together? Did you know Paul Hart was having an affair with Jason's wife Lucinda?

David: I'm sorry, what paper are you with? Are you with the *Inquirer*?

Bryan: Hart was cheating with Jason's wife, so the motive is clear —

David: Bye, I have to go. Get that phone out of my face.

I clicked STOP. The ante had just been upped. Krieger had blown my cover. Sooner or later, the FBI would learn that I had been at the scene. I had to assume that Dom and the FBI would connect my disappearance to the Hart hit-and-run. Any video would show I hadn't been the one to kill Hart, but it would intensify their search for me.

I reconsidered the implications. The FBI had said that GVO was trying to kill me, since Big George believed I killed his son. Now I was wondering if that was true. And if it was, why would GVO kill Hart? And who had chased me after the funeral? It was hard to imagine who in GVO benefited from Hart's death. Then I realized the answer:

Milo.

I reasoned it out, my heart beginning to

pound. Milo was a confidential informant, and Paul Hart negotiated the cooperation agreement. That information was dangerous to know. It could get Milo killed by Big George or anybody else in GVO. So maybe Milo had decided Hart was a liability, or maybe Hart had threatened to expose Milo to Big George, after Milo had double-crossed him by killing Junior, not me.

The realization sent a shudder up my spine. The only question was how Milo would have convinced Big George to have Hart killed. As far as I knew, Big George thought of Hart as his lawyer and had even invited Hart and his girlfriend to Junior's funeral. I couldn't understand why Big George would have him killed the same night.

Then it struck me.

Maybe Milo had lied to Big George about Hart, like with the botched carjacking. Milo could have made up some lie that would turn Big George against Hart. Or Milo had simply gone rogue and ordered the hit-and-run.

But now what?

My mind raced. If Milo had gone rogue, there were two possibilities. Either Big George would know GVO was responsible for killing Hart because he would know that the BMW driver was one of his own guys — or Big George would be too preoccupied with Junior's death to pay attention to a random hit-and-run in Center City, which happened to kill his lawyer. There were plenty of dark blue BMWs in the world, and the news hadn't mentioned a plate number.

My gaze returned to the TV, but my thoughts went back to the funeral today, about Hart and the girlfriend, then about the cards I'd taken from the funeral home.

"Remy?" I called out, heading for the garage.

Fifteen minutes later, I was on my second cup of black coffee and my brain was in overdrive. I had retrieved the box from the funeral home, and my task lay before me on the gritty tile floor.

First was a row of cards that I had taken from the floral arrangements on the first shelf of the display, laid out in order from left to right. Second was a row of cards I had taken from the second shelf of flower arrangements, also left to right, and the top row contained only three cards, from the flower arrangements that had their own easels in the back.

I scanned a few names in the first row:

Deepest Sympathy, Rachel & Big P
Love, Sonia & Little Jimmy
Condolences, RJ

I realized I was essentially looking at the inner circle of GVO, but I didn't know how to find out who they were. They hadn't signed the guest book, but they'd sent the flowers, trying to score points with Big George. There were no last names on the cards, so I couldn't look them up online, and most had only nicknames.

I sipped coffee, puzzling it out. Then it struck me that a nickname was also an alias. I reached in my pocket, pulled out my Tracfone, and logged on to the Internet. I went to the court records site, plugged in Marie's username and password, and searched under *George Veria.*

Onto the tiny screen popped the caption of the most recent criminal case against Big George, and there were other defendants, since he was part of a criminal conspiracy. Five codefendants were named, and as I had known, every caption in a criminal indictment listed the defendants, as well as last known aliases.

I rallied. To identify the members of GVO, all I had to do was use the captions on the indictments and compare them with the cards. I probably wouldn't get all of the members, but I'd take as many as I could. It would be tedious on a phone, but I had no other option.

I was about to get started, then stopped myself, remembering Hart. I scanned the cards and found his in the middle of the second row.

Deepest condolences, Paul & Contessa

I double-checked the cards to see if there was another Paul, and there wasn't. It was always possible that Hart's flowers had been brought to the cemetery, but I bet they hadn't. That was usually done for immediate family or those closest to them, like Milo. So Hart's girlfriend was named Contessa.

I jumped on Google and searched under *Contessa* and *Philadelphia.* There weren't that many Contessas, and I clicked on the first one, a Contessa Burroughs on LinkedIn, with her current employment:

Paralegal, White-Collar Litigation Team,
Lattimore & Finch, Philadelphia Office

I scrolled to whitepages.com and looked up her address.

Chapter Forty-One

I reached Contessa's neighborhood first thing in the morning. The sky was cloudy, but I had my sunglasses on, so nobody would see my face. I felt different with my head completely shaved. Freer, bolder, and onto something after last night. The car felt different, too; it had taken all night to dry, but it was credibly black. My new license plate was from New Jersey, a nice touch.

I circled the block looking for a parking space, my tires rumbling on the cobblestones in this old part of Philly, called Northern Liberties. It used to be the industrial section, marked by abandoned warehouses and the old red-brick Schlitz and Ortlieb's breweries, but had since been gentrified into a vibrant, hip neighborhood and the warehouses renovated into upscale apartments that attracted young professionals like Contessa. She lived in NorthLofts, overlooking the Delaware River.

The traffic was light, but there were people on the sidewalk. A woman ran by with a mutt, and two men walked uptown carrying messenger bags. I imagined Contessa wouldn't be going into the office this morning, since Hart had been killed the night before. The local news reported that the police had no further leads, though now I distrusted official reports. A reward had been posted by Lattimore & Finch, and official mourning press-released by the Philadelphia Bar Association, the Criminal Justice Section of the American Bar Association, and a host of prominent lawyers and law firms, as well as political types like Senator Ricks, Representative Caldwell, and the Governor of Pennsylvania.

I reviewed my plan. I assumed Hart trusted Contessa, since they were lovers and she worked for him. She probably knew Milo was a confidential informant, and his cooperation agreement had to be filed and saved online or in hard copy. Lawyers like Hart didn't do their own administrative tasks, so I was betting Contessa did. If she knew Milo was an informant, or even if she didn't, I was going to tell her so — and that I believed Milo was responsible for Hart's murder. I wanted her to give me a copy of the cooperation agreement, so I could show it to Big George and prove Milo's betrayal. She might do it because she would want to take down Milo, as revenge for killing Hart.

I spotted somebody leaving a space across from NorthLofts and waited to pull in. In the meantime, I sized up her condominium, a former warehouse about seven stories tall with large louvered windows. I spotted a boxy white security camera over the apartment entrance and put on my ballcap, pulled into a parking space, and left the car.

I kept my head down as I approached the building and reached the entrance, a modern glass door. On the wall to the right was a long panel of black buzzers. No names were listed, but I remembered Contessa's apartment number, 626.

I held my phone to my ear and pretended to call whoever I was visiting. I blocked the button panel from the security camera as best I could and pressed a button at random. I heard the buzzer sound, but nobody came on the speaker or buzzed me in. I pressed another button, waited again, but no answer.

Suddenly I saw a young woman in running gear approaching the door from the inside, and I kept talking on the phone. "Yes, honey, I'm sorry I'm late, I really am," I said into the phone, just as the woman opened the door. I made a help-me-I'm-a-bad-boyfriend face while I kept talking on the phone. "I know, but traffic was crazy, I'm really sorry."

The woman flashed a disapproving look and left the door open, and I caught the door, still talking.

"I'm coming in right now. The car is packed and we're good to go." I kept up the fake conversation inside the lobby, which was small and brightly lit with exposed brick walls and a mailroom. The elevator bank was ahead, next to the staircase, and I opted for the stairs. I slipped into the stairwell and took the steps two by two, taking off my sunglasses and cap. Reflexively I reached to smooth my hair into place, then remembered I didn't have any.

I reached the sixth floor. A sign on the wall indicated even numbers were to the left, so I went that way. The hallway was quiet and well lit, with pale blue walls and a turquoise patterned carpet. Morning newspapers sat in plastic sleeves outside many of the doors. At the end of the hallway, I could see a few items in front of one of the doors. When I got closer, I realized they were flower arrangements.

I reached the door with the flowers, 626. It was Contessa's apartment, and the flowers had to be for Hart's death. I knocked. There was no answer. I waited, then knocked again, harder.

"Contessa?" I called out, and in the next moment, I heard a door opening behind me. I turned around to find an older woman in a thick bathrobe standing in the threshold of the apartment across the hall.

"She's probably not home, don't you get it?" The woman's hooded eyes flashed with anger. She had a white towel wrapped around her head. "All morning, everybody's knocking! They woke me up!"

"I'm sorry —" I started to say, but the woman scowled at the flower arrangements in the hall, throwing up her hands.

"Everybody lets them in! Nobody follows the rules, her most of all! She leaves everything in the hall! Amazon boxes! Her bicycle! Muddy boots! Umbrellas! Recycling, *trash*! She's too lazy to take it to the incinerator! I tell her, it's a fire hazard!"

I didn't know what to say and wouldn't have gotten a word in edgewise anyway.

"I've had enough! You wait here!"

"What, why?" I asked, but the woman popped back inside her apartment, slamming the door behind her. She came out a minute later, holding up a key. "Pick those flowers up! We're moving her crap into *her* apartment." The woman charged past me, shoved the key in Contessa's door, and twisted the doorknob. "Put them inside! She'll see them when she gets home! I'm sick of this!"

I picked up the flower arrangements.

"Contessa, you home?" The woman flung open the door and stalked inside the apartment, with me on her heels. "Listen, you gotta get your—"

The woman gasped in horror.

I almost dropped the flowers.

Contessa was hanging from a ceiling fan in the living room, dead. Her face was a horrid blue color. Her eyes bulged from their sockets, her neck bent at an unnatural angle.

Horrified, I took in the rest of the scene. A wooden chair under the ceiling fan had been knocked over. An open Mac laptop and an empty bottle of wine sat on the coffee table. A wineglass lay on the rug in a circle of red.

The woman screamed. "Help! Help!"

I edged out of the room. I couldn't be here when the cops came. I left the flower arrangements.

I ran down the hall and into the stairwell. I could hear the woman screaming and the sounds of doors opening, then a commotion. I raced down to the third floor, then the second, then the first.

I stuck on my hat and sunglasses, then left the stairwell. I hurried through the lobby, keeping my head down. I hustled across the street, jumped inside the car, and drove off, taking my first breath.

CHAPTER FORTY-TWO

I drove under the concrete pillars of I-95 on Delaware Avenue, the wide boulevard that bordered the gritty underside of Philadelphia. My heart was pounding, my mouth had gone dry blocks ago. I couldn't get the horrific image of Contessa from my mind.

Clouds blanketed the sky. I passed Fishtown and Port Richmond to my left, and to my right the industrial riverfront was marked by warehouses, loading docks, and stacks of shipping containers. They lined the Delaware River, a murky body of water that curved east and divided Pennsylvania from New Jersey. Petty Island squatted in the middle, a gloomy, gray spit of land, dotted with oil drums.

I raced ahead in grimy truck traffic, sensing I had to get off the street. I passed a few storefront lunch places serving truckers and longshoremen, then the massive truck parking lot at Tioga Marine Terminal. I bypassed chain hotels and finally spotted a run-down two-story motel with a flat roof and water stains marring its concrete façade. An old-school neon sign read THE WATERBIRD.

I pulled into its lot and parked next to a row of trucks. I took my cardboard box from the funeral home, left the car, and headed for a glass door labeled OFFICE, which was covered with faded credit-card decals. It looked like the kind of place that wouldn't insist on ID if I paid in cash.

I turned out to be right.

My room was on the second floor, overlooking the parking lot and Delaware Avenue. The noise of the traffic rumbled through its thin walls, and I could hear raucous laughter coming from another room.

I took off my hat and sunglasses and set the box on a double bed with a ratty blue quilted cover. The room was bare except for a night table across from a matching bureau and boxy old TV on a metal cart. I turned it on and headed into the bathroom.

I went to the sink and splashed cold water on my face. What had happened to Contessa had shaken me to the core. Maybe because she was young, maybe because it came so quickly after Hart. And Allison.

I twisted off the faucet, dried with a thin

towel, and left the bathroom, sliding out my Tracfone. I had to understand what I had just seen. It made sense that Contessa would be in despair after the murder of her married boyfriend, but my suspicions were on alert. It might have looked as if she died by suicide, but I wondered if it had been staged.

I sank onto the edge of the bed, running over the possibilities. There was no doorman at Contessa's building. No check-in. Someone could have gotten into the building the way I did, then knocked on her door. She could have opened it, whether she knew him or not — assuming it was a man, which was likely given the strength that staging a suicide would have taken. It could have been two men, even three.

I followed the same analysis as I had with Hart, trying to figure who benefited from her death. I got the same answer: Milo. Milo could have been as worried about Contessa as he was about Hart. It was the same reason I wanted to talk to Contessa. I was assuming she knew Milo was a confidential informant and also where to find the cooperation agreement. So Milo had a motive to kill her, eliminating his last loose end.

I mulled it over. I didn't know if the killer had been Milo, the BMW driver, someone else, or all of the above. The BMW driver couldn't have been in two places at once — here *and* waiting for Hart until the fundraiser was over — but I didn't know what time Contessa had been killed. If she hadn't gone to the fundraiser, she could have been killed first, then the killer could have gone after Hart. She would have trusted him enough to let him in, or he could have overpowered her.

I could imagine Contessa's terror when she realized what was about to happen. I had seen it in Allison's eyes. The terror of knowing what no one wants to know. I felt a deep stab of grief, and the words came to me as if I were reading my daughter's mind.

This is how I die.

I couldn't stop thinking of Allison, then realized I was never *not* thinking of Allison. Maybe that was the way it was going to be from now on. Maybe that was the way I could keep her with me. Maybe there would come a time when it didn't make me feel broken, but I doubted it. Allison was younger than Contessa, but they were both too young to be gone.

I flashed on the scene in Contessa's apartment and the open laptop on the coffee table. I was sure that Lattimore & Finch, if not Hart or Contessa, stored files and documents on the cloud under a passcode. Maybe Milo, or whoever was working for him, had gotten her to delete the file before killing her. The Philly police or the FBI would figure out if it was suicide or murder, but that would come later. Now there was just the loss of a young girl, and that alone was awful.

I scrolled to the website for Lattimore & Finch, then searched under *Criminal Justice Team.* There were two lawyers and one paralegal — Contessa — in the section. It was a small section, since it existed to serve the CEOs who got target letters or when one of their kids got caught drunk driving.

I thought it over. It was a natural conclusion that probably no one other than Hart and Contessa knew about the cooperation agreement.

"Paul Hart," I heard someone say. I looked at the TV to see a red Breaking News banner, which read REACTION TO HIT-AND-RUN OF PROMINENT LAWYER. A female TV reporter stood in the drizzle outside of a gray stone edifice, and I listened idly to the report.

"I'm at the War College in Carlisle to speak with Senator Mike Ricks about Center City lawyer Paul Hart, who was killed in a hit-and-run last night. Hold on, here he is now. Senator Ricks, Senator Ricks? Would you like to comment?"

"Certainly." Senator Ricks appeared with the reporter, his expression somber. He had sterling gray hair, steely wire-rimmed glasses, and plain features with a strong jawline. His bearing was erect, which I recognized as former military. "I offer my deepest condolences," said the senator, "to his lovely wife and family. I valued Paul's support, as I do every lawyer and law firm working to support my campaign."

"Have you heard from the police about any leads?"

"No." Senator Ricks addressed the camera. "If you or someone you know has any information about this tragedy, please come forward and do the right thing."

"Thank you, Senator, and for another reaction, we'll switch to Representative Barbara Caldwell, who has finished speaking at Temple University Law School. Over to you, Tom."

The screen changed and a male TV reporter appeared, standing with a tall, attractive woman with tortoiseshell glasses, her dark hair pulled back. "Representative Caldwell, do you have any comment on the death of Paul Hart last night in Center City?"

"Yes, I extend my deepest sympathies to his family and his wife. I knew Paul, not just as a loyal supporter, but also as a fellow lawyer."

"Representative Caldwell, Mr. Hart was a supporter of Democratic causes as well as Republican, and public records show that Lattimore and Finch contributed to your campaign and Senator Ricks's. Do you have any comment on that?"

Representative Caldwell smiled tightly. "If you're suggesting that bothers me, let me assure you, it doesn't."

The TV reporter nodded. "Do you feel the same way if records show that Lattimore contributed five hundred thousand dollars more to candidates from the other party?"

"Of course," Representative Caldwell shot back. "Now, I must go."

"Thank you," the reporter said, and I shifted my attention to the task at hand.

I took the cards from Junior's flower arrangements out of the box. I had numbered them according to the way I had gathered them from the display, that night on the floor of Remy's office. I picked them up and started to lay them out in order, left to right: first row, second row, third row. On each card, I had written the name of the GVO member under his alias, which I had found on the indictments.

I scanned the cards, taking mental inventory. Now I knew the GVO members and their proper names, but I didn't know what else I had, if anything. Then I looked at the cards again, flashing on the display of the floral arrangements at the funeral home. The smallest ones had been on the bottom shelf, the medium-size ones on the second shelf, and the biggest ones on the top shelf. Behind the shelves had been the massive displays on easels.

I scanned the cards again and had another thought. The arrangement of the cards could be a reflection of GVO's organizational structure. It made sense that members who earned the most bought the biggest arrangements, the middle-types bought the medium arrangements, and those on the bottom shelf were the lowest-level members of the organization.

Retail level.

I separated the cards on the last row, presumably from the retail-level dealers, and took a look at the names and aliases. I realized I had to improvise, now that Hart and Contessa were dead. I would have to penetrate GVO, directly.

I turned to the box, dug under the folder, and found my new gun, an old Rossi revolver, .38 caliber, with a brown handle and a metal barrel. It felt heavy, and its steel chilled the palm of my hand. The gun had cost three hundred dollars, and the registration number underneath the barrel had been scratched off, which made it illegal.

I turned the gun in my palm, crossing a border for the first time. I was sitting in a cheap motel room in industrial Philadelphia, contemplating going into the belly of the beast.

No more playing it safe.

I turned the gun this way and that, then aimed it at the wall. A muscle memory came back to me. I had learned how to handle a rifle, growing up. I could shoot fairly well because we used to practice on cans. If I had to shoot, I could hit something.

I sat straighter, looking down the barrel. The sight was long and notched, and I imagined pulling the trigger in self-defense, or something darker. For the first time in my life, it didn't seem impossible. I thought about Allison, but this time, instead of breaking my heart, it opened my eyes. I had to do whatever it took to get justice for her. To save my family. To free them from the program.

I set the gun on the bed and rose, thinking about my next move. I found myself walking to the window and eyeing the traffic on Delaware Avenue. My gaze found my car in the parking lot, next to a dirty white Hyundai with a Phillies decal on the bumper, peeling at the top.

I found myself looking at the decal. Underneath it looked as if there was the shadow of a dent, but it was really a dark shape where the Phillies decal had been. Random dirt stuck to the residual adhesive, like a shadow.

I thought of the dark blue BMW, with its odd vertical dent. Maybe it wasn't a dent at all. Maybe it was a red *P,* for the Phillies. I flashed on the Phillies-themed flower arrangement on the lowest level of the display. It had been red roses in a baseball vase.

I crossed to the box of cards and picked up the card with a red Phillies logo. It was signed:

Condolences, from North Philly Phil

I put two and two together. The name of the BMW driver had to be North Philly Phil. I picked up my Tracfone and scrolled quickly to the court index. Now all I had to do was search the indictments for that alias to find the real name of the defendant.

I skimmed caption after caption. It didn't

take long to find Phillip Nerone, aka "North Philly Phil." I scrolled to the White Pages and plugged in *Phillip Nerone,* but a flood of entries came up. I narrowed the search to Philadelphia and still got several screens. I skimmed them, scrolling through one page and the next, but none of the addresses was close enough to be the same Phil Nerone. I assumed he lived locally, so his address must not have been listed.

A plan began to form in my mind. I scrolled back to the court site and plugged in *George Veria.* I should be able to take the details from the indictments and use them to make maps of where GVO was doing business. It would take some doing, but it was the only lead I had.

I needed paper, a pen, and black coffee.

It was time for Plan B.

Chapter Forty-Three

I waited until after midnight to drive through New Cumberton, dismayed at how run-down the town had become. It had once been a thriving farming community, but the hay and soybean fields had been plowed under for developments. The jobs had evaporated, and it was too far to be a commuting suburb, so its future held little promise.

I figured it was as good a starting place as any to see if I could find the BMW driver, Phil Nerone. I had prepared for the trip all day, rereading every indictment, pleading, or opinion relating to GVO I could find. The most recent pleadings showed GVO had been concentrating its business in New Cumberton, and I could see why. The town was located right off of Route 202, with its own exit, so there was easy on-and-off for anybody buying drugs.

I drove quietly through the town, passing

run-down brick rowhouses with old cars parked in front. Light glowed and TVs flickered from a few of the houses, but vacant ones remained dark, like missing teeth. Porches sagged, and windows and doors were barred. Streetlights were broken, and I was guessing it was intentional. Nobody on the street wanted a spotlight.

New Cumberton's town proper was a ten-block area, its streets a grid pattern typical of the agricultural and mining towns around Philadelphia, modeled on the city itself. Townsend Street was the main drag, containing a pizza place, a Dollar Store, a tavern, a hoagie shop, and a Goodwill store. Everything but the pizza shop and the tavern was closed, and no one was on the street except on the corners, where young men hung out, laughing, smoking, and talking.

I watched cars stop on the corners, talk briefly to the young men, then cruise ahead. I no longer wondered why the drug business was booming, or why the dealers weren't put away, because I knew the answer now. I lived the answer now. The justice system was broken.

I drove down Hunter Street, scanning the men on the corner. None of them were Phil Nerone or looked familiar, so I didn't know if they weren't GVO or simply hadn't been at the funeral. I took a right onto Twenty-Seventh Street and kept driving, scanning the men selling drugs, then the faces of the drivers stopping by, just in case. No luck.

I got to the end of Twenty-Seventh and turned onto Price Street, and there was a large man on the street wearing a red Phillies ballcap, but it wasn't North Philly Phil. I knew the big man watched me as I drove past because I could see the brim of the hat following me.

I took a right onto Donegal Street, where there were fewer parked cars. A quick scan told me the BMW wasn't among them, but I had known this wouldn't be easy. Phil Nerone could be anywhere, or he might not even be on the street. I had assumed he was a low-level dealer, but I could have been wrong.

I drove ahead in the dark, my thoughts grim. I used to think that law governed us all. I had thought that justice was an ocean, and that lawlessness was only islands in the water. The exception, not the rule — like Gitmo, an island beyond the reach of courts. Now I knew better, after Allison. There were no islands of lawlessness; the lawlessness was everywhere. An ocean of lawlessness, with no island in sight, no land anywhere at all.

I kept driving in light traffic, but I didn't see Phil Nerone. I continued for almost two more hours, then started to think that I should move on to another town. I hopped onto 202 for a stretch, then hopped off and on again in Ranston, another old farming town that had seen better days. It was laid out on a similar grid, though it had a nicer residential section of brick rowhouses and a longer main drag with a Wendy's, Mexican and Thai restaurants, bars, and other small businesses, closed now.

I headed for the rougher sections of town, where the houses were run-down and vacant lots left to rubble. The pattern was depressingly familiar: men hanging on street corners, cars stopping and starting.

I gave up eyeing the men, realizing it would be easier to spot the BMW than to spot Phil Nerone. I drove past slowly, going down one street, then the next, less familiar with the grid than New Cumberton's, since I hadn't looked up the map of every town.

Two hours later, I hadn't found the BMW or Nerone, but felt only more determined. I would find Nerone if it took all night, and if I didn't find him tonight, I would try again the next night and the night after that.

I stopped at a red light on Donegal Street, trying to decide if I should move on to the next town, so preoccupied that it took me a moment to notice a man with a goatee stepping out of the shadow on the corner. Phil Nerone. I had just passed him. He was alone, and there was no one else on the sidewalk.

The light changed, and I drove forward, spotting the BMW parked on Whitman. I drove around the block, then cruised down Donegal again, making a beeline for Nerone at the corner. He was leaning into the passenger side of an old white Altima, its brake lights glowing. The streetlamps were out, and the rowhouses dark. Two were boarded up with plywood covered by graffiti. A dog was barking, the sound echoing in the still night.

I told myself to stay calm. I had rehearsed this moment in my mind. It was do or die, but I was hoping for the former. In case of the latter, I'd left some letters.

The Altima drove off, and I steered toward the curb, lowering my passenger side window. Nerone turned to face me, dark narrow eyes, longish hair, and a scraggly goatee, wearing a black hoodie with jeans.

I braked, my engine idling. Nerone started to walk to my passenger window, then slowed his step. I assumed he was being cautious because I wasn't a regular. I didn't think he recognized me, newly bald. Either way worked for me.

I gestured him forward, and Nerone came over, shoving his hands in his hoodie pockets.

"Who sent you?" he asked flatly.

"I need to see George Veria. I'm the guy he's looking for."

Nerone snorted. "Move on, buddy."

"I'm Jason Bennett. Get in your car and call Big George. Tell him I want to meet him, alone. I'll follow you wherever he chooses."

Nerone's lips parted. He wasn't used to decisions, he was used to orders. He didn't understand why I was offering myself up, and it threw him off. Surprise gave me the upper hand.

"Is this a hard one, Phil? Call Big George."

Nerone moved his hand in his pocket, presumably aiming a gun at me. "Get out of the car. You're coming with me."

"No. Don't even think about killing me. You know he'll want to do it himself." I met Nerone's nervous gaze. "Either you get in that BMW or I leave now. You wanna be the one who let me get away?"

Nerone hustled to the BMW, sliding a phone from his jeans.

CHAPTER FORTY-FOUR

I followed the BMW down 202 South, and the drive gave me time to get nervous. I glanced at the dashboard clock. It was 4:25 a.m., and I was heading for parts unknown behind a killer, going to meet an even better killer. Hard to believe this was my plan, but it was all I had.

I clenched the wheel and straightened in the seat. Drizzle misted the air, and I turned on the windshield wipers, keeping the BMW in view. There was almost no one on the highway. My tires rumbled on wet asphalt.

I ran through the possibilities, my stomach tight. All I had to do was get to Big George and tell him the truth. If he came to the meeting alone, I had a shot. If he came with Milo, it could be lethal.

We got off 202 and wound our way through the suburbs, passing Cape Cods and McMansion developments, and in time the houses began to disappear. We reached the mushroom farms, passing their characteristically long, rectangular buildings of white cinder block. Their parking lots were full because the farms operated around the clock, but there were no signs of life. I knew if I lowered the window, I would smell the stench. I didn't lower the window.

We drove deeper into the countryside, then the field opened up on a night so dark that I couldn't tell the difference between land and sky. There was no moon, no stars, and the only light was my headlamps. Flies and moths flew crazily into the jittery cones of light. A car passed us, then another, and we came to a faded sign that read VALLEY COMPOSTING.

The BMW turned right at the sign, and I followed, heading uphill toward a massive structure of gray corrugated metal, several stories tall. It had vented chimneys and a long flat roof with large security lights at the corners. The parking lot was to the right, empty except for a few cars. My stomach tightened as I wondered if any of them belonged to Big George.

The BMW accelerated into the lot, then Nerone jammed on the brakes, parking with an unnecessary screech. He jumped out of the car, brandishing a gun, which I had expected. I didn't have the upper hand anymore, but I had expected that, too.

"Get out your hands up!" Nerone shouted as I parked the car, cut the ignition, and got out, raising my hands.

"Is he here yet?"

"Shut up!" Nerone patted me down with his free hand, then lifted up my shirt.

"I'm not armed." I assumed he was looking for a wire. I had guessed they'd pat me down. My gun was in the glove box.

"Get going!" Nerone waved the gun toward a door in the corrugated façade of the composting plant.

I went that way, with him at my heels. A motion-detector light switched on, illuminating the area, and I looked around quickly, getting my bearings. On the far side of the façade was a massive garage door, wide and tall enough to admit heavy trucks. The door was rolled up halfway.

Nerone opened the entrance door. We entered a dark hallway. I felt his gun in my spine. I walked down a hallway lined with windowless doors. At the end was a door with a plastic window. Light shone through the plastic.

"Go," Nerone ordered.

I opened the door onto a massive garage with a stained concrete floor, pooling water here and there. Two dump trucks were parked in bays on the right. The room reeked of mushroom compost, the stench intensified by moisture and heat.

"Keep going."

I walked the length of the garage, past racks of heavy-duty hoses. We reached another corrugated wall with a double door. We were near the end of the building. My gut tightened. Whatever was going to happen would happen here.

"Hurry."

I opened the double door onto a huge storage area with a corrugated metal ceiling. Bags were stacked in rows on wooden pallets reaching two stories high. Overhead a row of oversize industrial fans whirred, thrumming loudly.

"Up ahead."

I kept going. The storage area felt still, so I assumed we were the first to arrive. The stacked bags ended, and I stepped into the clearing. Opposite me was another stack of bags lining a center aisle, ending in a back entrance with another windowless door.

"Stay here." Nerone slid his gun into his waistband. "They'll be here soon."

They. So Big George Veria wasn't coming alone.

I braced myself.

Chapter Forty-Five

I saw the back door opening, and a silhouette entered the storage room. It moved down the center aisle toward us.

It wasn't Big George.

It was Milo. Alone. Big George wasn't with him.

My jaw clenched. It was my worst-case scenario.

My mind raced. I realized Nerone must've called Milo, who said he would call Big George, but he must not have. I was down to Plan Z.

I hadn't seen Milo since the night he killed Allison. I met his menacing gaze with a fury that I could barely suppress. "Where's the boss?" I made myself say.

Nerone crossed to Milo. "Yeah, I thought he was coming."

"Shut up," Milo snapped, never taking his eyes from me. Nerone stepped next to him. Two against one.

Is this how I die?

"It won't work, Milo," I told him. "I took care of it already, in case you showed up alone. Tomorrow Big George will know you lied to him. You killed Junior and you're an FBI informant."

Milo blinked.

"Wait, you're a *snitch*?" Nerone's mouth dropped open. He pulled his gun from his waistband and fired — a split second after Milo pulled a gun and fired first, blasting away. Orange flames flew from the muzzles. The sound deafened me, the fusillade echoing in the space.

Milo's hand flew to his upper arm. Nerone's chest exploded in bloody shots. He crumpled to the ground.

"Help!" came a scream from behind me. I had no idea anybody was there. It must have been a security guard.

Milo swiveled his head to the sound, momentarily distracted. It was my only chance. I turned around and ran for my life.

Milo chased me, firing. A bullet whizzed past my temple. I felt the hot, percussive wave.

Someone was screaming, "Help, 911! I'm being shot at! I'm at Valley Composting!"

I burst through the door and ran down the hallway. I heard shots behind me. Milo was killing whoever was calling 911. Their frantic shouting ended in silence.

I reached the exit door and flew through. I raced to my car, jumped in, and twisted on the ignition.

Milo ran from the exit door after me, blasting away. A bullet shattered a window in my back seat.

I floored the pedal and raced downhill to the main road. Momentum sped my way. There was no time to get my gun.

Headlights appeared in my rearview mirror. Milo was chasing me in a dark SUV.

I kept the pedal to the floor. I gripped the wheel with all my might. The tires bobbled. I had to get to the main road. I was getting closer and closer. Cars traveled back and forth, then a tractor-trailer.

I reached the road. Milo fired again, gaining on me.

A passing minivan swerved crazily, and I figured Milo had hit him. The tractor-trailer going the opposite direction stopped to avoid the collision.

I zoomed onto the road, fishtailing into a left turn. The minivan trailed off into a ditch. The driver of the tractor-trailer jumped out of his cab.

Milo kept firing. The tractor-trailer driver returned fire. Traffic stopped abruptly. The gunfight played out in the headlights of the cars.

I sped away to the lethal cracking of gunshots. Cars slowed to a stop. I weaved through them and kept pressure on the pedal.

I checked the rearview mirror. Behind me was darkness. So far, no SUV headlights. I didn't know what had happened to Milo.

I raced off.

Chapter Forty-Six

I sped away, one eye on the rearview mirror. Cars appeared behind me, but none was Milo. I didn't have time to process anything. I had to get away.

There was only one road heading out, and I kept going. In time I heard sirens. Their scream grew closer. I spotted police cruisers speeding toward me in the oncoming lane, heading to the composting plant. Their light bars flashed red and white. Traffic in their lane pulled over.

I slowed with the other cars in my lane, a temporary gaper block. Three cruisers with blaring sirens flew by, spraying gravel and silt.

I picked up speed when the traffic did, then drove as fast as I could. I turned off the main road at my first chance, heading for the back roads. It was farmland again, and the houses were far from the road and dark. I was one of the few cars, and the only sound was the shaky shuddering of my own breathing.

I drove along in the dark. I tried to control my respiration. I could feel my shirt soaked from sweat. I shook as adrenaline ebbed from my system. My body was coming to understand I was still alive.

I swallowed hard, trying to get some saliva going. I blinked my eyes clear, trying to focus. The road ahead was dark and empty, a single lane weaving through the country-side. I knew I was heading west, which was as good a direction as any. I couldn't go south because that way was Delaware, and the FBI.

I tried to process what just happened. Milo had known what I was going to tell George. He wanted to kill me before I got the chance. But I had busted him in front of Nerone. Unfortunately, Nerone had paid the price.

I flashed on the horrifying scene. Like with Hart, Nerone's death gave me no comfort. I felt stunned and shaken, driving forward. I thought of the security guard at the composting plant calling 911. Milo had killed him, too. My sole consolation was that I was trying to bring it to an end. I knew what I had set in motion and I could only pray it would work. All hell had broken loose tonight, but the truth was inching to the surface.

I tried to think what Milo would do next, assuming he hadn't been killed or arrested. Soon, Big George would be hearing that Nerone had been murdered at the composting plant and wouldn't understand why. His first call would probably be to Milo, but I couldn't imagine what kind of explanation Milo would come up with. It would take some grade-A bullshit and Milo had never been to law school.

I breathed slowly, and my brain began to function. At some point, police scanners would report a gunfight at the composting plant and a description of Milo's SUV. Milo had to know that he couldn't keep a lid on his secret much longer. Something told me he wouldn't be going back to Big George. It would be too risky. Milo would have to go on the run, and I didn't know if Milo would stay in contact with the FBI as an informant or break with them, too.

I realized that Milo would still be after me. I knew the truth about him and I wasn't stopping until I told Big George. The FBI would still be looking for me, and Dom would know exactly what I was up to, after the police figured out that my car was on the scene, too. The composting plant would have cameras and there had been plenty of witnesses on the road. Sooner or later, Dom would figure out that the newly black car used to be white.

The sky began to brighten as I headed uphill, on a single lane road that cut through a field. After a terrifying night, dawn was coming. The sun had yet to show its face, but its wispy golden rays brushed the darkness away, imperceptibly, inevitably.

I felt my hopes lift, without knowing why. My lungs filled, and a peace came over me. I realized I was thinking about Lucinda.

I reached for the phone, but stopped myself. I wanted to talk to her, but it was too risky. I didn't trust the FBI not to tap our phones or bug the house. I bet that even a text could locate me.

I returned my hand to the wheel.

I didn't know what I would say to her anyway.

Chapter Forty-Seven

The sun climbed the sky as I drove west, taking the route through small towns to stay off anybody's radar. I hadn't eaten in ages, but I passed fast food restaurants that might have security cameras. Finally, I found one that catered to truckers, judging from the parking lot, and I pulled in.

I slipped on my sunglasses before I got out of the car. The diner was a long rectangle with a single door on the left, crudely recessed in a dingy white clapboard front. There was a row of small windows cluttered by advertisements for cigarettes, beer, and chewing tobacco.

I pulled open the door, greeted by the aroma of brewing coffee and frying bacon, and the place was abuzz with a nervous tension. Truckers in baseball caps and flannel tops filled the booths and counter, eating breakfast, checking their phones, and talking excitedly, as if they knew each other, which maybe they did.

I crossed to the counter and sat down on the end, next to a trucker with a thick red beard like a Viking. He had on a denim jacket and a light blue cap that read COLLINS CONSOLIDATED TRUCKING, with capital CCs in the outline of a truck. He hunched over scrambled eggs and hash potatoes I couldn't wait to order myself.

I caught a snippet of his conversation with the trucker next to him, who had an Iron Man neck tattoo.

"That dude picked the *wrong* trucker. Jaybird doesn't take any shit."

"I know that's right. The only thing that man listens to is Carol."

They burst into tense laughter.

I blinked, surprised. It sounded like they meant the gunfight with Milo. I asked the bearded trucker next to me, "What's everybody talking about?"

"Oh, it's bad news." The trucker's expression darkened. "Just happened last night. One of us almost got killed. Some asshole shot up a composting plant in Chester County like it was the Wild West."

I realized it made sense. That would be all over the news. "Oh no. How's your friend? Is he okay?"

"Yes, thank God, he only got hit in the

shoulder. He's in the hospital in stable condition. The dude also shot a young girl and her grandpa."

The minivan. "How are they?" I asked, my heart in my throat.

"In the hospital. They're stable, too." The bearded truck driver scooped a forkful of eggs into his mouth. "That asshole killed two guys."

"It's a damn crime spree," interjected the trucker with the Iron Man tattoo.

"It burns me up." The bearded trucker gulped some coffee. "Jaybird only got out of his rig to help the girl. A Good Samaritan. No good deed goes unpunished, right? He'd do anything for anybody. A gentle giant, Iraq vet, too. Last week he got out to move a turtle off the road."

The tattooed trucker interjected, "Not just any road, the *turnpike.* Got out on the PA Turnpike to save a freaking *box turtle.*"

"So what happened to the shooter? Did they get him?"

"The cops? Nah. Jaybird thinks he hit him, but that coulda been an exaggeration."

The tattooed trucker interjected again, "Ya think? Jaybird and his tall tales?"

"Linda?" The bearded trucker motioned to a waitress in her sixties, and she came over with a pot of coffee. She had a sweet smile, a round, lined face, and spiky short blond hair. She poured me a cup.

"Thanks." I took a sip, and the coffee tasted terrific and hot.

"What can I bring you, sir?"

"The same thing, please." I gestured at the bearded trucker's plate.

"Sure." The waitress took off, and the bearded trucker shook his head, hunched over his eggs.

"Jaybird drives for us. We're with Collins Consolidated, outta Wilmington. We got one of the biggest private fleets in the mid-Atlantic, almost twenty-five thousand of us on the road. We'll find that asshole who shot him." The bearded trucker lifted an unruly red eyebrow. "We're on the lookout, all of us."

The tattooed trucker nodded. "You know that saying, he can run, but he can't hide? Well, he can't even run. He better *hope* the cops find him before we do. Dude's gonna get his, that's for sure. We even got a description of the car, black Lexus SUV, 2019."

"I'll keep an eye out, too," I said, sipping my coffee. I made a mental note that Milo's SUV was a Lexus. In truth, I wouldn't mind if the truckers found Milo and meted out justice, though I'd never felt that way before.

The bearded trucker called to the waitress. "Linda, where's that old TV? I want to hear if there's any news!"

"No more TV, it broke!"

"He ever gonna get a new one?"

"Not unless you give him one!"

"Damn." The bearded trucker clucked, and the tattooed trucker slipped on wire-rimmed reading glasses.

"What are you, *eighty*? You don't need to watch the TV news. Look it up on your phone."

"Screen's too small."

"I told you, get the glasses." The tattooed truck driver started scrolling on an iPhone in a heavy-duty case. "Here we go. They got an update."

"Any news about Jay?" The bearded trucker leaned over, and so did I. Heads turned in our direction, and conversations ceased. Eyes lifted from plates, and coffee cups stopped in mid-sip.

"Nothing new on Jaybird!" The tattooed trucker raised his voice to be heard. "Good news, the young girl's leaving the hospital tonight!"

A trucker called out, "Praise Jesus!"

Another called back, "Praise *Jaybird*!"

The truckers laughed grimly.

The tattooed trucker continued scrolling.

"Hold on, they ID'd the people that got killed at the plant! There were two! 'The victims have been identified as Phillip Nerone, thirty-four, of Avondale . . .' " The tattooed trucker stopped reading and scanned the crowd. "Anybody know a Phil Nerone? Kyle, you live in Honey Brook, right?"

The truckers shook their heads.

The waitress came over and set breakfast in front of me. "Here we go, sir."

"Thanks." I dug into the scrambled eggs, shoveling them into my mouth. They tasted warm, buttery, and good.

The tattooed trucker held up his phone, continuing his update to the crowd: "One more thing, they identified the other guy who got killed at the plant."

I paused, fork in hand over my hash browns. The second murder victim was probably the security guard behind the bags last night, calling 911. I shuddered at the memory. I could still hear him pleading for help, then the ringing of the gunshots, reverberating in my head.

The tattooed trucker pushed up his glasses. "Says here, 'The second victim found at the scene has been identified as Bryan Krieger, forty-one, of Brooklyn, New York.' "

Bryan Krieger? I set down my fork,

stunned. So, the desperate man calling 911 had been the citizen detective, not a security guard.

The truckers reacted.

"What's a guy from *New York* doin' down here?"

"Buyin' or sellin', take your pick!"

"Jaybird gets winged by a drug dealer? There's no justice, man!"

I slid out my phone, scrolled to Krieger's website, and skimmed the latest entry of his blog, posted yesterday afternoon, when I was at the motel:

> Gang, I told you last night the huge news that I saw Jason Bennett at the scene of the hit-and-run murder of Paul Hart, the big-time Philadelphia lawyer who was sleeping with Jason's wife Lucinda! I can't give you the details yet, but I'm following a major lead! Stay tuned!

I read it again, horrified. It was possible that Krieger had followed me, but I didn't know how or when he had started. He had seen me at Hart's hit-and-run, but how had he followed me thereafter?

I had no answers, only more questions. Had he seen me at Contessa's? How would he know to go there? What had he been up to? What lead was he following? And how did he get to Valley Composting last night?

I scrolled up through Bryan's website, and found the audio posted was his interview with Hart's wife Pam. I read the transcript that I had listened to earlier. I realized something I hadn't noticed before; Bryan hadn't posted the entirety of the interview, only an excerpt that began with his introduction. But the interview hadn't ended on air, a detail I'd missed before.

I listened to the audio file again, phone to my ear.

Bryan: I can see you're brutally honest —

Pam: That I am! I got honesty *and* brutality!

Bryan: I'm investigating whether your husband was having an affair with a woman named Lucinda Bennett. She's a photographer who took his photo last summer.

Pam: I don't know anybody named Lucinda, but if she had a pulse, I'm not surprised Paul's screwing her. She wasn't the first and she won't be the last! Ha! Ha! Are you trying to shock me?

It struck me that Pam Hart could've gone on to talk about other women that Hart had cheated with, possibly Contessa. If she had, then Krieger could've continued to track me, always one step behind. He could have gone to Contessa's apartment the next morning, just like I did, and he could have seen me leaving. After that, he could've followed me to the motel and waited outside until last night, when I left for New Cumberton.

I flashed on last night, driving through the run-down part of town after town. There had been traffic on all of the streets. I didn't I know what kind of car Krieger drove. He could have been following me last night, all the way to the composting plant.

I mentally retraced my steps inside the plant from when Nerone had taken me at gunpoint to the storage room where we waited for Big George. We had been there about twenty minutes, long enough for Krieger to pull into the lot, park, and sneak inside the storage room before Milo got there. Neither Nerone nor I would have heard him over the industrial fans.

I remembered Krieger's terrified shout when Milo and Nerone had started shooting, then the frantic 911 call. My heart felt heavy at yet another loss. Krieger was trying to get to the bottom of my family's disappearance, and it had led him to a horrible death.

My phone started ringing, and I scrolled to check the screen.

Unknown, it read.

But I knew who it was.

I pressed the green button to answer. “Yes?”

“This is George Veria,” said a gruff voice.

Chapter Forty-Eight

An hour later, I was sitting on the floor of an old van, with a black hood over my head and zip-ties cutting into my wrists behind my back. The floor of the van was hard, the air smelled of stale cigarettes, and the ride was bumpy. I braced my back against the side, scrambling to stay upright. Bottles rolled back and forth, clinking.

Two heavyset thugs were in the front. They'd taken my car keys, wallet, and phone. My gun was in my glove box, doing me no good. Still I told myself to stay calm. I was on my way to meet Big George Veria. I had willed this meeting to happen. Plan B was never going to be a picnic.

I had set everything in motion yesterday afternoon, as an absolute last resort. I had to get to Big George, without getting killed in the process. I had hoped to use Nerone to get to him, but that hadn't worked when Nerone had called Milo instead. I hadn't predicted how badly it would go wrong last night, but I always knew there was one simple, if insanely conventional, way to get to Big George.

By FedEx.

I wrote him a note in the motel, for early delivery at eight a.m. It read simply: *Please call me.* Then I had written my name and phone number.

And it had worked.

That is, if I lived.

I believed I had a chance of staying alive. I prayed that the murders at the composting plant would work in my favor. That was what I was telling myself, though I didn't know if everything was falling into place or falling apart. Either way, it was the only option left.

I didn't know where we were meeting or how long it would take to get there. I tried to see through the jersey weave of the hood but couldn't. I listened to the noise of the traffic like they do in the movies, but I learned nothing. There were no foghorns to suggest a river, nor were there seagulls or trains. It sounded like normal weekday traffic on a road shared by moms, accountants, sales reps, UPS, and homicidal thugs.

Our speed varied, so I couldn't tell if we were on a highway. I stopped trying to see through the hood and closed my eyes. I inhaled, calming down. I thought of how much had changed since I decided not to play it safe. I didn't feel brave, but I felt determined. I had one priority, Lucinda and Ethan. They had to be safe and they had to be free.

I thought of Allison, and for the first time the image that surfaced wasn't a heartbreakingly gruesome one. It was the Great Blue Heron that I had seen that first day, taking flight over the marsh, its beautiful wings angular and strong.

My chest felt full and tight, both at once. My heart was broken, but broken open. I hurt so much, but I *felt* so much, too. I felt *everything* more than I had before. I gave myself over — to what, I didn't know. To whatever happened next.

I was unarmed, with no way to protect myself. I was just a suburban dad who believed in the truth. I was about to see if that mattered anymore.

I turned my thoughts to what I would say when I met Big George. It would take everything I had, and everything I was, to survive. I felt strangely as if I had lived my entire life for this moment.

In time I noticed the sounds of traffic recede and I felt the van slowing, turning right, then left. I heard the faint keyboard sounds of someone texting.

I sensed we were almost there.

Life or death.

CHAPTER FORTY-NINE

The van came to a stop, and I heard the two thugs opening their doors, then slamming them, and their heavy tread on gravel as they walked around the back of the van. I heard the back door flung open, creaking at the hinge, and was yanked out by my elbow. I scrambled to get my feet under me and was pulled stumbling out of the van, then shoved forward.

My heartbeat thundered. My mouth was completely dry. I staggered a few steps, my wrists cuffed behind me. I could see sunlight through the hood. I tried to orient myself, but couldn't. There was no sound except birds chirping.

They started me walking by shoving something in my spine. A gun. The ground sloped downward, but I had no idea in what direction I was heading. I half-stumbled and half-walked downhill.

Suddenly a heavy hand gripped my shoulder, as if I were going to be held still while I was shot. I went rigid with terror. I didn't want to die. I thought of Lucinda saying that she hadn't wanted to die at the hospital. I knew exactly how she felt.

My hood flew off, and I staggered, blinking against the bright sun. I wheeled my head around, getting my bearings. I was in the woods on the bank of a running stream. Across the stream was a cabin of weathered wood with a front porch.

The thugs behind me left and went back to the van, as if dismissed, and I looked to my left to see a figure charging over a footbridge toward me.

George Veria. His silhouette was thick and wide, his build powerful. His black hair glistened darkly and his eyes were flinty slits in a fleshy face, with deep crow's feet. His eyebrows were graying, his nose bulbous, and his jowls loose. Close-up, he looked older than he had at the funeral, in a boxy black shirt with baggy jeans.

My gut clenched. I was handcuffed. I couldn't fight back. I couldn't protect myself. There was nowhere to run. I stood my ground. He advanced quickly, his bulky arms at his sides, balled into fists. He gathered momentum as he reached me, and

I could hear him panting, enraged, like an animal.

I had to talk fast. "Listen, I didn't kill your son, Milo did —"

George threw such a powerful punch that I felt every knuckle in his fist embed itself in my face. I flew sideways, knocked off-balance, barely managing to stay on my feet. I doubled over, weaving. Pain arced through my cheek, temple, and skull.

George lurched after me. He hit me with a powerful uppercut to my face. My forehead exploded in agony. I emitted a primal sound.

He grabbed my arms and hurled me to the ground. I rolled downhill, tasting dirt and grass. He charged after me. I tried to roll toward the stream. He kicked me, his heavy boot connecting with my hip.

I curled up in the fetal position, trying to protect myself. He kicked me again, grunting with effort. Pain radiated throughout my body. I folded up. I couldn't hold a single thought in my head except one.

This is how.

The realization triggered an adrenaline rush. I hadn't come this far to get kicked to death. My brain started working. So did my mouth.

"George, I didn't do it . . . Milo did it!" I

could barely talk. I had no wind left. "It's the truth! Would I come here . . . if it wasn't? I can tell you . . . I can explain —"

"Shut up!" George kicked me in the back, and I cried out, but kept talking.

"I was driving with my family . . . Milo and Junior, they pulled us out of the car, then the dog jumped on Milo . . . his gun went off and hit my daughter." I gulped, I couldn't catch my breath. "Milo killed . . . my Allison, he killed my *daughter,* he shot her, you sent him —"

"You killed Junior!" George tried to kick me, but I wriggled out of range.

"That's not true . . . Milo lied to you! I didn't fight . . . why would I, I'm just a guy, the car's insured . . . I was taking care of my daughter, she was on the street and —"

"You did it!" George tried to kick me again, but he missed, seeming to lose steam, his chest heaving with effort.

"I was trying to save my daughter. . . . We heard another shot and we saw it. . . . *Milo* shot Junior."

Suddenly George started coughing, and I shifted away, landing on the stones and silt at the edge of the water.

"He used . . . Junior's gun . . . then he drove away. Milo did it, I swear. . . . He wants to move up, he needs Junior gone . . . right?"

George doubled over, hacking from deep within his chest. He sprayed blood droplets onto the grass. The two thugs came running toward him.

"Get away!" George shouted, sputtering blood on his shirt. The thugs retreated hastily, and he wiped his mouth with a tissue he took from his pants pocket, still stooped over.

I lay on my side, in pain, but I made myself keep talking. "Milo's not returning your calls, is he? Last night I told him . . . I was getting to you today. He knows . . . I'm going to tell you the truth. He's an . . . FBI informant."

George stayed doubled over, his hands resting on his knees. His dark gaze shifted upward, boring holes into me. "How do you know?"

"I overheard it . . . it's true."

"So your family's in the program."

"Yes, but we have to get out . . . and I never did anything to you or Junior, and you have to let us be . . . let us get back to our lives." I settled in to my pain. "My wife can't take it, neither can my son. . . . We don't deserve it, any of it. We didn't even get to . . . bury my daughter."

George fell quiet. His lined face was a haggard mask of spent rage.

"You've done everything you can to me . . . to what's left of my family. I lost a daughter, you lost a son, it has to stop." I didn't know what I was saying anymore, I was throwing everything against the wall. "You have to believe me . . . it's Milo, he killed Nerone at the plant, he sent Nerone to run Hart over—"

"What about Hart?" George scowled, still doubled over.

"Nerone killed him . . . he was driving the blue BMW . . . I know Nerone killed Hart . . . I was there, I saw him run Hart over."

George's dark eyes flared briefly.

"I knew the BMW from Junior's funeral. I saw him. It was Nerone."

"You were at the cemetery? With the feds?"

"Not with them, on my own. . . . I wanted to figure out a way to get to you . . . to tell you about Milo. . . . Your guy chased me through a cornfield. He tried to run me . . . off the road."

"I don't know what you're talking about."

"You know Contessa . . . Hart's girlfriend . . . she died in her apartment. . . . They tried to make it look like a suicide."

George's fleshy lips parted, as if he hadn't known that, either. I sensed he was back on his heels, so I kept going.

"Milo killed Contessa . . . because she could prove to you he was an informant."

"No, that's not why. Something else is going on." George shook his head, and blood dripped from his lower lip. He straightened with a grunt, returning his tissue to his pocket. "I know Milo's a snitch. Whose idea do you think it was?"

"Yours?" I asked, astonished. "Milo was playing the FBI . . . for you?"

George didn't reply, but I couldn't process it fast enough, trying to refit the pieces of the puzzle, and all of a sudden, it struck me.

"Milo is playing you."

"Ya think?" George motioned me to stand. "Get up."

I tried to get my legs under me, but fell back again. George shuffled over, grabbed me by the arm. He started to hoist me up, and I finally got my feet under me, bringing me to his level, then I felt rage from deep within me.

"George, you're responsible for my daughter's murder. Milo fired the gun, but you sent him."

"No, I didn't. I didn't kill your daughter."

"I didn't kill your son." We faced each other, two grief-stricken fathers, barely able to stand. Every inch of my body was in pain, but I saw a way to get out of this alive. "George, take off these handcuffs. We need to sit down and sort this —"

"Were you an altar boy?"

"Yes, why?"

"It shows." George motioned to the thugs, and I felt panicky, so I went for broke.

"What's the point . . . of killing me? How much time . . . do you have left anyway?"

George's dark gaze shot to me. I heard the thugs coming from behind. I knew it was my last chance, so I took a flier.

"Milo killed Junior . . . because he wants your business. He knows you're dying, he's waiting you out. You just going . . . to let him take everything you worked for? I can help you . . . stop him."

"Why would you?" George asked, his eyes narrowing. He halted the thugs with a hand signal.

"You said, 'Something else . . . is going on.' If Milo's not working for you . . . he's working for somebody else. That makes him a threat to my family . . . as long as he's alive."

George lifted an eyebrow, appraising me anew. "Not such an altar boy, after all, eh?"

Chapter Fifty

The cabin walls were paneled, and the windows small, so it was dim inside. There was a living room that had a galley kitchen along the left wall with a round wooden table, and on the right, a plaid couch flanked by end tables with cheap lamps. There was no clutter, so I assumed it hadn't been used in a while. There was one bedroom and a bathroom that I had cleaned myself up in.

I sat at the kitchen table, in pain. My head throbbed. My right cheek was swollen, and there was a cut over my right eye. My side hurt every time I moved — a bruised rib or two, I figured. I had cuts and bruises on my face, but none required stitches.

George retrieved a bottle of Macallan from the cabinet, then set down two shot glasses decorated with black palm trees spelling out Montego Bay. He uncorked the whiskey bottle and filled my glass first, which I took as an apology for aggravated assault.

I downed the shot, ignoring the twinge in my shoulder. The whiskey burned, but I had no idea how much I needed the drink until it was gone.

George downed his shot, then sat down across from me. "I'll tell ya one thing. You got balls."

"You kicked the shit out of them, too."

George snorted. "You're a funny guy."

"My wife thinks so."

George poured us another shot. "I have a month, tops. It's pancreatic."

"I'm sorry," I heard myself say.

"No you're not."

"I am until you get Milo."

"Now, *that*'s funny." George smiled, then downed his second shot. "I had a good run. My wife's gone. My son, even my dog. I'm sixty-six. Nobody retires in my business. If it's cancer, you won."

This is how.

"So you believe me, that I didn't kill Junior."

"You wouldn't come if you had. I knew you were telling the truth about Milo being a snitch." George sighed, holding the shot glass between his thick thumb and forefinger. "I practically raised that boy. He worked for me a long time."

"How long?"

"Fifteen years. I took him in from his junkie mom." George shook his head, his face falling into resigned folds. "For what it's worth, I didn't send him or Junior out the night your daughter was killed. I didn't know it happened until after. I was home, puking my guts out. Nowadays that's what I do, that and go to doc appointments. MRIs, CAT scans, bloodwork. I gave up day-to-day operations a month ago. I let Junior run it with Milo."

"You make it sound like a corporation."

"It's a business like any other."

"It sells death and crime."

"Cigarette companies sell death. Drug companies sell rehab." George shrugged. "Anyway, I had to step off to give Junior his due. I was grooming him for the top spot, but the diagnosis sped everything up. He didn't consult with me. His mistake was he trusted Milo, too."

I believed him because it rang true. "What about the double homicide in Jennersville? You didn't know about that?"

"No."

"Why did they do it? Was it because those two guys were stealing?"

"That's what Milo told me, after. Now I

know it was a lie. He set Junior up." George shook his head. "Milo was the first one I told about my diagnosis. I didn't even tell Junior first."

I tried to get on track. "What's Milo's relationship like to Hart?"

"Hart and Milo are close. I'm close to Milo and Junior. I *was.*" George poured us another whiskey, and I could see grief ambushing him, coming for bad guys and good guys alike.

"Something must've been going on between Milo and Hart. I don't know what." I tried to think out loud. "I'm guessing if Hart has some dirty work, he gets Milo to do it."

"That could happen."

"If that's happening, Milo doesn't tell you, does he?"

"Hell, no."

"Has he ever done anything like that before?"

"Not that I know."

"So we have to wonder why would he do it now." I mulled it over. "With you getting sick, things are unstable, isn't that right?"

"Yes."

"So we focus on what Hart would want Milo to do. He's a rich preppy lawyer."

George poured me another shot, then

himself.

"Thanks." I hoisted my shot glass. "To the truth."

"Good enough." George drank, then set the glass heavily on the table.

"Here's what I figured out, with my wife. At first we thought Milo and Junior carjacked us to make it look like they needed to ditch the car after Jennersville. Then I found out she'd had an affair with Hart —"

"Whoa." George snorted. "Too much information."

"Hart sent Milo to kill me during the carjacking, so he and my wife could be together. We think Milo changed his mind and double-crossed him."

George burst into laughter that ended in a coughing fit. I rose in case he started spitting blood, but he didn't. He grabbed his tissue and held it to his mouth while his laughter subsided, then he used it to wipe his eyes. "God, you're funny. That's funny."

I sat back down. "I take it I'm wrong. How?"

"You're the one who wanted to talk." George shrugged. "So talk."

"I can't, I'm trying to understand if my theory is right. You're laughing. If you're not going to explain, then we're never going to figure out what Hart and Milo were up to."

George rolled his eyes. "Okay. Hart did not send Milo to kill you because of your *wife.* Hart doesn't love *any* woman that much. The only reason he does anything is for money or power."

"He already has both."

George smiled, amused. "Who has enough? Is there anybody with money and power who says, no, thanks, I'm good? Present company excluded."

I thought of the politicians on TV, talking about Hart. "Is that why he was political? Like with the senator? And the representative?"

George nodded. "He has his head so far up that senator's ass he'll never see daylight."

"What about that representative, the woman?"

"She's not the one he cares about, it's the senator. They know each other from school."

"Law school?"

"I think so." George snorted. "Hart will do anything for him. I think he's angling for attorney general or like that. I been with Hart when Ricks calls. He jumps."

"They know each other that well?"

"Yeah, I heard 'em once, on the phone

talkin' about the old days. Hart knows people in D.C. Once, Junior heard him talkin' about the CIA."

"The CIA? What about it?"

George shrugged. "I don't know. Something about the CIA and Gitmo."

My ears pricked up. "What about Gitmo?"

"I don't know. I remember because I thought Junior said Gizmo. Milo corrected me." George frowned. "Gitmo, Gizmo, who gives a shit? They had a good laugh at my expense."

"Was Milo at Gitmo?"

"No.

"Was Hart?"

"No, but I think the senator was."

"Ricks? Was he in the service, or a lawyer?" I had new questions. I needed my phone back. The answers could be public record.

"I don't know. I don't remember."

I tried to think back, my mind racing. There were a lot of lawyers at Gitmo during my time there. I tried to remember if the senator had been one of them, earlier in his career. "You know, I was at Gitmo, starting back in 2002, 2003, the early days after 9/11."

"The fucking terrorists. We go too easy on 'em."

"Not all of them were terrorists. The

government detained hundreds of people and sent them to Gitmo. The FBI handled the initial interrogations, but then the CIA came in, and all bets were off. They tortured those guys."

"Good." George poured another drink, but I kept talking, trying to figure it out.

"Anyway, the military started tribunals there, and they had to be transcribed. I was one of the court reporters."

"I don't know what it has to do with Milo."

"Neither do I. I'm trying to figure it out."

"Couple of my boys went to Cuba once. Said it was hot as hell."

"Did Milo go?"

"No, not Milo. He was pissed, too. He loves the beach."

I thought about Gitmo, casting about for ideas. "When I was down there, I didn't see anybody but other court reporters. We had an office to ourselves. We transcribed the audiotapes from the hearings."

George rolled his shot glass around on its bottom rim. "Hart loves that military shit. He used to call Ricks 'the general.' "

"Was he a general?"

"No, like, for a joke. But Ricks didn't like that. I got the impression he wanted to keep it quiet."

"Keep what quiet?"

"The military thing."

I didn't get it. "What candidate for president wants to play down his military service? Most of the time, they're waving the flag."

George shrugged. "Maybe it was Gitmo they kept on the down low."

"Well, if it's something to do with the detainees, they'd want to keep it *all* on the down low. None of that was good for the military, the CIA, or the CIA contractors."

"You would know, you were there." George's gaze narrowed. "What if it's about you?"

"Me?" I asked, surprised. "You think I'm the connection?"

"You thought Hart sent Milo because of your wife. What if it was because of you and Gitmo?"

I felt my mouth drop open. "Hart wants me killed because of something that happened at Gitmo?"

"Let me tell you something." George pointed a thick finger. "Hart screws women who can do for him. Like I said, money or power. His wife is rotten rich, that's why he married her."

"What about Contessa? What could she do for him?"

"She's the daughter of Penn PowerSavers.

Hart gets their legal business because of her. That's why he gave her the paralegal job. That's why he screws her."

I thought of Lucinda. "He just started seeing my wife a few months ago. She's a photographer, and they met when she took his picture."

"He called her for a *picture*?" George chuckled. "No, not Hart. He called her to get to you."

The notion flipped my thinking. "So it's not that Hart was having an affair with her, then tried to kill me. It's that he *started* the affair to get to me?"

George wagged a thick finger. "But remember he's working for the senator."

"So there must be a connection to Ricks. Something I know about Gitmo or something I have that Ricks wants."

"They could be looking for it."

"Or trying to hide it." I met George's eye. "You burned down my office. All my Gitmo files are gone."

"Shit happens." George cocked his head. "Now you mention it, it was Milo's idea."

"He could have been trying to destroy a document or get to me somehow. Maybe there's something I know, or they think I know, that they want to keep quiet."

"That's when shit happens, to cover up

for an election."

I tried to put it together. "So, Milo was working for Hart, and Hart was working for Ricks?"

George smirked. "What's the difference between a senator, a lawyer, and a career criminal?"

"Is this a joke?"

"Yeah. It's on you."

I couldn't deny it. "Here's the only problem. I don't have anything from Gitmo. They don't let you leave with anything. Everything was top secret. Classified. Every exhibit, every transcript, every photo, chart, whatever. I don't have any classified documents."

"What about unclassified?"

"Sure, but what of it?"

"Like what?"

"Administrative stuff. Schedules, travel plans, emails, correspondence. It could be something I have, but I don't know what. It was a long time ago. They're saved in the cloud, in archives." I starting thinking. "Can I have my phone back? I can access my files from anywhere."

"Everybody with the phones." George rolled his eyes. "I hate that shit."

"I can search the files on my phone."

"Not anymore. I told the boys to trash it."

"Thanks." I gave him a look. "Can I use yours?"

"It don't have Internet."

"Do you have a laptop?"

"What am I, a schoolteacher?" George snorted. "What do you think, we're gonna *work together*? What are we, the *Hardy Boys*?"

"Don't you want to know what's going on?"

"I know enough."

"So what about Milo?"

"Oh, I'll *find* him," George shot back.

"Where do you think he is?"

"Not your business."

"Do you think the FBI knows?"

"No, he's AWOL, but I know where to look. I got four guys loyal to me. Milo's got four, too."

"How will I know when you find him?" I realized we were talking about the murder of another human being. I didn't know if I had become a worse version of myself, or better.

"Oh, I'll give you a ringy-dingy." George mimicked a phone call with his hand.

I let it go. "I assume I'll find out from the FBI."

"Right, *they're* reliable. They flipped your daughter's killer. Did they ask you? Did they give a shit? Wise up, Bennett. They got their priorities, you got yours. Their priority is them. Yours is your family." George rose heavily, motioning me up. "Time to go."

I stood up. "Where are we going?"

"Not 'we.' *You.*"

I didn't like the new chill in his eye. "You're letting me go, right?"

George thought a moment. "Why not?"

Why not? I had just won a coin flip for my life.

"I'm letting you go," George repeated, musing. "Can't remember the last time I said *that.*"

I shuddered. "Look at you, goin' to heaven."

George guffawed. "Good one, altar boy!"

Chapter Fifty-One

I sat on the van floor with my back against the wall, feeling every bump on the road. It hurt if I moved to the right or left, and my skull throbbed. The thugs had handcuffed me and put the hood back on.

I was alone with my thoughts. All I had was questions. What happened in Gitmo? How was I involved? What possible document could I have that could get me killed? What was Milo after? Hart? A senator running for president?

I remembered back to the early days at Gitmo. I first went down there in the spring of 2002. The government had opened Guantánamo to high-value detainees, the so-called "worst of the worst," about seven hundred men from Afghanistan, Iraq, Pakistan, the UK, and all over. The FBI conducted the early interrogations, but then the CIA had taken over.

The government formed panels of military

judges, which began to hear proceedings regarding detainees. I transcribed the proceedings, which were endless, and none of them got anywhere near trial during my time there. The big case back then was Al Qahtani, a Saudi electrical engineer who had trained in bomb-making with Al Qaeda in Afghanistan. He was charged with terrorism and conspiracy with Osama bin Laden, Abu Zbaydah, and other higher-ups, but the trial never got underway, bogged down in endless procedural wrangling.

I racked my brain, but I couldn't see what my time at Gitmo had to do with anything. I met no lawyers or any military personnel except our handlers, and we court reporters bunked, ate, and socialized on our own. I made friends with two other court reporters, Sam Newman from Seattle and Rowena Boulton-Ramirez, out of Washington, D.C., but we didn't communicate otherwise, and I had heard they had both passed.

I felt stumped. "Hey guys, can you get me out of the hood and handcuffs? And lend me a phone? George said it was okay."

"Didn't say anything to us."

"Call him and ask him. He knows why."

"Shut up."

"He's going to be pissed. He wants answers."

I heard the faint *tick-tick-tick* of texting from the front seat, and not long after, an alert sounded.

One of the thugs said, "Okay, fine. When we pull over."

"Good, thanks."

"The boss must like you."

"How could he not?" I asked, amusing myself.

I scrolled to my Dropbox, entered my username and password, and read the phone in the moving van. All my files popped onto the screen, and I clicked to archived files, where I had saved unclassified documents from Gitmo, by year. I scrolled to the beginning of the Gitmo 2002 files and clicked.

The file was completely empty. The screen was pure white. The folder contained no files. I didn't understand. It should all be here.

I got out of 2002, went to Gitmo 2003, and clicked open. It was completely empty. I went to Gitmo 2004, and all of the files were gone. The same with 2005, 2006, and 2007. All of my documents from Gitmo had vanished.

My mouth went dry. I couldn't explain it. I hadn't checked these files in ages. I certainly hadn't deleted them. I had forgotten all about them until now.

I left the Gitmo folders and scrolled to archived Word documents from 2002 to double-check. I clicked, and a list of case names piled onto the screen. I opened one for a test, a massive pharmaceutical litigation. All of the correspondence and transcripts were there. The only archived files that had been deleted concerned Gitmo.

I went to my current files, opening them up, to triple-check. The list unrolled onto the screen, and I scrolled down to my Word documents. I opened one, and onto the screen came a transcript of a lawsuit for breach of a commercial contract.

I felt stricken. Somebody had deleted my Gitmo files. How? Why? I tried to think who had the power to do that. The FBI did, but I didn't see any connection, on the information I had. Then I remembered something George had said.

Junior heard him on the phone, talking about the CIA.

I felt my gut tighten. The CIA had the power, but I didn't know why they would want to, either. If somebody at the CIA was in my files, or going rogue, it had to be for a reason.

My mind raced. If the CIA had something

to do with this, Ricks would be a logical place to start. I left Dropbox, navigated to the Internet, and plugged in *Senator Ricks* and *Gitmo.* Instantly a list of articles came onto the screen.

I clicked the first one, which was from six months ago, in *The New York Times:*

RICKS SAYS GITMO ISSUE WAS PARTISAN EFFORT TO DISCREDIT HIM

The issue of Senator Mike Ricks's participation in the case of Rohan Doha has finally been put to rest. Mr. Ricks has repeatedly denied participation in the death of the detainee Doha on Guantánamo Bay Naval Base, which occurred in November 2003, after three days of enhanced interrogation methods. Mr. Ricks was serving as a military interrogator at the time, but records show that he was not involved in the interrogation of Doha. Exhibits from the infirmary on the base show that Mr. Ricks was admitted there for three days during that time period, for dehydration and severe intestinal flu.

Two other military interrogators, William Diebold, 24, of Phoenix, Arizona, and Martin Tornott, 25, of Paris, Texas, were convicted of dereliction of duty and assault in connection with the Doha interrogation and served time in military prison. Both Diebold and Tornott filed affidavits stating that Ricks was not involved in the interrogation and was in the infirmary.

I blinked, wondering if I had been at Gitmo then. My birthday was November 3, and I remembered that one of my birthdays I had been at Gitmo. Lucinda had been unhappy about it, but I had to go when they sent us.

I navigated out of the article and clicked the next link:

RICKS RESPONDS TO ALLEGATIONS ABOUT DOHA INTERROGATION

Senator Mike Ricks has come under fire for his alleged participation in the 2003 interrogation at Guantánamo Bay Naval Base, which resulted in the death of detainee Rohan Doha, 28, of Kabul, Afghanistan. Initially thought to be a high-value detainee, Doha was revealed to be a goatherd, having no connections to terrorism. His arrest was part of a mass roundup by Afghan authorities and tribal warlords, triggered by the U.S. government's offer of bounties for terrorists.

Mr. Ricks has stated that though he was a military interrogator at Gitmo, he was in the infirmary at Gitmo during that time. He will be releasing documents to that effect in the near future. He denied speculation that his status as the son of the late Senator Morrison Ricks afforded him special consideration.

I mulled it over, jostling in the back of the van. I didn't remember Senator Ricks at Gitmo, but it would've been unusual for me to meet him.

I scrolled down to the next article:

DETAINEE DEATH AT GITMO DISPLAYS HORROR OF SANCTIONED TORTURE

The case of Rohan Doha demonstrates what went wrong during those days when enhanced methods of interrogation were approved at Gitmo. The military interrogators trying to get information from Doha, later revealed to be an innocent goatherd, engaged in "pressure-point control tactics," mainly the common "peroneal strike," a blow to the side of the leg above the knee. Doha was subjected to leg strikes while in shackles and beaten until he lost consciousness. He was also sleep-deprived for three days, "sleep-depped" in the vernacular, and chained to the ceiling. Reportedly, Doha sustained over 100 strikes in a 24-hour period, and died from a blood clot lodged in his heart. The medical examiner specified that Doha's legs had been "pulpified." His autopsy states the method of death was homicide. More than one official spoke on background, stating that the murder of Doha was "sadistic."

I shuddered. It was coming back to me now, the fear and mourning in the wake of 9/11, the entry into Afghanistan and Iraq, the debate over whether enhanced methods of interrogation were torture, or were reliable. It was the days of Donald Rumsfeld, Jack Bauer, and the awful photos of Abu Ghraib, which took its cue from Gitmo, using the same methods.

I scrolled through the articles about Doha, getting the horrifying gist. Doha had been tortured to death in one of our darkest moments in history. It appalled me, but I didn't see what it had to do with me.

I kept going, reading the rest of the articles, and there was nothing more pertaining to Gitmo and Ricks. I searched under *Hart* and *Gitmo,* and got no results. I even searched under *John Milo* and *Gitmo,* but got no results. The only thing I knew that connected Ricks to Gitmo was the Doha interrogation.

I scrolled back to the initial article, where Ricks had produced affidavits stating that he was not involved because he was in the infirmary. The documents probably saved his presidential run. Nowadays there were precious few things that could disqualify a presidential candidate, but sadistically beating an innocent man to death was one of them.

I looked away, trying to collect my thoughts. My birthday kept sticking in my mind. It must have been the one in 2003 that I'd had at Gitmo. I scrolled to my online calendar in Dropbox, but it only went back as far as 2017. I had kept a paper Week-at-a-Glance calendar until then.

I thought back to that birthday. I remembered I had gone on a booze cruise on Guantánamo Bay to celebrate with Sam and Rowena, the two other court reporters. She brought a cake from the base, and he brought a bottle of cheap champagne.

I pictured it clearly, then remembered why. I had taken photos on a camera Lucinda had lent me. I had the film developed, but she had made a print for me as a keepsake. I had scanned and saved the photo digitally in my Gitmo archive, now deleted.

Then it struck me. I had saved a duplicate in Favorites because it was my birthday. I navigated to my photos and scrolled back to 2003, then to November. The wintry Pennsylvania thumbnails switched to the golden sun and palm trees of Cuba.

I reached November 3 and found photos from the cruise, scrolling through shots of the setting sun. I stopped at the last photo taken that night, of Sam, Rowena, and me. We were standing on a boat, smiling at the camera and toasting with plastic wineglasses. Two military escorts flanked us, since we weren't permitted to travel off-base alone, and a third had taken the picture. I didn't remember their names because we'd met them that night and hadn't seen them again.

I enlarged the photo and got my answer.

Happy Birthday to me.

CHAPTER FIFTY-TWO

I hit the road for Delaware, back in my car, my brain on fire. Now I understood why Milo tried to kill me on Coldstream Road. I had a photo of us with our military escorts, one of whom was a young Michael Ricks, who would later become a senator. The photo was taken on November 3, 2003, the day that Rohan Doha was sadistically killed during an interrogation — when Senator Ricks was claiming to have been in the infirmary.

I accelerated, heading east. My photo proved that Ricks was covering up any involvement with Doha's murder, which would torpedo his presidential run. Military interrogators worked with the CIA back then, and Ricks and his CIA buddies must have been revising the record to save Ricks's political future, getting the other interrogators to scrub Ricks's role. There was only one loose end. Me.

Ricks must have remembered my photo and gotten in touch with his old friend Paul Hart. Hart must have started the affair with Lucinda to get to the photo or find out if I remembered it, but when she broke it off, he engaged Milo to kill me. It was an open question whether Ricks knew, but I was betting he did. Milo had double-crossed them both.

I reached for my phone to call Lucinda, then realized I no longer had one. It was too risky to call her anyway. Her phone was probably tapped, whether by the FBI or CIA, I wasn't sure. The only thing I knew for certain was that a rogue CIA operator connected with Senator Ricks could still be after me. I was guessing he was the driver of the black SUV that had chased me through the cornfield. And he could even have been the old man in the cemetery.

I'll find him.

Suddenly I realized that the threat to my family didn't end with Milo. On the contrary, we were safe only if Milo was alive, so the FBI could question him and expose Ricks and the conspiracy.

My fingers tightened around the steering wheel. George would kill Milo when he found him. It was the last thing I wanted now, but I couldn't call him off. I had no way to reach him, even if he would've listened to me.

I had to get back and tell Dom everything. My family wouldn't be safe outside the program until the conspiracy had been exposed. It would end Ricks's presidential bid, and there would be one fewer criminal in Washington, D.C.

I weaved around a delivery truck and a minivan. I wondered how Lucinda would react when I told her. She had been blaming herself, but it had been my fault. My connection to Gitmo, my past on the island.

The revelation tightened my chest. I felt a wave of guilt and blinked tears away. I would spend my life trying to understand how a minor event in my past had led to the murder of my daughter.

All this time, I had been trying to decide whether I would forgive Lucinda. Now I wondered if she would forgive me. I didn't know what would happen to us. I didn't know if we would stay married. We both had choices to make.

The end of the program could be the end for us, too.

To me, it felt no-win.

I reached Delaware at the end of the day and pulled into our driveway. The front door was closed, which struck me as strange because the evening was so temperate. The van was gone, but the black Tahoe was there.

I cut the ignition and got out of the car. It was still and silent. Moonie wasn't barking. Instinctively I hurried to the house, ignoring the pain in my ribs.

"Jason!" Wiki shouted, and I looked up to see him hustling down the stairs. "Thank God you're back! I've been waiting for you! Where've you been? We've been calling and calling —"

"Wiki, what's the matter?" I asked, my heart in my throat.

Wiki hit the driveway and hustled toward me, his astonished gaze taking in my swollen cheek and the cut over my right eye. "What *happened* to you?"

"Tell you later. Where's Lucinda and Ethan? Aren't they here?"

"No." Wiki met my gaze, swallowing hard. "Milo has them. He has Dom, too."

"No!" I cried, stricken.

"Don't worry, they're alive. He wants to make a deal. Come on, I'll take you to the team." Wiki hustled to the black Tahoe, and I hurried to the passenger side, frantic.

"Go, hurry!"

CHAPTER FIFTY-THREE

Adrenaline flooded my body. My aches and pains subsided. "What happened to Lucinda and Ethan?"

"The bosses want to brief you." Wiki focused on the road. We zoomed past Thatcher's front yard. "Please don't get me in trouble. I was supposed to wait in case you showed up and —"

"Wiki, tell me!"

"But it's less than an hour away. We set up a command center, right over the border in Maryland —"

"Tell me!" I slammed the dashboard.

Wiki startled. "Jason, I'm not supposed to brief you. It's above my pay grade."

"I know why they said that! They want to break it to me that they flipped Milo! They were *working with* my daughter's killer! They knew where he was all along! He's not in Mexico, they lied to us!"

Wiki went pale. "I know, but I swear, I

didn't know they were running him until last night. Neither did Dom. They'd never tell us something like that, and we —"

"Whatever! This is damage control, all of it! Tell me what happened to my wife and son!"

"Okay, but don't tell them you already know."

"Fine, go ahead."

Wiki inhaled, his eyes on the road. "Bottom line, they're all there. Gremmie, Watanabe, and Reilly, our hostage negotiating team —"

"Negotiating for what? My wife's life? Ethan's? Dom's? What happened?"

"Okay. Lucinda sent me to the fish market last night. She wanted bay scallops, a pound. She told me, 'The sea's bigger than the bay —' "

"Right, right." I remembered with anguish.

"I know the difference between a bay and a sea scallop, though they're both bivalves. Bay scallops are native here —"

"Wiki, get to the point!"

Wiki blinked, flustered. "When I came back from the fish market, they were gone. Then Milo called."

My heart stopped. "Who did he call? Did he call you?"

"No, Gremmie, then Gremmie called me."
"When?"
"About ten minutes after I got back."
"When did this happen?"
"Before dinnertime. I left for the fish market at five-thirty. I got home at six forty-five, and they were gone. There were signs of a struggle. Dom must have put up a fight."
"How do you know? Was there blood?"
"No blood. The kitchen chair was turned over. There's more than one of them. Milo's not working alone."
"I *know* that! I could've told you that! He's working for Senator Ricks!"
"What?" Milo looked at me like I was crazy. "What are you talking about?"
"I don't have time to fill *you* in. Tell me what happened to Lucinda and Ethan."
I tried to picture the struggle. "How did they get Dom, too? Was he in the house with them?"
"We don't think so —"
"You must know! You have cameras everywhere! Where did they enter from? I know you looked at the surveillance tape!"
"They entered from the back door," Wiki admitted reluctantly. "The investigative team reviewed the tapes, and I didn't get to see —"

"How did they find us?"

"We're investigating that. I'm sorry, Jason, I know it's —"

"How many were there?"

"I think two, plus Milo. They had on ski masks. We know one was Milo because of the tattooed sleeves. He's not trying to hide. He's already negotiating. He called us right away."

I didn't get it. "So why did he wear a mask?"

"Scare tactics, we think. They carried AKs, but no shots were fired."

Oh God. I looked out the window, trying to compose myself. We were heading south past ritzy vacation houses. The sun was sinking, shooting bronze rays into the marsh, silhouetting the tall reeds and cordgrass.

"We believe they're alive and unharmed. There were no signs anyone was injured." Wiki glanced over, lips pursed. "Between us, the bosses are totally on board. They'll make the deal."

"For immunity?" I asked, anguished, but I knew the answer. I would have loathed the idea before, but no longer. "Fine with me. I just want Lucinda and Ethan back. And Dom."

"I know, we're on the same page."

"So they came in through the back door,

and Dom saw them on the monitors?"

"Yes, that's what we think. So don't worry, the negotiation team has been in this situation plenty of times. They have procedures, like any kidnapping. They're already negotiating the other terms."

"What other terms?" *Of course.* "Milo wants money, too? How much?"

Wiki gritted his teeth, his eyes pleading. "Jason, you're going to cost me my job. They didn't even tell me. I only overheard —"

"How much!"

"Twenty million, and out of the country."

"They'll give it to him, won't they? I'll give them everything I have." I thought of the smoldering ruins of the house. The business worth zero. "Anything in the bank accounts, and I can try to borrow —" I stopped when I realized. "Wait, I know what else they want. They want a photo from Gitmo."

Wiki frowned, confused. "What are you talking about?"

"They want to cover up for Ricks."

"Cover up what?"

"I'll explain later." I had a random thought. "What about Moonie?"

Wiki blinked. "Oh, Moonie."

I groaned, pained. "Oh no. What about

him? Is he hurt?"

"I don't know, I forgot about him. I think he ran away. He must have —"

"You think? Don't you know? I would've thought Ethan would've taken him."

Wiki shook his head, his eyes on the road. "I only saw part of the surveillance video. I don't remember seeing the dog. I assumed he ran away."

"Ethan loves that dog. *I* love that dog —" I looked around reflexively, as if Moonie would come running up. We were on a single-lane asphalt road, flanked by marshland. The sky was darkening fast.

"I'm sorry. I'll find the dog later. He'll probably go back to the house."

"But you've been there all day. Did you see him? Did you even try —" I didn't finish the sentence, it sounded silly. Lucinda and Ethan were more important than Moonie. Still. "I'm surprised the dog would run away. He'd be aggressive, like on Coldstream. He's even been aggressive with me."

"You can't tell what a dog will do in an emergency."

"That's true," I said, masking a newly uneasy sensation. I couldn't imagine Ethan leaving Moonie behind. Moonie wouldn't allow himself to be left behind. We were crossing a single-lane bridge over a narrow river. There was a fishing boat in the distance. Wherever we were going seemed deserted. I began to doubt Wiki was taking me to a safe house full of FBI agents.

"Sorry about Moonie. I was worried about you and everybody. I'll call animal control when we get to the house. Maybe somebody turned him in."

"Okay."

Wiki glanced at the dashboard clock. "You'll feel better when you meet the team. They're impressive."

"You're right." I pretended to ease back into the seat. "I need to calm down."

"Lucinda and Ethan are going to be okay."

"They have to be." My thoughts raced. My gun was in my car. Wiki was armed. I could see the bulge under his black polo, on his right hip. "How far away did you say we are?"

"About twenty minutes."

"Thank God." I had to do something. I tried to act natural. "Poor Lucinda. She must've been so scared. Ethan, too."

"I know. But Dom was with her. He'll take care of them."

"Will he? He messed up once already."

"He won't again."

"I guess you're right," I said, bracing myself for action.

"I know I'm right, and —" Wiki started to say, but suddenly I grabbed the steering wheel and wrenched it downward.

Steering the Tahoe off the road.

CHAPTER FIFTY-FOUR

"No!" Wiki shouted, shocked. The Tahoe swerved wildly downward into the muddy shoulder.

I reached for his gun with my left hand, a split second before he reacted the same way. His right hand clamped over my left, but I gripped the handle of the gun through his polo shirt.

The Tahoe lurched to a stop, jostling us both. I struggled to hold on to the gun. The Tahoe slid in the mud, tilting crazily to the driver's side. I fell toward Wiki, caught by my seat belt.

"Let go or I'll shoot!" I curled my index finger through the trigger guard.

"No!" Wiki shouted back. The Tahoe sunk into the muddy water at the shoreline. Frantically, Wiki unbuckled his seat belt with his left hand.

I punched him in the face. His head whipped backward. His grip on the gun released. I wrenched it from its holster and scrambled to free it from his polo shirt.

Wiki caught my hand, trying to pull it off the gun. We struggled. The Tahoe sunk deeper into the water. I held on to the gun with all my might.

Wiki hit me with a roundhouse left, connecting. My cheek exploded in pain. I squeezed the trigger involuntarily.

The gun went off. The report deafened me. Wiki yelled something I couldn't hear. Blood spurted from his upper thigh. The Tahoe halted its off-kilter descent. The engine stopped.

I scrambled out of the Tahoe, with Wiki behind. He shoved me into the mucky water, then lunged after me. He landed on me, punching me in the head. I struggled to hit him back, torqueing right and left to shake him off.

I swallowed water, gulping silt. I held my breath but couldn't much longer.

I swam for the surface, bobbing up. Wiki pushed me under. I punched him in the stomach. He doubled slightly.

I popped up, gasping, just in time to see him lunging at me. I raised my hand with the gun and brought it down on his head. Wiki landed on me, forcing me underwater.

I held my breath. I kept my arms up,

pistol-whipping him again and again. I was running out of air. I martialed my strength and fought back. I tried not to panic. I felt Wiki let go.

I popped back to the surface. I coughed, gasping. Wiki slipped under the surface, his head bleeding. He began to sink, unconscious.

I grabbed him by the shirt. The deadweight carried me downward. I treaded water frantically. I looped my arm under his neck so he stayed above water.

I looked around to orient myself. The shoreline glistened darkly, thirty feet away. The Tahoe was only partially submerged.

I swam for shore, gasping for air, my heart pounding. Every few strokes I went under, weighed down by Wiki. I kept the gun out of the water. I didn't know if it worked anymore.

I paddled to the shore, whacking reeds out of my path with the gun. I found my footing, tangled in the cordgrass. I clawed my way onto the slimy mud, panting. I inhaled and exhaled, recovering my strength.

I dragged Wiki partway onto land and turned him on his side, looking for his phone. I wrenched it out of his back pocket. Blood poured from the gunshot wound. He would bleed, but not to death. I patted him down for other weapons. I didn't feel any.

I climbed beside him and smacked him. "Wiki, wake up!"

Wiki regained consciousness, groaning.

I drilled the gun into his temple. "You were taking me to Milo. You were gonna let them kill me."

"They just want you to shut up. They were gonna make a deal."

"Bullshit! They were gonna kill me."

"No, no, they would've paid —"

"What happened at the house? Where's Lucinda and Ethan? Tell me or I shoot you, I swear."

"Dom got them out. He saw them coming."

"Who? Milo?"

"Yes."

"You told him where we were!"

"I had to —"

"Bullshit!" I let it go. I didn't have time. A car could come by. "How many were there?"

"Two plus Milo."

"Who? I want names."

"Carl. David."

"CIA?"

"Carl's ex-CIA. David's GVO."

"Last names?"

"That's all I know."

"Dom saved Lucinda and Ethan?"

"Yes, he got them out —"

"Where is he?"

"We don't know. We're looking for —"

"Where's the dog?"

"I don't know. I didn't see any video —"

"Did you call Milo before we left?"

"Yes." Wiki's terrified eyes shifted to the gun. "If you kill me, they'll come looking. If I don't show —"

"I'm not gonna shoot you unless you try and stop me. Stay here." I scrambled up the muddy marsh and ran to the Tahoe. I jumped in the driver's seat and started the ignition, but the big engine wouldn't turn over. The Tahoe didn't move.

Wiki started to get up, struggling to his feet.

I twisted the ignition again and again. Finally the engine came to life. I threw the Tahoe into reverse and hit the gas. The tires skidded, spraying mud.

The Tahoe lurched backward, stuck. Mud flew everywhere.

Wiki staggered toward me, clutching his hip.

I floored the gas pedal. The Tahoe shot backward in a shower of mud and water.

I slammed the Tahoe into drive, veered around, and hit the gas going north.

I glanced in the rearview mirror, spotting Wiki on the darkening road.

Chapter Fifty-Five

I raced north, breaking Wiki's phone on the dashboard. I couldn't risk being located via GPS. I was going back the way we had come. There was only the one street and I didn't see any route sign.

I accelerated through the marsh. My grip tightened on the wheel. I tried to process what I knew. Dom had gotten Lucinda and Ethan out in time. Milo and the others didn't know where they were.

My thoughts flew. I had to get to Lucinda and Ethan. To do that, I had to find Dom. If I knew him, he would protect them with his life. I trusted him, after everything.

I considered whether he would contact the FBI higher-ups. He didn't know who he could trust. He'd worked undercover. He was used to relying on himself. I assumed he was on his own, with Lucinda and Ethan.

I thought about whether he would contact the state police, or whether I should. I doubted he would, for the same reason. The first thing the state police would do was contact the FBI.

I zoomed through the marsh. The sky darkened, blackening the pools of water flanking the road. I had no way to contact Dom. I didn't have a phone and I couldn't remember his number anyway. I doubted he left his phone still active. I assumed he was driving the van, but I didn't remember the plate number. Not that it could've helped.

All I had to do was figure out where Dom would go. I racked my brain for what I knew about him. We'd run together a handful of times. He never revealed much about himself. I knew he had a wife and kids in Villanova. I would bet that his first thought had been for their safety. He would've told them to get out of town. Otherwise they were in jeopardy, because they couldn't have been hard to find, and Milo would have used them as leverage.

I tried to think of anything he had said that could give me a clue about where he would go. I remembered something about Will Smith. Dom was West Philly born and raised. Maybe he would go back to his childhood home, but then I remembered something else.

Still, I loved that job. I felt useful.

Dom loved his Uncle Tig, who had owned a check-cashing agency. It seemed like a thought that had come to him during the run. The kind of detail he might not have mentioned otherwise. It was possible that the FBI didn't know about that, or if they did, it was buried in some personnel file.

I wished I could look up the address but I didn't have a phone. Then I remembered. Dom had mentioned the address.

Gibbons and Masterman.

I felt myself rally. Maybe Dom had gone back to West Philly. Maybe the check-cashing agency was still there. Maybe he would remember that he had told me about it. He could be hoping I would remember and know where to find them.

I straightened, filled with new purpose. I turned onto the street that led to the houses, and took a right, avoiding our street, just in case. I kept driving past the ritzy vacation houses. I was finally leaving the marsh. I knew where I was going.

I could see smaller houses up ahead and beyond was civilization. I lowered the window. The wind blew from the right. The bay beach was east. If I stayed straight, I would find the main road into town.

I found the road and approached town

proper, but I could see cars slowing down ahead. It must've been an accident. I looked around for other routes, but I remembered there was only one way to the main road.

My chest tightened, thinking of Lucinda. How horrible it must have been for her, how terrified she must've been. I wondered if she had recognized Milo's tattooed sleeves. We had never really talked about Milo. There were so many things we never talked about. I never once thought they would be in danger. I thought they were safe in the program.

I fed the car some gas, then had to brake again. Ethan must've been scared out of his mind. He would've remembered Milo. He would've thought he was going to die.

I accelerated, then stopped again. I couldn't lose them, and nothing could happen to them. I glanced at the dashboard clock. I'd been stopped for fifteen minutes.

I tried to calm down, impatient.

I was losing my head start. I cursed, realizing that sooner or later Milo would come after me. I wouldn't be hard to find, on the one route. I didn't know how long it would take to clear the accident.

I switched on the radio to hear what was going on. A commercial came on for beer, then a weight-loss drug. Cars were beginning to pile up behind me. I scanned the row for a vehicle that Milo could be driving, like a black SUV. I didn't see one.

Suddenly my ears pricked up at something on the radio. "Police are on the lookout for a Jason Bennett, a Caucasian male in his forties, height six three, average weight. He is believed to be armed and dangerous. He was last seen driving a black Tahoe, model year 2020."

Me? I turned up the volume, appalled.

"Police believe Bennett may be responsible for the fatal shooting of an unidentified man found in the shallows under the Lenape River bridge. Local fishermen reportedly saw the vehicle stopped on the bridge. Police have established roadblocks on routes in and out of the marshland —"

Oh my God. It wasn't an accident. It was a roadblock, looking for me.

The report ended, and I lowered the radio. I was guessing the unidentified man was Wiki. He had been alive when I left him and I hadn't stopped on the bridge.

I shuddered. Milo must've killed Wiki, taken his body back to the bridge, and dropped him over the side. There had been a fishing boat in the river. Maybe the fisherman called the cops or Milo did anonymously, identifying the Tahoe.

I straightened to see the roadblock, but it was too far ahead. I had to get rid of the Tahoe.

I looked around wildly. Darkness was falling fast. Nobody was out. There were small houses on either side of the street, on the way into town. Only a random few looked occupied, with cars parked out front or in driveways.

I looked ahead at the line of traffic.

And something caught my eye.

CHAPTER FIFTY-SIX

I pulled over to the closest house and parked in front. I hopped out of the Tahoe and walked down the sidewalk. I kept my head down, hiding my bruises. I brushed mud from my arms. My wet pants clung to my legs.

I hurried along the sidewalk, passing one, two, then finally three cars until I reached a long container truck that read COLLINS CONSOLIDATED, with the large CC logo inside the truck outline. I hustled into the street, crossed in front of the rattling truck grille, and waved to get the driver's attention. I spotted a return wave but couldn't see the trucker through the windshield glare.

I hurried around the driver's side to find a skinny, middle-aged woman with bright blue eyes, long hot-pink hair, and a friendly smile that faded when she gave me a once-over. I said to her, "Excuse me, my name is Jason Bennett —"

"You need to step away, sir." The trucker eyed me hard, and a tan Chihuahua popped into view and started barking. "Quiet!" the trucker snapped at the Chihuahua, and the little dog quieted instantly.

"I know this sounds crazy, but I'm trying to get away from a man named John Milo, who shot Jaybird, one of your fellow drivers. Do you know Jaybird?"

"What? Hold on a sec." The trucker lowered an audiobook that had been playing in the background. She had on a pink T-shirt and jeans. The Chihuahua sat in her lap, his eyes round as black marbles. "Now, did you say Jaybird?"

"Yes, do you know Jaybird? Did you know he was shot? He's in the hospital. It happened last night, outside of Avondale, Pennsylvania. I was at a diner with two other Collins truckers, one had a red beard like a Viking and the other had an Iron Man tattoo on his neck."

"You mean Tony?" The trucker broke into a smile, her forehead relaxing. "You know him?"

"Yes, I know Tony!"

"What did you say your name was?"

I repeated it. "And you are?"

"Flossie Bergstrom."

"Flossie, please call Tony. He'll vouch for

me. We talked at breakfast." I checked the line of cars behind us, which was lengthening. Somebody honked. "Please, I need a ride to Philly."

Flossie paused. "I don't take riders."

"Couldn't you, this one time? For Tony? For Jaybird? I can explain."

Flossie blinked, thinking it over. "You like dogs?"

"Love 'em!" I answered, my heart lifting.

Inside the cab was comfy, with tan cushioned seats. The steering wheel was of polished wood, and the dashboard had a touchscreen next to a bewildering series of gauges. Atop the dash was an E-ZPass transponder and a radar detector, with a CB radio mounted at the ceiling, its microphone in a holster.

But now that I had a higher vantage point, I could see we were closer to the roadblock than I'd thought. I felt a bolt of alarm. Six Delaware State Police cruisers were parked on the shoulder, their rooftop light bars flashing silently. Three teams of two troopers stopped each car and talked to its driver in a smoothly coordinated operation. I would have to explain to Flossie quickly.

"Your dogs are so well-behaved," I said, trying to break the ice. It turned out Flossie had three Chihuahuas; one in her lap, one in the driver's seat next to her, and one sitting neatly on the console. The one on the console was missing an eye, his right lid sewn shut. The dogs sat preternaturally calm, their gazes fixed on me with an intelligent curiosity.

"They're rig dogs. They know how to act. Manny is my baby, and that one's Moe and the one-eyed one is Jack. They're good company."

"I didn't know you could drive around with pets."

"Nobody tells me what to do." Flossie petted Manny's smooth head. "Now, what's going on, Jason?"

"I'm trying to get away from a man named John Milo, who shot Jaybird. Milo wants to kill me."

"Why don't you call the police?"

I hesitated, unsure how much to tell her. "I can't trust them, and the lives of my wife and son are on the line. They're in hiding, and I have to get them before Milo does."

Flossie recoiled. "You mean this Milo guy wants to kill your wife and kid?"

"Or kidnap them, to use them as leverage against me."

"Why?"

"To keep me quiet about what I know."

Flossie's expression fell into deep lines. "I got a feeling I don't want to know what you know."

"You don't." I checked the roadblock. One of the troopers was motioning the line forward. I was running out of time. "Please get me through this roadblock. You can drop me off right after, anywhere. They're looking for me."

Flossie grimaced. "This is for *you*?"

"Yes. They think I killed somebody, but Milo framed me for it."

"Dude, you're *a lot.*"

"Tell me about it." I tried to smile, but it came out shakier than I hoped.

"You okay?" Flossie softened, cocking her head, and I didn't know how to answer.

"Will you just hide me, please? I'm begging you. Call Tony. He'll remember me. We talked at the diner."

"I don't have his cell."

"What about the CB?" I gestured to the CB radio.

"The range is only ten miles. Tony drives the middle of the state. I won't get an answer fast enough. There's an app, but I'm old school."

"Then please, trust me. Get me through this roadblock."

Flossie thought it over, patting Manny.

"How are you going to get to Philly?"

"I'll figure it out."

"That where your wife and kid is?"

"I think so."

Flossie hesitated, her gaze searching mine.

"Please, help me. I swear, I'm just a dad, trying to keep my family alive."

Flossie gestured behind her. "Okay, get in back. You'll see my bed. Keep quiet."

"Thank you." I scrambled between the seats and climbed into the back, which was roomy enough for a single mattress with flowered sheets, a pink coverlet, and two pillows. At the head and foot of the bed were cubbyholes that held a laptop, a row of paperback books, and a phone charger. A second bed, also cushioned, was folded flush with the back wall.

Flossie put the truck into gear, and I got under the covers and pulled them over my head. We lurched forward, the massive engine rumbling loudly. In the next minute, I felt little footsteps walking on my arm and opened the covers.

Jack slipped under the coverlet, made a circle, and curled up next to my body, placing one paw over the other daintily. I didn't know what to do but cuddle the dog, which soothed my nerves.

The truck stopped, its brakes squeaking. I

heard troopers talking outside. Flossie gave the truck gas, then braked.

We were getting closer. The troopers sounded louder, but I couldn't make out what they were saying. We inched forward, stop and go. I tried to stay calm. It felt like forever.

Finally I heard a trooper say, "Hello, Miss, how are you doing today?"

CHAPTER FIFTY-SEVEN

"I'm just fine, Trooper Davis," Flossie said, and Manny began to bark. "Please don't get too close. He's not friendly."

"Attack Chihuahua, eh?"

"For real, yes." Flossie snorted. Manny kept barking. I noticed she didn't tell him to hush. I tried to listen.

"License and registration, please."

"Here we go. What seems to be the problem?"

"This you? Flossie Bergstrom?"

"Yes, sir."

"Here we go, Miss. You may take this back."

"Thank you. So what's going on?"

"We're looking for a Caucasian male. He looks like this. Have you seen him?" I heard a paper rustle.

"Wow. Is he single?"

The trooper chuckled. "He was last seen driving a black Tahoe, 2020. You see a vehicle fitting that description?"

"Only about a hundred a day." Flossie snorted. Manny barked louder.

"If you see one with this man driving or otherwise behaving in a suspicious manner, please call 911 or the tipline on this sheet."

"Will do."

"Do not approach him. He's armed and dangerous."

"Trooper Davis, please back up. He bites."

"How many dogs you got?"

"Three."

"I only see two."

I gulped.

Flossie said quickly, "Third one's in the back. He's blind."

"Quite an animal lover, eh?"

"They're the only people worth knowing."

"Thank you, Miss. Move along."

"Jason, the coast is clear," Flossie called back, and I took off the covers, brushed mud from the damp sheets, and climbed into the passenger seat with Jack. The little dog resettled into my lap, crossing his paws with their cute brown toenails.

"I can't thank you enough."

"It's okay."

"Sorry about your sheets."

"Don't worry about it." Flossie handed

me the flyer, her expression grave. "I gather this is the Before picture."

I took the flyer, which read HOMICIDE SUSPECT at the top, above HAVE YOU SEEN THIS MAN? Underneath was a photo of me from my website, as if from another life. I was beaming, with a full head of hair, proud and happy in my best gray suit and silk tie, standing in my gorgeous new conference room. The caption was my name and birth date. I didn't have to remind myself who took the photo. Lucinda.

My gaze dropped to the text:

Delaware State police are seeking the public's assistance in locating Jason Bennett, a Caucasian male, age 47, 6'3", medium build, a resident of Chester County, Pennsylvania. Bennett is sought for questioning regarding the intentional murder of a man in Lenape, Delaware. The victim has not been identified, pending notification of next of kin.

Bennett is considered armed and dangerous. He is believed to be in the vicinity and has known connections in southeastern Pennsylvania. Anyone with information regarding Jason Bennett or this incident is asked to contact the Delaware State Police at our tipline. All calls will remain confidential. Anonymous tips can be sent by texting the word *TIP* to . . .

I felt stricken. I had gone from court reporter to Caucasian male.

Flossie said quietly, “They’re talking murder.”

“I swear I didn’t do it,” I said, sick at heart. The big truck rumbled at speed.

“I believe you. I’m a good judge of character. So’s Jack.” Flossie glanced over with a pained smile. “My husband John passed two years ago, throat cancer.”

“I’m sorry.” I thought again about telling her about Allison, but I couldn’t bring myself to say the words.

“Thank you. He used to say, ‘I know the secret to a happy marriage. Die two years after your wedding.’ ”

I laughed. “I’m sorry,” I said again. I could feel my chest tightening, thinking of Lucinda, then Allison. It was strange, driving down the road with a perfect stranger, who was as heartbroken as I was.

“I just keep goin’.” Flossie kept her eyes on the road. “I drive three hundred, four hundred miles a clip. I just go on. I have a good life, a heart full of memories. I was lucky, I got a good man. Third strike, but I got a good hit.” Flossie glanced over. “Jack was my husband's dog."

"Really." I held the little dog, warm and sleeping on my lap, his tiny jawline resting on my index finger.

"He's ten, my old man, and I don't know how much longer he has. I'm happy every morning he wakes up."

"I get that," I said, but it sounded like pre-grief. I wanted to tell her that there was enough grief in the world, not to anticipate it, but she knew that already. "We have a little white mutt, but I'm worried he ran away when this all went down. My son named him Moonie. He's crazy about that dog. It's a small town, I'm hoping he couldn't have gone far."

Flossie looked over. "Where in Philly are you heading?"

"West Philly."

"I can get you within striking distance."

"Thank you, I'd really appreciate that," I said, grateful. "Can I ask you another favor? Can I borrow your phone? I need to find the guy who's with my wife and son. He's protecting them."

"Okay." Flossie handed over an iPhone with a home screen photo of a gaunt man with a warm smile.

"John?"

"Yes."

"He seems nice."

Flossie smiled, nodding. "Genuine. That was him to a tee."

I went online, plugged in *check-cashing* and *Gibbons and Masterman,* but got no results. I set my location as Gibbons and Masterman and searched *check-cashing agencies near me.* None appeared. I went to Street View and scanned the street corner in West Philly, but didn't see a check-cashing agency.

I tried Tig Kingston in Philadelphia and got a slew of Kingston entries. I scrolled down but none had the first name Tig or anything that Tig could be a nickname for. If Tig was an uncle, it was possible he didn't share the last name Kingston.

I thought of another tack. I had to bet Dom would tell his wife where he was. I scrolled to the White Pages and searched *Dominic Kingston* and *Villanova, Pennsylvania.* No listings came up.

Denise likes it better than undercover.

I searched under *Denise Kingston, Villanova,* but again, no luck. Then a listing at the bottom caught my eye: Denise Kingston, Rosemont College, Admissions Office. I pressed the link, then drilled down until I found the phone number and called.

"Admissions," a woman answered.

"Yes, I'd like to speak to Denise Kingston. I'm a friend of Dom's, I work with him in procurement. I'm on the road and supposed to meet him, but I misplaced my phone and I don't remember his —"

"Denise isn't in."

"Did she leave for the day?"

"No, she had to go out of town. Her sister is ill."

"Oh, I'm sorry to hear that. Thank you." I hung up, my mind racing. I realized Dom probably told Denise she was in danger, and asked her to get out of town with the kids.

I racked my brain to think of another way to find Dom, but couldn't. I tried to remember our conversations, but nothing else came to mind. I handed Flossie back her phone. "Thanks."

"You know, I got a sweatsuit that'll fit you, one of John's. I keep it for cold nights. It'll feel better than those wet clothes."

"Great, thanks."

Flossie smiled slyly. "You can have it if I can watch you change."

CHAPTER FIFTY-EIGHT

I reached West Philly well after dark, which worked for me. I hustled down Banning Avenue with my head down, wearing John's boxy jean jacket over a generic gray sweat-suit. I had on Flossie's light blue Collins Consolidated ballcap, and we had eaten Filet-O-Fish sandwiches from McDonald's, so I felt almost human again. I kept my eyes peeled for a check-cashing agency, but so far hadn't seen one.

Banning Avenue was well-lit, a main thoroughfare I had driven many times, using it as a shortcut when the Schuylkill was congested. Lining the street were a variety of shops: a nail salon, a children's shoe store, a take-out place with a sign that read SOUTHERN STYLE COOKING, an old-school barbershop, a Jamaican jerk restaurant, and a storefront church. There were families shopping, talking in groups, or heading to cars at the curb. An old-fashioned trolley rumbled past on rails, and traffic was light but steady.

I walked under a blue scaffolding and reached Gibbons Street, so I took a left. The street turned residential, lined with brick rowhouses, each with a different door, window treatment, or front porch, typical of Philly neighborhoods.

I kept going, passing houses with porches or small front yards surrounded by wrought-iron fences. Light emanated from the houses with the sound of talking, laughing, music, or TV. I approached the intersection of Gibbons and Masterman, recognizing it from Google's Street View. There was no check-cashing agency.

I scanned the corners and noticed something that I hadn't seen on Google. The rowhouse across the street had new brick in its façade, a lighter color around a small window in the center, as if a storefront had been replaced. It could have been the check-cashing agency.

I crossed to the rowhouse, and a TV set flickered behind the curtains. The front door was painted black, next to yellow mums in a concrete planter. I rang the bell, and after a moment, a young woman in a T-shirt and jeans answered the door, with a baby in diapers on her hip.

"Excuse me," I started right in. "I'm looking for a man named Tig. I think he used to have a check-cashing agency here, maybe before this was a —"

"For real?" The woman stepped back and slammed the door.

I turned away, but I'd have to start knocking on doors. I had no other options. Sooner or later, maybe somebody would remember Tig. Philly was like that, if people moved, they didn't move far.

I knocked on five more doors, then another five, zigzagging across the block in an orderly fashion and getting nowhere. I struck out at the next five houses after that, beginning to feel desperate, but I stayed the course for doors 17 and 18. No luck.

I felt my heart lift when door number 19 was opened by an older African-American woman. She had steel gray hair, and she looked at me with dark, lively eyes through her bifocals. She had a kind smile, her mouth bracketed by laugh lines. In her hand was a thick hardcover, and she had on a white sweatshirt that read SO MANY BOOKS, SO LITTLE TIME and black leggings.

I started my spiel. "Excuse me, I'm looking for someone named Tig. He used to have a check-cashing agency on the other corner, over there."

The woman's face lit up. "Oh, Tig? I know Tig."

"Yes!" I almost cried out. "I'm a friend of his nephew Dom."

"Oh, I remember Dom, from when he was a little boy."

My heart soared. "Yes, he used to work for Tig when he was younger, after school."

"Haven't seen him around lately."

"Do you know where I can find Tig?"

"No, I lost track of him." The woman frowned in thought. "What did you say your name was?"

"John Flossie," I answered, to play it safe.

"I do know somebody who's good friends with Tig."

"Can you tell me, please? Or call them? It's really important."

"Hold on." The woman nodded. "You wait right there. I'm going to make a call, and I'll be right back."

The woman's name turned out to be Mary Ward. A retired library aide, she let me into the house and showed me to a blue paisley couch to wait for one Leonard Richardson. She said it wouldn't be long, since he lived only two doors away.

I thanked her, looking around. The living room was small and cozy, lined with books on three sides, and her reading chair was catty-corner to the couch. A framed poster of Van Gogh's *Sunflowers* hung above a walnut console table that held a boxy television and an old Dell laptop, with a chair underneath.

In no time, there was a knock on the door, and Mary answered it, admitting a balding African-American man in his seventies, lanky and tall in a tan windbreaker over a T-shirt and saggy jeans. His lined face was long, his lips pursed. Milky cataracts rimmed his brown eyes, and a scar nicked his top lip.

Mary stepped aside as he entered the living room. "Leonard, this is John Flossie, and —"

"Bullshit!" Richardson pulled a gun from his pocket and aimed it at me. "On your knees! Hands up!"

CHAPTER FIFTY-NINE

"Don't shoot!" I knelt down and raised my hands.

"No games!"

"Please, I'm just trying to find —"

"Shut up!" Richardson turned to Mary. "Woman, what are you *doing* lettin' him in? Look at 'im, beat to *shit*! What were you *thinking*?"

Mary's fingers flew to her mouth. "Leonard, put that gun away!"

"I tell you all the time! You're *too damn trusting*! Don't you know who he is?"

"I was trying to tell you, his name is John Flossie."

"That's not his *real name*! Soon as you said he looked beat up, I went on the computer. He lied to you." Richardson turned to me, glaring. "You say you're a friend of Dom's? Liar! You tell her what you did!"

"I didn't do anything! I swear —"

"Mary, where's your damn computer? Oh!" Richardson crossed to the Dell, keeping the weapon trained on me.

"Mr. Richardson, I can explain everything. What happened was that —"

"I said, shut up!" Richardson hit a key. "Mary, what's your password?"

"Mary123."

"How do you even *exist in this world*?" Richardson typed it in and scrolled to Google as I watched, worrying how this was going to turn out. I couldn't have him call the cops. Then Lucinda and Ethan could be gone for good.

"Mr. Richardson, I didn't tell her my real name because —"

"You're *damn right you didn't*!" Richardson hit another key, and onto the screen popped a headline: LOCAL MAN SOUGHT FOR MURDER OF FBI AGENT, then the subhead: JASON BENNETT AT LARGE AFTER FAMILY DISAPPEARANCE. Under that was my photo from the conference room.

"Mr. Richardson, none of that is true, and I can explain if —"

"What do you think I am, *stupid*?" Richardson whirled around to me, aiming the gun at my forehead. "You're a *killer*!"

"Mr. Richardson, do you know Tig? If you do, please call him. I can tell you what to say, to verify who I am —"

"I *know* who you are! You killed a *fed*!"

"No, they framed me for that —"

"You're stone-cold *crazy*! You killed your *whole damn family* —"

Oh God. "That's not true, I'm hoping they're with Dom —"

"It says it in the *dang newspaper*!"

"They're wrong —"

"The cops say it!"

"They're wrong, too! The FBI isn't releasing the information. They can't, because of the conspiracy." I sounded crazy, even to me. "Please get me to Tig —"

"Now, why would I take a crazy-ass *killer* to one of my *oldest friends*?"

"I think he'll know how to find Dom and —"

"What you need Dom for? You gonna kill him, too?"

"No, listen, Dom doesn't work in procurement. He's an FBI agent, protecting me and my family in the witness protection program."

Richardson blinked.

"Oh my!" Mary gasped. They both looked at me, shocked. The gun didn't waver from my forehead.

"Mr. Richardson, for the love of God, please call Tig."

■ ■ ■ ■

"It's ringing." Richardson held his cell phone in his left hand and his gun in his right, trained on me. I stayed on my knees, my hands raised. I'd noticed he'd called Tig with one touch, which meant he had him in Favorites.

Richardson said into the phone, "Tig, yo, I got a White guy here, name of Jason Bennett. He killed a fed in Delaware. He's been askin' about you, tryna get to Dom."

Richardson fell abruptly silent, then his graying eyebrows lifted in surprise. "No *shit,*" he said into the phone.

A brown Honda came to pick us up, and Richardson hustled to the passenger seat and I went to the back. The Honda took off, driven by an older African-American man, his features shadowed by a red Sixers cap. A short salt-and-pepper beard covered his chin, and gold rings glinted on his fingers. He seemed short, and his black leather jacket puffed around his shoulders.

Richardson turned to me. "Get down."

I lay down in the back seat.

"By the way, this is Skeet."

"Nice to meet you, Skeet. Thanks for

the assist."

"Welcome."

I felt the car accelerate. We turned left, then right. My heart pounded with anticipation. I couldn't wait to see Lucinda and Ethan.

Richardson clucked. "Tig shoulda told us Dom was in trouble."

Skeet snorted. "It's bad, that's why. He wants us clear."

"Bullshit on that. We're here. All for one."

"One for all."

"The Black Musketeers."

"The *sexy* Musketeers."

They both laughed.

I smiled. They sounded like old friends, the ease between them palpable. "How do you guys know each other?"

"Poker buddies," Richardson answered. "Before that, we were in 'Nam together."

"Three tours," Skeet added.

Richardson shook his head. "You always gotta say that."

"So what? I *elaborate*."

Richardson chuckled, and Skeet joined him.

I started thinking up a plan. I could count on Dom, but I needed an army.

Maybe I already had one.

Chapter Sixty

"Let's go!" Richardson motioned to me, and the three of us piled out of the parked car and hurried down the street. Most of the houses had been abandoned. One had been torn down, leaving a pile of bricks, rebar, and plaster. No one was on the sidewalk. The streetlights were out. I didn't know where we were and it didn't matter. Lucinda and Ethan were here.

We hurried to a dilapidated brick rowhouse, its front window boarded up. Richardson had texted ahead, and the front door opened as soon as we hit the stoop. Richardson and Skeet hustled inside with me on their heels.

We squeezed into a dark hallway, then the front door was closed behind us. It was pitch black. I heard a dead bolt being engaged, then the rattle of a chain lock being drawn. Nobody said anything. The air felt cold. It smelled dusty.

"Follow me," a man whispered, presumably Tig. We fell into step behind his shadowy form, left the hallway, and hurried through a large, empty living room, our shoes scuffling on gritty hardwood.

A door opened to our left, and a light emanated from the doorway, illuminating Tig in profile. He looked like an older version of Dom, with a neat balding head, round dark eyes set close together, a strong mouth, and a jawline with a cleft.

"Tig?"

"Yo." Tig smiled quickly. "Go downstairs."

"Thanks." I hurried downstairs, and my heart leapt at the sight. Dom stood with a smile beside Lucinda and Ethan, who were already in motion toward me.

"Jason!" Lucinda rushed to me, her arms raised, tears in her eyes, with Ethan by her side. I swooped them both up, feeling all of my senses exploding at once, love, gratitude, fear, and relief.

I kissed Lucinda's hair and held Ethan close, his spiny back racked with sobs in his Call of Duty T-shirt. I could feel the warmth of Lucinda's skin under my palm in her sundress. We clung together, and I never wanted to let them go. My family.

"Dad!" Ethan buried himself in my side, and I released Lucinda to hug him, wiping his tears away, then looking down into his face.

"It's okay, honey, it's going to be okay now." I held him again, meeting Lucinda's eye. Uncertainty flickered behind her teary gaze, and I knew why, but I wasn't about to go there now.

"I love you," she said, with a shaky smile.

"Love you, too," I heard myself say.

"Your face is all bruised! And your hair's gone! What happened?"

"I'm fine." I waved it off, then looked at Dom, throwing open my arms and giving him a big hug. "You saved their lives!" I let him go. "Thank you!"

"That's why I make the big bucks." Dom burst into laughter, then he gestured behind me. "Jason, meet Uncle Tig."

"Tig!" I threw open my arms, but Tig raised his hands, laughing.

"I'm not a hugger."

"You are now," I said, hugging him anyway.

Dom gestured to the men. "Lucinda, Ethan, let me introduce you to Tig's friends, Leonard Richardson and Skeet Dunwoody."

"Nice to meet you." Lucinda smiled, extending a hand, and while they exchanged introductions, I looked around.

The cellar was chilly and musty. The walls

were of damp plaster painted a grimy white and falling off in clumps. The floor was concrete, though it had been swept. A makeshift kitchen had been set up on the left with an old white porcelain table and wooden stools, a dorm-size refrigerator, and a hot plate on an orange crate. A laptop powered by heavy-duty extension cords and power strips led to a fuse box. Four heavy blankets and mismatched pillows sat under the stairway, makeshift beds. It killed me to think of them, hiding here in fear.

I returned my attention to the group, still smiling from the introductions, and I watched their faces fall as they read my expression. "Guys, we have to get you out of here."

Dom nodded gravely. "That's the truth."

"Did you send your family out of town? I tried to call your wife at Rosemont, but they said she had a sick sister."

"It's a cover story. She knows the drill."

I felt relieved. "And I guess you heard about Wiki."

"Yes." Dom's eyes narrowed. "He must have been with them all along. For the record, I didn't know we were running Milo."

"I know that," I said, meaning it. "But for the record, can they flip Milo without telling us? The victim's family?"

"Yes. It happens more than they'll admit." Dom frowned. "But I can't figure out what's going on."

"I'll fill you in, but first tell me what happened at the house, when Milo and the others came. How did you get Lucinda and Ethan out?"

"I was in our apartment, keeping an eye on the monitor. I saw something funny in the woods out back and just then I got a call from Wiki. He said he was calling from the fish store and started in with his usual science class — you know, mollusks, shellfish — but he sounded nervous. I thought, 'Something's wrong.' " Dom's expression tightened, suppressing the anger he must have felt at Wiki's betrayal. "I realized he was trying to distract me from the monitor."

"So what did you do?"

"I kept on talking, I didn't want him to suspect anything. I went to the house and got Lucinda and Ethan." Dom glanced in their direction. "To their credit, they moved fast and we rolled out."

"That's amazing." I wanted to hug him again, but didn't. "I'm so grateful, Dom. Thank you."

"Hey, all I did was follow procedure."

"For once, I'm good with that." I had a nagging question. "What about Moonie?"

Dom glanced at Ethan, pursing his lips. "Sorry, he took off after a rabbit while we were leaving. We called him but he didn't come back. We had to go."

"I get it," I said, pained, but Ethan looked down. I ruffled his hair and drew him close to my side. "Don't worry, honey. We'll get him back somehow."

"You think?" Ethan looked up, hopeful.

"Bet on it," I told him, confident all out of proportion, for some reason.

Dom continued, "I brought Lucinda and Ethan here to let the dust settle. Nobody at work knows about Uncle Tig. I didn't know where you were, but I knew I'd mentioned him. I was hoping you'd remember."

"And I did." I smiled, all proud of myself. Lucinda beamed, and our eyes locked, but I looked away, at Dom. "Not just another pretty face, eh?"

"Ha! Have you *seen* a mirror?" Dom laughed, and everyone joined him, including me, then I got serious.

"We need a plan, and I think I have one."

"I have one, too."

"It might be the same one." I met his eye. We both knew what had to be done, but neither of us said anything. I didn't know how to talk about it in front of Ethan.

Tig interjected, "Dom, whatever you need, you know I'm in."

Skeet nodded. "Me, too. All for one."

Richardson smiled grimly. "One for all."

I felt touched. "So we have the Sexy Black Musketeers."

They all laughed, and Dom nodded. "Jason, you need to brief me."

"Will do, but we have to do this tonight. The shit is hitting the fan."

"O-kay!" Dom broke into a grin. "I *like* the new Jason."

"Me, too," I said, smiling back.

Lucinda looked over, but she wasn't smiling.

I didn't ask her if she liked New Jason.

I was trying not to care.

Chapter Sixty-One

We sat around the kitchen table on stools, orange crates, and the dorm-size refrigerator, and I brought everybody up to speed. I started with Hart's hit-and-run by Phil Nerone and my finding Contessa dead in her apartment, then in the composting plant when Milo killed Phil Nerone and Bryan Krieger, and finally my meeting with George, which caught Dom up short.

"You *met with* George Veria?" he asked, his lips parting in surprise.

"Yes, at his cabin." I smiled. "What, did you think I beat *myself* up?"

Dom laughed.

Lucinda recoiled and Ethan winced, but I continued.

"Anyway, I'm off the hook with him now. I convinced him it was Milo who killed Junior, not me."

Dom blinked. "And he let you walk?"

"Why not?" I said, smiling, and Dom

smiled back, so I continued my update. I told them about how George got me thinking about Gitmo, then looking through my photos and finding them deleted except for the duplicate of my birthday photo.

Lucinda interjected, "Honey, I know that photo, I remember it."

Dom looked over. "You remember a photo from 2003?"

Lucinda nodded, her expression bittersweet. "I remember he looked good, that's all. I was sorry I didn't get to spend his birthday with him."

I let the awkward moment pass and resumed my update, telling them about Senator Ricks and how the photo busted him, proving he was lying when he claimed he wasn't involved in the Doha interrogation and death. When I was finished, I met Dom's eye. "So it all goes back to my time at Gitmo."

Dom nodded, gravely. "Right."

"They want that photo and they want me."

Lucinda looked stricken, putting an arm around Ethan, who kept his head down. During my recap, I'd downplayed the violence of the past few days, but the boy wasn't stupid.

"Buddy." I reached over, touching his arm. "I know this is scary —"

Ethan looked up. "I can handle it, Dad."

"Good." I turned to Dom. "If Milo isn't going to stop until he finds me, the plan is obvious. We have to let him."

Dom nodded, tense. "Yes. We draw him out, set a trap. Obviously, not here. I know a place from my undercover days, down by the airport."

Lucinda recoiled, aghast. "Wait, what? You're going to use Jason as *bait*?"

"Not exactly," I answered, though she was right.

"Are you crazy? It's too dangerous. You'll get yourself —" Lucinda stopped, glancing sideways at Ethan. "Jason, I don't know why you have to be there. Why don't you just let Milo think you're going to be there, but stay here?"

"I want to be there. This is my fight, not theirs." I gestured to Dom and the others.

"But they're professionals!"

Tig chuckled. "I'm no professional."

Skeet grinned. "That's the truth, I've seen you shoot."

Richardson laughed. "Me, I'm *better* than a professional."

"There we go." I smiled, grateful. "Thank you, gentlemen." I remembered they were armed and turned to Dom. "I need a gun."

"No. You'll be safely out of the way."

"But you need me, and I know how to shoot. I learned, growing up."

"I don't have an extra, anyway."

Lucinda leaned to Dom, upset. "I don't know why you can't get *somebody* in the FBI to help you. They can come with a SWAT team or whatever."

Ethan interjected, "Yeah, they call for backup, even with Pablo Escobar."

Dom turned to Lucinda. "Don't misunderstand. I am going to make a call."

"To who?" I asked, confused. "I thought we were doing this on our own."

"It may end up that way, but I have a better plan. We can't wait for Milo to find us, and I can't access files about confidential informants, so I don't know how to reach him."

"I assumed you could, somehow."

"No, but this is better. I'm going to call Reilly and say you haven't turned up. Play dumb, act like I don't know Wiki flipped." As he spoke, Dom's gaze was intense. "I'll tell him I have your family. I'll say I heard on the news that Wiki was dead and I think Milo must have killed him."

I followed his logic, watching Dom grow more animated, as if his undercover days were coming back to him. If I was New Jason, he was Old Dom.

"I'm going to tell him that I have your family by the airport, not here. Then we see what happens." Dom spread his hands, opening his palms. "If Reilly is clean, he'll show up, we'll have backup, and we'll find another way to lure Milo. If Reilly is dirty, then he'll call Milo and Milo will show up."

"You're going to call him right now?"

"No. We'll call him from there. I don't want GPS to give away this location."

Still upset, Lucinda asked, "Why don't you call the Philly cops? Have them in place?"

"The locals will never do that without contacting the FBI. They'll bust us."

Dom paused. "I figure Milo will come with three guys."

I thought back to my conversation at the cabin. "George thinks four of his guys are with him."

"Okay, four." Dom didn't miss a beat. "He'll come to use your family for a bargaining chip. He'll want to use them to draw you out."

"I get it." It was a great plan. "We're flipping the script."

"Exactly. We win either way. If Milo shows up, we take him down and contact the Philly cops."

"Yes, and I'll testify against him. But

Dom, we're not going back to square one. We busted the conspiracy, so there's no reason for witness protection. Agreed?"

Ethan turned to Dom expectantly.

Dom hesitated, then a smile spread slowly across his face. "Right. If it works, you're free."

"Done." My gaze found Ethan's, and I winked. He winked back.

Lucinda only frowned.

After Dom and the others had gone upstairs, I lingered to say goodbye to Lucinda and Ethan. I hugged Ethan, who still felt too thin. If I needed a reminder of why I was going, it was in my arms. "I love you."

"I love you, too."

"See you later."

"You said that before, remember?" Ethan's young face was drawn, exhausted, and scared.

"Yes, and I came back. So count on it. When this is over, we'll go get Moonie." I touched his cheek. "Now, go sit at the table while I talk to Mom, okay?"

"Okay." Ethan walked away, and Lucinda stepped forward, taking my arm.

"Jason, you can't do this." Her eyes were wide with fear, and her fair skin mottled. "This is *crazy.*"

"No, it's not. There's no other way. I haven't come this far to quit now."

"It's too dangerous."

"I'll be fine. You heard the plan."

"Stop calling it a plan, it's not a plan. It's practically suicide."

"Shh." I glanced across the room at Ethan.

"Jason, this isn't happening because of Gitmo. Like you said, Gitmo is only the 'but for.' "

"It *is* because of Gitmo. 'But for' is lawyer bullshit. I got you and Ethan into this mess and I'm going to get you out."

Lucinda frowned, agonized. "You don't have to be a hero."

"I'm not trying to be a hero, I'm trying to solve a problem." I felt the truth of my words as they left my lips. Maybe a hero was just a guy who solved a problem. A regular dad, trying to fix things for his family. I fixed the water leak, I fixed the plaster. Mr. Fixit, writ large.

"Honey, please —"

"I don't have time to argue. They're waiting." I nodded toward Ethan. "You're making him worry."

Tears filled Lucinda's beautiful eyes. "I love you."

"I love you, too."

"You'd better come back to me." Lucinda

kissed me, with more feeling than she had in years.

"Wow," I said, when she let me go.

It was all I could say.

Chapter Sixty-Two

We drove together in the white van that had first taken us to the house in Delaware, and I felt we had come full circle. We started our nightmare on Coldstream Road and we were going to end it, one way or another, tonight.

We were rumbling around the ragged back of the Philly airport, situated at the southeast end of the city, on the industrial banks of the Delaware. We were one of the few cars on a service road used by UPS, FedEx, and container trucks going to and from the cargo depots. We rode in silence past crane and rigging facilities, empty parking lots for corporate jets, a sheet-metal fabricator, and truck and equipment warehouses.

Dom drove, I was in the passenger seat, and Tig, Skeet, and Richardson were in the back seat. Richardson nodded off, snoring softly, and nobody woke him. I marveled at their calm, wondering if it had been seasoned in Vietnam. I had never been in a war, but I knew what heroes were. They were heroes.

Dom didn't say much either, but I could read his demeanor. He perched at the edge of the seat, driving inclined over the wheel. His gaze swept the surroundings, but his sight kept returning to the middle distance, maybe even turning inward, into his own past. He knew this dark and dirty terrain, and he emanated excitement like a steady electrical thrumming, as if he were a powerful, professional, machine.

I was in good hands.

I had to pray that was enough.

I wanted all of us to get out of this alive.

We reached a faded sign that read ROPER CRANE & RIGGING and pulled into a large, empty parking lot surrounding a corrugated metal building, about three stories tall. We drove past the building, took a right, and parked in front of a massive crane, which was even taller than the building. Its cab was almost a story high, the undercarriage five feet tall, and its tracks about twenty-five feet long. Black-tarped scaffolding encased the crane, its fabric tattered and torn. An American flag flapped at the top, fraying.

"Everybody out of the pool." Dom cut the

engine. "Tig, the toolbox."

"Okay," Tig answered, and we piled out of the van. No motion-detector lights went on, and Dom left the van doors open for light.

I looked around, orienting myself. The entrance to the building was across from us, a double door chained with padlocks. Above, at the upper reaches of the building, was a skinny catwalk that extended the length of the front and near side, with a series of doors and broken windows.

Otherwise the area was dark and deserted, with no ambient light from the businesses, since they were too far away. Thick clouds covered the sky, a darkly orange haze from the refineries, their stacks billowing ghostly white. The wind carried their chemical odor, overpowering the briny smells off the water. There was no sound, and the stillness felt settled in, as if the property had been abandoned for years.

"What you guys think?" Dom asked, his hands on his hips.

Tig nodded, setting down the toolbox. "It's good."

I turned to Dom. "What's the deal with this place? This real estate has to be valuable. Who can afford to abandon it?"

"It's in bankruptcy litigation. I used it back in the day and followed it since then in the paper." Dom pointed up at the catwalk. "Those are the offices. That's where you watch from, Jason."

"Thanks," I said, my emotions mixed. "You sure I can't help?"

"You'll help by staying out of the way."

Richardson turned to Dom. "How long will it take until Reilly, or whoever, gets here?"

"Two and a half, three hours."

"So we got time." Richardson shrugged. "Maybe we'll play a hand. Anybody bring cards?"

They all laughed, and Tig opened the toolbox with a soft grunt, took out flashlights, and gave them to Richardson and Skeet. He tucked a bolt cutter under his arm, then closed the box and straightened up. "Okay, time to make the donuts."

Richardson turned his flashlight on the building, running a jittery circle of light over rust and grime on the weathered metal. "Hope there's no rats. I don't mind mice, but rats, no. Can't take 'em."

"I'm with you." Skeet shuddered, his gold earring glinting. "I'll take mice any day of the week. I tell my wife, they're Mickey Mouse, only no pants."

Tig chuckled. "I'm sure there's no rats. No mice neither. Prolly fresh and clean inside like the Ritz."

Richardson snorted. "Who you kidding? You never been to the Ritz."

"Have so," Tig shot back. "Had drinks there, many times."

"You didn't *stay* there."

"Why would I? I got a house." Tig clucked. "If I hadda stay there, I could stay there. What're you saying? I'm a piker?" The three men walked to the entrance, their voices receding.

Dom slid a flip phone from his pocket. "I'm gonna call Reilly."

"Should I go with them, or stay here, in case you need me?"

"Stick around." Dom flipped open the phone, its faint orange screen shadowing his smile. "You can hear what a good liar I am."

Chapter Sixty-Three

I sat next to Dom on the floor of the office, our backs against the wall of corrugated metal. The office was one of a row of offices on a cantilevered balcony of concrete, which was accessed by a long, rickety metal stairway. The space below was empty, but I assumed it had once held heavy equipment. The air smelled of dust, dirt, and dead mice. We'd heard telltale scuffling, but nobody wanted to know if they were rats or mice. I was guessing both.

We had been over and over the plan, discussing every particular, and there was nothing to do but wait in the dark. Tig, Richardson, and Skeet sat catty-corner to us, having dozed off. Dom rested with his eyes closed, but I knew he wasn't sleeping. I left him to his own thoughts. Planes flew overhead intermittently, some closer than others, and one rattled the walls.

All I could think of was Lucinda, Allison,

and Ethan. I tamped down any emotion that popped up, threatening to sidetrack my focus. I tried not to think about Hart, either. Or Contessa or Nerone. The face that kept coming to mind was Milo's, his glittering eyes surfacing from my subconscious. I shifted position, unable to get comfortable.

"Jason, you okay?" Dom asked quietly.

"Yes. How about you?"

"Fine. Don't worry, we got this."

"I don't want anybody to get hurt."

Dom smiled. "We won't. They might."

I couldn't find a smile. "You think Reilly is dirty?"

"Yes."

My gut clenched. I had been holding out hope the good guys were coming. "Why?"

"Little things, thinking back. Like, he wanted Wiki to partner with me on this job."

"I thought Wiki was your partner."

"No, we switch around for each job. I've worked with a couple guys. This time Reilly wanted me to take Wiki. Said he was young, that I could bring him along, all that." Dom shook his head. "He talked to my ego, and it worked. Anyway. What's done is done. Milo and his crew's on the way."

"And the plan is —"

"Your plan is you stay here. Right in this office."

"I really can't help?"

"Absolutely not."

"Dom, I really think you should reconsider."

"No."

We both fell quiet, tacitly agreeing to disagree. I reviewed the plan in my mind. Everyone but me was supposed to take their positions twenty minutes before the expected arrival of Milo and his gang. Tig, Richardson, and Skeet were to wait behind the crane while Dom flagged Milo down. Then on his signal, they were all to rush the car. I was supposed to wait up here and call 911 in case it went south. They had guns; I had Dom's flip phone.

Dom looked over. "By the way, I want to tell you, I got to know Lucinda. We had some good talks. She told me what happened between you two."

I felt my cheeks warm. "So you know she cheated? Did Ethan hear?"

"No, he was asleep."

I breathed a relieved sigh. I didn't know why it mattered. I didn't know what mattered and what didn't anymore.

"I gotta say —" Dom shook his head. "I like her. I admit, I didn't in the beginning, but I like her now. She didn't like me in the beginning, either. She told me so. Not that she had to." He paused. "I'm not getting in the middle between you two, I'm just saying. Things happen."

My mouth tasted bitter. "She cheated on me with an asshole."

"It happens, even in a good marriage." Dom's tone softened, which struck me.

"Your wife cheated, too?"

"No, I did." Dom looked over, and though I couldn't see his features, I could feel his gaze take on a new weight.

"Really." I didn't know what else to say. I was surprised. He seemed like such a straight arrow.

"I screwed up, after my partner got killed. That's no excuse, I know it. I lost my way. I wish I could say it was only one woman, but it wasn't." Dom sighed. "But one day we talked, and I came clean. We went to counseling, the whole nine. The thing is, she forgave me. Now it's behind us, and I'm grateful to her, every day."

"I don't know if I can forgive Lucinda. I don't know how you get past that."

"That's your pride talking."

"Fair enough. My pride has a say."

"Okay, tell you what I learned from an applicant. The man was a stone-cold killer. Gangster of the highest order. I was best man at his wedding."

I smiled, intrigued. "Wiki told me that. It was true?"

"Yes. Now, this applicant was no sage philosopher. But I never forgot something he told me. He said, 'Decide what you want and do what gets it.' " Dom nodded. "Nothing else matters. No rules, no laws. Not what you *should* want. Not being right. Not your pride."

I thought a minute. "That's sociopathic."

Dom chuckled. "In the wrong hands, maybe. I take the truth where I find it, regardless of the wrapper. It's not always easy to tell the good guys from the bad guys."

"Agree. We're living that."

"So here's what, with Lucinda. Decide what you want. Decide what matters to you the most. Your pride — or your family."

"It's not that simple."

"Then it's not, for you." Dom shrugged. "But I see what you went through for Lucinda and Ethan. You risked your life. Hell, you're risking your life tonight. If you forgive her, you get your family back."

I couldn't reply.

"She'll never forget it, ever. In here, I *never* did." Dom pointed to his chest. "And I never will."

We both looked over when Tig clucked

under his breath. "Dom?" he said, his tone incredulous. "You really believe that shit?"

Dom laughed. "I thought you were asleep."

"No, I was just restin' my eyes."

"Me, too," said Richardson.

"I heard every word," added Skeet.

Dom laughed again, and so did I.

"Excellent," I said, embarrassed. "To review, my wife cheated on me."

"So what?" Tig shot back. "Jason. Do you love the woman, yes or no?"

I flashed on that kiss. *Wow.* "Yes."

"Then you forgive her. That's what love is. Forgiveness. Judgment belongs to God Almighty. Not you."

Dom chuckled. "Okay, that works, too."

"Amen," said Richardson.

"Boom-shaka-laka!" added Skeet.

Only fifteen minutes later, we were on our feet. It was go-time. Without another word, Dom, Skeet, and Richardson started downstairs to take their positions.

Tig lingered behind, rubbing his knee. "Dom," he called down, "I'll be right there. My knee's actin' up. All that sittin'."

"Okay," Dom called back, heading downstairs, and Tig bent over the toolbox, took something out, and crossed to me.

"Jason?"

"Tig, thank you for what you're —"

"Here." Tig put something in my hand, and I looked down to find a gun, heavy and cold, its black metal barely visible in the darkness.

"Whoa," I said, surprised.

"Dom doesn't know. The other two do." Tig kept his palm over mine, atop the gun. "Here's the new plan. You don't stay up here. You come downstairs. We do like Dom says, the three of us take them, nice and easy. If anything goes wrong, come out shootin'. Not too early, not too late."

"Okay." My heart started to pound.

"You know I raised Dom. My late sister's child. He's not only my blood, he's my heart. You dig? My *heart.*"

"I understand."

"You were right, what you said before. This is your fight. If it comes down to you or Dom, I pick Dom. You do, too. It's only right." Tig held my hand on the gun. "Understood?"

"Understood," I said, swallowing hard.

Tig patted my hand. "Good man."

Chapter Sixty-Four

I hid downstairs behind the entrance door, looking through a patch of corroded metal to see outside. Dom was standing in front of the crane, next to the parked van. Tig, Richardson, and Skeet were out of sight behind the massive counterweight of the crane.

I heard a car pulling in on the left side of the building. Its high beams threw light on the back of the parking lot. Its big engine roared. Its tires rumbled on the gritty asphalt.

My heart thundered. My mouth went dry.

Dom stood ready, his hands on his hips.

A black Escalade turned around the building, its high beams sweeping the lot in a blinding arc. Its dark silhouette and chrome grille came into view, but I couldn't see inside the car. I couldn't tell who was in there or even how many.

The Escalade cruised to a stop, its high

beams blasting Dom. He raised a hand to shield his eyes, which was the signal. Suddenly Tig, Richardson, and Skeet showed themselves, pointing guns at the Escalade.

"Come out with your hands up!" Dom hollered, aiming his gun. "Nice and slow!"

Three doors of the Escalade opened slowly. The driver's door remained closed.

Two men emerged from the back of the Escalade, one on the left and another on the right. A man came out of the passenger seat. I couldn't see their features, but they had on street clothes. They weren't FBI.

Dom shouted, "Milo, out with your hands up!"

I kept my eyes glued to the Escalade's driver's side. I raised my weapon. I stayed put, sticking to Tig's plan.

The driver's side door opened.

I held my breath. My heart hammered. I didn't know if I could restrain myself when I saw Milo. I had a loaded weapon.

The driver emerged, a bearded White man. Not Milo.

If Dom was surprised, it didn't show. "Lie down!" he shouted. "Everybody, down on the ground!"

My mind raced through the possibilities. Milo could still be in the car. Or he hadn't been in the car in the first place. I stayed put, gun at the ready.

Suddenly I heard another car on the left side of the building, moving fast. Smaller and lighter than the Escalade. Its engine made barely a sound. Its headlights were off, trying not to signal its arrival. I didn't know if Dom and the others heard it over the Escalade's big engine.

Milo had to be in the car, with more men.

I couldn't wait another second.

I raced out the door.

And everything happened at once.

Chapter Sixty-Five

A dark sedan veered around the building, spraying gunfire. I was already in motion when Dom was hit. He fell to the ground, holding his arm.

I returned fire, aiming at the sedan in the dark. I ran to Dom and grabbed him by the other arm. He scrambled to his feet, holding his gun.

The men in the Escalade started shooting. Orange flame popped like firecrackers. Dom and I returned fire. Richardson went down, doubled over. Tig and Skeet grabbed him on the fly, blasting away as they dragged him behind the crane.

The dark sedan screeched to a halt. Milo flew from the driver's seat.

"Milo, over here!" I shouted, showing myself by stepping away from the crane.

"Jason, no!" Dom shouted. "Get down!"

Milo's head whipped around. He aimed at me and fired. I felt the percussive wave of a bullet whizzing past my temple. I returned fire, aiming in the dark.

Dom yanked me behind the crane. I kept firing around the side.

Milo advanced on the crane, spraying gunfire from an assault rifle. A bolt of terror ran through me. Things were going south. Suddenly the parking lot came alive with light and action. SUVs were racing into the driveway.

"Milo!" I heard somebody shout.

But it wasn't one of Milo's men.

It was a voice I recognized.

Chapter Sixty-Six

It was George Veria.

I looked at Dom. "It's George. He's here for Milo."

"Good." Dom turned to the others. "They're with us."

"Thank God!" Tig gasped, surprised. "Watch your friendly fire!"

A deafening barrage of gunfire exploded from the far side of the parking lot. I peered around the crane to find George and his men shooting at Milo and his crew, caught between us and them. Milo and his crew turned around, firing back at George and his crew.

Dom, Tig, Skeet, and I kept shooting. Dom hit one of Milo's men, who went down. George and his crew whipsawed assault rifles back and forth, mowing down Milo's men. The first one dropped, then the second. One of George's men fell.

Milo fired back, aiming at George's stocky

shadow, silhouetted by the SUV headlights. I spotted George aiming back at Milo, a lethal standoff.

I held fire, watching.

George got off a single burst. Milo went down, shooting.

George crumpled to the ground a split second later. The firing stopped as abruptly as it had begun, the violence deadly and convulsive.

I turned to Dom, but he was bending over Richardson, who was sitting down, his back against the undercarriage of the crane. He had been shot in the stomach, and Dom was checking the wound, with Tig and Skeet hovering.

Dom looked up. "He'll be okay if we hurry."

Tig put a phone to his ear. "I'm calling 911."

I turned to Dom. "How's your shoulder?"

"Flesh wound." Dom rose. "I'm going out."

"Right behind you," I said, and we took off.

Chapter Sixty-Seven

Dom and I hustled from behind the crane, weapons ready. Nobody was moving around us. Bodies lay still on the asphalt, blood pooling around them. A smoky haze drifted in front of the headlights. The air smelled of cordite.

Dom started checking the men, and I hurried past Milo, who lay on his side, motionless. It was George I wanted to see. I spotted him lying on his back, illuminated by the SUV's open door.

I shoved my gun in my waistband and hurried to his side. His big chest was moving in a halting manner. Shuddering, not rhythmic breathing. His shirt was blackening with blood. It looked as if he had been hit in the chest three times. His wounds were catastrophic. A tourniquet wouldn't help.

I felt his wrist for a pulse. It was faint under my fingers. "George, I'm here," I heard myself say. "It's Jason."

His eyes fluttered open. He breathed through his mouth, his lips parted slightly. "Bennett."

"Hang in. We called 911."

"I'm gone . . . either way. This way's . . . better."

"Don't say that." On impulse, I picked up his rough, meaty hand, slick with warm blood.

"Bennett . . . did you see?"

"Yes." I knew what he meant. That he killed Milo.

"I did it for Junior. For your kid, too."

I wasn't sure how to feel about that. Gratitude, and guilt. "How did you know we were here?"

"Take a . . . guess."

I would have laughed, in other circumstances. "George, we don't have time for guessing games. Please don't die before you tell me."

"You crack me . . . up." George managed a smile. Blood pooled in the left corner of his mouth.

"I'm trying to."

"Okay . . . I called . . . the agent . . . who worked with Milo. Reilly. I knew he wouldn't need Milo . . . after Milo got rid of . . . you."

I understood. "You saved my life. Thank you."

George smiled again, with bloody satisfaction. "We win."

Nobody wins, I thought, but didn't say.

George began to breathe harder, emitting a sucking sound. He winced, frowning in pain. "You remember any . . . prayers?"

"Sure." I swallowed hard. "How about Hail Mary?"

"Whatever."

"I got you, pal." My throat thickened, unaccountably. "You're a good bad guy."

So I prayed for him for the next few moments, holding his hand, until his breathing stopped.

The next hour was a blur of police activity, blaring sirens, flashing light bars, uniformed Philly cops, and ambulances. Dom took command, tasking me with putting Richardson in an ambulance, and Tig and Skeet in a cruiser. Dom briefed the cops and medical examiner, then made phone calls. The EMTs insisted he go to the hospital, but he made the ambulance wait, coming over to me.

"Jason, you're all set. I talked to the U.S. Attorney. He's sending someone to pick you up and bring you downtown. They want to take your statement. Tell him everything."

"Okay." I nodded. "We should tell Lucinda —"

"I texted her you're okay."

I smiled. "Did you tell her I love her, too?"

Dom chuckled. "I'm leaving that to you. The Philly cops are sending some uniforms to sit with her and Ethan until you're done."

"Did you text Denise?"

"You know I did. I'll see you at the U.S. Attorney's as soon as I'm finished at the hospital."

"Okay, good luck."

"You, too." Dom turned to go, then stopped himself. "Hey, where'd you get that gun?"

"Don't worry about it."

"You didn't follow my plan."

"I'm a badass court reporter."

Dom snorted, holding out his hand. "Gimme the gun, so I can give it back to Tig."

Chapter Sixty-Eight

Half an hour later, I found myself sitting in a large conference room in a modern concrete monolith at Sixth and Chestnut in Philadelphia. It was harshly bright, lit by recessed fluorescent panels and dominated by a large walnut table. The walls were lined with watercolors of an idealized City Hall, Boathouse Row, and the Benjamin Franklin Parkway, and there was a floor-to-ceiling glass wall with a view of the southeast part of the city, where our gunfight had taken place. It looked better from a distance.

I was introduced to Rob Forman, the United States Attorney for the Eastern District of Pennsylvania, a fortysomething go-getter with quick dark eyes, slick black hair, and a gym-trim build in a dark suit and tie. He introduced me to his best and brightest AUSAs, male and female lawyers in casual clothes. I shook hands all around, and they congratulated me, which felt vaguely surreal. Nobody remarked that I looked like hell, but I'd washed up in the bathroom, so I knew my face was bruised, my bald head scraped, and my clothes spattered with blood.

Once the introductions were over, we all sat down, and the last person to enter the room was a friend of mine, John Colasante, one of the best court reporters in the city. He looked surprised to see me, and I would have been surprised to see me, too. Of course the lawyers didn't introduce him, because they never bother to introduce the court reporter. We all joke they think we're part of the steno machine, but it's not funny. John and I nodded, acknowledging each other as kindred spirits, about to suffer fools.

I sat on one side of the conference table, and the lawyers sat on the other. I gave a full accounting of everything that had happened and eventually drank three cups of vending machine coffee. Dom arrived as I began to answer their follow-up questions, and they greeted him with hearty congratulations, which made me like them better.

Dom sat down next to me, the questions continued, and the night sky surrendered to a purplish gray dawn in the window behind them. Finally the sun climbed the clouds, and by eight o'clock in the morning, the lawyers were out of questions.

I sensed we were finished. "So what happens next?"

"We're going to hold a press conference today with the officials from DOJ and the FBI Director —"

"I meant, what about Reilly?"

"Already in custody."

"Anybody else?"

"Our investigation is ongoing. At this juncture, we believe Reilly is the only individual left involved in the criminal conspiracy."

"Will you give them the photograph from Gitmo, of me with Senator Ricks?" I had pulled it from a laptop they had supplied during my statement.

"Yes, we passed it up the chain. We will share any and all evidence."

"Do you think it will bring Ricks down?"

"I don't know."

"It better." I still believed in justice, even in a world that didn't know the difference between right or wrong, or the good guys from the bad.

"Now, about our press conference." Forman picked up a sheet of paper and skimmed it quickly. "We're going to say that you and your family were the victims of a botched carjacking that took place on Friday night, two weeks ago, on Coldstream Road in Chester County. The perpetrators were John Milo and Junior Veria, members of the George Veria Organization, or GVO." Forman checked his paper. "We're going to say that Milo and Veria attempted to carjack your vehicle because they were fleeing the scene of a double homicide in Jennersville, which they are believed to have committed."

"So you're going with the carjacking story."

"Yes."

"Not the truth?"

"Not for now."

"Why?" I found myself wondering if Forman was a good good guy like Dom, or a bad good guy like Wiki. So far the only good bad guy I knew was George Veria, but I was keeping an open mind.

"As I said, Reilly is in custody, but it will take time to prepare the case against him. The same is true of any case against Senator Ricks, since at this juncture, the extent of his involvement in the conspiracy is unknown." Forman squared his jaw. "We will say nothing about the photo you gave us, your time at Gitmo, or the Doha interrogation. Similarly, we will say nothing about the hit-and-run death of Paul Hart or the apparent suicide of Contessa Burroughs. We don't want to publicly connect these dots. To do so could imperil the investigation of Senator Ricks."

I got that. "What will you say about my daughter?"

"We're going to say that the carjacking was botched, and it resulted in the murder of Junior Veria and your daughter, Allison."

It hurt to hear it. Now it was official. I felt a wave of grief, but stayed in emotional control.

"We're going to say that subsequent to the events of that night, you and your family entered the witness protection program. Your house, office, and your wife's studio were destroyed by GVO, a form of witness intimidation that you and your family resisted. We will say that you and your family are currently in an undisclosed location. We will ask that the press respect your privacy during this difficult time."

"What about the murder of Bryan Krieger, the citizen detective? Milo killed him at the composting plant. Phil Nerone, too." I flashed on the horrible way that Krieger died.

"We won't make any statement about that

today. We're saying only as much as we have to."

"You might want to rethink that." I sighed inwardly, since they had learned exactly zero from what had just happened with us. "There's a citizen detective community online, and they're not going to let this go. It's like our friends. It's the same thing, all over —"

"We'll take it under advisement." Forman nodded. "We're going to address the rumors regarding you, Jason. We're going to say that you are guilty of absolutely no wrongdoing. That should clear your name and rehabilitate your reputation, to the extent it's necessary."

"Okay," I said, though it was hard to care about my reputation right now.

"That's basically it." Forman set the paper aside. "On a personal note, you must be wondering about the settlement regarding the damage to your house, your office, and your wife's studio. I've already contacted the powers that be in Washington. They feel confident we can reach a financial settlement that will enable you and your family to start over."

Start over. I didn't even know how to respond to that. I hadn't thought about a settlement yet.

"I spoke with the FBI Director, and it is his opinion that GVO is out of business, given those killed at the scene last night, in addition to the prior deaths of Junior Veria and Phil Nerone."

I heard an unmistakable note of triumph in his voice, but I flashed on the scene in New Cumberton and the other towns I had been through, watching the drug business on street corners. I knew another organization would emerge sooner rather than later, filling the void and meeting the demand.

"We will announce that thanks to the teamwork of the FBI, the Delaware State Police, and the Philadelphia Police, GVO no longer poses a threat to the citizens of the tristate area. Our heartfelt thanks to you and your family, too, Jason. We appreciate everything you have done. I assume you do not want to appear at the press conference."

"I don't, thank you."

"Good. Then that's it, for now." Forman linked his hands in front of him.

"Wait, what about Dom? You're giving credit to the FBI, when Wiki and Reilly tried to kill Dom and my family?"

Forman blinked. "We're not in a position to reveal —"

"Yes you are, you just don't want to." I felt angry all of a sudden. "Is Dom even going to be at the press conference? Is the public ever going to know what he did? He got my wife and son out before Milo got there. He hid them. He saved their lives."

Dom waved me off. "Jason, it's okay."

I faced Forman. "Dom put his life on the line for me last night. He got his uncle and his friends to put their lives on the line. If that's not a hero, I don't know what is."

"You don't need to tell me." Forman flashed Dom a professional smile. "Special Agent Kingston is already an FBI legend."

"Does that mean he gets credit? A raise? A promotion? Because whatever you're paying this legend, it's not enough."

"We'll take that under advisement, too." Forman cleared his throat. "Moving on, Jason, we would request that you and your family relocate to a hotel near this office for the foreseeable future. We can shield you from the press and you'll be available to answer our questions as the investigation launches, leading up to trial."

"No, thanks," I found myself saying. "We'll go back to the house in Delaware and lay low. I'm not disrupting my family any more than they have been."

"Jason, as a favor to the department, I would request that —"

"No, but thanks again. Nice meeting you

all." I rose, brushing down my bloody clothes. I nodded goodbye to John, who nodded back from behind the steno machine.

Forman looked up, blinking. "What if we have questions before the presser?"

"Call me. You know where I am."

Dom rose beside me. "I can field calls for him and take him back to Delaware."

Forman stood, smoothing down his tie with a frown. "Jason, if you wait until the press conference, you can meet the Director —"

"I have to go find my dog," I told him.

Chapter Sixty-Nine

"Jason!" Lucinda rushed out of the brick rowhouse, throwing open her arms, and I caught her, holding her close, trying to swallow the lump in my throat. Two cops stood in the doorway, smiling.

"Let's keep the drama to a minimum," I heard myself say, without knowing why. It wasn't because the cops were there.

"Dad!" Ethan hugged me, and I pulled him close to my side.

"Everything's okay, buddy. Everything's okay."

"Can we go find Moonie?"

"Sure we can," I told him. All that, but what he cared about was the dog, and I understood why. "Let's go home."

We headed south under cloudy skies on the route we had taken that first day, except I was driving and Dom was in the passenger seat, since his shoulder was hurting. Lucinda and Ethan fell asleep in time, and the only sound was the steady rumble of the van and the gentle snoring of my wife, which made Dom smile.

He said, "I love me a woman who snores."

I smiled back. "Me too. Does Denise?"

"Totally." Dom chuckled.

"Thanks for doing this. Sorry to put you out."

"Not a problem. She and the girls are going to stay at her sister's for a few days."

I glanced at the dashboard clock. "Think we'll make it back in time for the press conference?"

"I don't care. They're all the same. Blah-blah-blah joint effort law enforcement God country apple pie."

"It bugs me that they're not giving you credit."

"First off, you're the one who busted GVO, Jason. You met with George. You figured out the Gitmo connection."

"Only because I *was* the Gitmo connection."

"Anyway, I don't need credit. I have a bigger ask in mind. I want out of The Babysitters Club."

"Why?" I asked, but I wasn't completely surprised.

"I missed the action. I *need* the action. I

realized it in the past few days."

"What do you want to do instead? Go back undercover?"

"No. It's too hard on Denise and the kids. I promised her. I want to be in the field." Dom glanced over, his eyes twinkling. "In layman's terms, a good old-fashioned FBI agent, out of the Philly office. I think I'm ready."

"Ready?" I almost laughed. "What are you talking about? You're a bona fide *hero.*"

Dom hesitated, his smile fading. "I didn't tell you everything that happened with my partner, undercover."

I blinked, caught up short, but didn't say anything. I didn't want to pry. I had yet to figure out if we were friends. Rather, I knew I was his friend, but I didn't know if he was mine.

"The day my partner was killed, I was supposed to go to the buy, but I had car trouble." Dom shook his head. "Typical undercover issue. It's always the little things that get you. Cheap-ass car goes with the cover. The engine doesn't turn over that morning. It's too cold out. So my partner goes instead." He winced. "It messed me up, that it was supposed to be me. After he died, I went back undercover, on a new job. But I was hesitant, a split second behind. It wasn't grief. I was scared. Like, phobic. That's when I got out." His lips flattened. "I joined The Babysitters Club, and all this time, I've been hiding. It's ironic. I haven't been protecting my applicants, I've been protecting myself."

My heart went out to him. "I get that, though."

Dom straightened, turning to me. "I'm changing things because of you."

"What?" I asked, surprised.

"I was stuck in The Babysitters Club, like you were stuck in the program. It's no good. You can't stay stuck, you have to move on. Like you did. I decided to move on. I have to forgive myself for not being there, when he died. I have to set it down. I carried it long enough." He nodded, his eyes flashing with new animation. "I'll always mourn the man. But grief is one thing, and fear's another. I'm moving on."

"Well, jeez." I felt touched. Maybe I was his friend, too. I could think of only one thing to say. "Damn, I wish we had a Tate's."

"Now you're talking!" Dom said, bursting into laughter.

Chapter Seventy

The sky had cleared by the time we got to the house, and I pulled up in front, scanning the area for Moonie. I had half-expected the dog to be on the front step, but he wasn't anywhere in sight. Lucinda had called the local shelters on the way down, but no dog fitting his description had been turned in.

Ethan threw open the back seat door. "Moonie! Moonie!"

I turned to him. "Check out back."

"Okay!" Ethan ran toward the house. "Moonie!"

Lucinda emerged from the van, glancing around. She looked tired, her hair in disarray and her dress rumpled. "It's weird, coming back."

"I bet." I didn't move to comfort her, my feelings bollixed up. I had tabled thinking about us until we were safe, but I couldn't ignore it any longer. Maybe I was compartmentalizing, but the walls of the compartment had collapsed.

"Moonie! Moonie!" Ethan shouted, behind the house.

"Are you sure we're safe now?" Lucinda asked Dom.

"Absolutely." Dom placed a hand on Lucinda's shoulder. "You have nothing to worry about."

"Thanks, Dom." Lucinda gave him a brief hug, evidence of a new closeness, and I didn't mind. If I couldn't comfort her, Dom could. He was good at telling my wife I loved her when I couldn't.

"GVO is defunct, thanks to your husband, who keeps trying to give me all the credit."

"You deserve it," I interjected.

"No, you do," Dom shot back.

Lucinda smiled at me, shaky. "So do you, honey. You got us out."

"Moonie!" Ethan called from the backyard.

Dom turned from Lucinda to me. "You know, I can go get you guys some food."

I sensed he was trying to give us time alone, which was the last thing I wanted. "You don't have to run our errands anymore. Later I can wash up, change, and go."

"I don't mind. I'll run to the store, and you guys look for the dog."

"I'm worried he's really gone." Lucinda met my eye. "Jason, I wish you hadn't promised Ethan."

"Let's stay positive," I said, even though I was wishing I hadn't promised him, either. "I'll go change, then go look for him."

Lucinda checked her watch. "The press conference is on in half an hour. Aren't you going to watch?"

"No," Dom and I answered in unison, but Lucinda looked at us like we were crazy.

"Don't you want to know what they say, about us?"

"We know what they'll say." I didn't want to watch the press conference, and truth to tell, I needed distance from her. I had to get my bearings and I was worried about the dog. Not just for Ethan's sake, but for my own. I hadn't realized how much I loved the damn dog until this very moment.

Dom's expression softened. "Lucinda, I'll watch with you, then go to the store."

"Okay," Lucinda said, looking away from me.

I interjected, "I thought you'd want to call Mom or Melissa. Or hop on Facebook and get back in touch with everyone."

"Not just yet."

"I thought you were champing at the bit to —" I started to say, but it was coming out like criticism, so I shut up, newly awkward with my own wife.

"But then again, I don't want them to find out from TV." Lucinda bit her lip, uncertain. "I'll call Melissa first. My mom won't get it, over the phone."

"Well, your choice. I'll go with Ethan." I hustled off toward the house.

Lucinda called after me, "Don't you want to eat something first?"

"No, thanks!" I hurried under the house, feeling Lucinda's eyes on my back.

I loved my wife and wanted to forgive her.

But I wasn't Tig, and I wasn't Dom.

So I had to figure out how.

CHAPTER SEVENTY-ONE

Ethan and I looked for Moonie in the backyard, then all around the property, and finally at my spot on the beach, where I had come our first day. The sun glistened on the bay, and a breeze rippled across its surface, making wavelets with twinkling crests. Seagulls squawked overhead, but there was no Blue Heron in sight.

Ethan took off, calling for the dog, but I stood on the sand, trying to swallow the lump in my throat. I was supposed to be returning to my life, starting over, coming back to the things I could and couldn't fix. I couldn't fix the fact that Allison was gone. Or that I couldn't find it in my heart to forgive my wife. Or that the dog was missing.

"Dad, this way!" Ethan called, motioning back to the house.

We went back out to the street, calling for Moonie. We walked up the street and didn't see him anywhere, nor did we see anyone else until we got to Thatcher's. The old man was sitting in his ratty recliner, smoking a cigar, and we walked onto the lawn, where I waved to get his attention.

"Mr. Thatcher?"

Thatcher looked over, unplugging the cigar, and if he recognized me it didn't show. Either he was keeping our secret or I looked that much different, which was entirely possible.

"Excuse me, have you seen a little white dog?"

"Nah!" Thatcher called back, so we kept going. The sun climbed the sky, and the air grew heavy with humidity. Ethan seemed not to notice, focused on finding the dog, calling and calling.

We circled the block, going down streets I had never been on, lined few and far between with empty vacation houses. Ethan was getting more upset as the afternoon wore on, and I was kicking myself for being so confident before. I didn't know how much more loss the kid could take.

Two hours later, I was exhausted, aching in the ribs, and worried we weren't going to find him. I stopped Ethan and put a hand on his shoulder. "Honey, maybe we should go back to the house, get something to eat, and —"

"I know, we should try the Ghost Forest!" Ethan brightened, newly excited. He wiped sweat from his forehead. "Remember when we went there, how Moonie was sniffing around? What if he remembered it?"

"It's possible, but we shouldn't get our hopes up —"

"Come on!" Ethan charged ahead, going back to the house. His skinny legs pumped, and I fell into stride behind him.

"Honey, I know I said we'll find him, but I'm starting to worry we won't. I could have been wrong."

"We'll find him, Dad. We're going to find him." Ethan nodded, leading with his chin. "I bet he's in the Ghost Forest. He liked it there. Allison's there. Remember we said we could feel her there?"

"Yes," I answered, my heart sinking.

"What if Moonie could feel her too, and he wanted to be with her? I bet he misses her. Do you think he does?"

"I'm sure he does, but —"

"I think so too. He won't forget her. He loves her. Like you said. You always have someone if you love them."

"We're going to find him. Don't worry." Ethan charged ahead, pushing his damp bangs from his face. "If he's not in the

Ghost Forest, he coulda gone home. You know, back to our real house, the one that burned down."

Oh no. "Honey, that's not possible."

"Yes, it is, Dad. Dogs do that all the time. They go find their home, even if it's far away. They know."

I cringed, inwardly. "Our house was too far away. He doesn't know the way and he couldn't —"

"He knows a lot, Dad. He's a smart dog. You didn't think we'd get the cedar boxes, and we got them."

"That's true, but this is different."

"Dogs have superior powers of smell, Dad. That's their superpower, like yours is reading lips." Ethan looked over with a grin, and I managed a smile, fresh out of superpowers. And compartments.

"I still don't want you to keep your hopes —"

Ethan kept walking. "You know what's my superpower, Dad?"

It struck me that we had never talked about his superpower. "No, what?"

"I never give up. Allison told me." Ethan smiled. "We got in a fight and she said, 'You never let it go,' and later she said she was sorry and she said, 'It's good to never give up. It's your superpower.' "

My throat caught. "She was right."

"She was." Ethan picked up the pace. "We'll find him in the Ghost Forest."

"We'll see," I said, praying.

The Ghost Forest looked even more desolate in the daytime. The dead trees with their smooth white trunks and limbs looked like so many bones reaching into the sky, the fingers of a skeleton trying to pull heaven down. Or maybe it was my frame of mind. Despair and exhaustion swept over me, and I realized we weren't going to find the dog.

"Moonie, Moonie!" Ethan kept calling, hoarse.

"Ethan, I think we should go back."

"Not yet, Dad. You said not until dark."

So we looked everywhere for the rest of the afternoon, getting bitten by horseflies and mosquitoes as we sloshed around in the brackish muck, our shirts clinging to our bodies and our sneakers tugged off our feet. The marshy water reeked, murky and black in large patches, even as it rushed out to the bay, obeying the laws of the moon.

Finally, the sun dipped behind the line of bare trees, and it was time to call it quits. I went to Ethan and gave him a hug. "Honey? Let's go back, for now."

"No, he can still be out here." Ethan pulled away, looking up at me, his eyes filling with tears.

"He'll be fine for the night."

"Something could get him, snakes or eels or things like that."

"Ethan," I said firmly, "we're going back now."

"Can we come back tomorrow?"

"Yes, of course."

"We have to come back every day until we find him. We'll never give up. Okay, we can never give up?"

"We'll see," I told him, and Ethan seemed to collapse, his head dropping forward and his knobby shoulders slumping. I scooped him up and held him the way I used to when he was little. He started to cry, his light frame racked with sobs, and I hugged him tight, feeling his warm tears as he buried his face in my neck. He wrapped his legs around my waist, and I linked my hands under him, ignoring the ache in my ribs.

I carried him toward home, and in time he stopped crying, so I set him down. We trudged through the muck in miserable silence. The house came into view, its lights shining through the darkness. When we got closer to the backyard, I heard talking and laughter from the kitchen, carried on the night air.

We reached the backyard and were going through the gate when I noticed something on the street in front of the house.

I realized what it was, surprised.

I picked up the pace.

Chapter Seventy-Two

"Flossie!" I opened the back door to find my trucker friend in the kitchen with Lucinda and Dom, talking and laughing around a table dotted with wineglasses and plates of goat cheese, cherry preserves, and stone-ground crackers. Dozing on the floor were Manny, Moe, one-eyed Jack — and Moonie.

"Moonie!" Ethan bolted for the dog, and Moonie scooted barking into Ethan's arms, licking his face.

"What's going on?" My mouth dropped open. "Where did Moonie come from?"

"I found him." Flossie rose, beaming in her pink top and jeans.

"My God, thank you!" I felt so happy I gave her a big hug. "How did you find him? When?"

"You said what he looked like, so I put out the word. One of the other Collins drivers spotted him near the on-ramp, so I picked him up last night."

"Amazing!" I laughed with relief, touched by her kindness. "You drove back for him? Thank you!"

"I told you, nobody tells me what to do."

"But how did you find us?" I glanced at Lucinda, who stood smiling by the table. She had changed into her blue sundress, looking fresh and pretty with her hair pinned up. She rested her fingertips on the back of the chair, as if waiting for something, and I realized I had hugged Flossie instead of her.

Flossie was saying, "I heard the press conference on the news, so I called the FBI and they called Dom." She chuckled. "Moonie's a great little dog. You shoulda seen him in the rig. Quiet as a mouse."

"Moonie? Quiet?"

"*Our* Moonie?" Ethan looked up while the dog licked his cheek.

"Yes, *your* Moonie." Flossie lifted an eyebrow. "He needs limits, is all. He barked a lot, but my boys taught him how to act. I gave Lucinda a few pointers, so he'll behave better for you."

"I got it, I'm on it." Lucinda smiled, going to the sink, and Manny and Moe watched her with their characteristic curiosity. Jack got up on wobbly legs and wandered over to me, his tail wagging.

"Hey, buddy," I said, charmed. I scooped him up and on impulse, gave him a little kiss. Then it struck me that I had now kissed a Chihuahua before my own wife.

Ethan snuggled Moonie. "I'm so happy. Thank you, uh, lady!"

I said, "Ethan, her name is Flossie Bergstrom."

"Thank you, Flossie Bergstrom!" Ethan sang out, and we all laughed.

"Jason, here." Lucinda came toward me with a glass of water.

"Thanks," I said, taking the glass. She looked away just as I managed to meet her eye, so we didn't make eye contact.

Flossie added, "Jaybird's doing great, by the way. He sends his regards. They all wanted to come by to thank you, but Dom said only me."

"How long have you been here?"

"Only two hours. We had a nice visit." Flossie's expression softened. "I'm sorry about your daughter."

"Thank you," I said, realizing I hadn't told her about Allison. Lucinda must have, but she had returned to the sink, her back to me.

Dom interjected, "I would've called you, but you didn't have a phone. Wiki took the laptops, so I couldn't find you on the monitor."

I waved him off. "No worries, I'm happy to get the dog back."

"Ethan, drink some water." Lucinda set a glass of water on the table, then smoothed back his sweaty hair. "You must be starving."

"I am!" Ethan picked up the glass and drank thirstily.

Flossie checked her watch. "Well, I have to hit the road. I gave Lucinda my number. Maybe we can see each other again."

"I'd love that," I said, meaning it. "I owe you big-time."

"No, it was the least I can do. Collins Consolidated loves you." Flossie smiled warmly, then her gaze shifted to Jack. "He loves you, too."

"Talk about a great little dog." I smiled, with Jack nestled against my chest. "I didn't know I was a Chihuahua guy, but I am."

"That's what my husband used to say." Flossie came over and stroked Jack's domed head. "To tell you the truth, this dog is partial to men. I think he still misses my husband. He'll look for him in the truck. He never really warmed up to me." She smiled, sadly. "The others pick on him, too. They figure he's the weakest one, on account of his eye, but Moonie was gentle with him. Jack bonded to Moonie, too. They slept together in the back."

"Aw," I said, touched.

"Aw," Dom said, teasing me.

Flossie smiled. "You know, Moonie could use a friend. He's calmer with Jack, and Jack looks happy with you. He's got his man buddy."

Dom laughed. "Jason, do you see where this is going?"

I blinked, surprised as it dawned on me. "Flossie, what are you saying?"

"I'm thinking you should keep Jack." Flossie shrugged. "I wasn't planning on it, but seeing him here with you, I'm thinking yes."

"But Jack belonged to your husband."

"I know, but he'd be happier with you." Flossie nodded, puckering her lower lip. "That's what my husband would want."

"Are you sure?"

"Absolutely. Do you want to keep him?"

Lucinda looked over, beaming. "I'd love to keep him. He's adorable, and I do think Moonie likes him. They've been sleeping under the table, curled up together for the past hour."

Ethan gasped, delighted. "Can we keep him, Dad? Please? I like his closed-up eye.

He looks cute, like a stuffed animal."

Dom grinned at me. "You gotta say yes, Hershey. You got that soft, gooey center."

Everybody laughed, including me, then I looked down at Jack.

Jack looked up at me.

We both knew the answer.

Jack knew it first.

Chapter Seventy-Three

After Dom and Flossie left, Lucinda and I started cleaning the kitchen, falling into our standard division of labor. I cleared the table and scraped scraps into the trash. She rinsed the dishes and loaded the dishwasher. We both knew each other's moves, but our rhythms were off. I picked up a plate of cheese, bumping into her on the way to the sink.

"Sorry," I said, realizing it was the first time I had physically touched her since the rowhouse, and that kiss, earlier. I wondered where the *wow* had gone. I didn't know if it would come back.

"Here, I'll take that." Lucinda held out her hand for the plate without making eye contact, and I handed it to her, turning away.

Ethan sat cross-legged on the floor, playing with Jack and Moonie, who really liked each other. "We need to get some dog toys."

"Good idea." Lucinda rinsed a plate.

"Yes, it is," I said, a fraction of a second later. I picked up another plate, and the only sound was Ethan talking to the dogs. I couldn't remember the last time we had been so silent in the kitchen. It was usually the time we caught each other up on our day, so I tried to go back to that routine, like a factory default setting for a marriage.

"Lucinda, did you watch the press conference?"

"Yes."

"How was it?"

"What you thought, no surprises. Dom said they say the same thing every time."

"Right, he said that to me too."

"They said nice things about you, which was good. They made it clear you hadn't killed us."

"Oh good." I managed a smile. "Low bar."

"I went online and got back in touch with everybody, and of course we're blowing up on social. Facebook comments, lots of talk about us on Instagram."

"Oh?" I threw the dirty napkins in the trash. "Good or bad?"

"Good, so that was nice. Wishing us well, sending prayers, all that. So many nice things about Allison. It was lovely. Lots of the moms, a lot of parents from school.

Neighbors. Even our UPS guy." Lucinda put the plate in the dishwasher. "I responded to as many as I could, then Dom came with Flossie and Moonie. He wanted to surprise us."

"He did."

"Flossie seems really nice."

"She is."

Ethan looked up. "Mom, what about Zack's parents? Did they say anything?"

"Yes, that they're happy to hear we're okay." Lucinda put another plate in the dishwasher. "Mr. Sullivan posted something very nice about you. They can't wait to see you."

I picked up the silverware. "How about Mom? Did you get in touch with her or what?"

"Back on track, thank God." Lucinda brightened. "I talked to her on the phone, no FaceTime, but she sounded good. She's not following the news and they're not going to put it in front of her, so that's good."

"That's good," I said, realizing I was echoing her. Everything was *nice* and *good.* I didn't know when we started talking like preschoolers.

"I talked to the supervisor, who's new. The mean nurse has already been let go. You know, the one who took her lavender lotion."

"Did they get the lotion back?"

"Yes."

"Good. Nice." The kitchen fell silent except for the clatter of dishes and Ethan's baby talk to the dogs. I put the last plate on the counter, then plastered on a smile. "I'm going to go take a shower."

"Okay," Lucinda said, closing the dishwasher.

Ethan looked up. "Are you guys going to get a divorce?"

Lucinda recoiled, her lips parting slightly. The faucet was running behind her.

My chest tightened. I didn't know if Ethan knew about Lucinda's affair, but he was addressing me. His expression was pained, but his eyes remained dry. As anxious as he had been lately, my son looked oddly mature, the man inside the boy emerging, as if the future were testing the waters of the present.

"Dad, are you?"

I knew I had already made the decision. "No, of course not," I answered.

"Good." Ethan returned his attention to the dogs.

Lucinda met my eye, with a look I recognized.

We have to talk, it said.

CHAPTER SEVENTY-FOUR

I led Lucinda to the beach, instinctively wanting to have our talk away from the house. It turned out to be darker than I expected, the only light emanating from an ivory moon behind sheer clouds. The wind rippled a black bay, lapping against a beach that vanished to a hidden point. I couldn't see Lucinda's features clearly, but I knew them so well, from the curve of her cheekbone to the contour of her smile, absent now.

"Lucinda, I don't want a divorce."

"Do you love me?"

"Yes, of course," I answered, my chest tight. "That's not the problem. The problem is I don't know how to forgive you. I think I can but, man, it's hard, right now."

"But you know you don't want a divorce?"

"Right."

Lucinda cocked her head. "Why not?"

"Is this a quiz?" I shot back, edgy. Because

if it was, I hadn't studied. I couldn't show my work. I only knew the answer.

"No, it's a discussion."

"I love you, I love our family, and I can't imagine doing that to Ethan, not after . . ." My throat caught, and I couldn't finish the sentence. We had gone through so much, but we had lost Allison. Our hell wasn't over, it was just beginning. I felt a wall of pain and hurt and anguish coming, as inevitably as a tide. "I mean, we lost our girl."

"I know," Lucinda said quietly, sniffling, and I found myself reaching for her hand. But she didn't reach for mine.

"What?" I let my hand drop. I could see her lower lip trembling.

"I know I did something terribly wrong. I know I hurt you and I'm very sorry for that, but Ethan isn't a reason for us to stay together."

"Why not? I think he is. He needs us now. I mean, we all lost her." My heart hurt when I said it out loud, anguished. "We lost her together."

"I know that, too." Lucinda cleared her throat. "But Allison isn't a reason, either. Neither of our children is a reason for us to be together."

"It's not only the children. We're a family.

We make a family."

"Not if you and me aren't a couple, we don't. I mean a real couple, a loving couple. A couple that should be together." Lucinda's hand fluttered to her cheek, wiping a tear away. "At the studio, I see families before I take their portrait, and I see the way they are, how they relate to each other. I see love when it's there, sure, but I also see resentment, and hurt, and history." She wiped away another tear. "Sometimes, after I finish the shoot, I have no idea why some couples stay together. I don't want to be them, ever. I want to know why we're together."

"Okay," I said, listening.

"I know why I had an affair." Lucinda sniffled. "I think I was taking care of Caitlin for so long, then Mom got sick, and I'm not complaining, but you know, I just thought, life is so short. Anything could happen, I could get sick, I could die. I needed to do something for me, and when I met him, it was all about me, and only me. It's as pathetic as that. Now that I know it wasn't real, it's even more pathetic."

I understood. She had taken Caitlin to every chemo appointment, gotten her through surgery, then taken care of her mother. And all the time, there were the kids, the games, the homework, the PSATs, the permission slips. I knew it had taken a toll, but maybe I hadn't appreciated how much. Lucinda was so capable she made it look easy, but it hadn't been.

"I feel different now, and I have to ask myself if this is the marriage I want —"

"Wait, *I* didn't do anything wrong," I blurted out, but I knew it wasn't completely true. I thought back to my realization that I had been playing it safe. My dropping out of law school had been me opting for the safer route, just like my father.

I'm a scenic-route kind of guy, I remember saying that awful night.

But I was New Jason, and I could acknowledge I had made a mistake or two. And as soon as I had that thought, my heart softened and I began to forgive her. Not all the way, but I could see a path to follow, like a way home.

Lucinda straightened. "I'm saying if we're going to stay together, it has to be because we want to for *us,* and not the us from before, but who we are now."

"Okay."

Lucinda fell silent.

I asked, "You mean you want to, kind of, renew our vows?"

"Yes. Only if we both want to."

"Do you want to?"

"Yes, I love you and I want to stay married to you. And I want to rebuild our life and our house, right where it was, and I want us to live there. Is that what you want, too?" Lucinda held out her hand, a pale, open palm in the moonlight, and I reached out my hand and took hers.

"Yes, I love you, and that's what I want, too. We'll rebuild everything." I took her gently into my arms, and I held her against my chest while she began to cry. I rocked her back and forth, feeling the tears in my eyes and the love in my heart and the grief we shared, the two of us standing between the land and the water, clinging to each other under the moon.

Wow, I thought.

She could make me feel that way, even without a kiss.

My wife.

My love.

Chapter Seventy-Five

I sat at the conference table alone, and the packed gallery was restless, waiting for the hearing to begin. The Senate chamber was vast and impressive, its ivory walls adorned with oil portraits in gilded frames and finished with crown molding. Rings of polished walnut desks filled the space, and the blue rug that looked dark on TV was bright. Photographers crouched in front of me, forming a veritable wall of cameras, and I could imagine how I would look in their photos. Grim, grieving, and purposeful.

Today I was going to get a father's justice.

Six months after Allison's murder, criminal charges against Senator Ricks had yet to be filed, so I had pushed for a congressional investigation, supported by public outcry, media coverage, and political pressure. The party wanting to tank Ricks's presidential run backed me, but I didn't expect purity of motive. They had formed a Select Committee on the Doha Interrogation and decided I would be the first to testify.

They didn't know I had a litigation strategy of my own.

The senators found their seats, a slew of dark suits and lapel pins scrolling through their phones and finishing conversations. I recognized some of them from my lobbying efforts, but the one senator I wanted to see hadn't yet arrived.

I glanced at Lucinda, who was sitting in the front row next to Ethan, in the new suit and tie that he had worn at Allison's funeral, which we had held privately a few months ago. She smiled slightly, but her gaze remained impassive, because we'd kept our plan to ourselves.

Suddenly heads turned to the back of the chamber, and a murmur rippled through the crowd. I felt my jaw clench as Senator Ricks appeared and made his way down the aisle, his silvery hair glinting in the overhead lights. He greeted members of his party, nodding and smiling, and they clapped him on the back as if he had won something rather than masterminded a conspiracy that killed Allison. Most of them supported him, and he led in the polls, but I was hoping to change that today.

I had imagined this moment so many

times, thinking I would look away, but something primal took over and I glared at the senator as he took his seat. Ricks avoided my eye, even though I was squarely in his sight line. The cameras clicked away, since the media had hyped the standoff, the-father-versus-the-senator, designating us good or evil depending on which news you consumed. I knew who was good and who evil. Soon the world would, too.

The photographers were shooed away, and the Speaker gaveled the hearing to order and made an introductory statement. I was sworn in, eyeing Senator Ricks, who still looked everywhere but at me. He knew the gist of my testimony and was spoiling for a credibility contest, but we hadn't revealed our evidence. Our primary exhibit was on a poster, and my backers were keeping it under wraps until later, for dramatic impact. But I had other plans.

The Chair of the Select Committee on the Doha Interrogation leaned in to the microphone to make his introductory statement, and my heart began to pound. It was go-time. I rested my hand on my phone casually, then scrolled to the text function, which was already loaded with the photo I had taken on my birthday, proving Senator Ricks a liar when he'd claimed he was in the infirmary at Gitmo.

I pressed SEND.

I kept my eyes on Senator Ricks, and in the next moment, one of his female assistants received my text message. I'd been able to get her cell number but not his, and I'd typed under the photo: Show this to Senator Ricks immediately.

I sat back to watch, and Lucinda looked over too, because what unfolded was for our satisfaction alone. The assistant frowned at her phone, leaned forward, and showed the screen to Senator Ricks. He glanced over, then the color drained from his face. He grabbed the phone, his lips parting, and looked up, his shocked gaze finally meeting mine.

I got him.

Epilogue

I stood with Lucinda and Ethan in the dappled sunshine of the backyard. We had just planted a magnolia tree in memory of Allison, next to the two trees that were her goalposts, Scylla and Charybdis. They had survived the fire, though much of the yard had to be re-landscaped. Moonie and Jack were off investigating the new hydrangea in the back.

We had moved back in two days ago, and the first order of business was honoring Allison. We had held a vigil for her at school, inviting her friends, teammates, and the entire community. Nine hundred people had shown up, a touching tribute to her. But they had moved on, and the three of us felt torn up inside, our guts wrenched. We grieved because we loved her and she didn't get to live the full life she deserved. Our feelings were bittersweet, all the time. I was hoping that someday, there would be more sweetness than bitterness.

I had picked up the pieces of my business, and Lucinda had picked up the pieces of hers. We didn't host the holiday party last winter, using as an excuse that the house wasn't finished. We weren't ready for company on our first Christmas without Allison, and her birthday had broken our hearts. When spring came around, my office resumed its softball team, but we needed a slogan for the T-shirts other than OUR WORD IS LAW. I didn't believe in law the way I used to, so we went with WE'RE YOUR TYPE. What I believed in was truth, justice, and love. Sometimes I thought those were three different words for the same feeling.

Lucinda and I had joined a support group, meeting weekly with a group of heartbroken parents who had lost children to every calamity imaginable, fully aware that we were every parent's worst nightmare. But we were also proof that there was life afterward, diminished though it might have been. We survived week to week, helping each other through, bound together by our love for our children, who would always live in our hearts.

Senator Ricks had left the presidential race and resigned from Congress, and it was only a matter of time until he was indicted.

FBI Special Agent Matt Reilly had gone to prison for twenty years, having pled guilty to his role in the conspiracy. Dom and I talked it over sometimes, and I was letting go of my anger at the system. I knew that nothing would bring back my baby girl, and Allison would never again kick a soccer ball between Scylla and Charybdis.

"What do you think, honey?" I asked Lucinda. "You like the tree where it is?"

"Yes, it looks good." Lucinda smiled softly, her eyes glistening. She had on a yellow dress for our little ceremony.

"So do I." Ethan nodded, straightening. Back in school with his friends, he had gained weight, and the therapy had done him good. It had done all of us good, and we went faithfully every week.

"Then we're ready for the tag. You want to hang it?" I met Lucinda's pained gaze, feeling our shared grief, but also the warmth of our bond. We had grown closer over the past year, and I had learned that forgiveness had a power of its own.

"No, you hang it." Lucinda took my hand and put the tag inside.

"Okay." I went to the tree, knelt down, and hung it on the matching holder. The silver tag was shaped like a Great Blue Heron, custom-made for the memorial, and it gleamed in the sunshine. I read the beautiful inscription, which we had written together:

WE WILL ALWAYS LOVE YOU, ALLISON
SOAR HIGH, SWEET GIRL

My eyes filled with tears, and I felt myself surrender a sob, then another, and soon I was crying in earnest.

Lucinda and Ethan came to my sides, lifting me to my feet and holding me close, and it struck me that we would always do that for each other, lift each other up and hold each other close. That's what a family was for, even when the worst thing possible happens.

We were a family, still.

The four of us.

Forever.

ACKNOWLEDGMENTS

My first thanks go to you, my readers. So many of you have followed and supported me as I expand the type of book I write, and I feel so grateful to each and every one of you. So you get my first thanks, always.

What Happened to the Bennetts required research outside my expertise, so thank you to those experts who helped me, named below. And, of course, if there are any mistakes in this novel, they're on me.

Thank you, dear John Colasante, friend, chef, and court reporter extraordinaire, and my friend Raymond Carr, who retired from the FBI after a stellar career. Thanks to my pal legal eagle Nicholas Casenta, Esq., Chief Deputy District Attorney of the Chester County District Attorney's Office. Thank you to Lieutenant Robert P. Klinger, of the Willistown Police Department. Deepest thanks to Susan Kehoe, my dear friend and proprietor of the wonderful independent bookstore Browseabout Books in Rehoboth Beach, who helped me with details of the Delaware beaches and kept me supplied with great books about the region. Thanks to my gal-pal photographer April Narby for her help, and a big hug to Annabelle Rinda, who helped so much, too.

Thank you to the great Ivan Held, publisher of G. P. Putnam's Sons, who inspires and supports me at every step. Thank you to the wonderful Sally Kim and to my genius editor Mark Tavani, who guided and improved this manuscript so much.

Thanks to Alexis Welby and Katie Grinch for all of their hard work in publicity. Thanks to Ashley McClay, Emily Mlynek, and Nishtha Patel, the goddesses who come up with new ideas for marketing. Thanks to Anthony Ramondo and Christopher Lin for their sensational work on this cover, and thanks to audiobook mavens Karen Dziekonski and Scott Sherratt. Lots of gratitude and love to everyone at Putnam, who works so hard on my books!

Thanks and love to my terrific agent Robert Gottlieb of Trident Media Group. Robert is absolutely dedicated to my career, in addition to being a wonderful human being. Thank you to his colleague Erica Silverman, who has worked to make progress in Hollywood. Much gratitude to Nora Rawn in Foreign Rights and to Nicole Robson in Digital Media, who has been absolutely essential on marketing. Lastly, thanks to Aurora Fernandez, Andrew Jason Jacono, and Sarah McEachern for their hard work on behalf of my books.

Finally, thank you so much to the team at my company, Smart Blonde LLC. (Yes, that's the real name. LLC LOL.) My bestie/assistant Laura Leonard supports me every day, and I love her and can't thank her enough. Thanks and love to Nan Daley and Katie Rinda, who help with research, marketing, and every other kind of support.

Thanks and love to my bestie Franca Palumbo for her love and support, and, finally, big thanks and even bigger love to my amazing daughter Francesca Serritella, a novelist in her own right. Everything changed for me the day Francesca was born, in ways too numerous and wonderful to recount here. She's truly a gift, graced with intelligence, a kind heart, and a generous soul. I've been writing about family all my life, because that's what matters most to me. That's her.

Love you, honey, and deepest thanks.

ABOUT THE AUTHOR

Lisa Scottoline is the *New York Times*–bestselling author of thirty-two novels. She has 30 million copies of her books in print in the United States and has been published in thirty-five countries. Scottoline also writes a weekly column with her daughter for *The Philadelphia Inquirer.* Lisa has served as President of Mystery Writers of America and has taught a course she developed, "Justice in Fiction" at the University of Pennsylvania Law School, her alma mater. She lives in the Philadelphia area.

The employees of Thorndike Press hope you have enjoyed this Large Print book. All our Thorndike, Wheeler, and Kennebec Large Print titles are designed for easy reading, and all our books are made to last. Other Thorndike Press Large Print books are available at your library, through selected bookstores, or directly from us.

For information about titles, please call:
(800) 223-1244

or visit our website at:
gale.com/thorndike

To share your comments, please write:
Publisher
Thorndike Press
10 Water St., Suite 310
Waterville, ME 04901